"Filled with history, romance ... drew me in and held me captive.... Ms. Rice makes the Revolution come alive. I can't wait for the next installment in the amazing Mystic Isle series! I am hooked!"
—Romance Reader at Heart

"With whimsical and subtle touches of humor and memorable characters, [Rice] cleverly blends the paranormal with the historical events of the French Revolution in this passionate, very sensual romance. Her powerful voice and talent as a great storyteller make this one another keeper." —*Romantic Times* (Top Pick, 4½ stars)

"An enthralling tale that should not be missed."
—Romance Reviews Today

**Mystic Guardian**

"*Mystic Guardian* will enchant readers."
—The Romance Readers Connection

"Set against the background leading up to the French Revolution, Rice's book boasts a pair of extraordinary characters.... Her flair for subtle touches of humor and clever dialogue ... draws you into this magical, mystical, and sensual paranormal historical romance."
—*Romantic Times* (Top Pick, 4½ stars)

"A fine, fresh series kickoff, Rice's latest is passionate, rich in historical detail, and peopled with enough captivating secondary characters to pique readers' curiosity for many volumes to come." —*Publishers Weekly*

"Charming, magical." —*Midwest Book Review*

*continued ...*

### Magic Man

"Never slows down until the final thread is magically resolved. Patricia Rice is clearly the Magic Woman with this superb tale and magnificent series." —*Midwest Book Review*

### Much Ado About Magic

"The magical Rice takes Trev and Lucinda, along with her readers, on a passionate, sensual, and romantic adventure in this fast-paced, witty, poignant, and magical tale of love." —*Romantic Times* (Top Pick, 4½ stars)

### This Magic Moment

"Charming and immensely entertaining." —*Library Journal*

"Rice has a magical touch for creating fascinating plots, delicious romance, and delightful characters both flesh-and-blood and ectoplasmic." —*Booklist*

"Another delightful magical story brought to us by this talented author. It's a fun read, romantic and sexy with enchanting characters." —*Rendezvous*

### The Trouble with Magic

"Rice is a marvelously talented author who skillfully combines pathos with humor in a stirring, sensual romance that shows the power of love is the most wondrous gift of all. Think of this memorable story as a present you can open again and again." —*Romantic Times* (Top Pick, 4½ stars)

"Rice's third enchanting book about the Malcolm sisters is truly spellbinding." —*Booklist*

Other Historical Romances by
Patricia Rice

The Mystic Isle Series
*Mystic Guardian*
*Mystic Rider*

The Magic Series
*Merely Magic*
*Must Be Magic*
*The Trouble with Magic*
*This Magic Moment*
*Much Ado About Magic*
*Magic Man*

Other Titles
*All a Woman Wants*

# Mystic Warrior

## A MYSTIC ISLE NOVEL

# Patricia Rice

A SIGNET ECLIPSE BOOK

SIGNET ECLIPSE
Published by New American Library, a division of
Penguin Group (USA) Inc., 375 Hudson Street,
New York, New York 10014, USA
Penguin Group (Canada), 90 Eglinton Avenue East, Suite 700, Toronto,
Ontario M4P 2Y3, Canada (a division of Pearson Penguin Canada Inc.)
Penguin Books Ltd., 80 Strand, London WC2R 0RL, England
Penguin Ireland, 25 St. Stephen's Green, Dublin 2,
Ireland (a division of Penguin Books Ltd.)
Penguin Group (Australia), 250 Camberwell Road, Camberwell, Victoria 3124,
Australia (a division of Pearson Australia Group Pty. Ltd.)
Penguin Books India Pvt. Ltd., 11 Community Centre, Panchsheel Park,
New Delhi - 110 017, India
Penguin Group (NZ), 67 Apollo Drive, Rosedale, North Shore 0632,
New Zealand (a division of Pearson New Zealand Ltd.)
Penguin Books (South Africa) (Pty.) Ltd., 24 Sturdee Avenue,
Rosebank, Johannesburg 2196, South Africa

Penguin Books Ltd., Registered Offices:
80 Strand, London WC2R 0RL, England

First published by Signet Eclipse, an imprint of New American Library,
a division of Penguin Group (USA) Inc.

First Printing, July 2009
10   9   8   7   6   5   4   3   2   1

Copyright © Rice Enterprises, Inc., 2009
All rights reserved

SIGNET ECLIPSE and logo are trademarks of Penguin Group (USA) Inc.

Printed in the United States of America

PUBLISHER'S NOTE
This is a work of fiction. Names, characters, places, and incidents either are the
product of the author's imagination or are used fictitiously, and any resemblance
to actual persons, living or dead, business establishments, events, or locales is
entirely coincidental.
  The publisher does not have any control over and does not assume any
responsibility for author or third-party Web sites or their content.

# Acknowledgments

Despite my whining, I'm grateful to my editor, Ellen Edwards, who provides the left brain for detail that my big-picture right brain desperately needs.

And to my agent, Robin Rue, my gratitude for not laughing too hard when I say, "And now for my next act . . ."

And most of all, to my faithful readers who follow me anywhere, no matter how high I fly or how low I go. . . . If you're the wind beneath my wings, these books are all your fault! You've spoiled me. Hugs.

# Prologue

•

"*Don't touch me!*" Lissandra Olympus commanded with the arrogance of a queen. Moonlit locks scraped back from her fair face, she stood tall and regal against the tropical forest, bestowing the same expression on Murdoch LeDroit as Eve may have on the serpent in her garden.

As usual, Murdoch looked like a pirate. Barefoot, he dwarfed Lissandra's willowy height. A swath of peat-dark hair curved across his unshaven jaw as if he'd just climbed, rumpled, from his bed. The sword held ready at his side belied his sleepy-eyed appearance.

Only recently back from his long journey into the world beyond the Mystic Isle of Aelynn, he still wore the billowing shirtsleeves of the Other World that emphasized his muscular shoulders. He sported neither neckcloth nor waistcoat, so the ocean breeze was free to plaster the thin linen against his wide chest and reveal much of his sun-bronzed throat.

His face—the dark-lashed, sea-smoke eyes narrowed with seductive intent, the amused twist of sculpted lips promising delectably sinful delights, the cheekbones honed to a knife's lethal edge—caused women to swoon and men to scowl in wariness.

*Most* women to swoon. Not Lissandra, the Oracle's Daughter.

Appearance didn't matter on the Mystic Isle. Ability did. And because of her family's reputation, Lissandra's abilities were believed by Aelynners to be superior to those of a mere Agrarian upstart.

Undeterred by anyone else's beliefs, Murdoch was confident that he had more than proved his superiority—physical, mental, and supernatural. Both isle and woman were the prizes he intended to claim. Was destined to claim, although only he seemed certain of his ability to See the future.

He'd been away at sea a long time, waiting for his princess to grow up. It was gratifying to recognize that the desire simmering between them had only increased with separation. She held him at arm's length for good reason. The air crackled between them. He knew she curled her slender fingers into fists to prevent them from pushing his uncut hair out of his face as she had done countless times in the past.

He and Lis had grown up together like puppies in the same litter. Adolescence had shown them how pleasurably the hot wind beneath her cool reserve could feed the flames of mutual lust. Learning the painful lessons of their unequal positions had halted their youthful experimentation. The difference in their ages had made him careful.

But she had become a woman while he was gone, one who knew her own worth.

He admired the way his princess held her ground, forcing him to step back, knowing he had not yet earned the right to touch her. He respected her ability to resist temptation, although life would be much simpler if she could accept his wisdom and let go of her inhibitions.

His mouth quirked as he imagined the uninhibited Lis he'd once known. At his half smile, she retreated cautiously, increasing the gulf between them, depriving him of the fragile floral scent that belonged only to her.

She wore her ethereally lovely silver-blond hair stacked high and caught up in a coronet of island pearls. A tropical breeze molded her white cotton sarong to her curves and long legs. The twilight shadows hid her eyes, but he'd seen the liquid blue of longing in them after he'd sailed his ship into port. Their desire was a tangible thing, but until tonight, he'd not been in a position to act upon it.

Tonight, he meant to change their relationship.

"I'm the only man who *can* touch you, Lis," he reminded her with a laugh. "Your sharp tongue is no match for my rapier wit. My fire melts your frost. I've watched you weep when you've Seen a child's impending death, and I know your suffering when you See that a man's destiny lies beyond Aelynn. You are not your unfeeling mother, no matter how hard you try."

"Then I must keep trying, mustn't I?" she answered coolly. "Your destiny remains as black as your heart. I will not doom Aelynn for your ambition."

It was an old argument, a verbal sword that had held him at bay since adolescence. They were adults now. The argument had lost its usefulness.

"It is not ambition that makes me See that our world is limited and a new leader must change it. If I don't act now, you will become as narrow-minded as our Oracle." His voice softened. "You're better than her, Lissy."

Without waiting for her defensive retort, Murdoch walked away. He didn't want to take out his frustration on the woman who least deserved it, a woman as trapped by circumstances as he was. Tonight, by all the gods, that would change.

Purpose pulsed beneath his skin as his instinct for Finding led him to the man he needed to confront— Luther Olympus, Lis's father and the only father Murdoch had ever known. His own father had died before his birth. Murdoch's lack of powerful parentage had created a barrier between him and Lissandra so immense that it would take a wizard of great genius to surmount it. He intended to be that genius.

Luther stood on a rocky outcropping overlooking the black sand of Aelynn's port, where Murdoch's crew was preparing a feast to celebrate the success of their sailing venture into the Other World. Normally, Lis's mother, their Oracle, would have blessed his ship's safe return, but Dylys Olympus had found duties on the other side of the island.

Lis's mother knew what Murdoch was going to ask, and she did not approve.

He respected the Oracle for her experience and knowledge, but though she had raised him, Dylys could never be his mother. He had a mother, one he'd been forced to abandon so he might learn from the mighty Olympians. But tonight . . .

He was a free man, and he would have the prize promised by the gods.

The Council Leader acknowledged his approach with a nod. "I hear you have already purchased land from Waylan's father."

"Waylan isn't interested in land, and his father has no other offspring. You know why I have purchased it, don't you?"

Years of responsibility had etched lines upon Luther's face. He did not smile as he nodded. "I fear you expect more than you can command. It would be far better if you waited for my son, Ian, to choose a wife who can lead the Council. You and Lissandra are too young for the responsibility that comes with authority."

"You and Dylys have decades in the future to teach us. And it may come to pass that Ian is chosen by the gods, so you worry overmuch. I have worked hard to earn Lis's hand. I have land now. I can join the Council. The only obstacle that remains is you. She will not go against your wishes."

Luther looked out over the waves lapping against the shore. "The only obstacle is you," he said gently. "Your skills lie in war, not peace. This is a peaceful island. Instead of seeking compromise, you demand your own way, and your anger scorches the ground you walk."

"It is the anger of frustration. You know I would harm no one here. Would you have us wait until we are old and gray? There would be no chance of children to lead us into our future then." Murdoch clenched his fingers into fists, and despite the ever-simmering turmoil beneath his skin, he forced himself to remain outwardly composed.

"It is for the sake of those children that I go against my instincts." Luther studied the crowd gathering around the bonfire. "Take your seat on the Council, prove you can act responsibly, and I will allow you to court Lissandra."

Shocked at such an easy surrender, Murdoch staggered backward, nearly falling from his precarious perch on the rocks. Then, as joy washed over him, he pumped his fists into the air, safely dispersing the electricity of his angry frustration into the atmosphere.

Worried glances turned their way. It was not unusual to see Murdoch and Luther arguing, or to see lightning

sizzle in their vicinity. Aelynn's inhabitants had learned
the wisdom of staying a safe distance from the habitual
explosion.

"I would hug you, but it would be most unseemly."
Murdoch held back his laugh of relief as Luther regarded him with the dry fondness of approval.

"You have not won her yet," Luther warned. "Casting your lightning to the sky is a wise ploy, but it is still
not proper control. You must practice restraining your
powers when in the grip of strong emotion."

"Practice, I can do! Thank you, sir. I must oversee the
celebrations. You will speak to my crew?"

"As always," Luther agreed.

In afterthought, Murdoch realized asking Luther to
speak was his first mistake.

Purchasing fireworks in anticipation of his victory
was his second.

Underestimating Luther was his third, but not his
most fatal one.

His arrogance in believing he had learned to control
his tempestuous gifts was Murdoch's undoing.

Focusing all his joy on Luther's promise, knowing Lis
was watching nearby, Murdoch located the fireworks
he'd placed behind the speaking platform and concentrated. He could channel his fire better if he had his
sword in hand, but swords were weapons of war, and
he must act in peace. Giddy delight probably wasn't the
best conduit for channeling energy, but it was less erratic
than fury, and Lis adored the colorful jewels of light he
brought back from his travels. He would gift her with
fireworks nightly, if she would let him.

Perhaps Luther would grant his public blessing to
their courtship tonight, along with his formal acknowledgment of the success of the voyage. In expectation of

defeating his competition for Lis's hand, Murdoch stood with his bare legs apart, arms crossed, waiting for the right moment to express his elation.

He hardly heard the greetings and congratulations for a safe journey. At Luther's words "I would like to announce . . . ," Murdoch's spirits rose, and he concentrated on the celebratory Roman candles stored behind the platform.

With his extra perceptions, he studied the winds and verified that the fireworks would be safe among the rocks, away from the crowd. Even if he accidentally shot off three at a time, he'd harm no one. He raised his hand to focus on his target.

". . . that I have accepted Trystan the Guardian's desire to court my daughter. . . ."

Red-hot anger burst behind Murdoch's eyes. Even if Luther meant this as a test, Murdoch couldn't dampen his shock, rage, and disappointment fast enough. The fiery lightning that was his greatest gift shot from his hand as surely as cannonballs ignited by gunpowder.

The entire box of fireworks erupted in one brilliant blast of red and blue. Colored fire burst across the midnight sky, setting their world ablaze.

Unholy wails and screams of terror almost drowned out the rapid percussion of exploding skyrockets. The platform on which Luther stood above the rocks tilted, cracked, then collapsed. Luther was already crumpling to the ground, a hand over his heart.

Frozen, Murdoch could only watch the horrified expression bloom on Lissandra's face as her father landed in a bundle of fine clothes on the sand. Unable to move, Murdoch continued to watch as Healers ran to the Council Leader's aid.

Even before Lis shoved through the crowd to kneel

beside her father, Murdoch knew what she would find. Luther was dead. Appalled at the atrocity he'd unintentionally committed, Murdoch couldn't even pray that Lis would understand.

And when she looked up with condemnation darkening her eyes, he deserved the words she flung at him.

"Damn you into eternity, Murdoch LeDroit," she cried in heartbroken ferocity. "If you don't leave my sight now, I will kill you myself!"

# One

"**Y**our documents, *mes frères.*" Three soldiers, muskets raised, blocked the road to the village.

From the back of his stallion, Murdoch LeDroit regarded with disgust the rogues aiming sword and musket at him and signaled the driver of the wagon to rein in his mule. He had places to be, messages to deliver, a life of sorts to get on with. He didn't have the time or patience for fools.

Despite their pretense, the soldiers weren't protecting the village from traitors by asking for documents proving the cart's passengers were loyal citizens. They were intent on robbing Murdoch's weary charges of purse and life.

This was what France's glorious Revolution had come to—highway robbery. For four long years Murdoch had ridden as an officer in support of the noble ideal of taking wealth from greedy aristocrats to feed the starving and downtrodden masses. Four long years of penance for his sins had deteriorated to a farce in the face of France's monetary and moral bankruptcy. Without wealth, power always fell into the hands of the best-armed bullies.

Two of the cart's more elegantly garbed passengers, helpless despite their once-great riches and prestige, cursed the thieves and began hunting for the few gold coins sewn into the hems of their fashionable attire— their only fare for passage to a safer life.

The youngest traveler, a small girl in a bonnet spilling golden curls, fell into the arms of her shoemaker father, who was driving the cart, and buried her face in terror. Wearing a moth-eaten frock coat, the driver hugged his child and stared defiantly through sunken eyes at the thieves. He had no money to bribe anyone, but the shoemaker had once given Murdoch a home and a helping hand when he'd needed them most. He would not desert the man.

Wearing the coat of the Revolutionary army, Murdoch had been using his disguise to lead escaped prisoners to safety. His charges were idealistic political leaders and innocents who had been unjustly incarcerated by power-hungry officials little better than the lawless miscreants who were confronting them now. Murdoch worked to see justice prevail—if only because he knew what it was to be denied an impartial trial.

Ever since the French king's execution at the beginning of the year, Murdoch had been unable to reconcile the Tribunal's penchant for blood and revenge with the principles of equality, fraternity, and liberty for which the original revolutionaries had fought. He'd envisioned Aelynn's leaders crippled and brought low in the same manner as France had assaulted theirs, and he could no longer stomach the bloodshed.

Saving refugees from the methodical madness of Madame Guillotine was his only means of holding the tattered remains of his soul together these days. That, and the message he meant to carry to his former friend Trystan, warning him of the latest outrage that would endanger his fellow Aelynners. He hoped Trystan wouldn't hold the past against him and would listen to his warning.

Aware of his own unpredictable gifts, debating his choices in this all-too-public venue, Murdoch held his temper and did nothing in haste. Still wearing his officer's braid, he insolently slouched on his horse while considering his prey. The angry fire of his youth had been diluted by experience—the people outside his island home were no challenge except to his imagination. His caped greatcoat hid his weapons and disguised his tensing muscles. He'd learned to conceal his taut, angry jaw behind a week-old beard, just as he hid the burning flare of his Aelynn eyes in his hat's shadow.

"I carry their documents," he informed the soldier with cool scorn that hid his fury. "What right have you to demand them from your superiors?"

"We demand equality!" the heavyset rogue shouted. "They're naught but a bunch of filthy aristos. Why should you or Paris share their wealth when we starve out here?"

"Justice demands they be tried fairly," Murdoch replied with insulting insouciance, slapping the reins of the stallion so that it pranced nervously.

The younger soldier dropped back a step to avoid the huge beast's hooves. "What care we?" he called in contempt. "They're naught but fodder for Madame Guillotine."

"So you choose to terrorize them for fun and profit. How industrious of you." Murdoch had spent these last months pretending he was one of these soldiers while he helped prisoners flee, but he lacked the patience for further charades. Making his choice, he departed his saddle in a leap so swift as to be invisible. His polished Hessian boots landed a full length in front of his horse, in the dry brush at the side of the road, beside the trio of lackwits. Sweeping back his greatcoat, he revealed the braid on the red and white officer's uniform he wore.

The thieves stumbled hastily backward, their gazes widening at the costly sword and rapier being bran-dished in their faces. Although the Revolutionary army was so poorly supported that they wore whatever uni-form they could find, men saw what they wanted to see, and these men saw authority. To be fair, they lacked any knowledge of Murdoch's homeland, so they could not grasp his gift for illusion or his powers—despite his swift, nearly invisible leap.

Murdoch sensed four other scoundrels hiding behind the hedgerow, their murderous intent clear even to his less-than-perfect ability to read their puny minds. He ca-sually tossed his weapons from hand to hand, letting his fury build while assessing his foes.

One of the renegades he faced had a few inches of height over him, but like many tall men, the soldier lacked muscle. The sergeant wasn't tall, and packed more strength. The third was a mere stripling. The boy's hot-tempered anger and fear were more dangerous than his aging musket. Disarming these three might terrify the hidden ones into running, if they were lucky. Boldly, Murdoch stepped forward, pushing the brigands back-ward with the points of his blades.

The heavyset soldier with a sergeant's stripes recov-ered sufficiently to scoff at Murdoch's presumption. "Do you think a lazy officer can take on three armed soldiers, all trained and experienced in fighting?"

"Experienced in theft, more like," Murdoch replied. "Be gone with you before I carve out your livers and feed them to the ducks."

Insulted, the heavyset sergeant ordered, "Shoot him, Jean."

The stripling aimed his musket and fired. The cart's passengers screamed.

When the smoke cleared, Murdoch remained un-harmed, leaning against the donkey's neck, some dis-tance from his last position. He tipped his tricorne from his face with the edge of his rapier, knowing he revealed the controlled fires of his fury as he regarded the stunned soldiers. "Do you have any more ammuni-tion to waste?"

The trio darted frightened gazes from the spot where Murdoch had been standing to where he stood now—twice the distance of a donkey's length. Again, they hadn't seen him move. "How did you do that?" the boy asked.

"Just kill the blackguards and be done with it," one of Murdoch's passengers shouted.

The child continued to sob into her father's coat. The shoemaker and his daughter were guilty of noth-ing except trying to make an honest living in a cesspool of mob mentality. Wasting diseases ran rampant in the filthy prisons, and the innocent died without trial or ver-dict. Murdoch refused to let these two die, as they surely would at the hands of these murdering thieves.

He rotated the point of his rapier in a tight, furious circle. If he focused on the weapon, he might be able to control his anger and prevent himself from inadver-tently killing everyone in the vicinity, including the cow-ards still lurking in the hedgerow. Keeping his temper was imperative.

Before the stripling could jump out of range, Mur-doch cut off the buttons at the boy's waistband and split

the string of his drawers. Both garments fell into the
dust at his feet.

While the youth cursed and bent to gather his clothes
and his wounded dignity, Murdoch swung sword and rapier in tandem, a feat few others could imitate. In a whirl
and slash of silver blades, stripes disappeared from uniforms, buttons flew, and more drawstrings were severed.
The soldiers were suddenly too busy covering their in-
decency to aim their muskets. With an assist from his
boot applied to a fat derriere, Murdoch tumbled the sergeant headfirst into the parched weeds.

"Gentlemen, I suggest you stand back so we may be
on our way," Murdoch thundered, his greatcoat flaring
around his boots as he swung up in the stallion's saddle
without need of stirrup. Disarming his foes hadn't eased
his ire. Violence too easily became a way of life when one
faced it daily, and he'd been facing it for four years now.
Four years in which he'd learned violence wouldn't win
him what he wanted. Rather than risk venting his volatile
temper, he would let the scoundrels live another day—
provided the ones in the shrubbery didn't interfere.

Standing in the stirrups, he held his saber in one hand
and urged his mount on with the other. Beside him, the
wagon lurched forward. The defeated soldiers rolled
and scattered from their path. The cape of Murdoch's
coat fluttered in the dry wind.

Still standing so he could better flourish his weapon,
Murdoch urged the wagon's animal into a close approxi-
mation of a gallop, aiming for the safety of the nearby
village. The passengers gasped and grabbed the cart's
sides. Dust flew in a cloud, separating them from the humiliated thieves.

As his stallion raced down the dirt road, Murdoch
flashed a wicked grin of triumph through the stubble of

his beard. "Praise Aelynn and may the road rise up to greet us!" he shouted to the heavens.

The heavens responded by releasing a ball of blue flame.

It arced toward Murdoch in a shower of sparks, igniting a host of memories—of legends he'd heard of the blue spirits of the gods wreaking their revenge or issuing their blessings. Legends of gods he no longer believed in. Only, instead of striking him down, the light bathed him in warmth before coalescing in the black pearl of his Aelynn ring, a ring that had been part of him since birth. Dazed and bewildered, he dropped back to his saddle.

A gunshot exploded, blasting him from his high perch and knocking him to the ground.

In a rage of agony and disbelief, Murdoch rolled across the grass, flipped over onto his uninjured shoulder, and with a power he could no longer control, conjured up lightning from the clouds that had been gathering since the encounter had begun. Thunder boomed as the first bolt struck. The wind hit the treetops in gusty gales.

The rotten wood of a hollowed-out tree trunk erupted in flames. Sparks spread to drought-stricken weeds. In seconds, fire raced with the wind of the rising storm— not in the direction of the villains, but directly toward the nearby village and its unsuspecting inhabitants.

Once again, Murdoch's good intentions had ended in disaster.

# Two

Standing over her mother's deathbed, swallowing a lump of grief, Lissandra Olympus looked out over what had once been Aelynn's lush jungle. Now brown palm fronds drooped onto wilting gardenias, baked by a relentless sun. Since the disappearance of the Chalice of Plenty four years ago, the volcano had rumbled and spilled ash as it never had before, and the island's temperate climate had become increasingly unpredictable.

The marriage of Lissandra's brother, Ian, to Chantal two years ago had pleased the gods enough to make them return the summer rains that fed the river and wells, but now the water was drying up in the excessive heat. Last spring a late frost had blackened fruit blossoms, and before that, winter storms had begun to wash away the sandy beaches that protected their shoreline. The people's anger and fear stirred unrest throughout the island. With their chosen Oracle incapacitated by a stroke, the island's solidarity had cracked. People fought over who would best lead them from disaster.

"Praise Aelynn," the dying Oracle whispered from her bed on the sacred altar. An instant later, Dylys's life-affirming grip on Lissandra's hand fell loose.

Tears rolling down her cheeks, cries of protest choking her breath, Lissandra repeated the Oracle's final words, "Praise Aelynn."

The temple swelled with glorious sound from a hymn written for the occasion, sung by the choir led by Chantal.

Lissandra's tears dampened her folded hands. She prayed for a cloak of authority to fall upon her, to give her the strength her mother had possessed to lead the island back to health and happiness. But Lissandra felt nothing except soul-deep grief.

Ian hugged her, but Lissandra fastened her gaze on the still figure of their mother, unable to grasp that the holy woman who had been central in her life was gone. Never again would she hear her mother's praise or admonishments, see her bathe a newborn or lead a crowd in worship. Never again would her mother speak words of wisdom to remind her of her duties.

She didn't need any reminders of her duty now. She simply didn't wish to do it—to close her mother's eyes for the final time.

Lissandra blinked, disbelieving, as a shimmer of blue flame rose from the Oracle's lifeless figure. The crowd gasped, and the choir faded into silence as the illusion flickered and coalesced into a solid core over the late Oracle's heart.

Finally grasping the miracle, Lissandra gulped and stepped away from Ian. She straightened, standing ready. Perhaps this was the moment when she would be granted the confirmation from the gods that she needed to carry on. Neither she nor Ian had ever been present at the death of an Oracle, but they had been forewarned by the legends telling of the blue spirit flame.

*The gods were about to choose the next Oracle.*

Beside her, Ian tensed. Lissandra knew he didn't want

the task. He'd rejected it by marrying Chantal and moving off the island. Yet, if the flame chose him, he could not deny the gods. He would have to return and take up their mother's role.

Selfishly, Lissandra almost prayed that would happen.

The blue flame gathered and formed a ball. Silence grew as the crowd focused on the translucent radiance, praying a true leader would be appointed to guide them to prosperity again.

The blue spirit flame rose steadily from the altar, then hovered, before shooting forward to circle Ian's head.

Lissandra gasped as the flame darted upward in rejection, and Ian's shoulders slumped in relief. She stood alone and accepting as the flame grazed her hair. She could actually feel a beneficent wave of energy as it descended. Even so, she felt resignation rather than anticipation as the mist of Seeing spilled across her sight, revealing other places, other times—

*A flash of silvered swords. A roar of smoking cannon. Soldiers—so many colors, red, and blue, and green. White splattered with blood. A battle-hardened Murdoch, there, raising a terrified stallion on its hind legs, leading the charge . . . his saber slashed downward, disarming a ragged peasant who charged at him with a wooden pike. Using his muscled thighs to bring the horse under control, he leaned forward with fury to drive his rapier into the throat of a man raising a musket.*

*The battle re-formed and became a wooded forest, the vision blurred at the edges. In the thunderclouds hovering above the woods, her spirit guide pointed urgently at a cart progressing toward a village in the distance. There, on the same white stallion, rode Murdoch.*

*The bucolic scene burst with an explosion of thunder, gunfire, and flames.*

Abruptly, the illusion dissipated. Above her hair, the ball hovered. Lissandra felt it grow cold, leaving an emptiness inside her. She almost touched the top of her head, but the ball shot forward, dashing in front of her eyes before arcing upward and disappearing into the unrelentingly blue sky—toward *Murdoch.*

Toward the Other World beyond the invisible barrier that guarded Aelynn.

People stared at her as if she were a stranger, as much in shock as she was, waiting for her to tell them what to do, to explain what had just happened.

Lissandra crumpled to her knees, scarcely hearing the crowd's shocked cries over her own confusion. *The gods had rejected her.*

Everything she'd been, everything she'd believed, had vanished in a puff of blue flame.

The spirit of the gods had deserted Aelynn—for a man who had turned his back on all they represented!

Days later, with the volcano rumbling ominously and spewing black fumes into the once-clear air, Lissandra remained stunned and in shock.

*Could Murdoch save Aelynn?*

She'd had the time between her mother's death and interment to accept what the gods had shown her. And if she had dreaded becoming Oracle, she dreaded even more the duty that had been bestowed upon her now.

No amount of meditation had changed what Lissandra's spirit guide was insisting she do—she must leave Aelynn and find the new Oracle . . . find the one person she wished never to see again. Then she must bring him home, to see him and work with him every agonizing day.

She couldn't do it, but she had to do it.

Even though her actions went counter to everything she believed, Lissandra squeezed the last piece of clothing into her medicinal case.

Waiting for her outside her cottage, Ian frowned when she emerged carrying the bag.

Lissandra faced her older brother with equanimity. "I will need to exchange my pearls for your foreign coin."

*Always divert attention from oneself*, her mother said inside her head. *Give them tasks they understand. They will believe in your omniscience and that the gods speak through you.*

But the gods had deemed her unworthy to speak for them. That she was almost relieved by their rejection only added to Lissandra's abject misery and bewilderment.

She pulled her cloak closer against the recent summer chill. In the distance, the volcano glowed a dull, angry red beneath the heavy clouds, as it had been since the spirits had departed. Lissandra and Ian passed a group of muttering men, who, instead of greeting the last of the Olympus family with pleasantries, as they once would have done, now turned aside in bitterness.

"Where are you going?" Ian demanded, following her down the path to the harbor.

"I'm leaving Aelynn, of course," she replied.

She said it simply, as if she were announcing her intent to breakfast rather than dashing centuries of tradition to the ground and stomping on it. Worse, she was doing it to seek a rogue who could destroy them all.

Fighting her fear, she kept her back rigid, knowing that if she hesitated, all was lost.

"I can't leave the island if you do," Ian pointed out reasonably enough, since the two of them were the last of a long, proud line of Aelynn's spiritual leaders.

She could sense he was playing along with her, thinking her actions were a riddle to be solved, since she had never before left the island or expressed a desire to do so. "I am sorry," she said in all sincerity, "but you have had these past two years in the Other World with Chantal, returning only now for Mother's funeral, while I have dealt with Mother and the Council and healed the ill of mind and spirit in your absence. It is your turn to stay."

If she died in the pursuit of her insane quest, Ian's "turn" would last a lifetime. Sorrow welled up in her at the thought that she might never see her home again, or that she might cause harm because of her decision. But beneath her grief and sorrow, a shred of relief remained. If she wasn't to be Oracle, she was no longer bound by duty. It was as if the weight of an island had been removed from her shoulders.

"Don't be foolish." Ian spoke sharply. "You are the only one who can step into our mother's shoes. I will stay and direct the Council if that is your desire, but you cannot leave."

"Try and stop me," she said, placing one foot firmly in front of the other despite her fear.

She was aware of resentful glares as she strode through the maidens' village, looking to neither side, hiding her heartache beneath practiced dignity. She veered past stunted crops toward the sandy path that would take her to the harbor. Every grain of wheat, every family behind every door, every flower along the path, were engraved upon her heart. She knew them as intimately as another woman would know her lover, had blessed them, healed them, watched them grow. She *belonged* here.

But not now that she had been charged with locating the real Oracle. At least, that was how she read the signs. Aelynn help them all if even her ability to See glimpses of the future was wrong. Then she truly would be purposeless.

That thought made her stumble. Tears seared her eyes, but she refused to acknowledge them. For the sake of her soul and pride, she must believe the gods meant for her to carry out this one last duty.

She'd learned the hard way that honorable people paid the highest price in this cruel world. They lost what they most wanted to men who were greedy for power and eager to take what wasn't offered. Men like Murdoch LeDroit.

There, she'd thought his name.

The knifing pain was as intense as it had been when she'd first banished him from her mind four years ago. In fact, it was worse. Already bruised and bleeding from grief, her heart nearly broke in two under the additional burden of knowing she must once more face the angry man who had brought about the death of her father.

"You are not well," Ian argued. "You should rest."

"No one thinks *you* ill when you wish to leave the island," she retorted. As she'd been taught, she hid her inner turmoil with a raised chin and haughty tone.

"I always ask the Council's permission before leaving," Ian reminded her. "I do not have a hysterical fit and pack my bags."

"I am not hysterical." She wasn't having a fit, much as she would love to do so—a display of emotion was unbecoming to an Oracle's daughter. "I am following the path I've Seen. I will sail with whatever ship is anchored in the harbor."

Ian caught Lissandra's elbow and directed her into an orange grove, out of sight of passersby. Like many of the crops on the island, the blossoms had been blasted by an unusual frost and had produced no fruit.

"It's unwise to make decisions so soon after a loss," he told her.

Although Ian kept his voice neutral, Lissandra heard in it a gentle request that she be realistic, which undermined her determination. Fighting for strength, she remained stubbornly silent.

Still grasping her arm, Ian grimaced and ran his free hand through his dark hair. "Where will you go?"

"To wherever the gods lead me ... to Find the new Oracle," she replied, speaking from deep in that place where her spirit resided. She withheld the name of the man in her vision. Ian and no doubt every other man on the island would tie her up and confine her to the house if they knew she meant to bring Murdoch LeDroit back to Aelynn.

"I thought you didn't know who the Oracle is," Ian said, releasing her in surprise.

Now that she didn't have to physically fight him, Lissandra hastened to return to the path. "I will know him when I Find him."

"Him?" Ian stopped in his tracks.

Lissandra glanced impatiently over her shoulder. "Oracles need only be wise, possess foresight, and speak for the gods. They do not need to be female."

Ian was no fool. He fell in beside her. "You think it's Murdoch! Believe me when I tell you that you're wrong."

"I have been wrong before." Very, very perilously wrong. And about the same man of whom they spoke now.

"He's a dangerous rogue," Ian protested. "I have seen him since his banishment, as you have not. He lives the life of a warrior, pursuing greed and ambition without thought to others. His powers have become even more violent and unpredictable than they were before his banishment. Even he admits as much. He spurned my trust and returned to France when the Chalice of Plenty vanished in England. The gods *cannot* have chosen a man who has rejected everything we stand for."

Every word stung like a barb in Lissandra's heart. She'd heard all this before, but that did not ease her sense of injustice. "He did not reject Aelynn. He was banished and dispossessed. He is the only one of us, besides you and me, who has an Oracle's ability to See the future, and he is the only one with that ability who is not on the island. Unless you wish to believe the spirits have deserted us entirely, I must see if they have gone to him."

"I will Find him," Ian said. "You stay here. You need not do this yourself."

Lissandra halted on the edge of the cliff overlooking the harbor. Below, a circle of jagged dark rocks formed a natural cove for Aelynn's ships. Beyond the rocks shimmered a barrier of rainbow mist that shielded the island from human sight.

She fought to prevent her voice from breaking. "It is you who does not understand," she said. "I have been a hostage here all my life, chained to these rocks by duty and responsibility and my love for my family and the people of Aelynn. I did it because I thought I belonged here, because I thought I was needed, and because I believed the gods had chosen me to be their next Oracle. And I was *wrong*!"

This last came out as an anguished cry and spurred her to flee down the rocky path to the black sand beach below.

Ian rushed after her, grabbing her elbow. In his eyes was compassion. "I will take you wherever you like, I promise. Just do not ask me to take you to Murdoch."

Her own eyes bright with unshed tears, she glared at him. Her voice blazed with a lifetime of suppressed emotions. "Don't you see? *I no longer know who I am!* There is no *me*! I do not know what I want or where I'm needed or why I even exist." Her voice cracked with her despair. "I only know what my spirit guide shows me I must do. If Murdoch is not the man I believe he can be, then this island is doomed."

She tore away from Ian's grasp and fled to the ship bobbing in the harbor.

# Three

Stealing through the gloomy twilight of the small Breton town of Pouchay, Lissandra stumbled on a loose cobblestone and nearly fell into a malodorous puddle of— *Ewww*. She grimaced as she recognized the smell. Did these people not know such filth caused disease? It was bad enough that this barren bluff lacked palm trees and jasmine-scented breezes, but now the stench of offal and coal smoke choked her lungs.

She contemptuously dragged the billowing bulk of her clumsy Other World clothing from the gutter. All the studying she had done about the Other World—its arts and its sciences—had not prepared her for the reality. Reading books in a library was not the same as walking the streets of a foreign land. After spending her life in sandals and a sarong, she had had to learn to walk all over again, weighed down by heavy petticoats, stiff corsets, and heeled shoes—dodging the filth.

To make it this far, she'd had to prevail over the vociferous arguments of Waylan the Weathermaker and Trystan the Guardian against entering a country torn by civil war. If Ian hadn't changed her mind, did they really think their masculine illogic could persuade her?

Honestly, one would think they'd know her better by now. Murdoch would have.

*Murdoch.* Once, he had nearly torched this primitive town because of his inability to control the Greek fire he'd set loose upon the water. Trystan had clearly described how the renegade had nearly killed Mariel, Trystan's wife, in that disaster. The Guardian would not easily forgive Murdoch, even though he was convinced the havoc had been unintended. Murdoch had set the fire on purpose, and that was enough to condemn him.

Murdoch had even dared fight Ian, nearly killing him with a *pistol.* Aelynn men did not use such weapons in an honorable fight. But there had been nothing honorable about Murdoch's attempt to command the fate of France, nearly killing her brother in the process.

Lissandra had no idea what Murdoch had been doing in the two years since he'd spurned Ian's forgiveness and trust and given up on their desperate search for the missing Chalice of Plenty. Had the miserable scoundrel actually applied himself to tracking the holy relic, he might have returned it to Aelynn and restored the island to its former prosperity and health. But no, he had set off on his own path, abandoning all he'd ever been taught. Abandoning *her* along with all he'd once known and loved.

She shuddered at the memory, and at the mental blasts coming from the arguments in a smoke-tainted tavern ahead. The men of Aelynn could be loud and boisterous, not to mention dangerous when riled, but they concealed their emotions behind walls of silence. Other Worlders did not. Turbulent waves of anger, greed, and jealousy spilled from the tavern along with a ferocious din and the stench of ale and pipe smoke. Even with her mental shields in place, the emotional havoc pierced Lissandra like the sting of a thousand jellyfish. How did Ian bear it when he came here?

*How did Murdoch bear it?* Gritting her teeth, she marched on. Anything he could do, she could do better.

She had hoped Trystan and Mariel would invite her into their home and take a few days to help her acclimate to this strange new world. Instead, they'd been forced to load their young family and friends on Waylan's ship and flee the danger posed by the newly arrived Surveillance Committee from Paris, which was charged with checking travel documents of foreigners within France's borders. Fearing spies on every sand spit, France had closed its shores to strangers—and executed anyone who did not carry the appropriate papers.

Lissandra doubted the committee would find anyone stranger than Aelynners. If a man as experienced in Other World affairs as Trystan feared this *committee*, she would have to be doubly wary. She couldn't, after all, prove she was a citizen of a country that didn't exist on any maps.

She hesitated outside the tall, forbidding stone structure of an inn, her extra senses picking up an odd vibration. Had she just sensed another Aelynner in the vicinity? Surely Trystan had made sure that all their countrymen had left the dangers of war-torn France.

The fleeting impression of grief and rage vanished as if a wall of silence had descended when she reached out with her senses. She didn't think an Other Worlder could create a mental wall of silence, but what did she know? She'd never been here before.

She shivered, hating the damp chill, hating being intimidated by the loud and violent inhabitants of this place. She debated whether to seek this person out and decided against it. It challenged her best abilities to accomplish her one task—locate Murdoch, verify that the gods had chosen him, and if so, drag him home. She would allow no distraction.

She picked up her pace and marched on. First, she would find transportation. At least her Empathy should lead her to choose a decent guide. Unless that, too, was as skewed as everything else here.

The cart Lissandra rode in rattled over a barren hill, crossed a ridge, and descended into a forested valley. A smudge of smoke hovered over the treetops below, blocking the scenic view.

Her heart skipped a beat. For the first time in four years, she could *feel* Murdoch's presence. He'd been part of her life since childhood. No matter how much her memories hurt, no matter what people told her, she couldn't stifle this unwarranted longing to see him again. The man Ian had described had lost the laughter in his eyes and become a fountain of hostility. Had he grown worse since Ian had left him nearly two years ago?

She was about to find out. He was down there somewhere, although the dynamic life force that had driven him since childhood was oddly banked.

Considering the lightning and explosive fireworks he'd set off to cause her father's death, the smoke shrouding the forest did not bode well. The horrific memory shredded her thin confidence.

"The village is through the forest, near a lake," the driver told her as he clicked his mule past a tumble of boulders that looked as if the gods had heaved them there in a Herculean tantrum. "It is usually a pretty picture this time of year."

At the bottom of the hill, the driver rolled the cart off

the main road and took a meandering dirt lane through scorched fields, skirting the still-smoldering forest.

"It is a miracle anyone survived the fire," the driver said. "Lightning struck the woods that terrible day. We've had a dry spring, and the sparks set fire to the weeds and spread to the wheat straw that our young men hadn't been home to plow. It carried across the fields, then leaped to the roofs. They lost only one bed-ridden old woman. They would have lost more had it not been for the stranger."

Lissandra sensed the presence that *ought* to be Murdoch. But his essence seemed to be a mere cinder of the white-hot heat she remembered. Or perhaps, she thought acidly, he'd burned out his rage on a village. That would be typical of the dangerous man he'd become. She had no illusion that the *lightning* had natural origins, not with Murdoch in the vicinity. Not after the vision she'd had at her mother's deathbed. Her vague hopes slipped into despair.

"What stranger?" she asked, if only to prove her theory.

"He gives us no name, so the priest calls him Abel. Old women call him a saint, but they are romantic fools. I call a man who is strong and skilled enough to drive off a half dozen thieves a warrior, not a saint. He was only passing through, but those he saved claim he single-handedly fought a troop of deserting thieves before the storm struck. They went on, but he stayed to fight the fire, and now he is helping the village rebuild."

*Murdoch.* It had to be Murdoch, although she could make little sense of his actions. With his gifts, he could have ruled all France. Was she wrong and the spirits had *not* descended on him? If so, what must she do?

As the old mule ambled around a bend, Lissandra

calmed her growing panic by admiring a row of sunflowers emerging along the edge of a field sprouting new green wheat where smoke still smoldered. How could life return so quickly to the scorched earth?

It couldn't. *Unless an Aelynn Agrarian lived here.* Murdoch had never shown any talent in that direction—although he did have destructive earth skills. Had he found an Agrarian Crossbreed here? One who might be responsible for the rapid new growth? Had he found a Crossbreed wife, as Ian and Trystan had? Lissandra clasped her fingers tighter and focused on doing her duty.

She'd told the driver that her husband had taken ill along this road, and she required a man to drive her from town to town so she might seek him. If Murdoch was married, a public encounter could prove embarrassing. "Where do those who were burned out live now?" she inquired to prevent her thoughts from straying.

"Most share the cottages that survived the fire. Others live among the ruins." The driver shrugged. "We are too poor to own land, and these days, who knows who is responsible for repairing the houses? Our landlords have fled France. Our so-called leaders argue in Paris, telling us we must pay tithes to a church that no longer exists and rents to a government that cannot help us. They send deputies from the Tribunal to make certain we do not complain as we pay. Good Bretons rise up in arms against the patriotic Guards, but here, in this village"—he shrugged again—"we simply wish a roof over our heads."

She had seen the soldiers—the National Guards—in Pouchay, heard that angry villagers throughout Brittany had risen up in revolt against them, but she had not yet seen an outbreak of the violence that she could feel simmering across the land.

As they approached the village, she could see burned-out shells of stone houses, their ancient thatching gone, their contents scorched beyond repair. She was relieved she'd reached her journey's end, but this disaster crippled her hope that perhaps Murdoch had miraculously changed and thus earned the regard of the gods.

Despite the temptation, she refused to turn back without personally confronting Murdoch. Dreading the encounter, she picked at her cloak and scanned the street in search of his familiar form.

"Do you know who I might talk to?" She glanced at the two-story inn ahead. The fire hadn't reached its tall roof, although the whitewash on its lower walls was blackened with soot.

"You may need to offer coin for answers," the driver said. "They are isolated here and not likely to speak with strangers."

She had exchanged her pearls for a purse of coins at a moneylender's, as she'd learned to do from Mariel. Using her Empathy to judge the moneylender's greed had resulted in a fair trade, but avoiding the thieves who had followed her had been daunting. Aelynn law required she not cause harm or display her supernatural abilities in this world. But just thinking that an Olympus of Aelynn was reduced to *hiding* from miscreants because of an irresponsible bastard like Murdoch deepened her anger and resentment.

She produced the small silver coin Trystan had said would buy almost anything. "Is this enough?"

The driver nodded curtly. "Do not display more than one. The world is full of thieves."

She shuddered, knowing the truth of that. In just two days, she'd had thieves attack her for the coins she carried, and seen the fire damage caused by deserters. If deprivation drove people to such levels, what would become of Aelynn should its crops continue to fail, or the volcano continue to spew its deadly lava?

As they drew closer, she could see a man in a neat blue uniform lounging at the tavern door, watching her arrival with suspicion, reminding her that this village was not any safer than the port she'd left behind. She had already discovered that uniforms did not mean security.

Also noticing the soldier, her driver spit on the ground and guided his cart down an alley, out of sight of the main street. "There are committees for everything these days. Here, they send the Committee of Public Safety to conscript our men," he explained with bitterness. "In the name of the Revolution, they have been licensed with the power of life and death, but they do naught except harass the innocent when they should be fighting for our country. It does not matter who you are—they will ask for your documents. Do not go near them if you're alone."

Having no documents to show, Lissandra found it far simpler to travel unobtrusively and pray no one noticed her. It had worked thus far, but it wouldn't if she stayed in any one place for very long.

Her driver pointed to a row of attached stone houses covered in soot and scorched in places, but relatively intact in comparison with those on the main street. "The widow Girard is a respectable woman with a young son she raises alone. Tell her Luc sent you."

Lissandra handed him a coin and let him assist her from the cart. Given that she had the strength to knock the driver over with a slap, Lissandra found quaint the custom of treating women as weak, inferior creatures, but she had spent a lifetime disguising her inner self while studying others. She was an adept student.

*An Oracle must be cold and harsh to be heeded*, she heard her mother say. *An Oracle must be superior to those she would lead.* And so with discipline and hard work, Lissandra had made herself superior, which had put her on a lonely pedestal. Now that she'd stepped down, it seemed practical to be unassuming—provided she was offered no provocation to act otherwise.

The widow Girard was a small wren of a woman who checked the alley before opening her door. "There are too many prying eyes these days," she whispered after Lissandra introduced herself. "They seek spies and traitors around every corner. And the elders whisper of witches and demons."

Lissandra had no understanding of the subject or any interest in it, but she listened politely until she was offered an opportunity to speak. "I seek the stranger that Luc tells me has recently arrived. I had word my husband was ill along this road, and I hope the stranger might tell me of his whereabouts."

"The stranger is everywhere," the widow claimed, with a broad sweep of her hand. "He never rests. He is in the fields when we rise, and hauling broom for thatch when we go to bed. He fights the fires that linger in the peat fields."

Lissandra found it hard to fathom a warrior like Murdoch building instead of destroying, but she decided to reserve judgment until she saw it for herself. "Where does he sleep?" Or, *when* does he sleep? might be a better question if she was to believe one man could do all that the widow claimed.

The woman shrugged. "No one knows. You might ask at the church. The priest has been staying there to guard the statues from the thieving deserters who hide in the woods."

After obtaining directions to the church, Lissandra began her search. She prayed that it was her smoke-filled surroundings and her need to block the villagers' belligerent emotions that prevented her from sensing Murdoch clearly. If she let down her shields, the grief and hatred spilling from an entire town would incapacitate her.

When she saw no one at the church, she set out along a back way into the countryside, following her meager Finding instinct. She'd been warned that wolves and wild boars still roamed this wilderness, but she sensed few creatures of any size except some men in the distance—where her instincts told her she would find Murdoch.

Taking a deep breath to steady her ragged nerves now that she was so close to her objective, she entered the edge of the woodland.

As if a fire-breathing dragon lurked in the shadows under the trees, a cloud of smoke engulfed her, and she coughed harshly. Curse the gods, but this was worse than climbing the volcano's slope. She could feel the heat through the soles of her shoes.

A rabbit dashed across her foot. She tripped and caught her balance on a tall standing stone. The rock was so hot, she quickly withdrew her palm before it burned.

She dragged her gown up from where it tangled her feet, and held the fabric in her hands, using her Aelynn strength to stride faster. She doubted anyone could see her abnormal speed in this murk, and her lungs would appreciate a hasty departure.

A geyser of fire flamed upward through the layers of decaying vegetation on the side of the road. Startled, she halted. Was Murdoch out there, warning her to leave?

The devil she would.

Determined, she marched on, coughing harder in the

thickening smoke. She would have this confrontation done with. The setting might be ominous, but it was certainly fitting—

A demon shot through the smoke at inhuman speed. Lissandra glimpsed only a blur of broad, filthy bare chest before iron arms tackled her waist. She shrieked as the creature tore her heels from the ground and tumbled with her into the ashes on the far side of the lane.

Another fiery geyser spewed into the air on the spot where she'd just been standing.

Muttered curses assaulted her ears. With bare arms propped on either side of her head and muscular thighs pinning her legs, the demon prevented her escape. In shock, Lissandra closed her eyes and screamed at this smothering male proximity. Her attacker covered her mouth with his hand.

Refusing to surrender, she locked her mental shields against any emotional assault and shoved at broad— naked—shoulders, with the intent of flinging her assailant into the air with her superior strength. Beneath her palms she encountered the grit of soot and ash and the powerful play of muscles, but no matter how much strength she applied, her attacker merely beat the ground with his fist.

The ground trembled. She opened her eyes in terror.

And watched the geyser of fire die.

Cursing tonelessly in several languages with phrases so vivid they scorched her ears, her attacker trapped her between his bulging arms, glared down at her through the smoke, and, after only a moment's hesitation, covered her mouth with his.

Stunned by this invasion of her sacred person, Lissandra grabbed the monster's arms and tried to pry him away. She kicked and struggled, but her screams were smothered by lips so commanding she almost forgot to fight.

She *did* forget to fight. Senselessly, she clung to the strong support of his arms and kissed him back. Or maybe not so senselessly. This kiss lived inside her heart. . . .

. . . and her memories. She had dreamed of this kiss so long. . . .

His mouth tasted of strong wine, his beard bristles chafed her skin, and the heavy desire consuming them erased rational thought. She parted her lips at her assailant's insistence, drank his breath into her lungs, mated her tongue with his, and almost burst into flames.

Only when all the alarms clamoring in the back of her mind merged did sense return. With a cry of outrage, Lissandra summoned her strength and brought up her knee.

The confounded skirts hindered her effectiveness. Before she could emasculate the bastard, he rolled off her. Lying flat on his back, he stared at the leaves above them, loudly repeating his curses of earlier.

Undeterred, Lissandra turned on her side and glared into the piratical unshaven features she knew too well. Rising up on one arm, she smashed her fist into his iron-hewn abdomen. He merely *oof*ed and grabbed her elbow, pulling her off-balance and across his bare torso.

"By all the gods in this universe and the next," he roared, "this is the most asinine, ridiculous, inane, spectacularly stupid behavior I've yet encountered! What the *devil* was Ian thinking to send you here?"

Three more fiery geysers burst from the earth's floor.

Lissandra had found Murdoch.

# Four

*L* *issandra.*
   In the Other World. Alone. This could not be good.

Cursing the peat fire, her presence, and his stupidity in kissing her, Murdoch sat up, dragging Lis with him. If she wanted to run away from Aelynn, there was an entire world she could have chosen to explore. Why had she come here?

Another geyser of flame erupted from the peat bog of the forest floor. He'd spent months practicing self-control, and he lost it with one glance at Lis.

Shoving her into a hummock above the peat bed, he grabbed his temples and concentrated with all his might. With Lis, he didn't have to pretend he was dousing the fires with dirt, but she shattered the concentration he needed to mentally snuff the fire.

Once the danger was past, with only a vague ache at the back of his head as a reminder of his incompetence, he had time to contemplate Lis's improbable arrival, but he was too stunned to do more than act on instinct and help her from the filthy ground. The reality of her slender hand in his callused palm jarred him even more than the delicious, unbelievable taste of her kiss.

*Lissandra? Here?*

The possibility that Aelynn had somehow exploded and existed no more—for what else could have brought her to leave it?—froze his soul. His home had always been an oasis in the back of his mind, an idyllic place he dreamed about to which he did not belong.

But if the princess had left her throne . . .

Then he remembered. Wincing, Murdoch rubbed his still-healing shoulder and, with horror, glanced at the glowing ring he'd been trying to ignore since he'd been shot. His Aelynn ring of silence was so much a part of him that he'd have to cut off his finger to be rid of the glow of condemnation that had settled there.

If there were gods, they obviously hated him. Nothing else could account for Lis's arrival now, after all these years, when he was in the midst of another odious disaster of his own creation. The blue flame hovering over his ring taunted him with his guilt.

Scalding memories tore through Murdoch's soul: of Luther falling to his death at his hands; of leading a troop to hunt down his former friend Trystan and setting fire to a harbor; of wearing a French uniform and shooting Ian, his brother at heart. Even conjuring up his pride in his officer's stripes as he'd ridden his valiant steed into battle, rapier flashing, could not ease the pain of knowing he'd fought for the wrong reasons. And then there had been the final horror that even he couldn't justify or understand. . . .

If the blue flame meant the gods had targeted him for retribution, they'd found no surer vessel of revenge than Lis. Regrettably, he knew that if Lis had made up her mind to hunt him down—for whatever reason—she would follow him to the ends of the earth. And Murdoch would lie down and die rather than harm Aelynn's goddess.

Yet she'd kissed him in all his unworthiness, with a hunger to match his own. *Impossible.*

He'd hoped for far too long that she would forgive and forget and send someone looking for him. He'd given up that hope after he'd abandoned her brother in England.

He stamped out embers, trying not to recall how right her mouth had felt on his.

As usual, he hid his real feelings behind sarcasm when he finally spoke. "What the devil is the high-and-mighty Oracle's daughter doing here?"

"And a pleasure it is to see you, too," she said, adjusting her foolish hat and shaking leaves and sticks from her garments. "Do you always greet visitors with fountains of fire?"

Lis never wore skirts and petticoats. He stared at the ethereal silver and gold woman he remembered, now weighed down by the crude heavy garments of this world, and couldn't integrate the two images. Even covered head to toe in clothing filthy with ash, she was the tropical goddess he remembered, and his heart was still blacker than her skirts.

He picked up his shovel and ax and looked for more hot spots. "The peat burns underground. Unless you've come to help put it out, you need to leave."

"I see your charm has not improved during your years away." Ice dripped from her tongue.

And still he smelled the scents of sea air and jasmine of the girl he'd once known. She was like a breeze straight from Aelynn, and he defied his longing by pretending to search for any lingering fire. "Have you come to punish me for my sins?" he asked coldly. He needed to walk away before he fell into his old role and reached out to rub a smear of soot from her beautiful peach-flushed cheek. She wouldn't appreciate the caress.

"I doubt that's possible." She rubbed the dirt smear away herself. "I understand this time your fire killed an old woman."

"I saved the woman," he protested. "But she died of natural causes before I could carry her out of the flames."

"And I'm sure there is an excellent explanation for the conflagration also," she said in a rational tone that taunted him with his faults. "As I'm certain there was a logical reason for nearly killing Trystan and his wife with Greek fire, and attacking Ian with the intent to maim, if not kill. You always have an excuse."

She sounded just like her condescending mother. He needed the reminder that she was no longer the adoring playmate she'd once been—and that he'd been the one to turn her cold.

He set the wind to clearing the murk around them so he could see her, really *see* her. Overhead, branches swayed and rattled in the breeze he'd summoned, but at least no more embers flamed to life.

With the smoke gone, the full impact of Lis's slender, radiant beauty an arm's breadth away nearly crippled him, but Murdoch refused to falter in her eyes any more than he would in the face of danger. As usual, her proud mask of scorn and arrogance tarnished the gentle spirit he had once known. Or thought he'd known. The last he'd seen of her, she'd been well on her way to becoming as judgmental as her harridan of a mother.

Lissandra studied him as he studied her. He dripped sweat, he stank of smoke, and his crude homespun trousers were plastered to his legs. Murdoch wickedly considered embracing her again, although finally having Lis in his arms would no doubt ignite his lust like dry tinder, and he still had the result of his last error to clean up. "I repeat, what the devil are you doing here?"

Her gaze finally found the blue flame flickering on his finger, and her expression of dismay was so poignant that he almost walked away.

"I was right," she whispered. "The gods *have* chosen you."

He snorted rudely. "If there are any gods, they wish to destroy me." And had almost succeeded, if he accepted the glow as anything more than a lightning strike. Lightning was the only explanation that he could accept right now.

Lissandra had learned what she needed to know. The spirits had rejected her and Ian as Oracle and had chosen Murdoch.

Given that the spirits had not yet *entered* Murdoch, she supposed some doubt about his suitability must linger. For good reason, she knew. His crimes were many. It served him right to be reduced to a mere woodcutter instead of taking over the world as he'd probably intended.

She fought her feminine interest in the way Murdoch's muscles rippled beneath his soot-blackened skin as he swung an ax to level a scorched oak. She'd grown up in a land of giant men, some larger and more muscled, but none as bronzed and hardened as this rogue had become. It had ever been Murdoch who had held her interest, who had laughed with her, teased her out of her sulks, taught her to ride the wind currents off the cliffs, into the sea.

Of course, she'd broken her wrist attempting to match his accomplishments, but for one lovely summer before he'd sailed away the first time, she had believed the gods had intended him to be hers, and she'd felt blessed. That had lasted only until he'd sailed back and killed her father.

And still, even seeing Mighty Murdoch reduced to this, she knew he was the only man who could stir her desire. At least she'd had the sense to end that self-destructive kiss before the longing in her lower belly consumed her. The flare of lust in Murdoch's eyes had almost melted her shields.

She watched as he did his rude best to pretend she didn't exist. Had he caused the flaming geysers—or was he curbing them? With LeDroit, it was always hard to tell.

"My *mother* tried to destroy you," she said, acknowledging his earlier assertion, forcing him to admit the obvious. "I think the gods have other ideas. They left the island to seek you."

Wiping his brow with the back of his arm, Murdoch glared at her through narrowed eyes. "Dylys wouldn't allow the gods to do such a thing."

"My mother is dead," Lissandra said flatly. "She suffered a stroke two years ago and never recovered. She died a fortnight ago." She'd tamped down her tears on the journey here, but even a hint of sympathy from him would raise them.

Murdoch didn't provide it. Without any sign of regret or sorrow for the woman who had mentored him since youth, he swung back to splitting a fallen oak tree into planks. Lissandra winced as the ax slammed into the wood with such force that it stuck. Murdoch pounded the scorched heel of his boot against the tree trunk until he'd dislodged the blade. His trousers tightened against the powerful muscles of his thigh and calf, and Lissandra closed her eyes against the memory of him striding bare-legged and strong across the island.

She ought to leave. She couldn't subdue Murdoch, truss him up, and haul him back to Aelynn on her own. If his control of his gifts was still unpredictable, she wasn't even certain that returning home with him would be a wise idea. She had hoped . . .

She didn't know what she had hoped. She'd been a fool.

Resting his hands on his thighs, Murdoch paused as if to catch his breath. "May the gods take her and bless her," he murmured quietly. "I am sorry for your loss."

As she had feared, tears flowed down her cheeks at just this hint of the considerate man she had once known. Lissandra picked up her hated skirt and petticoat and prepared to drag her ridiculous heels back down the rutted path. "The gods want you to take her place," she informed him in arctic tones. "Anytime you're ready to come home, just let us know."

Murdoch swung his ax again and again, splintering the scorched tree into a stack of lumber, determined not to soothe the tears he heard in her voice. Lis's kiss still burned his lips and smoldered his insides. Loneliness for the family and friends he'd left behind swamped him as he watched her stride away, out of his life, her ridiculous skirts swaying. She belonged in loose linen tugged by a warm breeze, her hair flying like spun silk. He'd spent nights dreaming of his home and the woman who was meant to be his, imagining what it would be like to finally wrap her in his arms, and teach her the pleasures of her body.

He tried not to wonder who had taught her those pleasures in his place, but pain grabbed his heart in both hands and twisted until he almost howled at the injustice of gods he didn't even believe existed.

Lifting the stack of lumber, he strode after her—only because her path was the same as his, he told himself. And possibly because he would never see her again and needed time to soak up this brief memory.

He saw her ahead, fighting with her clothing and not attempting to use her Aelynn speed. He no longer cared if eyes watched them from beyond every bush. Even carrying a load too heavy to hold by normal standards, he covered the ground at a superhuman pace. Let them burn him as a devil. It would be simpler than living this life of torment.

He could have passed Lis by and strode on into the village, but he'd never been one to resist temptation. Despite the ashes she'd rolled in, the scent of the sea clung to her like an exotic perfume, and he breathed in deeply as he drew alongside her. Lis had the ability to stand straight and tall and glare down at everyone as if from a summit. He'd forgotten how small she really was. Even though she wore heels and a hat, the top of her head barely reached his eye level. He shifted the stack of lumber to a more stable position and fell in stride beside her.

"Who brought you here?" he demanded. "They should not let you wander alone."

"Why do you care?" she asked snidely. "It is evident you prefer grubbing in the dirt to the duties for which you've been chosen."

"I don't believe in gods or tall tales," he said with a scorn he'd developed over these past years. "Legends are just that, legends. If we believed them all, we'd believe giants once walked the earth, the world was covered with an ocean, and unicorns gamboled about with fairies."

"Just as there are no mermaids and Weathermakers,

Healers and psychics—all with gifts beyond ordinary human comprehension on an invisible island called Aelynn," she retorted.

Aelynn was *home*, not a fairy tale. He was so pathetically eager for news from home and conversation with his peers that he nearly revealed too much without thinking. He bit his tongue and walked faster. If he worked quickly enough, he'd complete repairs on another roof by morning. If he stayed away from Lis until she left, he might even survive her visit.

Ian was likely waiting in town, prepared to slit his throat. Despair washed over Murdoch. He'd let down everyone he'd ever loved or admired, and failed to accomplish anything in the process. He would do this one thing, rebuild the village he'd destroyed, if it killed him.

Undeterred by his rudeness, Lis caught up with him. "To these people, *we're* legends. Our history may not be written, but Aelynn exists. How can you ignore what we are, what we are meant to be, in favor of . . . ?" She gestured to the burned-out fields and the desolate village ahead.

He gazed at her incredulously. "Your mother *banished* me from Aelynn. She attempted to strip me of my powers and leave me useless. I am hated by every man, woman, and child on the island. Have you become so arrogant as to believe you can just present me to the Council and say, 'Here he is,' and they will accept me as the chosen one?"

"They *have* to accept you!" she cried. "There is no one else."

He snorted and walked faster. "Then Aelynn is as doomed as France. At least here, I can be of some use."

In this world, redemption was still possible.

"What happened to set the village on fire?"

"Nothing extraordinary," he said, refusing to mention the blue flame that had distracted him, almost causing his death. To admit it existed was to accept the plausibility of Lis's theory. He swallowed to clear his suddenly obstructed throat. "I left Paris with a cartload of escaped prisoners, thinking I could take them to the coast. We ran into brigands. I inadvertently started a fire." If that didn't send her fleeing, he couldn't imagine what would.

She shot him a quelling glance that said she hadn't expected less.

Once they reached the village, he flung the boards down in front of the priest's house and waited for her to go back to Ian. He refused to open his psychic senses to Find her brother's whereabouts. Being scolded by a woman was bad enough. He didn't need it from a man who had once been his friend.

She looked down her nose at him as only the queenly Lissandra Olympus could do. "If you are the one who burned the village, I am sure they will be delighted at having a destructive monster like you to aid them."

He refused to wince as her barb hit its mark. Turning his back, he began scaling the stone wall of the parsonage with a board over his shoulder.

He knew the instant she strode off.

Once safely on top of the wall, Murdoch threw the plank over the post he'd already nailed in place, satisfied he'd done the right thing. Just to test that he wasn't losing his instincts, he opened his mental barrier to the town below. Immediately, he wished he hadn't.

*Hell and damnation.* Lis was storming blindly down the street with her Empathy sealed off, and the Public Safety Committee had started drinking early this evening. The simmering hatred and violence of the uniformed squad rose above all the everyday emotions of the townspeople. The committee had already condemned the mayor for "never having good republicans at his table" and sent him off for execution before Murdoch had arrived.

They were bloody-minded tyrants, bored and waiting to pounce on anyone for the least infraction. Their Parisian arrogance and hatred for those unlike themselves put them at odds with the simple people they'd been sent to protect.

Murdoch tried to tell himself that Ian would defend Lissandra, but his senses Found no trace of her damned brother. What the *devil* were they thinking to let her out here on her own? Lis knew nothing of the hazards here. She evidently couldn't even *walk* without being forced to shut off the Empathy that would warn her of danger. The chaotic, often violent emotions of this world must be pure torture for someone of her sensitivity.

Uttering another curse, Murdoch scanned the scene below—and found Lis wisely skirting the tavern. He was already halfway down the wall before a pair of soldiers sauntered from the inn as if they'd been watching— which was what they were paid to do.

Murdoch's keen hearing picked up their words even before he reached the ground.

"If it's a man you seek, I'm at your disposal," the older soldier called. He swaggered into the street to intercept Lis's progress, clutching the hilt of his sword as if it represented his masculinity.

If Lis refused the invitation, he would demand to see her papers. And she wouldn't have any. That was all the excuse needed to condemn her as a spy and be treated as worse. Even though Murdoch raced to join her, he had no way of stopping the confrontation. One threat to Lis and he let months of practicing composure and stifling his temper go by the wayside.

He curled his fingers to restrain his lethal instincts, but the fury he worked so hard to bank combusted, and a wind howled down the street in the direction of his rage. Intensifying with distance, it bent tall trees, rattled doors, blew off hats and shingles—and blasted the uniformed soldier out of his boots.

The soldier's terrified shriek as he flew backward pierced the stormy air.

Having served its purpose, the wind died as abruptly as it had begun. After peering from their doors and windows, the villagers left their hiding places and crept into the street, gawking at the debris that lay scattered in the wake of the sudden wind burst, then glancing around until they found the source of the screams amid the tree branches.

The soldier dangled by his bandolier high above the tavern roof. The limb supporting his weight bent dangerously low, in imminent peril of snapping.

Lissandra sensed Murdoch's approach even before he grabbed her arm and jerked her backward into the gathering crowd as men raced to find ladders and rescue the shrieking soldier.

She'd dropped her mental shields at the first sign of danger. Now, buffeted by the piercing agony of the mob's fear, she could barely stand, and she clutched Murdoch's arm rather than brush him away.

"You protected me," she accused him. That he had done so—again—in a tempestuous manner that only he could generate weakened her knees as much as the chaos did.

"You thought I would not?" he asked coldly. "Or that I couldn't?"

She needed to keep her wits about her. This was no time for their argument to boil to a head. They'd called attention to themselves. Not good.

People turned to stare and whisper as the crowd's fears found a focus on the strangers among them. Lissandra, not Murdoch, had been the one standing closest to the soldier. She could sense their fear of her, which had only escalated with Murdoch's abrupt arrival.

This incident seemed simple to resolve without their immediately running away.

Lissandra leaned her weight on Murdoch's arm until he was forced to hold her upright. He seemed prepared to do so, but she abruptly grabbed her hat to straighten it, hoping to distract the mob with the mundane.

"The wind," she exclaimed loudly. "I've never felt such wind! Is this place cursed?" With what little mind control she possessed, she nudged the villagers to look back at the man in the tree and associate the curse with the villain they all feared.

They did so with gratifying alacrity, murmuring among themselves, shaking their heads in bewilderment.

The second soldier glanced suspiciously from the place where she had been standing to the screaming man in the tree, then back to the two of them edging out of the crowd.

Before the soldier could speak, a priest pushed through the throng, quieting his more-frightened parishioners. He, too, glanced at the screaming bully, then at the second soldier.

"We are blessed," the priest declared loudly, stopping beside Lissandra and Murdoch. "The saints protect us from drunkards. Come, my friends, you are fortunate you are not harmed." He offered his arm. It took a moment before Lissandra realized she was meant to take it.

She dropped a little curtsy that Ian's wife, Chantal, had taught her. "It was most frightening, monsieur."

"*Père* Antoine," Murdoch whispered in her ear, falling into step beside her as the crowd parted, their fears apparently relieved by the priest's presence. "Or *citoyen*, if you wish to respect the new republic."

It was almost like having the old Murdoch back, whispering wicked commentary in her ear through Council meetings. She swallowed and fought her gratitude at his correcting her error. She had once been easily swayed by him. Never again.

"I apologize. I am much shaken, Père Antoine," she said to the priest.

"Of course, mademoiselle," he said, proving he preferred the old terms, "it is understandable. Where do you stay? I will take you there."

She had left her bag at the widow's, prepared to remain there until she found Murdoch. Now that she'd found him, she had no reason to linger. Except that going home without Murdoch, no matter how far he'd fallen, felt like failure, and she refused to accept defeat so easily. She ignored the priest's question while pondering her choices. "Do you often have winds like this?"

"Only since Abel has come to stay with us."

Abel? She glanced at Murdoch, but his expression remained enigmatic.

"Abel," the priest continued, "it would be best if you stay in the chapel until I can speak with you again."

Lissandra understood the priest's fears. She knew enough of the ignorance of the Other World to grasp the danger they faced if Murdoch refused to leave the village and couldn't restrain his gifts. And if he refused to leave, she could not either. Despite all rationality, her decision was made without a second thought.

"He is my husband," she told the priest, defying Murdoch's fingers digging into her upper arm. "I heard he was ill, and I have been looking all over France for him." There, let Murdoch react to that declaration.

He released her arm, and faded into the shadows of the alley where they walked. He was still there, listening, *judging*, but not interfering.

The priest stopped short and stared at her in dismay. "Surely he did not abandon you, madame. He is a paragon of strength who mends our village as our government will not."

"Paragons don't throw men into trees," Murdoch corrected with sarcasm, crossing his arms and leaning his wide shoulders against the burned-out skeleton of a house. "It is only a matter of time before the committee decides I am a demon traitor."

"That is ridiculous," the priest argued. "What you have accomplished in so short a time is a miracle blessed by God. The whole town supports you."

At being called a miracle, Murdoch shot Lissandra a glance that should have sizzled, but she ignored the warning. "My husband"—she sought some explanation for Murdoch's behavior—"seems not himself. Was there some accident in which he was hurt?"

Père Antoine's eyes widened. "He was shot from behind while saving his friends from thieves. He healed so well. . . ."

Shot! Someone had almost killed a potential Oracle? Lissandra glanced in horror at the half-hidden man, but he offered only an angled eyebrow, daring her to comment. Aelynners healed quickly, and Murdoch faster than most, since he possessed Healing abilities of his own. She shook her head free of fretting thoughts to concentrate on getting what she wanted.

She touched the priest's arm earnestly, willing him to believe her. "I don't think it's wise for my husband to travel until he recovers fully."

The priest relaxed. She felt sorry for the man. The villagers' homes and livelihoods had been ruined, and only Murdoch had come to their aid. The priest protected his people as fiercely as she guarded hers.

"Your ... husband ... has gifts that we need," the priest murmured, "gifts from God. I do not understand how he does it, but in only a few days, he has restored the church. And in the absence of our menfolk, he has begun replanting the wheat fields all on his own. He is a miracle worker."

"He has studied under great men from around the world," Lissandra assured him.

Murdoch coughed to cover a snigger. She knew him that well, even after all these years. At least he wasn't raging and throwing a tantrum at the lies she was telling. She would no doubt pay for them later. If human behavior was the same here as at home, he'd be scorned by all if he did not eventually leave with his "wife."

"Ah," the priest said. "That explains much." He looked at Murdoch sharply. "Perhaps we will not say this too loudly for a while yet. These are simple people who need a miracle to believe in. If you are to stay for any length of time, you will need to behave more circumspectly."

"I will attempt to refrain from heaving scoundrels into trees," Murdoch said with insouciance, daring the priest to believe the impossible. "But I would house my lady wife safely."

Lissandra suspected she was about to regret her impulsive decision to become his "wife."

"Of course," the priest agreed, pulling on his bottom lip in thought.

"The woodcutter's cottage will suffice," Murdoch continued as if he'd not been interrupted. "It is some distance from town, so I cannot get into too much trouble."

"But the fields . . ." The priest looked up anxiously.

"He is injured," Lissandra reminded him. "It is far better if he imparts his wisdom to your people rather than do it all himself."

"Fair enough. We will provide the cottage and what food we can in return for his lessons. Knowledge can be passed on, and we will be richer for it."

"Wise man, Père Antoine, not to argue with the lady. We wouldn't wish her to lose her temper." With a smirk, Murdoch straightened from the wall he'd been leaning against. "It might be best if the committee does not know where we are. I'll come to town instead."

"Perhaps that is best," the priest agreed. "But if you need anything . . ." The priest made the sign of the cross. "In this time of trouble, you have been our savior. Go with God."

He blended into the shadows in the direction of the chapel, leaving them alone, together.

# *Five*

Murdoch grabbed his *wife's* elbow, and dragged Lis toward the stable. She resisted. He tugged. She practically flew through the air, and he cursed his own strength. He set her down and released the slender hand to which he'd become attached so quickly.

He'd overcome his disappointment that he couldn't shove her back into Ian's custody. Given Lis's tenacity, what she hoped to accomplish by coming here alone did not bear scrutiny. No matter how high-and-mighty and powerful she thought herself, he knew he couldn't let her roam loose in a world of chaos she didn't understand and would probably want to Heal. He snarled in exasperation.

She wrestled with her filthy skirt, and he could almost feel the withering frost of her glare. To have Lis find him in the midst of yet another disaster peeled off his callous hide and left him raw and exposed.

He'd already discovered that he could never have a real relationship with any woman in the Other World. Sooner or later he always revealed himself for the monster he was. With Lis, however . . . she already knew him, inside and out, good and bad. There were far larger reasons why he couldn't have her, yet it was a comfort to be *known*.

"I assume you have some means of transport?" she asked.

"And you knew this how?" Acknowledging the correctness of her supposition, he grabbed her arm and steered her toward a structure the fire had not harmed.

"Because that is what you do—plan and scheme and look so far into the future that normal people do not understand your intent. Most of the time, it is vastly frustrating because you do not communicate well."

Entering the stable, he lit a torch hanging on the wall just inside the door. "I doubt that I have improved since you saw me last."

He set the torch in a bracket. A horse whinnied and kicked its door, and he scooped a handful of oats from the barrel.

"Was hanging that soldier from a tree branch intentional or accidental?"

"A little of both," he said. "I wanted to kill him but restrained myself."

"Before, you would not have bothered restraining yourself. Perhaps you exhibit signs of improvement."

He knew his flaws better than she did. He deserved her scorn and so did not respond to it. He reached for the homespun shirt he kept in the stable, and shrugged into it, not wanting to feel so naked in front of her. Under the circumstances, he couldn't expect to start up where they'd left off.

He led the mare out of its stall and fed her oats. She bucked her head affectionately, hitting him in the chin. Murdoch scratched behind her ear and in the torchlight considered his "wife" with an interest he could barely conceal. What the hell should he do with her?

He knew what he would *like* to do with her, but that would be perilous for all concerned.

She offered her hand for the mare to sniff, then rubbed the horse's white-striped nose. "I've wanted to learn more of these horses Ian told me about. She has a delightful mind."

Her gesture of friendship to an animal destroyed all his belligerent defenses just as her kiss had shredded his wits.

"You didn't come here to learn about horses." He brought out the small cart he'd made. "So why are you here?"

"Because it is my duty." Then she added, in that studious, observant manner he would have given years of his life to hear again, "The gods must be testing you."

If he still believed in fair and just gods, he'd have to agree with her.

"You've been planning this hiding place," Lissandra said without inflection, sitting stiffly beside him on the narrow bench as the cart rolled up to a woodcutter's cottage.

The floral scent that was Lis's own spun Murdoch's head so thoroughly that he could scarcely think straight. "Of course I planned it," he snarled in retaliation for what she was doing to him. "It is only a matter of time before the committee decides I am a spy or worse." He jumped down to tie the mare to an oak sapling. "This place is well concealed, and they're too lazy to look for it."

She ignored the hand he offered and stepped down on her own, retrieving the satchel he'd stopped to fetch from the widow's. She halted in the doorway of the musty cabin, waiting for him to locate a candle or lantern. "Why stay at all? Wouldn't it be simpler to just leave?"

"I'd forgotten how heartless you and your family can

be." With his mind, he lit the kindling he'd left in the fireplace—one small task he managed without creating an inferno. "It is my duty to fix what I have harmed."

"Are you to blame for that ugly pair of soldiers?" she asked while looking around at the hovel.

"The committee arrived before the fire. France is currently being governed by a Tribunal that is desperate for more cannon fodder for its war against Austria. Bretons and much of the western part of the country have ever despised the control of Paris. The provinces gathered an army of their own some months ago to march against the Tribunal, but the National Guard annihilated them. So when the Tribunal's committee arrived to conscript all able-bodied men, they disappeared into the forest. The town has no desire to sacrifice their men for a war created merely to ease the fears of cowards and bullies."

Lissandra looked at him blankly. "Are there ever good reasons for war?"

"Self-defense, perhaps." He waved away the question as irrelevant.

She nodded and returned to the subject at hand. "And so you are helping the village rebuild? How do you avoid this committee?"

He watched in fascination as Lis unfastened her crushed hat and set it on the rickety table. In the firelight, her lustrous blond hair sparkled like ocean pearls and crystals, even more so when she pulled out the pins and shook the tresses free. He almost bit his tongue when she dragged her fingers through that waterfall of shimmering light to massage her scalp. How could she not know she was crippling him with her provocative gestures?

She couldn't still be that innocent, could she? He preferred not knowing the answer to that question. He threw another log on the fire and watched it flare. "I pretend I'm a simpleton, a beast of burden, useless for conscription."

"And that's why the priest believes you are a miracle worker?"

He could tell she didn't entirely believe him, but he refused to explain himself. It was not as if he'd given his actions a great deal of thought. He just knew the violent life he'd been leading had to end. He'd hoped he could find peace in this remote village surrounded by mountains, hidden from the world. "I plant their fields, and they feed me with their best bread. The loaves they eat in their homes are hard and full of weevils. I'm not the saintly paragon here."

She smiled, and Murdoch realized he was pacing. He'd nearly burned out the soles of his best boots fighting the fire, and his feet had blisters that didn't need further irritation. He halted and glared at her. This was an impossible situation. He couldn't stay here. Not with her. He'd explode into a thousand tiny bits. Or blow the roof off the house.

"You're no saint," she agreed. "You had a white horse of your own, did you not? What became of it?"

He didn't ask how she knew that. Lis had always been able to See him—if she put her mind to it. He was just surprised that she'd tried. "I sent it to the coast with some . . . friends."

"Then how did you acquire the horse outside?"

He headed for the door. "I didn't steal it, if that's what you think. She was badly abused and kicks or bites anyone who comes near her. Except me, so I adopted her."

He strode out before he could hear her opinion on that.

\*    \*    \*

Lissandra sighed and released the tight clasps of her fitted jacket. She supposed, in this cooler climate, more layers were required than at home, where they wore little in the way of clothing. Murdoch was accustomed to seeing her with her hair down and barely clothed, so it wasn't as if modesty was necessary.

But tonight, his reaction to her loosened hair had been so strong as to seep through his Empathic barriers, warning her that his self-control was fragile. His gifts had always been erratic, but until her mother had attempted to strip him of his abilities before she banished him, he'd always possessed a formidable restraint around her.

How could she possibly persuade him to come home and save his people with this . . . awareness . . . between them that blocked reasonable discussion?

It would be easier if she kept her distance, but that did not seem likely in these close quarters—and given their explosive reunion. She had *known* it was Murdoch and still had not resisted his kiss. She might have killed him, but she had surrendered like a fool instead.

Still picking twigs out of her hair and clothing, she deflected her self-recrimination by studying the hut to which he'd brought her. A new, well-stuffed mattress rested on leather thongs bound to stout tree trunks. That showed signs of Murdoch's creation. On the island, wood was rare and expensive, so furniture was usually not elaborate.

The table had a plank top and was aged enough to be something the woodcutter had left behind, but the gray wood had been neatly sanded and polished to resemble one of Aelynn's communal tables. At home, they believed that food and company mattered more than the decor.

But Murdoch was a warrior trained since childhood

to wield knives and swords like extra hands; he was not a farmer or carpenter. Despite their peaceful neutrality, Aelynners were bred to protect the sacred chalice and sword. Murdoch had been the most powerful warrior on the island until his banishment. This humble abode revealed an interesting domestic side of him she'd never expected, but where were his weapons? Both Ian and Trystan had said he still used them. She shuddered. She had *Seen* the warrior's bloody weapons at work.

Murdoch returned from putting up the mare in the shelter beside the cottage. She watched him warily as he flung logs on a fire and dumped a bucket of root vegetables on the table. That he knew his way around a kitchen didn't surprise her. He was trained for survival, and one must eat to survive. That he ignored her was unsettling. She'd expected fireworks and fury, not this frigid indifference.

"How long will it take you to repair the village?" she asked, determined to have this discussion done.

"As long as it takes." He took the empty bucket, threw aside a cloth covering the wall beside the fireplace, and disappeared into another room she hadn't realized was there.

Following him to peer into this new chamber, Lissandra gasped in surprise when a dozen tiny candles flared into life, illuminating a rock pool of steaming water. "A hot spring! No wonder you chose this place."

All Aelynners were accustomed to the luxury of hot springs and regular bathing. She had discovered such niceties were hard to come by in the Other World, but apparently Murdoch had learned to provide his own. She longed to shed her clothes and plunge into the bath, but the awareness between them was such that she could actually feel him daring her to indulge.

She might not be able to read his mind, but now that she knew about the bullet wound, she sensed the pain in his shoulder, and the ache of muscles he had strained with his hard labor. She would not be a Healer if she didn't know these things. He wanted the bath as much as she did. "I've brought my medicinal bag with me. A hot soak in water laced with herbs would ease your soreness," she suggested. As a Healer, she could do no less. As a woman—she was asking for trouble.

Maybe it was time she asked for trouble.

His crude shirt prevented her from admiring the play of his muscles in the dim light. He filled his pail and waited for her to step aside so he could return to the main room. "I don't need your help, but the water is warm. Use it if you wish."

At his harsh tone, Lissandra retreated and let him carry the bucket to the fire, where he dumped the water into a kettle. A bath could wait until she was alone. "How long have you lived in this village?"

He shrugged. "Long enough to know I'm not leaving. Ian can have his castle in England. This place suits me. I've been looking for an excuse to claim the cottage, so I thank you for it. It's built into the side of a hill, and the bathing chamber once stored vegetables. It's warm on cool nights, cool on warm ones. Now that I have water, I have all I need."

As he spoke, his Aelynn ring of silence flared with blue fire. Fascinated, Lissandra couldn't drag her gaze away. Were the gods warning that he lied? Or that he had just denied the obvious? She swallowed hard and sought words, but they wouldn't come.

If she remembered her legends correctly, the blue glow proved he was not ready to accept the gods, so the spirit stayed with the ring that had been a part of him since it had been placed on his finger at birth. No wonder his essence had seemed so dim. His inner demons were battling with the gods.

"I see that you and France have self-destruction and denial in common." She was no simpering miss terrified of Murdoch's black glares and masculine sulks. Defying his challenge, she removed her confining jacket and returned to examine the bathing room, feeling his tension escalate as she did so.

This root cellar couldn't duplicate the spacious grotto they had enjoyed on Aelynn, but his ability to produce a hot spring where there was no volcano said much of why the gods had chosen him. His ability to manipulate earth, wind, fire, and water went well beyond that of any other man she'd heard about. If anyone could save Aelynn, it had to be Murdoch.

And he had every reason to wish them all dead. She had to be crazed to believe he'd help.

"I have nothing on you in pigheadedness, if you think you can change my mind." Murdoch leaned his shoulder against the doorjamb and watched her. She'd almost swear his penetrating stare could see through cloth, and she shivered a little despite the heat. "Is Waylan waiting for you at the coast?" he asked. "I can take you back tomorrow."

Lissandra unfastened a tie holding together her skirt and bodice. "Waylan should be halfway to England by now. Something called a surveillance committee has been hunting for spies to torture and kill, and it seemed safest for all concerned if Trystan and everyone else left France."

"I am glad they escaped, but why on earth would Trystan allow you to stay behind?" Murdoch asked in genuine surprise. "Has he lost what few wits he possessed?"

"Do you think me so weak as to let Trystan stand in my way when the survival of my home is at stake? The gods have designated you as our next Oracle. The volcano threatens our existence. Bad weather is ruining our crops. The Council is paralyzed by bickering over what we should do, while our *Oracle* hides in rural anonymity. Either the whole world is mad, or I am."

He snorted. "I am no more an Oracle than the priest in the village, so it must be you who is mad. I have work to do. You can stay here until I am done, and then I'll take you back to the coast and look for someone to escort you home." Turning his back on her disrobing, ignoring her pleas, he walked out.

"I did not risk my life so you can send me home like a lost child!" Beyond aggravated by this day's events, not knowing how to deal with all the agitation Murdoch aroused in her, Lissandra removed her hated shoe and flung it after her oblivious host. The shoe flew through the curtain and swerved harmlessly away.

Nothing touched Murdoch unless he wanted it to.

# Six

The next morning, Lissandra stirred the simmering cauldron of root vegetables Murdoch had prepared the night before. At home, a hearth witch would have fixed his meals, or he would have eaten with his friends. Wasn't he lonely living in isolation like this, hiding what he was?

This strange attempt at domesticity would never last. Inevitably, Murdoch would grow restless and incite trouble by demanding that wrongs be righted. And since he made no pretense at diplomacy, his methods of accomplishing what he wanted were always inflammatory. She'd yet to see evidence that he'd learned better in the years since he'd been banished.

Last night, he'd insisted she take the bed while he'd strung a hammock across the room for himself. Sometime after she'd fallen asleep, he'd departed and he hadn't returned. She had wanted to use her Healing powers to relax him, so they could have a rational discussion this morning. Stupid of her. He was a bundle of nerves and muscle so tense that it was a wonder he did not explode like the Roman candles that had killed her father. Oracles were men and women of peace. What on earth were the gods thinking to choose a man who was more likely to erupt like a volcano than call a quiet convocation?

Lissandra knew she didn't qualify either. An Oracle needed the wisdom and strength to calm a volcano, return their tropical weather patterns, and heal whatever was wrong with their crops. She came into her own only when she could lay her hands on people and feel the blood move beneath their skin, feel their pain and surround it with her energy. Healing was her true gift. Then, she felt useful.

Yet Aelynn had other Healers. They needed leaders, and by birth she should be one. By birth, Murdoch should not. The blue glow of the spirit flame contradicted everything she knew about how things *should* work.

After covering the cooking pot and banking the fire, she donned her sandals rather than wear the painful heeled shoes. She didn't dare revert to her simple tunics, but last night she'd cleaned her French gown, taken up the hem, and reduced the width of the skirt so she did not need billows of petticoats to hold it off the ground. She'd used some of the excess material to create inserts at the bodice waist so she did not need the restrictive corset, and covered the neckline with lace scraps from her petticoat to hide her unfettered breasts so she could be comfortable in this world.

If Murdoch would not stay with her, she must go after him. As irritating as it was to be ignored, she saw no other means of understanding what the gods intended.

He'd left the horse and cart, but now that she was rested, she didn't need an animal any more than he did. They would require transportation to reach the coast, but otherwise, she was accustomed to walking miles of Aelynn's roads each day, Healing the sick and delivering babies. Although, admittedly, she usually walked at a speed much greater than Other Worlders. Sensing that no one was about, she set off quickly, and slowed down as she approached the village.

Lowering her shield slightly, she sensed Murdoch in the fields beyond the village. She glanced warily at the tavern, but it was closed and dark at this hour of the morning.

The roof of the priest's humble cottage had been replaced overnight. Père Antoine stood outside, gazing upward in awe. Lissandra knew very little of roof construction, but the rough-hewn timbers looked more solid to her than the thatch she saw elsewhere.

"Good morning, Père Antoine," she said courteously, refraining from asking all the questions that were on the tip of her tongue. She was too new to this world to understand its customs, or how the people built their houses. She hoped that what Murdoch had done—for no one else could have repaired the roof so quickly—was satisfactory.

"It would take five men weeks to build that," the priest murmured in an amazed tone. "There is never enough time or materials. I had despaired of ever having a roof again." His voice broke with emotion.

She pretended to understand. "It is how we do things at home. Is it not done right?"

He finally looked from his roof to her. "The former thatch was so old, it leaked in a fine mist. A roof like this . . ." He looked as if he would cry. "It will last for decades. It will hold tile if we can buy it. He has reinforced the inside so we can add another floor for a loft."

She nodded as if that were to be expected, and handed him a bag made from a scrap of her petticoat. She'd filled it with an herbal remedy that she thought might be useful to these people. "I would thank you for being so kind to my husband while he was recovering."

She had decided last night not to let Murdoch's perversity stand in the way of her duty. Let him pretend to be a simpleminded laborer. She would stay and haunt him until she could convince him to come home. She would have to learn how to live here—although it did seem a trifle awkward having to hide their unusual skills.

"Mix a pinch of these herbs with a cup of water, and drink it down to ease the aches of a hard day's work. My husband swears by it," she said crisply, not asking for gratitude but expecting to be obeyed.

The priest looked at her gift as if it contained the Holy Grail. "If this is what keeps him going, we should be able to restore half the town on our own."

"It takes practice," she warned. "He is driven by near madness, so do not try to keep up with him."

"I will help him, whatever it takes," the priest said fervently. "His traveling companions said he was skilled with swords as well, but weapons are dangerous in these times."

Ah, finally, some glimpse into what had happened here. "He seldom lets his weapons out of his sight," she said carefully. "I am surprised that he does not wear them."

"He gave them to me in atonement for what he calls his sins. They are well hidden," Père Antoine assured her. "Far better that he apply his energies to constructive work, especially if his mind is injured."

The priest had hidden Murdoch's sword, and Murdoch had let him? Wasn't it Euripides who first said, "Those whom the gods would destroy, they first make mad"? Surely the ancients did not mean that literally! Had they brought her here to kill a madman? Or ... to Heal him? "And his traveling companions?" she asked, hiding her uneasiness.

"Once they ascertained his injuries were not fatal,

they went on without him. It wasn't safe here for them."
He tilted his head meaningfully toward the tavern where
the soldiers stayed.

Lissandra would have liked to know more, but the
priest did not seem inclined toward explanation, and she
was anxious to see what Murdoch was up to today.

"I give you good day, Father." She hurried off, leaving the priest to his roof gazing. It did not take much to
make an Other Worlder happy, it seemed.

Following her Finding instinct, Lissandra wandered
down a back lane until she reached a field sprouting new
green wheat. She frowned and calculated how long it
took for wheat seed to germinate. Recovery from the
fire seemed extraordinarily quick, unless the wheat here
was different from what they used at home.

Wandering farther into the field, she found Murdoch
plowing the furrows with a primitive farm implement
that he pushed with both hands. Today, he wore a pair of
crudely made sandals. As before, his chest was bare, and
his impressive shoulders strained at the plow. Only, this
time, she saw him in full sunlight without a thick layer
of soot. She gasped at the many scars marring his once-
smooth skin. Ian had mentioned wounding him when he
was here, but how many injuries could one body take?
The healing scab of a wicked graze still tarnished one
broad shoulder.

Murdoch turned as if he'd heard her thoughts, and
bestowed a black gaze on her. "I told you, I have work to
do. If you keep interfering, it will take longer."

The furrows he'd just plowed had no green seedlings,
but they appeared moist, as if he'd planted the seed and
watered it as he worked. A hint of steam or mist rose
from the furrows, and she crouched down to feel heat
rising from the fertile soil. She watched and thought

she saw green pushing through the dirt in a recently plowed row farther down the field. She'd never actually *seen* plants grow. "What are you doing?" she asked in fascination.

"Planting." He returned to pushing the blade into the ground. A sack tied to his waist dropped a thin line of seed as he walked.

"You're not an Agrarian," she called after him. "How did you learn to do this?"

He didn't reply. Frustrated, she wanted to beat her fists upon his back until she had answers, but even if she hit him with all her strength, Murdoch had the power to fling her away as if she were no more than an irritating insect.

All right, if he insisted on repairing the village before he would listen to reason, then she must help speed his efforts. What could she do? She knew how to plant herbs but had few Agrarian gifts as spectacular as Murdoch's for tending them. She had no knowledge of construction. She enjoyed working with fine fabric, and could sew and mend, but that required materials she didn't possess. She could predict the future, but telling people their future was usually more depressing than useful. Her gifts were exceedingly impractical in this world.

Which made her feel more inadequate than ever.

Sensing a muffled cry and the mental anguish of pain from some creature nearby, she glared at Murdoch's naked back, hoped she scorched a hole in it, then deliberately worked her way across the field toward the forest and whoever had been injured. She could still Heal.

Murdoch knew the instant Lis turned away. Since her action immediately followed a cry of pain, it didn't take much logic to know where she was going. The damned woman simply didn't understand that this wasn't safe, peaceful Aelynn, and there were monsters everywhere.

He threw down his plow, found the homespun shirt he'd tossed onto a branch, and jerked it over his head. The fire had destroyed the fine clothing he'd once carried with him. He'd been reduced to the crude hand-me-downs the villagers provided, and he tried to take care of them.

He stalked after Lis, cursing under his breath. Until her arrival, he'd been coping. He'd even convinced himself to quit pretending he could ever change the world. He'd hoped if he could make himself useful, he might be welcome here long enough to make a difference. Fixing one small village, repairing some of his mistake, was all he'd asked.

And then Lissandra had arrived, shattering his illusion.

He stifled his inappropriate temper and caught up with her where he'd expected she'd go—the encampment of local men who were hiding from conscription. He knew they watched him from the shadows during the day, then came out and hoed the fields at night after he had gone, aiding him as best they could when the committee wasn't looking. Torn between wanting to lower his mental shields in order to know who was around him, and fearing the barrage of grief and anger that would assault him when he did, Murdoch had refrained from getting too close. Lissandra, of course, waded right into the emotional tempest.

"The wound requires stitching. If you'll hold this pad tight over it, I'll fetch my bag." Crouching beside a young lad with a bandage wrapped around his hand, Lissandra straightened, observed Murdoch's arrival, and, ignoring him, strode off toward the village.

He stepped in front of her. "If you go parading back and forth from a supposedly empty forest, carrying a medicine bag, and anyone sees you, they will be suspicious. The committee doesn't know these men are here."

"Shall I turn invisible?" she inquired with the cool demeanor she'd apparently chosen to keep him in line. "The wound needs tending or it will become gangrenous."

Murdoch glanced over her shoulder at the small band of men. "Take the lad to the woodcutter's cottage," he ordered them. "My wife and I will meet you there."

He grabbed Lis's arm and hauled her out of the forest, toward the field where he'd been working. "You are wasting your efforts," he muttered for her ears alone. "There is an entire world of people who need Healing and only one of you. You may as well try to eradicate the world population of flies by swatting them one at a time."

She applied her not-inconsiderable strength into digging in her heels and yanking her arm from his grasp. She nearly toppled when he released her. Murdoch refrained from catching her when she stumbled. The more he ached to hold her in his arms, the more he knew he must let her go, for her own good.

She righted herself and, hands on hips, glared at him. "You should know about Healing—your back is covered by scars! Are they wounds that do not Heal?"

He hadn't wanted her to see his scars, not the physical *or* the emotional ones. That she *had* seen them humiliated him even more. "I still have some ability to Heal," he growled at her. "One does not go to war without injury."

"You would have served this world better as a Healer than as a mercenary."

He crossed his arms and regarded her with the same arrogance she employed. "I made an honest living."

"Killing?" she retorted, not acknowledging his loftiness. "I have spent these last years attempting to understand how you could have done what you did to my father."

Refusing to let her force a fight, Murdoch turned and stalked through the field, avoiding the new seedlings.

She followed on his heels. "We have nothing in our texts about aberrations like yours."

Murdoch snorted. Aberrations! Accidentally killing a beloved leader and setting a village on fire were *aberrations*.

"I need you to talk to me!"

He could practically feel her breathing down his back. He was glad he'd remembered his shirt so he did not remind her again of whatever had set off this charming chat.

"I've studied other kinds of mental abnormalities," she continued, despite his silence, "and observed the phenomenon among some of our people. Did you know your father was an Agrarian with Navigation abilities? That's an aberration."

"He should have stayed an Agrarian. Then he wouldn't have fallen overboard and drowned before I was born." He caught her elbow and dragged her to the road.

"But, see, that's what I mean." She shook him off again, matching his increasing pace. "Agrarians aren't *meant* for life on the sea. He got seasick and fell overboard. But he could Navigate! He shouldn't have been able to."

"No more than I should be able to do what I do." Murdoch dismissed her absurdity with a gesture. "I'm not an Olympus. Only your family should be able to See. The gods laugh at us."

"No, we laugh at the gods," she argued. "We ignore what we don't understand. Your gifts are too great to be dismissed, but there may be others like your father, people who are expected to continue as their families have for centuries but who could be so much more!"

"Who could be dead like my father," he said indifferently. "None of this matters to me. My place is here, and I'm trying to make the best of it. Your place is on Aelynn. You need to go home and do what you can there."

"I can do nothing!" She threw up her fists in a gesture of despair and frustration that he had never seen in the ice queen before—then she proceeded to walk away from him.

She could do *nothing*? An all-powerful Olympus could do nothing? Murdoch frowned and caught up with her. "You can do everything your mother could do. Quit feeling sorry for yourself, grow up, and go home."

She spun on her heel so fast, her palm cracked against his jaw before he could halt her. Murdoch staggered more from surprise than pain. He rubbed his face with his fingers to take away the sting and shook his head. "What the hell was that for?"

"Because I can't blow up rocks or set fires to express how I feel," she said with the stone-cold voice of her mother. "Because violence seems to be the only way to hold your attention."

Lis stalked off, practically racing into the village. He caught the back of her bodice and tugged her to a halt so they could proceed at a normal pace, without attracting unnecessary notice. His action pulled her gown tight against her unbound breasts, and cursing, he hastily released her. Lissandra had definitely grown up—and filled out—in the years he'd been gone. His lust for her escalated so swiftly, it drained his head and made him dizzy.

The damned woman made him dizzy just by existing.

"You make no sense," he complained. "Blowing up rocks serves no purpose."

"Isn't that what you do when you lose your temper? Blow up things? Set them on fire? That must be extremely gratifying, far more so than arguing with a senseless donkey who kicks and brays and resists doing as it's told."

"You no longer have any right to tell me what to do," he pointed out, logically enough. "I was banished from Aelynn, and thus am free from your authority. And that's making you crazy, isn't it?"

As they reached the far side of the village, she picked up her speed again. "You were never under my authority. No one is. Yet an entire island needs me to bring home an Oracle to save them from destruction. You see my problem?"

"Your problem is that you think what I do actually matters, and it doesn't. I can't go home. Besides, it wouldn't solve anything. It won't bring your father back."

They were nearing the cottage. The young man and his friends would arrive soon. This painful argument wasn't going anywhere. Murdoch increased his pace.

Lis didn't. "Ian says if you find the Chalice of Plenty, you can do anything you like," she called after him with a decided tone of resentment.

He'd tried that. Even the chalice had hidden from him. If that didn't prove the gods had forsaken him, he didn't know what did.

# Seven

Even Healing in this world was a painful chore. Clenching her teeth against the sensation of the boy's knifing pain, fighting the waves of anguish emanating from his friends, Lissandra rubbed an unguent over her patient's wound. Leaning his broad shoulders against the doorframe, Murdoch crossed his arms and watched the proceedings like a jealous lover. Not that he gave off jealousy so much as impatience and frustration. If that much leaked past his mental shields, she was glad she could not feel the full fireworks going off inside him.

"The wound needs time to mend," she reminded the youth while his companions hovered anxiously. With the bandage applied and her work done, she mentally shut out the farmers, as well as Murdoch, and sighed with relief at the return of serenity. "Keep the wound covered. Don't get the bandages wet. If you see the flesh turn red around the wound, come to me at once."

"Yes, madame," the boy replied, bowing his head gratefully. "I thank you. I will chop some wood for you when my hand is better."

She hoped she wouldn't be here long enough to need any more wood than the pile Murdoch had already built, but she nodded at the boy. "I would appreciate that, thank you." She looked at the two men who had brought him here. "You cannot hide forever. You know that, don't you?"

Thin and careworn, their faces revealed no expression. "We can do more by hiding than by going to war," one replied. "Our families need us more than the army does."

She couldn't disagree. France's war was one of aggression, not defense, fought for glory and greed, as far as she had been able to discern from Ian's explanations. The idealism of the early revolutionary years was lost in cynicism and violent dissension among factions. Murdoch was well out of it—if that was what his retirement here meant.

She stood, and the men passed by her, tugging their forelocks in farewell. Murdoch stepped out of their way. They didn't address him, but they offered nods of what appeared to be respect to the man honed like a blade of steel, standing aloof and alone.

Lissandra repacked her bag once their guests had departed, and when Murdoch continued his stoic silence, she approached their earlier argument from a different angle. "You've been raised as a leader of men. I cannot understand why you reject the opportunity the gods offer."

"I've always been a peasant," he said in evident displeasure at the topic. "My father was an Agrarian and my mother is a hearth witch. They're called farmers and maids here. You're the closest thing Aelynn has to a princess. Should you be Healing peasants?"

"Aelynn doesn't have nobility or peasants," she protested, then frowned at the sound of her mother speaking through her. "The gods give us only the burdens that we can bear. It would be far easier if I were just a Healer, but they chose some of us for heavier loads. We all work equally, each according to our ability."

"Some people are more *able* than others, then," he said sarcastically. "Did my mother have any choice when your mother took me away?"

Lissandra stared at him in puzzlement. "I was barely old enough to speak at the time, but I do not remember any argument over your joining us. Your mother should have been pleased that you were given the best education possible. Would she rather you plowed her fields?"

"She doesn't have fields. Hearth witches may eat at your table and walk through your homes, but they cannot earn land with their labors. Which means she had no vote and no say in what your parents chose to do. You need to look beyond your own privileged life, princess." He walked out.

*Drat the man!* If she had to follow him to the ends of the earth, they would have this discussion. He had avoided the subject of leadership with his ridiculous arguments about equality. He'd been immersed in revolutionary ideas for too long. She caught up with him as he turned toward town. "I am not a princess."

"Be glad of that. The average citizen here despises the aristocracy. In Paris, the nobles are paying for their arrogance by losing their heads." Murdoch had forgotten how blind Lis's naïveté could be. She needed to see the world from a fresh perspective.

Lis nodded as if he had imparted nothing new. "Trystan and Mariel explained that to me. I don't think anyone would mistake me for a noble."

"They'd be fools if they didn't," he muttered. "You haven't a subservient bone in your body."

"Nor do you," she said with a hint of amusement. "I traveled from the coast with everyone thinking me a poor widow. You are not the only one with unexpected talents."

*Talents.* An odd description for the things he did. Calling up a wind and flinging men into trees was a *talent.* Setting fires with his mind was a *talent.* Talking to horses in his head—

As if conjured by his thoughts, a pony with a small boy on its back raced to meet them. Murdoch caught Lis's arm and pulled her to the side of the road. She shook him off, as usual, and approached the widow Girard's son, who spoke to her quietly, throwing nervous glances in Murdoch's direction.

"That is thoughtful of your mother," Lis said, accepting the basket the boy removed from his saddle. "I have made the tisane I promised her. If you'll wait a moment . . ."

The lad stared at Murdoch while Lis returned to the cottage to gather some packages. With nothing better to do, Murdoch stared back.

"My mother says you're a saint," the boy said.

"Boys should not argue with their mothers," he replied. Lis was right, damn her. He didn't know how to converse.

"Do not let anyone follow you here, Jean," Lis warned, returning to hand the refilled basket to the boy. "We cannot have too many people visit."

"My pony is fast," the lad said with confidence. "No one can follow me. Père Antoine says that when Abel has time, he can teach me to grow giant beans for my mama's cassoulet."

"Save your pony's manure," Murdoch told him. "Let it rot behind the shed. Add old bean vines and scraps from your table until it all composts into a dark soil for your garden. Then plant the beans beside your garden wall so they will stay warmer in spring."

The boy beamed. "Thank you, monsieur. *Citoyen,*" he

corrected in confusion, before tugging the pony's reins and galloping off toward town.

"Changing the world takes time," Lis remarked. "The people of France do not even know what to call one another."

Murdoch shook his head. "Making up new names changes nothing. The people would be fine if their leaders listened to them instead of serving their own selfish greed and ambitions. But people who fight for power are the least likely to be reasonable about sharing it."

Lis studied him as if he'd just sprouted wings. Only then did he remember she was an Olympus with the power he'd just disparaged. So much for communicating.

"An interesting theory," she said noncommittally. "If you are returning to the field, I will remain here to plant a few seeds for our own use, in case we must stay for any length of time."

"There is a manure pile behind the stable," he called mockingly as she departed.

The moment she shut the door between them, Murdoch's whole world emptied, and he slipped into a pit of despair. He'd thought if he isolated himself in rural tranquility, he could smother his unpredictable reactions and live normally—until Lis walked back into his life, reminding him of all he could not have.

No matter how wrongheaded she might be, Lis was the one shining, pure vision in his life. And he must not sully her—which he would certainly do if he couldn't chase her away.

Curse it all, it would be easier to move an island than Lis once she made up her mind.

Kneeling beside the newly turned earth, patting her precious rosemary seeds into the soil, pondering whether she could summon heat and moisture as Murdoch did, Lissandra glanced up at a sudden gust of wind.

In minutes, dark clouds scudded across the sun, and thunderheads loomed over the trees.

She would think France had unusually swift storms, except she sensed the explosive tension that could be only Murdoch approaching. He'd been gone most of the day, but it was not yet dark. She hadn't expected him to return until he could no longer see to plant.

Alarmed at the pain she sensed in him, she gathered up her skirt, leapt to her feet, and raced down the road. She should never have left him alone for a minute.

"Go away," he ordered, holding his hand against his chest awkwardly. "I can Heal myself."

He probably could, and had frequently done so if the scars on his back were any evidence, but Lissandra couldn't bear to feel pain and do nothing. She clenched her fingers in her skirt to prevent herself from reaching for him. "What happened?"

"A minor altercation. It is nothing. Go burn some soup or something." He strode faster while the sky darkened.

"It is *something* if you end up flooding the valley with the storm you're conjuring." She danced in front of him, attempting to get some glimpse of the hand he hid—the hand with the ring on it.

He glanced skyward and shrugged. "I didn't do that. It's a summer storm."

He lied. Or refused to accept the truth. "Look at your ring."

He glanced at the glowing black pearl on his finger. "It could light a cave. I'll save on candles," he said dismissively.

Lissandra watched as the glow faded with his distraction. "When you are calm and accepting, the spirits enter you and the ring's light diminishes. When you reject the gods with your fury and frustration, the spirits flee to the ring."

"Superstition," he muttered, stalking into the cottage.

"How can you deny the gods?" she asked in exasperation. "Superstition is merely ignorance mixed with old wives' tales to explain the inexplicable. Some people blame their troubles on evil forces, but the most evil force I've ever met is human nature. Magic exists in all the beautiful gifts from the gods, the twinkle of stars and a baby's smile. They've given you more than you deserve."

Without asking permission, he rummaged through her bag for a bandage. "You sound like the priest."

"That's because I am the closest thing to a priest that we have on Aelynn. People need explanations, and I've been trained to provide them. Are you going to tell me what happened?"

"No." He threw back the curtain over the doorway to the bathing room.

Determinedly ignoring his hostile vibrations, Lissandra followed him. "If you're spilling all your energy into raising a storm, you won't have any left for Healing."

He knelt down beside the rock pool and dipped his injured arm into it. She winced at the bloody gore and torn tissue visible beneath the thin cloth of his sleeve. "Shall I help you off with your shirt?"

He shot her a scathing look that said he'd drown before he'd let her help him.

"Oh, botheration." Without a second thought, she stepped forward, planted her foot between his shoulders, and shoved Murdoch headfirst into the pool. Only because she caught him unaware and off-balance did she succeed. The splash caused by his massive weight soaked them both.

"What in Hades did you do that for?" Cursing, flipping his wet hair out of his eyes, he floundered to a seated position, keeping his arm below the water's surface.

His crude shirt clung to his broad shoulders and was plastered to his chest, revealing the dark whorls of hair there. Lissandra fought her attraction by firmly thinking of him as her patient. "Stubborn cantankerousness harms the Healing process but usually dissolves in hot water. You are not the first recalcitrant male to refuse my services." She knelt beside the pool and reached for his wrist.

He ought to smell of sweat and blood and anger, but to her, he smelled of musky masculinity sweeter than flowers in spring. She wanted to splash the warm water in frustration, but that was not how an Olympus behaved. *Dignity and decorum at all times*, her mother's voice said inside her head. Shoving Murdoch wasn't dignified, but she considered it justified.

"Services? Is that what you call it?" He leered down her wet bodice while she raised his arm to examine it. "Had I known you offered *services*, I would have helped myself long ago."

She'd earned her icy reputation by freezing rowdy men into silence with a practiced glare, which she granted now, while she slid her fingers over the irregular tear in his flesh. "You've cracked a bone. You can't Heal this yourself."

Applying her energy, she knit the fracture to give it strength, then located and sealed torn blood vessels, concentrating on taking away the pain. He threw back his head and grimaced at the ceiling, and his wet hair streamed down his neck. She had to let down her shield to Heal, so she was grateful he kept his in place.

"Look at your ring," she ordered, distracting him from what she was doing.

He glanced at it and scowled. "It's not as bright as it was outside."

"Do you hear thunder?" His sword arm was so heavily muscled that she had some difficulty mending the torn ligaments. Her own flesh sang with the joy of stroking his. The connection between them was so close that she could feel his heart beating in tandem with hers.

But years of restraint had taught her well, and her placid demeanor revealed none of her inner turmoil while she applied her skills.

He concentrated on the blue glow on his ring. "I only hear light rainfall."

"The thunderheads must have spread into normal rain clouds. I'd love to know how you do that without even thinking about it."

"The same way I create wind and fire." He allowed no regret to tinge his harsh words. "My energy builds until it finds some release. I can suppress it only to a point."

Ian had warned her that Murdoch's powers had lost almost all focus, even more so than before their mother had banished him and attempted to strip him of his gifts. Lissandra wondered whether she could somehow heal Murdoch's inner wounds and give him the control he needed. But believing she could do what her parents had not was no doubt arrogance on her part.

"I don't think there is anything innately wrong with strong emotion, even fury, if that's what stokes your energy," she said, thinking aloud. "But the energy is more useful if directed toward a purpose. Say, if you're angry because your ax has become stuck in a tree—instead of calling up a storm, you could direct all that pent-up frustration toward tugging out the ax."

"Or splintering the tree," he corrected. "How should a skilled swordsman direct his frustration? Removing the blade from a dead body won't bring it back to life."

"Rain rusts metal, so calling up a storm is scarcely a productive direction if you wish to control your sword."

"Maybe I wish to destroy it." His pent-up storm of emotion finally dissipating with the rain, he leaned back against the rocks and let her work her Healing on his arm.

She heard the thoughtful man she'd once known behind his comment, and wished she knew what had finally evoked his attentiveness. "We generally don't cast off our hands if they offend us," she replied carefully. "A warrior's swords are extensions of his hands."

"But if I react with anger, with weapons in my hand . . ." He frowned and didn't finish his thought, no doubt contemplating the destruction he could wreak. Had wreaked.

"From what I know, your weapons are the only thing you *can* control. You use them as your focus. Perhaps we ought to find you a magic wand if you don't wish to use a sword again."

He snorted and picked up a candlestick, waving it as if it were the wand of which she spoke. "You are toying with my mind."

"Somebody needs to. You're not using it." Now that she knew he was not seriously injured, Lissandra had difficulty restraining that part of herself that admired Murdoch's physical attributes. He was sprawled in the water, his clothes plastered to his long limbs, narrow hips, and . . . aroused masculinity. Desire coaxed her to join him, to show him that she was all he needed. She wanted to know how it would feel to have his hands on her. . . .

Common sense warned she would be playing with fire . . . literally. Sensing the bullet hole in his shoulder, she sent Healing energy up his arm.

He lazily pointed the candle at her as if it were a magic wand. "Ka-zaam, you're a beautiful princess."

She laughed, well aware of the dirt she'd rubbed into her cheeks and her hair straggling from its pins. "You would have to turn me into something I am not if you wish to prove your magic wand works. Perhaps turn me into a *clean* princess."

"Not modest, are we? Do all men proclaim your beauty these days?" he asked, finally succumbing to her soothing energy and relinquishing the violence in him. Momentarily.

"I've seen my reflection and will not deny what gifts the gods have given me." She ignored the jealousy leaking from him and brushed a stray lock of hair from her nose, leaving a streak of diluted blood on her cheek, while she sought an answer he would accept without anger. This business of tamping down her own temper so as not to escalate his didn't ease her frustration. "Men who admire power and prestige will always see beauty in the person who possesses both. I'm sure that in this world where I have no authority, I am seen as no more than a pale, skinny wench."

"Men aren't that blind," he scoffed. "Is that what you thought I saw in you—power and prestige?"

"Of course," she said matter-of-factly. "But they're also what kept us apart, so there was no beauty in them." She returned to applying pressure to his arm.

"I was not such a dolt as to ignore your true beauty," he protested. "Even a man with no eyes must see the worth of a woman who is willing to track him down to the ends of the earth."

That declaration would have thrilled her, except there was nothing beautiful about their hopeless situation. Until Murdoch accepted the gods and learned to control his dangerous energies, he could not return to Aelynn. Could she admit failure and return without him?

# Eight

"Quit treating me like a piece of porcelain." Murdoch shrugged off Lis's aid in applying the confounded bandage.

Physical torture by gods would have been less excruciating than the tempting scent of Lis beneath his nose and having no means of touching her. Or, worse yet, having the means and not the right. He'd escaped the bath to get away from her, but she'd followed him back into the cottage instead of staying behind to take advantage of the warm water to bathe.

Stripped of his torn shirt, his loose peasant trousers still soaking wet, painfully aware of his physical reaction to her presence, he backed off far enough that he couldn't reach out and grab her, then finished wrapping the wound himself.

"You must learn to control *all* your passions, not just your temper," she replied obliquely, without any indication that his words had affected her. He'd believe the woman was made of solid ice except her remark alluded to his obvious state of arousal. His ice princess knew what she was doing to him. Even years apart hadn't reduced their physical attraction—a no-doubt fatal attraction, should they act on it. Half Aelynn would have his head if he touched their princess with his tainted hands. But the temptation was very real ... and very powerful.

He retreated as she approached to help him, until he hit a wall. Which meant he needed to consider an escape route. "You say the gods wish me to contain my *passion*?" He repeated the euphemism with mockery. "You may as well ask me to fetch the moon."

"Other people do it all the time," she replied mildly.

"Not me. I'm a man. You're a woman. If we share meals and a roof, the natural way of things is to think of sharing a bed."

"Do you really want to find out what happens when you express your lust and I resist?" she asked in the dispassionate tone he despised.

He didn't need her veiled allusion to know that without some measure of restraint he might easily crack Lis in the same inexplicable manner he cracked the earth. Frustrated, he flexed his bandaged arm. Every sore tendon protested. "I'll go flaccid if I can't exercise this."

She assessed his near nakedness, no doubt with professional interest, but his pride preferred to believe it was prurient.

"You once had the strength of ten men. Does it matter if one of them is currently weak?"

That she recognized his superiority despite his *aberrant* status caused need to rumble through him again. He wasn't imagining her desire. It was real. He'd tasted it when he'd kissed her. Despite everything he'd done to her, the magnetism between them hadn't changed.

Acting on a surge of renewed confidence—or stupidity—Murdoch reversed his tactics and stalked his tormentor. She backed away until he had *her* up against a wall for a change. It felt good to trap Lis exactly where he wanted her—in his arms.

"Let us see if the earth trembles." He bent his head and placed his mouth on hers.

To his bliss, she didn't fight him. She succumbed willingly to his rough pressure. Her lips were pliant and parted as if she was as eager as he was. She accepted the thrust of his tongue, matching it with a greedy demand of her own that thrilled him to his marrow. Her breasts were inches away, and he willed her to arch toward him. Too bad mind control didn't work on Lis.

As much as he longed to grip her sweet-smelling shoulders and drag her against him, he didn't dare test his luck by touching her. He restrained himself by digging his fingers into the timbers while he leaned in and drank deeply of the nectar he craved more than the breath of life.

She pressed her palms against the wall also, denying him further contact. Murdoch wanted her to caress him first. He wanted her to need the brush of flesh against flesh as much as he did. He gentled his kiss, almost pleading for her to break through that restraint between them.

Instead, she slipped away, ducking beneath his arm so quickly that he didn't see her move. He missed her immediately, and the longing nearly spilled out of him before he shut it off. He turned and glared at her, hiding his pain. "Why did you do that?"

"To show you I can. And will." She glanced appraisingly at his accursed ring. "I must return to Aelynn. If you won't come with me, then you have no right to touch me."

"You'd have to be insane to ask me to return." He paced the floor, frustrated on so many levels he couldn't stand still. The ground trembled and a hairline crack appeared where he walked. He didn't do these things on purpose. They simply happened when he confined his excess energy too long.

He drew a deep breath and sought a release to keep from opening up the floor. He raised an image of Lissandra in his head, pictured cupping her breasts, stripping back the cloth. . . .

Throwing him a look of outrage, she cursed and walked out.

Now, that was an interesting twist. She'd *felt* his thoughts? He didn't think she'd done that even when they were young and reckless.

She'd just said he had no right to touch her . . . *if* he wouldn't return to Aelynn. The significance of her earlier statement finally filtered through his lust. Was there a chance in hell that he could have her if he did return? He almost blacked out from holding his breath as he considered the possibility.

Lis had *left* Aelynn—an unthinkable act in itself. And she'd done it for *him*. No, she'd done it for Aelynn, because she believed that balls of blue flame carried the spirits of the gods. Considering his fiery state of arousal, he would soon suffer from blue balls of a different sort.

With the first insane niggling of hope prying at his skull, Murdoch strode after her.

"I directed my energy as you suggested," he called when she headed into the woods.

"Find another damned direction besides me," she shouted back, clearly as aroused as he and running from temptation.

He crowed in unholy triumph at having finally cracked her icy shields.

Then he stopped to consider what he'd done. He'd never affected anyone with his thoughts before. Why Lis? He was prone to raising thunderclouds and splitting open the earth. What kind of monster did that make him when he used his uncommon abilities to pressure a woman into a sexual relation?

One who wouldn't let his woman walk off into the woods alone. He started to storm after her like a love-sick youth and slowed when he realized what he was doing. *His woman?* He no longer had the right to play slap and tickle as if they were still children, regardless of the desire he sensed in her with every fiber of his being. He couldn't resist following, but he slowed his pace—until her shout of alarm startled birds into flight.

Murdoch broke into a run. Trees whipped past him in a blur, and he burst into a clearing, prepared to tear the head off any molester without regard to his injured arm.

He slammed to a halt, fisting his fingers so tightly they should have broken in an effort to prevent calling down lightning. Instead, the earth trembled.

Lissandra calmly gripped a bearded stranger by his beaked nose and, even as Murdoch watched, brought her knee up in a direct blow to the man's groin. Her attacker collapsed on the ground, curling up with a groan, before Murdoch could assimilate the string of events.

Wincing over the other man's pain helped to restrain the urge to smash her attacker into bloody pulp. "I warned you about these woods."

"And I told you that you didn't have to worry," she retorted.

With his first irrational urge to kill conquered, he studied the moaning man, not recognizing him as anyone from the village. But strangers escaping Paris, running from the Tribunal, or deserting the army often kept to these wilderness areas. "We'll need to haul him off to the authorities."

"Leave him. He'll not be assaulting another woman anytime soon." With composure, Lis brushed her hands on her skirt as if halting rapists were an everyday event. She glanced at him. "That's the third time you've tried to protect me."

"It's what I do," he grumbled. It was what he'd give his life to do if the damned woman would let him.

She slanted him a look that he couldn't easily interpret. "You have obviously forgotten the many ways I can neuter a man's desire."

Murdoch squeezed the bridge of his nose rather than cover his privates as he had a sudden inclination to do. "If I'd remembered, I would have thought twice about kissing you."

"You couldn't have kissed me if I hadn't wanted it," she corrected. "That part of a man's brain is very simple and straightforward. When I touched the villain's nose, I directed all my energy to the overheated element. Depending on how much energy I direct, I can neuter him for life or merely turn off his interest."

Murdoch processed this information against his memories of their stolen kisses in a country far, far away and in a time that no longer existed. She'd never neutered *his* desire. "Is that why you didn't touch me just now?"

"Of course not. I have no need to exercise such restraint. *I* learned to control my energies." She left the thought dangling with the implication that, unlike her, he had no such discipline. "If you push too hard, as you often do, I prefer to walk away. Would you rather I release my restraint and twist your nose?"

He winced. "Ours was never an easy relationship."

"It is no relationship at all. We want each other. We can't have each other if we live in different worlds with different goals. There is no future for us."

"Sensible," he agreed bluntly, hearing the finality in her voice and resenting it, even though he knew she was right.

Except she kept saying *if*, as though an alternative existed in an impossible world where he'd killed her father and earned the hatred of an entire island's people.

She sighed and picked her way daintily across a fallen log, apparently deciding it was safe to leave her moaning molester behind and that Murdoch was no longer a danger to her virtue either. "I could call up my spirit guide again," she said, "but the answer is always the same—our paths are dark. Apparently even the spirits don't know how our story ends."

He laid his palm across the small of her back and steered her around a puddle, and when she didn't resist, he kept his hand there, absorbing her heat and the graceful sway of her hips. It had been too long since he'd had reasonable discourse with a woman who understood exactly what he was. If she meant to leave, he'd steal every pleasure he could now.

Behind them, the would-be rapist cursed and staggered to his feet. Murdoch glanced back to see the coward lurching through the underbrush, apparently intent on putting as many miles between himself and Lis as possible. An excellent result, and done without swords. Interesting.

He returned to following the path of Lis's devious mind. Normal women thought in roundabouts he couldn't follow. Lis added depth and volume to the spiraling paths. "I'm a danger to everyone around me. You would do better to go home."

"I will not return without an Oracle. I believe the gods have given me this duty as a test."

"Gods are just a woman's feeble attempt to make sense of the universe," he argued.

She cast him a disbelieving look. "Look at your ring and tell me that."

The ring glowed malevolently. He glared back at it. "My life is not dictated by a piece of onyx and pearl." Nor a pretty face, he added mentally, but he was a little less sure of that as the ice in Lis's eyes froze his soul.

"Onyx and pearl that are so much a part of you that you can't take them off," she reminded him tartly. "No matter how much you tamp it down, your anger consumes you. It is in everything you say and do. I assume that wound on your wrist is a result of temper, and that is the reason you won't tell me about it." She entered the cottage and rummaged about in their supplies for the makings of dinner.

"One of the committee clowns watched me work all morning," he muttered, as if that were an answer to her inquiry.

"Oh? Is a mortal responsible for wounding a warrior?" she taunted, producing an onion and peeling it.

"A load of timber is responsible," he muttered. He didn't want to talk about it, but he didn't want to leave her here alone either. "It fell from a roof."

"Timber? And you had to catch it? Why?" She peeled another layer.

He paced. He could ignore her questions and walk out, or stay and let her irritate him into responding. He didn't want to leave her alone. Stupid of him. "There were children playing in the lane. The boards could have fallen on them."

Only the bloody tear in his arm had prevented the villagers from screaming sorcery at his swift action in diving from the roof to catch the stack of falling timber. Apparently his injuries made him human in their eyes.

Had he been truly human, he would have broken his neck leaping from the roof, and the timber would have crushed his arm and no doubt his head and rib cage, but the villagers lacked the imagination to grasp that.

Lis threw an enigmatic glance in his direction, as if she knew what he wasn't saying. "Saving the children was heroic. But why did the timber fall?"

"Because the clown stared at me all morning."

Her face lit with mischief and understanding, and he almost chose Lis's method of nonconfrontation and walked out right then.

"Your temper built until the foundation shook," she guessed, rightly.

He paced some more. He ought to kill a rabbit or catch a fish or do *something* useful, but he was oddly compelled to see where this conversation would take them. He hoped it would take them to bed. "I may hurt myself, but I never intentionally hurt others. I would never hurt you."

She stopped chopping the onion to look at him through eyes the glorious silver blue of a morning sea.

"No, you can't hurt me. I have always known that under your anger is a man who simply wants to be loved and respected. I gave you that when I was a child. In return, even when I was six and you were twice my age, you let me follow you everywhere, and challenged the other boys to swordplay if they laughed at me. I *know* you, as no one else does."

Back then, he would have killed to protect the fascinating fairy child she had been. They were not children any longer. She was wrong. He could hurt her now. He'd already done so, and he doubted that she'd ever forgive him.

He released his tension by clenching and unclenching his fists over his head, then lowering his arms slowly. He looked for a heavy weight with which to repeat the exercise.

He needed his sword. He placed his pillow against the wall and smashed his fist into it, releasing his bottled-up energy in an act that harmed no one but himself. His knuckles suffered pain, and he dislodged one of the solid timbers. That satisfied his frustration, temporarily.

"You used to punch noses instead of walls."

"Everyone thinks I'm some kind of freak, and they're right. I'm no Oracle."

"You're the next-best thing we have to a god, yet you insist on throwing your gifts away."

He couldn't take it anymore. Not her apparent serenity over the sins of his past. Nor his knowledge of the violence simmering so close to his surface that it could turn to evil in the blink of an eye—as it had done too recently for him to even think about.

And most of all, he couldn't tolerate his damnable weakness in playing house with her as if they were still innocents.

He stormed out, slamming the door behind him.

Wooden shingles slid from the roof.

# Nine

Lissandra let the tears leak down her cheeks and blamed the onion.

Nothing had changed. She still adored the man Murdoch could have been. He still hated the man he was.

She was still frustrating him with her reasonableness. He was still tearing her into pieces with his unsettling turbulence.

The list could go on, but she was tired of analyzing why they'd grown apart—even before her father's death.

Only when they kissed did everything seem possible. She had all too often wondered what might have happened when they were younger had they acted on their urges and engaged in sexual congress. But the temptation had become a trap around which they'd continually danced—using desire as blackmail and bribe for what they wanted and couldn't have. Had Murdoch been any less honorable, she would no doubt be his slave by now, so hungry for satisfaction that she could not see right from wrong.

Which made it even more difficult to reject him now. The look he'd given her when she'd pulled away after his kiss had been so wistful.... She'd hurt him, and he'd understood why she'd hurt him. The loss of her childhood hero pained her. The child in her ached to believe again.

The *woman* in her just ached. Especially after the stunt he'd pulled in mentally disrobing and caressing her. She'd actually *felt* his touch. She'd be lucky if she ever slept again without the image of Murdoch's hand on her breast haunting her, drat the aggravating creature. If she knew how to inflict the same tormenting mental image on him, she would return the favor.

How long could she turn her back on Aelynn's problems while waiting for the perverse man to admit the gods had chosen him? Or must she abandon him here to find his own way?

She snorted in cynical amusement. She didn't need her Sight to realize she would never desert Murdoch. Until she understood differently, she had to assume the gods wished him to be Oracle. For now, she must be a true vestal virgin and sacrifice herself to Healing Murdoch's emotional wounds for the good of Aelynn.

Gods forbid that she do what *she* wanted for a change.

Not that she knew what she wanted.

She threw together flour and lard and began crumbling it between her fingers. If she had yeast, and an oven, she would punch bread dough as Murdoch punched walls. Lacking essential ingredients, she would have to be content with flat bread.

She had time to ponder why the villain she'd unmanned had been looking for them. He'd been paid, she was certain. Money had been the thought uppermost in his mind when he'd grabbed her. Beneath that had been the usual male lechery. She supposed she should have questioned him. Murdoch would have. But her attacker had left an unpleasant taste in her mouth, and she'd wanted him gone.

Coming from a land where men were giants of

strength, she scarcely considered the incident more than squashing a bug in the woods. She knew he wouldn't be back. She simply disliked a world in which people would cause harm for something so vulgar as coin. Telling Murdoch would only exacerbate his fury, which would not be conducive to achieving her goals.

Murdoch didn't return until sundown. Unshaven, his dark hair covered in sweat and twigs and bark, he'd evidently set himself some Herculean task to test his wounded arm. His shoulders strained the seams of a shirt he hadn't been wearing when he'd left. Did he keep an endless supply in saddlebags somewhere? More likely, lonely village women were sewing for him.

Lissandra was grateful he wore the loose trousers of a peasant and not the knit breeches of a gentleman. She didn't think she could resist this longing to linger in his arms if his masculine physique were any more visible.

"I'll take you to the coast in the morning." After throwing that startling announcement into the air, he drew off his shirt and crossed the room toward the bath.

He smelled of perspiration and male musk, and Lissandra's knees weakened. She clenched the table until her knuckles hurt to prevent herself from going after him.

He meant to abandon her on the coast and return?

"I will follow you back here," she warned. "You risk reopening the wound by overexerting yourself," she continued, admonishing him for his filthy state rather than cursing his intent to send her away. "You might be strong, but you're not immortal."

"I'm not stupid either. The committee is seeking me. I don't know if it has anything to do with the incident in the woods, or my catching the timber, but they have concluded I'm not a simpleton after all. The next step is to demand my documents, then conscript me. Would you like to imagine what will happen then?" He called this last from the pool.

No, she wouldn't like to imagine what would happen if soldiers attempted to drag Murdoch off to war if he didn't want to fight. If he could call up thunder over a mere wound, his fury would most likely eradicate the village.

"I'll need to hide until my task is done, and you're too visible," he called from the bath.

She tried to block out the distracting image of a naked Murdoch in a heated pool. While she worked her Healing, she could look on him as a patient, but not now. Now, he was all perfectly formed male, and the only one she'd ever craved. Rather than wallow in lust, she needed to consider this new development.

Had the villain in the woods been the first sign that they were being spied on? If so, she agreed that she needed to leave. She might have been isolated on Aelynn, but she'd listened to the crew of every ship that had arrived, and read the newssheets they'd brought back. She was aware of the fear and anger driving the vengeful actions of the Paris Tribunal, which preferred imprisonment and bloody executions to impartial trials. They *both* had to leave.

And she realized she didn't want to go, that she was enjoying this respite. Was that selfishness? She wanted Murdoch to herself, to share the bath he'd made with his own two hands, to watch her rosemary seeds grow, to live as a normal person did, for just a little longer.

She had thought she was running to find Murdoch. Was she, instead, running away from herself? She acknowledged the possibility. To endure the duties of an Oracle without any of the recognition or authority seemed pointless. She'd done that all her life, with no reward but the loss of the one man she wanted. Here, she was in charge of her own destiny, and she was developing a taste for it. And a hunger to know more of what she'd been denied.

Perhaps . . . if they had to leave this place, she could accept that Murdoch was right—she couldn't take him home, not while his suppressed angers caused unpredictable destruction. If her task was to help him learn to control his talents, then she had reason to linger in this world a while longer.

Unthinkingly, she rubbed her aching nipple as she wanted Murdoch to do. Recognizing her desire, she acknowledged that staying with Murdoch tempted fate.

Lissandra knew about the physical attraction of an *amacara* bond—those whom the gods intended to mate for life had instant, magnetic pulls that were difficult to resist once they were recognized. And the bond was impossible to break once they indulged in sexual congress.

The physical bond between her and Murdoch had always been that strong. She feared that if they made love, the gods would unite their fates for eternity.

Being physically bound to a dangerous man like Murdoch, one who could capture her heart, would be suicidal. No matter how much she desired to learn the pleasures of lovemaking, she'd not enjoyed her freedom long enough to wish for that form of slavery.

She heard Murdoch splashing in the warm water, felt the physical draw of his presence. Even as she went outside to cool off, she wondered: how could she Heal him if she had to keep him at a distance?

Later, when it came her turn to bathe, Lissandra applied a mental bolt to the curtain. She didn't have to read Murdoch's mind to grasp the reason for his restless pacing. Their proximity affected him as much as it did her. She'd left him testing his Healing arms by pushing his weight up from the floor. She suspected the instant she left the room, he used the kitchen knife as a sword to practice his thrusts and lunges. Perhaps she should find some way of retrieving his weapons. If only she knew why he'd given them up.

She needed guidance—should she leave this humble cottage as Murdoch insisted? Could she possibly take him back to Aelynn while his gifts were still so volatile?

She sank beneath the water scented with herbs of peace, felt the tension seep out of her, and let her mind drift to that cloud where she could converse with her spirit guide.

The imp whirled with impatience. Nothing new. It was one of the reasons Lissandra had learned outward serenity, to conceal her inner impatience.

*How can I help him?* she asked.

The mental image of a fairy that Lissandra had given to her spirit guide shook her tiny head and pointed through the clouds.

Sighing, wishing she would get answers to her questions instead of being shown paths that led to even more bewilderment, Lissandra mentally drifted to follow her spirit's direction. She should have been more specific as to whom she wished to help.

The vision was alarmingly clear for once: the priest, bound to a chair with a cloth tied over his mouth. The priest's eyes were wide with terror as one of the soldiers poked a knife threateningly at his throat. She could not hear the words, but the soldier's expression grew angrier as the priest kept shaking his head in denial.

Trying to restrain her panic, she edged backward

from the vision, scanning the room. More soldiers. More than the lazy two she had encountered earlier.

And another presence—one she could not see but who seemed more menacing, more smug, as if he had arranged the priest's capture and torment.

She renewed her concentration, sending her senses in all directions. It wasn't as easy here as it was on Aelynn. Her powers were more diffuse the farther she traveled from home. Of course, she usually sought counsel only on individuals she knew. She didn't think she knew the shadowy man.

Or did she? There was something vaguely familiar....
*He was an Aelynner!*

Her spirit guide leapt up and down in agreement.

Lissandra struggled to identify the stranger, but he was not someone with whom she dealt regularly. A sailor, perhaps, one of the men who were not happy to stay in one place, who traveled to all parts of the world, returning only occasionally to visit with family.

Why was an Aelynner with the soldiers? Aelynners were expected to do no harm in the Other World. As far as she knew, only Murdoch had dared defy the gods' edict. What powers did this man have to threaten soldiers and a priest? And *why*?

Were the soldiers torturing the priest in hopes of finding Murdoch? Or—she remembered her sense of an Aelynn presence when she'd arrived in Pouchay—were they looking for *her*?

Her spirit guide nodded approval and popped into oblivion, dropping Lissandra abruptly back to earth.

She stared at the dancing candle flames around the pool and tried to pull together her vision, but fear throttled her thinking. Had she Seen the future or—worse yet—the present? The peril seemed imminent.

She needed Murdoch's advice, but she could no longer trust it. He would do anything to send her home.

She couldn't let that poor priest come to harm. This was why Aelynners did not belong in this world. How could she ignore injustice and *not* use every power within her grasp to help—even though revealing their gifts was forbidden by Aelynn law?

Lissandra smacked her hands on the bubbling water and pushed out of the pool. What good did a spirit vision do when she had no understanding of what she was shown? She was useless in this foreign land. Her education was lacking.

Which was what Murdoch had told her for years.

Mind screaming with frustration and uncertainty, she dried off and donned a tunic rather than take the time to wrestle into the heavy Other World gown.

She returned to the cottage's main room to discover Murdoch lying flat on his back on the floor, lifting the heavy bed for exercise. The tendons of his bare arms bulged and strained, and his wide chest swelled with his efforts. The display of strength incited an unholy desire in her, nearly distracting her from her purpose.

She almost vowed to become his sex slave right there.

Only the way he deliberately ignored her and continued to overexert his newly mended wounds reminded her of the pigheaded man she was dealing with. She kicked the sole of a sandal he'd obviously made himself, for no cobbler would claim its workmanship.

"Stop that. You will pull apart every bone in your body. I need to speak with you."

She'd never know whether he would have obeyed. A rapid pounding and a frightened cry from outside drew their attention.

Murdoch lowered the bed and scrambled to his feet, placing his bulk between her and the door. Lissandra glared at his broad bare back and debated kicking him again, or biting his tempting shoulder and licking his brown flesh. Wondering how he would taste was not logical.

"Who goes there?" he called.

"Me, monsieur," piped the widow's son. "The committee has found our men in the forest and summoned many soldiers to arrest them! Even now they hold Père Antoine for questioning. Mama says they will send them all to the Tribunal!" His fear was tangible in his choked words.

Lissandra edged around Murdoch and opened the door. She had little understanding of the Tribunal or its formidable *committee*, but her vision had enlightened her to the reason for the boy's terror. She had Seen not the future, but the present. The soldiers must be torturing the poor priest in pursuit of any other secrets the town held—like Murdoch. And his weapons.

Murdoch reached for his shirt. "I'll be there shortly," he told the lad. "Do you know where Père Antoine hid my swords?"

Jean shook his head. "No, monsieur."

"I'll find them. Stay with the lady," he commanded.

Lissandra considered giving the imperious idiot a mental swat, but she decided it would not be conducive to peaceful understanding. "You know it is more than the priest they want, Murdoch," she warned. "Use your head instead of your strength for once."

He swung around and glared at her, but she could tell she'd curtailed his natural propensity for violence. His eyes narrowed as he pondered the problem.

"Why did you give the priest your swords?" she demanded.

He shot her a glare. "After seeing the damage I can do, you have to ask? I had hoped to mend instead of destroy for a change."

He was even more appallingly attractive when admitting his faults. His dark hair had dried and curled loosely around his bronzed throat and intelligent brow like some Roman god of old. Every feature of his lean face was chiseled stone, with nothing soft about it, unless he smiled. At the moment, his mobile mouth was stern and taut with concentration.

"It is not the swords that cause harm," she reminded him. "It is the anger in your heart."

He scowled at that. "I told you, the committee has been watching me," he said, dismissing her admonition. "If they have found the others, they will blame me and will not let the priest go until they have me. He has not sworn loyalty to France. They may have discovered this also."

She could not speak of her vision in front of the boy so she chose her words circumspectly. "There is some possibility ... I have Seen that one of our people followed me to this village," she warned.

Murdoch nodded as if he understood what she did not. "I had already planned to take you away. Now there is more reason. But first, we must rid the village of a plague of rats."

Lissandra sighed her regret at having the decision to leave made for her. She began to move about the room, gathering their scattered belongings. "Jean, tell your mother the herbs I've planted are valuable. Someone must tend them."

The boy nodded fearfully. "You are going? What will happen to us?"

"You will follow the lessons LeDroit has taught you.

You will carry water from the river for the fields if it does not rain. You will share the houses that have new roofs until others can be mended. In time, you will be fine."

She hoped. She disliked abandoning anyone in need. But her duty was to Aelynn.

She sensed Murdoch's suppressed rage that he could not complete the task he'd set himself, but there was no help for it, not when others might be threatened by their presence. Even the villagers would fear them if she and Murdoch used their terrifying gifts to drive off a troop of soldiers. Truly, Aelynners were not meant for this world—

Midthought, it struck her—Murdoch had actually conceded to her logic and agreed that *he* must leave. The situation must be dire indeed.

"Follow behind us," Murdoch told the boy. "Slip away only when we are close to the village and it is safe."

The boy nodded worshipfully. "What will you do about Père Antoine, monsieur?"

"Nothing saintly," Murdoch retorted.

For better or worse, the Warrior had returned.

# Ten

Murdoch clenched his fists on the mare's reins and did his best to ignore the goddess of justice perched beside him. His inner turmoil shielded him from Lis's righteous anger, but not her beauty as the evening breeze blew strands loose from her moonlit braid.

She'd succeeded in forcing him to face his past ambitions when all he'd wanted to do was hide from the results. When he'd first arrived in France, he'd been filled with idealistic notions of freeing the downtrodden from the yokes of tyranny. At first, he'd aided the rebel cause from within the powerful court. After it became apparent he could not save France entirely on his own, he'd attempted to work within the system forged by the revolutionaries.

It had been nine months since he'd ridden into Paris, escorting recalcitrant Bretons who'd denounced the glorious new government. Nine months since his stomach for revolution had been purged in blood ...

*Wearing the blue uniform of the Breton fédérés instead of that of the king's men he'd worn more than a year before, Murdoch led two coaches carrying a fractious priest, a few defiant aristocrats, and several tradesmen accused of counterrevolutionary crimes. His men drove the* coaches and rode alongside in an orderly manner. Their long march from the far reaches of France would end at l'Abbaye prison in Paris, where these plotters against the new government would be tried for their crimes.

Unease shuddered down Murdoch's spine. He'd avoided Paris for this past year since the king's arrest. Even his ironclad mental barriers could not keep out the writhing torment of hundreds of thousands of panicky, tense, and violent souls all in one festering sore of a city. The malevolence of the mob crept along his skin as he guided the entourage through streets packed with hostile citizens watching the small parade of hated aristocrats and landowners.

Using General Lafayette's methods as his template for turning rabble into a real army, Murdoch had done his best to train his men to follow orders and resist the mob mentality that controlled the city. But even the horses danced nervously at the curses being flung at his prisoners. The Breton dissidents had been tried and found guilty in the newssheets and political pamphlets before they'd even entered the city gates.

The revolutionary government wanted blood—the king's, the nobility's, that of any who defied them. And lacking that, they would take the blood of any traitor to the cause. Murdoch had known that when he'd ridden through the city gates. And he was helpless to change the course of events now.

Then again, not entirely helpless. He'd forsworn using his erratic gifts in his effort to establish a place in the Other World, but he had his swords and his men and his pride.

Cheers and shouts from the crowd behind him were his first warning of trouble. Murdoch reined his stallion out of the procession.

Standing on the footboard of the second carriage, a violent protester stabbed a sword through the window at the unarmed passengers. Murdoch battened down his volatile wrath and urged his drivers to speed while he forced his mount through the mob, ordering his outriders to hold back the wave of people. Standing in his stirrups, he whipped out his saber and flashed it in the faces of the hordes, but his men were wildly outnumbered.

The mob spilled into the streets, heedless of the danger of galloping horses, heavy coach wheels, and Murdoch's steel.

Ratcheting down his fury until his head pounded with the pain of his effort, controlling his urge to hurl fire and lightning, Murdoch yanked the stallion's reins, forcing it to rear up on its hind feet, pawing the air and opening a path to the last coach. Sword raised high, he shouted curt commands to his men to close ranks around the coaches, but it was too late, had been too late before he'd even entered the city gates. No militia stepped forward to aid his men. No National Guard swarmed to protect the prisoners.

Soon the coaches would be overrun by a mob that smelled blood.

Murdoch rode down the line of his men, encouraging them to stand strong. But the rage of the mob and the release of long-pent-up hatred spilled through their ranks. In an instant, his trained revolutionary forces turned from fighting the mob to joining them—ripping open coach doors so they could seize their prey.

Enraged by their treachery, Murdoch whipped out his rapier, slicing both of his weapons through the air, hacking and stabbing at his own men to drive them back from the screaming, terrified prisoners he'd sworn to protect. Blood spilled down his hands as his greater strength decapitated a villain who was strangling a white-faced jeweler inside the coach.

Abandoning his horse, Murdoch leapt to the roof of the rear carriage. Sun flashed off the gold braid of his uniform as he swung his saber. His arms ached with the force of cutting through muscle and bone. Men cried out in death, falling to the streets, but more ran up to replace them. No longer able to hold back his inhuman strength, Murdoch wielded rapier as well as saber with the speed of a demon. Mercilessly, he gutted and pierced while the cowering prisoners prayed and wept.

The coaches raced faster. The mob surged behind them, only a few madmen still daring to challenge Murdoch's uncanny weapons. They were almost at the gates of the prison—

Where another mob rushed out to meet them, weapons in hand, bloodlust in their eyes.

Upon spearing a soldier who turned on him, Murdoch realized he'd once trained the boy, and the shield inside his head exploded. In truth, the Revolution had sown the wind—and reaped the whirlwind. Violence had no end until all in its path was destroyed.

In the anguish of realization, Murdoch's repressed energy blasted free of its confines, whipping the frenzied air into a funnel of wind, rain, and hail. Unable to control the weather any more than he could control a mob, he mentally drove the frantic coach horses into a gallop, over the screaming remains of the crowd, and past the prison gates, while wind and rain bowed trees, ripped at roofs, and swept the streets clean of both blood and mob.

Leaping from the roof of the rear coach to the forward one, Murdoch scrambled down to reclaim the reins, and steered the team down a narrow, deserted alley, safe from the tumult. The mob fell behind them, racing for *shelter from the howling fury he'd set loose. Halting the exhausted horses, Murdoch jumped down and flung open the doors of the prison coaches.*

*"Run!" he shouted. "Run, hide, leave France before you become victims to their madness again!"*

*Terrified, bleeding, and pale, his prisoners stumbled for freedom. The lone priest stopped to make the sign of the cross and bless Murdoch before he, too, hurried after the others.*

*Murdoch didn't feel blessed. Like victory, the use of power always had a price. With his prisoners released, Murdoch walked through the ruins wreaked by the storm, past bodies of men he'd trained these previous months, past the lifeless forms of women caught in midscream. Despair wrapped around him. Again, he'd tried to do the right thing—and ended by destroying all.*

After that, he'd changed his politics and his tactics, hoping to save lives instead of take them. He'd spent these last months rescuing innocent prisoners from the bloody mobs of Paris, sneaking in at night, risking his life again and again to carry out those who had been incarcerated for being born into the wrong family or for not crossing the right palm with gold. And still, all his erratic strength and mighty weapons hadn't been enough. Would never be enough against the unremitting tide of violence.

When he'd inadvertently set fire to an entire village, he had been forced to admit that he and his weapons were as damned as the Revolution was. He'd thought to set warfare aside and seek peace.

Only for Lis's sake would he take up a sword again. He didn't know where he'd go after this. He hated abandoning his task here, but once he rid the town of its infestation of human rats, he would have to set Lis on a ship for home.

"You can run faster than this cart can roll," Lis murmured, jolting him from his reverie. The boy rode obediently behind them on his pony and couldn't hear their conversation.

"I can't leave you alone," he growled back.

"You'll need your weapons if we're to have any chance of winning. There are more than a half dozen soldiers guarding the prisoners." She grasped the reins in front of his hands and tugged to slow the horse. "Just don't let anyone see you run. It raises too many questions."

"As does flinging men into trees?" He regretted the sarcasm after the words were said. She wasn't objecting to his weapons. He was the one who had reservations about their use.

She didn't appear to take his sharpness personally. "Exactly. I'll let the horse pull ahead around the bend. The shrubbery will hide you."

Murdoch had to believe a woman who could mentally geld a man could take care of herself for the few minutes it would take for him to run into the village. He leapt from the cart the moment it turned the bend. Landing on his feet, he entered the shrubbery before the boy could see him. He reached town within minutes and raced through the shadows he knew well, approaching the priest's humble abode from alleyways, moving silently. Opening his mind, he could feel the apprehension of the people hiding behind closed doors. Most were women and children and old men who were terrified of what might happen to their sons and husbands and fathers. And the priest. The bloody tales from Paris had reached even this isolated area, giving them good cause to fear the fate of any prisoner the committee took.

The priest's cottage was left unlocked, as always. Murdoch slipped through the kitchen door, knowing the place would be empty. In his head, he pictured a sword, and his nose led him straight to the priest's Spartan bedroom. The neat cot hid nothing, but the bare floor . . .

Using the kitchen knife he'd stuck in his belt, Murdoch pried at an irregular crack in the boards. In moments, he'd found the mechanism that opened the trapdoor. Lighting a candle, he leaned over the hole and caught the gleam of metal. The priest was hiding an arsenal.

Finding his leather scabbard among the hoard, Murdoch strapped it on before spreading the remainder of his loot across the floor. His weapons had been made to his specifications, so they stood out in this pitiful collection. Claiming his most prized possession, he stood with legs akimbo and with both hands swung the golden hilt of his well-balanced saber. It felt like a natural extension of his arms. He shoved the sword into its scabbard, adjusting to the weight on his hip, then inserted his rapier into his belt.

Swinging his arms and working through the tension in his muscles, he practiced whipping out both weapons and slicing them through the empty air. He hadn't exercised his skill since the fire, but the motions were ingrained in him from a lifetime's experience.

He scanned the rest of the hoard, found a knife more suited to his needs than the kitchen blade he carried, then hastily returned the remaining weapons to their hiding place.

He could hear the pony cart arriving on the edge of town. The boy would be riding off to his mother, leaving Lis alone.

Weapons in place, Murdoch hastened toward the front door and slipped into the street. Others peered out from behind closed shutters. He had an urge to call to them but refrained. The fewer who were involved, the better off everyone would be. He just wished he could stuff Lis in a cupboard and keep her safe until this fight was over.

She would no doubt knock him over the head if he tried. That she was here at all still shocked him unutterably.

Lashing the reins of the horse, guiding the cart, she sat tall and proud, like a warrior queen riding to battle in her chariot. Her silver-blond braid reflected the moonlight. She'd chosen to pack the petticoats and gown that offended her, and concealed her lightweight Aelynn garments beneath a cloak. The loose clothing would be easier for kneeing groins, Murdoch suspected.

He strode with confidence out of the shadows, realizing he understood Lis better than he had known. He stepped up on the cart and surprised her with a swift kiss on the mouth.

She caught his shirt; whether to draw him closer or push him away became moot. They both lost themselves in a hungry blending of breath and tongues—a heaven he didn't deserve.

Reluctantly, he set her aside before he committed a lewd act in public. If he was ever to be allowed to embrace her in the way he wished, he wanted it in private, where only the two of them could enjoy the moment. He caressed her jaw with his rough hand and brushed her swollen lip with the pad of his thumb to bring them both back to reality.

"Do you intend to enter the tavern and slay men with your eyes?" he asked, not entirely in jest. He had yet to determine how much she could or would do besides Heal. Growing up together, he and Ian had learned weaponry, studied the stars and the ocean currents, while Lis's path had led her to learn herbs and medicinal skills. She'd played with dolls. If she'd ever learned to fight, he didn't know of it. Perhaps she could teach him the path to peace. He took his seat beside her and usurped the reins while they both adjusted their breathing.

She eyed the weapons strapped to his hips. "I do not have your experience, but I should be able to tell you where the villains are and how many men surround the inn and some of what they're thinking. Would any of that be useful?"

"I sense two men besides the priest in the private room behind the tavern, plus a void that must be your Aelynner. They keep the farmers from the woods imprisoned upstairs. I don't need to read minds to know the committee and the soldiers around the inn are thinking about blood. Whose blood is the important question."

"Any blood will do, I'm sure," she said. "The committee has been humiliated and someone must pay. That is a very primitive form of thought."

He tied the horse to a post some distance from the inn. By now, the whole town knew of their arrival—and were waiting to see what their resident paragon would do to save their men. But he'd rather the soldiers not see them until it was necessary.

"And your intent is to incapacitate these forces and escape without a trace?" he asked.

"Or not get captured, at least," she agreed. "I dislike that the newcomer is an Aelynner."

An Aelynner holding a priest hostage did not make sense. If any of their countrymen had come to find Lis or kill him, they would do so directly, without involving Others. But in this matter, he trusted Lis's Sight more than his own.

He didn't like fighting one of his countrymen. He'd seen more blood lost than he cared to see again, and he had no desire to resort to his unpredictable energies if it could be avoided. The element of surprise could save lives. "Stay with the mare. I can do this alone."

"I have no doubt you can free the men, but can you do so without killing anyone?" She followed him from the cart against his express orders—while echoing his own fears.

Her presence hindered his actions. Although he didn't wish to kill anyone, such a promise would tie his hands behind his back. He started down a dark alley behind the greengrocer's. "If they're torturing a good man, why shouldn't I kill them?"

"Because killing is wrong," she insisted. "It is not our place to be judge and jury. Usurping the rights of the gods is arrogant."

"If they were fair and just gods, they would not allow good men to be harmed." He halted at the end of the alley, irritated with himself because he was actually heeding her foolishness.

Incredibly, he trusted Lis to know what he no longer understood. No matter how much he objected to her foolish female whims, he sensed that turning his back on her would be akin to turning his back on salvation.

"Are you prepared to bring a man to his knees without my aid?" he asked, not knowing whether he could save himself at the risk of Lis. He halted at the corner and peered over the wall into the tavern's kitchen yard. Little light flickered from behind the shutters of the private room in back.

"I am," she said, with such assurance that he actually believed her. He'd watched her bring a man down with a twist of the nose. She wasn't helpless.

"Then wait here while I survey the grounds. Do you need any weapons?"

"I can find what I need. How will you draw the soldiers away from the priest?"

"They stink of fear as well as greed. It's easy enough to act on both." He kept to the shadows, gliding away from Lis. He'd lived by his sword for years. Lis's belief that he had no right to be judge and jury resounded hollowly in the face of all he knew. Yet he wanted to believe her. To shed no more blood had been his hope when he'd retired his weapons.

He simply didn't see any way of saving the priest and freeing the prisoners without bloodshed. Bribery was the only nonviolent option his cynical mind could summon. He had little experience in peaceful solutions.

Locating the guard closest to the inn window where the priest was kept, Murdoch slipped silently up behind him, wrenched the man's sword arm behind him so he dropped the weapon, and placed his own blade against the guard's neck. "Not a sound or you'll never speak again," he murmured. He twisted his hand so the moon's light caught the polished onyx and pearl of his ring. "This is yours if you can hold your tongue until I return."

He had no intention of parting with the ring, since it would mean parting with his finger as well, but the eerie blue light cast by the pearl stifled the terrified guard's natural urge to argue. He nodded sharply, and satisfied, Murdoch slipped from the shrubbery to the shadow of a lilac bush outside the window. He couldn't sense the Aelynn presence as Lis did, but he did sense the movement of three men when he could hear the thoughts of only two, plus the priest's prayers.

Three against one wasn't bad odds, if he could avoid

the attention of the guards posted around the inn. He slid the point of his blade between the shutters, un-latching them and letting them bang inward. Before the guards on the outside could react, he swung his leg over the low sill and entered the room.

A shadow departed through a partially opened in-terior door, leaving only the bound priest and the two committee louts staring at him in disbelief. The older one grabbed the priest's hair and jerked his head back to hold a knife to his throat at the sight of Murdoch's weapons.

The priest immediately began muttering prayers for Murdoch's soul, which didn't much aid his temper. Sti-fling his irritation and desire to blast the lot of them through the wall, Murdoch maintained a menacing purr. "Leave quietly, and I will not kill you." He pointed the rapier at the fat soldier and glared at the older one threatening the priest.

The fat one staggered backward, away from the deadly steel. "You cannot get away with this! You are surrounded."

"Do you really think so?" Murdoch asked, stalking farther into the room. "Then how is it I am here?" In a movement faster than the human eye could follow, he switched the rapier from his right to left hand and slashed it across the arm of the older soldier holding the priest, forcing him to drop his knife from the priest's throat and wail in pain. Murdoch's right hand now held the saber on the stout guard.

"Jacques! Émile! To me," the older soldier shouted, holding his wrist and backing away from Murdoch's merciless weapons.

"That was very badly done," Murdoch admonished, slicing with a single cut the ropes binding the priest. "Now people will have to die, and my lady disapproves."

He could blast these fools to kingdom come with the point of a finger, but he could not prevent the blast from destroying the inn and everyone in it. He had to repress his angry energy.

As two more soldiers rushed through the door, Murdoch shoved his growing rage into the lockbox of his soul. He wanted no more whirlwinds or lightning bolts. He kicked the priest's chair until Père Antoine stood and limped toward the door. Then, lips set in determination, Murdoch began coolly swinging his weapons in defensive arcs, giving the priest space to escape.

Blood spurted from the wrist of the first guard who entered. He cried out in agony, grabbing his spurting artery before sliding toward the floor. Before his opponent's posterior so much as hit a floorboard, Murdoch had swung around to disarm the soldier he'd flung into a tree, leapt to the seat the priest had vacated, and stabbed his rapier at the two remaining men who were stupidly dashing to the rescue, causing them to fall back in their haste to escape the point.

A pistol shot rang out, and Murdoch felt the ball slam into his shoulder. Anger instantly burst through the chains in which he'd imprisoned it. Someone was going to regret that. And even though his already weakened left arm would be incapacitated in moments, he wouldn't be the one who repented.

White-lipped with the effort of tamping down the erratic gifts that could slaughter every man in sight, Murdoch relied on his superior strength to fight back. There was still the matter of the terrified men imprisoned upstairs to settle, but that would be better accomplished from outside. Once assured the priest had stumbled to safety, Murdoch leapt through the open shutters and into the night.

Where a half dozen more men raced toward him.

Where was Lis?

Instinct forged of a thousand battles and years of practice shattered his last remaining constraints at the need to
see Lis safe. Without a single thought, he aimed the sword
in his right hand at the closest guard and called down a
wind. A gust of icy air propelled Murdoch forward while
blasting the guard backward into the lilac. Flying tree
branches and a bolt of lightning provided cover so Murdoch could hit the ground and roll into the shrubbery.

*Where is Lis, bloodydamnhell!*

"Is that the demon?" someone cried in a fearful
voice.

"We still have the rest of the prisoners. Let him come
to us," a voice he didn't recognize said with assurance
and command. Lis had been right. This new person was
different. Murdoch could not sort out an emotion to
identify him, but he was preventing the soldiers from
fleeing as Murdoch had counted on. The inn should be
swarming with angry citizens overcoming the guards to
free the prisoners by now—had the soldiers retreated.

Crawling through the hedge, he checked to see if Lis
was anywhere close to where he'd left her. She wasn't.
He cursed and scanned the yard while the guards re-
formed on the inn side of the hedge. He wished he could
read her presence as easily as he read others', but her
Empathic barrier prevented it. His shoulder burned
with all the fires of hell as he scrambled to his feet, but
his fear for Lis burned worse.

Suddenly she was there, touching his elbow from behind. Her Healing energy found his wound and began
to seep through the blood vessels and torn muscle. "I'm
here. I didn't want you worrying that I was in the path of
whatever you're doing."

He rolled his eyes. As if he'd ever *not* worry about her. But his relief was immediate, allowing him to concentrate again. "Stay behind me!" he ordered, assessing the situation on the other side of the hedge.

Soldiers were spilling to the right and left of the shrubbery under orders of the Aelynner. They had to leave *now*. Even he couldn't fight his way free with only one arm. But he didn't want those poor farmers being marched to prison. If ever there was a time to use his corrupted powers . . .

Torn between the damage he could do and the lives of innocent farmers he could save, Murdoch braced his legs and focused on the slender steel of his rapier as he had not done in years. Grasping the hilt with both hands, he aimed the weapon at the inn and prayed with all his might.

The wind gusted behind him, flattening the branches of the hedge and rattling the inn's windows. He fought to hold back his energy, groping for some semblance of control so he didn't blast the village into the sky. The hilt shook with the force of his restraint, and the brisk breeze began to rattle the inn's walls and the rotting tree above it. He stifled an urge to grin in satisfaction at this small victory.

Conscious that Lis was clasping his injured arm, Murdoch gritted his teeth and maintained a breeze instead of creating a tornado. Dead branches flew through the yard, assaulting anyone foolish enough to approach him. Overlong limbs brushed at the inn's shingles. Stone walls did not shake so well, but the roof . . . Ah, there was an easy target, if he could keep it from flying away completely. The prisoners were being kept in those upper rooms.

He heard more shouts as the wind steadily increased,

and he debated how to free the farmers. He couldn't use
fire. Not again. He could try cracking the earth, but falling walls might injure the innocent.

Murdoch felt his temper rising as the guards pushed
against the wind and kept coming, but he continued to
aim his rapier at the tavern. Summoned by his instincts,
a wind howled through the trees, gathering a swirling
force across the town.

Lis gripped his elbow. "Think of good things, not
death," she demanded.

Had it been anyone but Lis, his temper would have
escalated. Instead, rather than lash out at her, he focused his ire along the rapier's edge, and directed the
wind to spiral across the rafters.

Ancient shingles and boards were ripped from their
nails, causing screams from all beneath the inn's roof.
The wind shattered windows and blew open shutters. He
almost gawked in astonishment at his own accuracy as
interior doors blew off their hinges, allowing men to spill
from every nook and cranny. Even the soldiers halted
their advance to stare in disbelief.

Lis's fingers bit into his upper arm, whether in fear
or awe he didn't bother to ascertain. She kept his sword
arm steady. Clinging to his phenomenal restraint, he held
his rapier as if he were shooting targets and blew down
one soldier after another, even though he could only feel
their panic and not see them through the tall hedge.

The freed prisoners scattered like ants from their
nest.

Amused by this result, Murdoch narrowed his gaze,
sighted along his rapier, and aimed at a uniformed figure crawling through the hedge. The wind blew the fool
backward into the privy.

"You're enjoying this!" Lis hissed in protest.

"There is nothing wrong with enjoying one's work," he retorted. If he'd had this kind of restraint all along, he would have enjoyed it sooner. The unusual exertion would have a price, he knew, but he couldn't stop now.

Ignoring the pain shooting up and down his arm, concentrating on the miraculous touch of Lis's hand, he aimed his rapier once more—at the troop of soldiers advancing from the street. A blast of stormy wind and a lightning bolt scattered them like bowling pins.

One side of Murdoch's skull felt the throb of a punishing headache, but his task wasn't done yet.

"Truly brilliant," Lis murmured. "I have never seen you at work, but that was amazing. You held your temper and harmed only one man."

At a cost, but he wouldn't confide his weakness to an infallible Olympus. "The Aelynner fled outside. I want a glimpse of him." Ignoring the pulsing beat at his temple and the aura of color ringing his vision that always followed intense concentration, Murdoch edged toward the street, hoping to discern his enemy among the people who were spilling from the tavern.

She caught his arm. "No, you have done what you set out to do. We must leave now."

"I have only freed a priest and a few farmers," he argued. "The monsters are still there."

"You can do no more. It's up to the men and their families now."

It hardly seemed sufficient, but her words fought past the pain in his head and brought him back to reality. He must think of Lis first. Her importance to Aelynn was far greater than his insane desire to save the world.

"Will it be safe to take the cart and horse?" she asked. "Or should we just run before the soldiers re-form and come after us? I'm not as fast as you."

"It would be faster to steal horses and ride. Or ..." Wincing at having to concentrate again, he opened his mind to the few animals in and around the village. Another burst of energy, and the headache from his exertions became excruciating, to the extent that he scarcely noticed his throbbing shoulder.

Grabbing Lis's arm, for support as much as to lead her, he fought waves of pain. As they ran toward the waiting cart, Murdoch reassured their mare while he sent every other possible animal that could be ridden racing for distant fields. It would be noon before the horses and mules could be rounded up, if at all. That should delay anyone from following them.

They reached the cart, and Murdoch collapsed into a moaning ball on the seat, leaned over, and threw up the contents of his stomach onto the ground as he hadn't done since youth. With effort, he held his throbbing temples in hopes of preventing his skull from exploding. He lost his grip on his rapier, letting it clatter to the floor of the cart.

"Overexertion," Lis whispered, touching his hunched shoulders after climbing up beside him. "I wish we could go home."

So did he.

Instead, he clung to his pounding head like a weak child, forced down the nausea, and allowed Lis to whip the cart into motion.

The jarring movement nearly split his head wide-open.

There was a reason his gifts were erratic. The intense concentration needed to control them debilitated him to the point of helplessness.

# *Eleven*

In triumphant joy at having finally seen the warrior at his best, Lissandra sent the pony racing down the lane. She disliked the sword-rattling contests that Aelynn men relished, but Murdoch had displayed both restraint and strength in saving the priest and the farmers—the ideal gallantry of his trade.

She wished they could return to the Healing pool of the cottage, where she could lay her hands on Murdoch and ease his suffering. His big body had collapsed into a semiconscious heap in the cart after emitting a groan of agony that seemed ripped from his soul.

She had never seen him in such torment.

Or maybe she had, and she'd wiped the memory from her mind, preferring to think of her hero as invincible. She'd been a little girl when she'd last watched an adolescent Murdoch suffer. He'd yelled and chased her away that day, and she had never seen him like that since.

He had deliberately never let her—or anyone—see him weak again, she wagered. She had known he lacked control—but no one had realized that the cause might be physical.

If there was something physically wrong with the gods-appointed Oracle, what would happen if Murdoch exceeded his limits and his own energy killed him? She stifled the horror welling in her soul and considered the thought from a different perspective.

Did she dare believe that the gods had sent her to Heal the suffering that could be causing his inability to contain his energies? She had never encountered such a problem before. He must have learned at an early age that focusing his energies resulted in pain, which made him vulnerable, so instead, he simply sent his excess energies into the universe.

She didn't know if she could limit herself to just *Healing* him. Even seeing Murdoch defenseless, she craved the physical connection between them. Her lips still throbbed with the passion of his earlier kiss. She threw him a surreptitious look, but his wide shoulders were hunched. Blood seeped through his shirt. She needed to bandage his wounds. In frustration, she forced herself to think of him as her patient, not the lover she couldn't have.

Finding some way that he could control his dangerous gifts without suffering crippling pain had to be her first priority—before he inadvertently killed himself or her.

In any event, their idyll had ended. Whoever the other Aelynner was, he wasn't their friend, and she wouldn't worry about him while Murdoch lay in agony.

Heading west, in the direction from which she'd arrived, she sent mental farewells to the village. It had been lovely having no real responsibility for a few days. She would have liked to have seen her herbs grow, experimented with this world's healing medicines, taken more time to observe the differences between Other Worlders and Aelynners. . . .

"Keep going," Murdoch said, lolling his head backward. "As long as the mare is able, keep going."

"You're in pain," she argued. "I need to touch you."

"I'd rather suffer the pain," he countered.

His words knocked the breath out of her, and tears rimmed her eyes. Usually, he couldn't hurt her with his ugly moods, but this uncalled-for remark hit a tender spot. She'd done what he'd asked and stayed out of his way. Had she been wrong to do so?

She whipped the horse to an even faster pace and didn't cringe when he groaned. She'd already wept entirely too many tears over the surly bastard.

The mare had grown weary by the time they traversed the hills out of the wilderness near the coast. The stars revealed an abandoned cowshed Lissandra remembered from her earlier journey.

"It's too dark to go farther." She used her best tone of authority at Murdoch's grunt of protest. "I don't know where I'm going, and the horse needs water and rest. Lie there and suffer if you like, but I won't mistreat an animal."

She let Murdoch stay collapsed on the seat while she unhitched the horse and led it to a small spring. Oddly, she felt as comfortable on this land as she did on the ground of Aelynn. She felt the holy spirits lingering in the spring, and she said prayers of gratitude just as she would have done at home. Her strength might be less this far from Aelynn, but her faith remained strong.

Even though her faith had led her to rescue an ungrateful wretch of a man. Maybe she'd pound his head with *her* anger for a change.

Except it was hard to be angry with a man who had controlled his wind-raising abilities with the expertise of a true Weathermaker to save innocents from harm, even knowing he would suffer excruciating agony as a result. The Murdoch she'd known had never possessed that much control or concern. Or that much power.

He'd changed.

True, he was still an irascible bastard, but then, her father had never been the most considerate of men either. Men of power had much on their minds, and it was difficult for them to set aside the problems of an entire world to consider the feelings of individuals.

Or so her mother had always told her.

Lissandra had her doubts. Her brother had never been harsh, and Ian's mind roamed far freer than that of most men.

Pondering the mysteries of the universe was exhausting. She tethered the mare in the spring-fed grass, and made her way back up the hill to the cowshed.

Murdoch had managed to exit the cart on his own. He slept now in the shed on a mound of rotting hay he'd apparently gathered from remnants scattered across the earthen floor.

In a protected corner well hidden in the back of the shed, he'd built a similar mound for her, added grass, and laid his shirt over it.

Her heart softened at the considerate gesture. Had any other man done this for her at home, she would have taken it as her due and thought nothing of it. For Murdoch to offer this kindness when he was in debilitating pain . . .

Sadness seeped through her protective frost as she realized that because of her unwise attraction to a man who could not or would not return to Aelynn, she might never have the home and children that came so easily to others. She could choose to take a husband from among the other men at home, but how could she ask a man to be content with a woman who neither loved nor needed him?

Even as a child, she had known that Murdoch was the only man who could possibly be her equal. She'd never found another to compare, no matter how hard she tried. It seemed cruel of the gods to match her with a man who despised all she loved, but it was probably her own stubborn perversity that made her yearn for what she couldn't have.

She cut through his blood-soaked shirt and cleaned his wound. The bullet had gone straight through, and even in his weakened state, the injury had begun to Heal. After applying a bandage, she threw her cloak over Murdoch's hunched shoulders and brushed his forehead with Healing energy. His tensed muscles relaxed, and he slipped into a deeper sleep, rolling more comfortably onto his back.

She smoothed his brow and caressed the thick length of his dark hair, sending Healing thoughts and prayers. He sighed and groped for her hand, and she retreated. She longed to touch him as woman to man, curl up next to him and let the heat of his big body melt the cold shell of her resistance, but the physical connection between them was much too dangerous. Neither of them was prepared for the results. If he wouldn't—or couldn't—go home, she had to leave him free to find a woman in this world.

France's spies and soldiers posed a threat unconducive to her Healing whatever ailed Murdoch. She'd have to take him to England, where Ian and his wife, Chantal, had a home, where Trystan, the island's Guardian, had taken his Crossbreed wife, Mariel, and their children to escape the bloodshed Ian Saw in France's future.

She had no choice. Murdoch may have been chosen by the gods, but he'd made it obvious that he was too dangerous to take to Aelynn until he was cured of whatever crippled his concentration.

*      *      *

Remnants of his dream lingered when Murdoch woke. Pressing his eyes closed against the painful light, he tried to retrieve the whole—Lis stroking his forehead, touching his hair. . . .

His already-aroused body didn't need encouragement. He rubbed his crotch to ease the throbbing and returned his thoughts to more practical matters. What had happened last night?

He'd overexerted himself—by *controlling* the wind. Instead of unleashing destruction, he had deliberately called up a wind, given it direction and speed, and saved the farmers. He'd channeled his rage through his sword before, but never with such precision.

*He'd revealed his sickening weakness to Lissandra.*

A low thud of pain took up residence in the back of his head, but he forced his mind to examine everything that had brought about his miracle of restraint—and his incapacitation.

Instead, he found himself recalling Aelynn, the home he'd banished from his mind as thoroughly as he'd been banished. He remembered Lissandra's mother, the all-powerful Oracle of Aelynn, the woman who had raised him.

Fury buzzed along the edges of his memory, but he kept probing at it like a sore tooth. Dylys had tried to train him as she had her own son and daughter, but he'd never taken orders well. She would tell him to concentrate on his task, and he would focus on a bird in the sky instead—because concentrating his energies *hurt*. Besides, he'd felt a child's resentment for having been taken from his real mother, which had manifested itself in disobedience. Resentment had eventually built to anger and then into a festering fury in adolescence. By that time, he and Dylys had gone head-to-head over his recalcitrance in refusing to follow her training. He'd quit his lessons and taken up sailing for profit the day Dylys had informed him that she would never allow an insolent devil like him to court Lissandra.

Those were distant memories, old pains from childhood, bitterness from adolescence. He'd grown cocky and arrogant once he realized he didn't need Dylys to have what he wanted. By then he'd learned that, despite his handicap, he was stronger than everyone else he knew.

And then he'd killed Luther, and in her grief and fury, Dylys had done her best to divest him of his strengths. He'd been banished from paradise and left to survive on his own. No one—not his friends, not Lis, *no one*—had come after him to hear his side of the story, to share his anguish. Not that explaining would have changed what he had done.

Time had not healed his emotional wounds, but the futility of war had eventually stripped him of much of his arrogance. Last night . . . miraculously, he'd almost been his old powerful self, only . . . better. Not a lot better, but just enough to make him crave that kind of accuracy and control again. If there was any hope that he could learn to direct the power as he had not been able to before his banishment . . .

He still wouldn't . . . couldn't . . . return to an entire island of people who despised him. He heard Lissandra moving about and contemplated lying here, waiting to see if she'd touch him again, but that was the arrogant ass thinking. Or his reproductive organs.

Just the memory of their kiss last night had him rising up on his elbow. He searched for a glimpse of her through the stripes of morning light shining through the drafty walls of the shed.

She was already dressed—in a garment that wasn't quite what he recalled. He rubbed his temple and tried to gather his scattered wits. He distinctly remembered her wearing the loose white tunic gown of Aelynn last night. And she'd packed a less-than-stylish gray gown, the kind that required corsets and petticoats and lengths of muslin or lace to fill the bodice.

What she wore now seemed to combine the two in some unfathomable manner that flattered her high breasts and slender figure. He recognized the gray fabric from the French gown, but unlike the earlier version, it displayed the sway of her hips beneath the cloth, and he had to rub his breeches to push his unruly organ out of sight.

"How did you do that?" he mumbled, rising into a sitting position. Amazingly, although his shoulder still ached, last night's headache had dissipated. He could remember spending days of his childhood curled up in agony after a particularly difficult feat. His Healing abilities had never extended to his head.

Startled, Lis stopped whatever infernal puttering she was about and turned to stare at him. "Do what?"

He gestured vaguely at her gown. "Create a gown from nothing."

She glanced down at the high bodice snugly outlining the shape of her breasts and shrugged. "This is similar to gowns that Chantal wears. I thought it might be more comfortable than that bulky mass of fabric, while being less distinctive than my tunic."

Murdoch snorted. "You will have men crawling on their hands and knees with their tongues dragging the ground should you walk about in that. It's little more than underwear."

He thought he caught her startled reaction before

she dismissed his comment with the imperial authority she wielded so well.

"I've created a wrap to go over my shoulders. I don't think it's any more revealing than Chantal's gowns."

He wanted to tell her that Ian's wife wore gowns from Paris, a completely different world from the villages through which they traveled, but he didn't wish to dilute her pleasure in her accomplishment.

"Do you have any idea where we're going?" He changed the subject rather than argue. He would cover her with a cloak when men were about and enjoy the view when they weren't.

He was waiting to hear her say they were returning to Aelynn, as she'd said earlier. His sudden impossible longing for home caught him by surprise.

"England, I think, to join Trystan in Ian's home."

Disappointment swamped him, even though he had known he would have to argue over any other answer. If there were gods, they laughed at him. England was where he had lost track of the sacred Chalice of Plenty—the chalice that was both his punishment and a lure of power.

Ian and Lis believed that returning the holy relic to Aelynn would restore the island to its rightful order. Murdoch had spent years chasing the chalice, alienating his friends, nearly destroying an entire village, hoping the relic would save the larger world, or at least France, but in the end, he'd lost all awareness of its existence, as if the gods had decided he was unworthy to possess it.

Did Lis know that? Ian would surely have told her.

"Trystan isn't likely to welcome me," he warned. He had no friends left. Not since he'd killed her father, at least.

*He'd killed her father.* The memory stabbed him with

the agony of a knife. His overexertion yesterday must have breached a wall he'd shut between himself and Ae-lynn. Or opened one between him and Lis. His grief and loss were almost palpable, even after all these years. Luther had been arrogant and obstinate, but a good man, in his own way. He'd been the only father Murdoch had ever known.

His sadness and guilt had been tempered by anger for so long that with the shield of resentment gone he was left stripped and more vulnerable than he liked. But hiding his pain from the world was second nature to him now. He stared blandly back at her.

"Trystan was once your friend," she said, watching his reaction with caution. "He will take us in if I ask him to. I know you almost destroyed Mariel's home and Trystan's ship with Greek fire when you thought they'd misappropriated the chalice, but I don't think Ian or his wife have any reason to turn you away, and it's their home."

"You believe in the bluebird of happiness, don't you? The valiant Trystan would never stoop to *misappropriating* the chalice. I believed it had come for me, and I wanted it back."

Leaving her to mull that over, Murdoch gathered up the shirt he'd left on her bed last night, and walked out of the shed and down the hill to where he sensed there was a stream. The unsettling emotions pouring through the newly opened barrier in his mind needed to be walled off again before they crippled him.

He washed, but the shirt he carried was too bloody to bear. The sun was hot enough that the linen should dry rapidly, so he wet the cloth in the spring and beat it against some rocks.

When he returned to the cowshed, stripped to the waist, Lissandra was waiting there with a clean muslin shirt that wasn't his own. She handed it to him, then gathered up the horse's harness, preparing to leave.

Startled by the offering, he didn't know how to react. "Sit down," he ordered, glowering at her. "You haven't had a bite to eat. I'm capable of catching rabbits and even cooking them."

Only after reestablishing his authority did he examine the shirt she'd given him. She'd obviously created it from the acres of fabric in the muslin petticoat she'd cut apart. Her generosity was overwhelming in the face of his surliness. "How did you make these garments so swiftly?"

"You use swords. I use needles. I've found mending more useful." Unmoved by his snappish manner, Lis waited for him to try on the shirt.

He slipped the soft fabric over his head and admired the way it fit the breadth of his shoulders and gave his sword arm ease of movement. The intimacy of her gift disturbed him in a manner he didn't know how to handle.

"Very useful," he agreed, smoothing the muslin over his chest, not ready to meet her eyes. "I can't remember the last time someone made something just for me." That wasn't a lie. Even the villagers had given him hand-me-downs.

"I made a shirt for you once before, but you left before I could give it to you." She abruptly broke off the dead branch of a shrub, apparently for firewood, since she threw it on a bare spot of earth.

*Left*—which time? When he'd sailed off to make his fortune, or when Dylys had mentally stripped him of his powers and banished him? He suspected the first. Lis had been too furious with him on the second occasion.

He couldn't hide what he was from her any longer. He'd killed her father, and still she'd come after him. Even after he'd revealed his weakness last night, she believed in him. If the only way he could have her was to be the Oracle she thought she needed, he had nothing to lose in trying.

Taking a deep breath, he offered up his soul. "Can you Heal me?"

# Twelve

Lissandra knew she'd planted the notion that she could cure him. She should be ashamed of herself, but Murdoch, the all-powerful warrior, looked so amazingly earnest and concerned. . . . Her pulse raced faster at his courage in asking. She simply stood there and admired the vulnerable man waiting for her answer.

A hank of his long mink brown hair hung damply across his sun-bronzed forehead, emphasizing his razor-sharp cheekbones and unshaven jaw. He'd pulled the rest of his hair into a knot at his nape so it fell down the back of the shirt she'd sewn for him. The flimsy fabric revealed his muscular strength.

She'd always seen Murdoch LeDroit as invincible, the hero of all her dreams, the powerful man who would rescue her from herself. By admitting that he was flawed, he became more . . . *real* . . . somehow. And more self-assured than any man she knew.

But no matter how brave he was, Murdoch was still wounded in so many ways she didn't dare count them. She could tend his visible injuries, but she feared she didn't possess the knowledge to heal his mind or his spirit.

"I am not my mother," she replied softly. "I cannot act as judge in place of the gods or wish you dead for what you have done. My duty is to Heal."

Murdoch's long lashes swept briefly downward as if he gave prayers of thanks, then lifted to reveal the startling indigo of his eyes. Against his dark coloring, the luminous effect was astonishing. She'd never before seen his eyes reflect the color of Aelynn's clear blue harbor. Usually, they resembled the sky on a stormy midnight.

"It seems the gods have tried to kill me and thus far, I have defeated them," he said. "Perhaps you will be more successful in Healing than killing me." A familiar insouciant grin crossed his face, returning him to the youth he'd once been.

"I'm thinking your arrogance would prevent you from realizing you were dead if you didn't wish to be," she countered. "But if there is some means of helping you control your unpredictable energies and their after-effects, then I must try. Still, you must know my Healing is often Empathic. If I'm to help, I must *feel* what you're feeling. You cannot block me out."

"You don't really want to know what I'm feeling right now," he boasted with a lustful leer that she knew was sheer mischief. When Murdoch really wanted her, he didn't waste time with leers.

"Then you'd better work on feeling things that I *do* want to know about," she retorted. She returned to gathering wood. "If you are going to hunt rabbits, you might wish to remove your clean shirt."

He chuckled. Sardonic Murdoch actually *chuckled*. She must be hearing things.

When he returned later with his catch, he was back to the brisk, efficient warrior who revealed nothing of his inner turmoil. That she knew he was in turmoil spoke only of their long-standing familiarity and little of his willingness to share his thoughts.

They ate silently and quickly in the early-morning

fog. When it came time to harness the horse, Murdoch took over the duty, leaving her to remove all evidence of their campsite.

"How is your head?" she asked, standing beside the cart.

"I'll live. We need to be on the road. I don't know if our mysterious Aelynner will bring others in pursuit, and I'd rather not find out." Holding the reins, he waited impatiently.

She climbed up on the seat beside him. "You used strengths last night that I didn't know you possessed. I can't tell if that was the cause of your headache or not."

"Define *strengths*," he demanded curtly, guiding the horse down the overgrown path.

"You have always been an expert swordsman and capable of defeating anyone in all physical exercises, but you have never been focused enough to direct lightning or wind against a specific target. Last night, you matched a Weathermaker's ability."

He snorted in dismissal. "Calling down lightning on Aelynn is a worthless skill, and in this world, it would have me burned for witchcraft. I see no point in crippling myself by practicing it."

She raised her eyes to the heavens for patience. "The gods gave you gifts for a good reason. Unfortunately, your idea of a good reason seems to be saving the Other World instead of Aelynn."

"Which is why I cannot go home."

"Precisely." She ignored his taciturnity. "You seem to believe everyone ought to think like you, and they don't. It has always annoyed you, and I cannot see that that has changed."

"Because they are wrong, and I am right," he said with his usual confidence.

She mentally swatted him.

He ducked as if the blow were physical, then shot her an aggrieved glare. "Why did you do that?"

"I'm thinking I ought to let my spirit guide out more often," she grumbled. "All my life I have listened to others tell me what is right and how to think. I'm tired of it."

He shook the reins. "Keep the damnable creature under control while you practice independence. I don't need another headache. Explain why you are really here if I'm so unsuitable for your precious island."

There was the crux of the problem she'd been avoiding. "I'd hoped for a miracle," she grumbled. "But I see that I was asking for too much."

He shot her a dark look. "What kind of miracle?"

How could she phrase it? It wasn't as if the island's problems were within her ability to comprehend, much less correct. "Ian must have told you that we have been effectively leaderless for years. When the chalice departed after Luther's death, people decided that we'd been abandoned by the gods. Lacking the benediction of the Chalice of Plenty, our weather has deteriorated. We go from scorching droughts to floods to freezing frosts. Ian and Chantal ended the drought, but the heat still bakes the fields. And then our Oracle died, and the spirits flew away. Now rebellion simmers in Aelynn much as it does in France."

"And you thought I could fix it?" he asked in derision.

She shrugged. "It does seem far-fetched, I admit."

He snorted at her bluntness. "You just wanted someone else to deal with it."

"The moment my mother died, the blue spirit ball circled Ian and me, rejected us both, and departed. We *saw* the gods leave," she retorted, "and now they're there, in your ring. What else am I to think?"

"That the only path to finding a suitable Oracle is to kill me so the gods are free to look elsewhere?"

She gave him a scorching look. "That is one way of looking at it, but killing a chosen Oracle to see if we receive a better one in your place is probably not the wisest alternative. My spirit guide insists you are the Oracle the gods want."

"Spirit guide?" he scoffed. "They are good for naught but mischief."

"Perhaps you have not tried to animate your Sight." There was a topic that she could confidently discuss without conflict or anger. "I've animated my mental picture of my spirit, given her a character and image that reflect my desires. That may be why I'm limited to Seeing only the paths individuals are destined to take. Your vision has always been broader, not directly affecting Aelynn, possibly because you sailed beyond our borders."

"In your less-than-direct way, you are saying that even though my vision may run true, it's not useful, and my gifts were never reliable."

She gave that some thought. "You must admit, it would be difficult to accept that killing my father was the right thing to do."

He scowled. "Because killing Luther wasn't my intent."

"Had you honed your Healing skills instead of your violent tendencies, you might have saved him," she countered, wondering how they'd returned so quickly to an even more volatile subject than Aelynn's lack of leadership.

"Would you have let me near him after I blew him

off the rocks?" He snorted without waiting for her reply. "You told me to get out of your sight. So I did."

Lissandra rubbed her eyes to hold back the tears. "And so you offered no argument in your own defense before my mother blasted you with her energy, nearly killed you, and sent you away."

She understood, or she'd tried. She'd spent years trying to hate him, and had succeeded only in shutting herself behind an icy shield of righteousness. Had he just once attempted to send word, offer an apology ... but he'd left her without a farewell, forgotten her, forgotten Aelynn, forgotten all that she'd hoped they shared, and he hadn't looked back.

"Even if killing Luther was not your intent, the result was the same," she continued. "Your unpredictable gifts and temper cannot be allowed on Aelynn." And she could not let them destroy her.

He sank into a black study. She was accustomed to caring for the weak, not the stubborn. Murdoch must accept his flaws before she could even try to improve upon them.

Lissandra turned her attention to their current predicament and the oddity of an Aelynner turning against them. It bothered her that the man had been in the room with the bound priest last night. She would like to believe that he'd been caught in something he could not avoid, but although she couldn't sense the Aelynner's emotions, somehow, it had not felt as if he were innocent.

It did not bode at all well if Aelynners lost sight of their mission and struck out on their own—as Murdoch had done. Had Murdoch's disturbing presence in the Other World disrupted some invisible barrier that had held Aelynners back all these years?

Such questions were well beyond her scope.

She knew only that after last night she was even more frightened of the future than she'd been before.

Murdoch's wounded arm and shoulder ached from guiding the horse over rough terrain, but they didn't hurt nearly as much as what felt like cannonballs of revelation exploding against his skull. Directing his energy last night had crippled him with more than pain; it had sent his emotions spiraling crazily out of control.

He wished he could empty his brainpan of all but simple needs—food, rest, desire for the woman beside him.

The desire burned hotter now, fed by the memories her presence unleashed. He'd had women before, many of them. None of them stood out in his mind as Lissy did. He might recall a woman's laugh, the flash of passionate eyes, or the roundness of a breast, but nowhere in his mind did an entire woman come to life like Lis, and not just because she sat next to him—but because of who she was.

The proud woman sitting stiff and cold was *Lissandra*, the Oracle's obedient daughter, who would always do what duty required, the woman who could not take him as a lover because her loyalties lay with a country that had rejected him.

*Lis* was the tenderhearted girl who once danced on hillsides, the nurturing Healer who loved to learn and wanted a home and family and the freedom to care for all who hurt, without thought to politics, class, or authority—the woman who wanted him as he wanted her.

Unfortunately, no matter what she might or might not want, Lis was too intelligent to have anything to do with a man who would tear her from her home and her people. He might be an undisciplined half-wit, but even in his rash youth, he'd known that Lis lived for the people of Aelynn. And he didn't.

No wonder he fought any belief in gods that would create such injustice.

The light of his damnable ring began to glow brighter, and he stifled his anger before he alarmed his all-too-observant companion. He turned his thoughts to more practical matters. "The English have blockaded the Channel. Sailing there will not be so easy."

"I know very little of the Other World," she acknowledged, "but I assume you can think of a way around that. If it helps, I'm fairly certain that somewhere beyond the blockade our ships are waiting for us."

Of course. Every man on Aelynn would be trying to find Lissandra and haul her home. And willing to kill him in the process. That wasn't an outcome he was prepared to risk. He wanted time with Lis, and an opportunity to learn how to maintain the cool concentration he'd applied last night. He would avoid Aelynn ships, by all means.

Allowing himself to *feel* meant recognizing with awe that Lis had actually left Aelynn for him. He couldn't see his way around the breadth of such a cataclysmal occurrence. It *felt* like a miracle. Of course, if he believed in miracles, he'd have to believe in her cursed gods.

Worse yet, *feeling* meant recognizing the trauma Lis must have suffered to force her to do something so out of character as to defy all Aelynn precepts—

*Dylys was really dead.*

For days, he'd deliberately avoided thinking about the woman who had banished him. But sorrow welled up in him now, and anguish for Lis, who had been her mother's shadow all her life. He knew Lis had to be here in defiance of her late mother's wishes—to prove, even in her grief, that her mother was wrong about him.

*The Oracle of Aelynn was dead.*

He and Dylys had ever been at odds, but she had done her best to teach him. The loss of her brilliance left a hollow place inside him. He had so many memories of her, if he allowed them in—of her patiently teaching his dirty childhood self to find the center from whence came his gifts, of her holding him as a frustrated lad when he'd overexerted his abilities, of her scolding him when he'd nearly killed himself trying to fly.

But the agony of her refusal to believe him after Luther's death, followed by her furious judgment resulting in his banishment, stood in the way of his mourning. That, and her rejection of his birth mother, although that was an ancient argument, one that proved they'd never truly understood each other. He'd always been no more than another responsibility for the Oracle.

But Dylys had at least recognized his abilities and tried to teach him, and for that, he was grateful. He said a prayer to the gods for the Oracle's soul and hoped Dylys had found a happier place—and more grateful students—in the next world. Her absence left a void in his world as well as Aelynn's. He was starting to grasp Lis's desperation.

And if he acknowledged Lis's faith in her gods, and him, then he had to consider the compelling beliefs that came with her: the meaning of the blue spirit flame's presence, the truth of his powers, and his responsibility to channel them . . . *responsibly*.

He shuddered at the enormity of what she asked.

"Swat me again," he muttered. "Swat me a half dozen times and clear the cobwebs from my wretched brain."

She cast him a startled look, deservedly so. Wrapped in defiance, he'd denied the full import of Lis's arrival until now. She had come here to see if he could replace *her mother*.

He handed her the reins so he could drive his fingers into his hair.

"Your head hurts again?" she asked cautiously.

"A headache would be easier," he countered. "Believe me, right now, I'd rather you just chopped off my head than Heal it."

"The opportunity might yet arrive," she said with a careless shrug.

He snorted. "You never had any delusions of my grandeur."

But hearing the confident Lis he remembered, Murdoch couldn't resist reassuring her with a hug as he used to do.

She sat stiffly and didn't relent when he squeezed her shoulders. "No, I never had any delusions about you," she agreed. "Don't think anything has changed."

But she was wrong. Things had changed drastically. He just didn't know what to make of them yet.

Her clothing prevented him from feeling the heat of her flesh, but the simple touch eased his isolation, and he rubbed her arm just for the solace of her softness. For four years he'd been without her. Knowing she wanted him and not taking advantage of it was the hardest task he'd ever been set.

Rather than disclose all the shattered, confusing emotions he'd let in, Murdoch changed the subject. "Do you know anything about the port where you landed?" He hadn't considered their destination, but it made sense that she had disembarked where she had friends, and this road led to Pouchay, where Trystan had once lived.

"Very little. I was limited in my movements when I finally escaped the ship. I know Trystan and his wife have a house nearby, but I have not seen it."

"I know the village." He and Trystan had not parted as friends, but Trystan hadn't rejected the refugees Murdoch had sent to him, even though helping them escape France went against the Aelynn dictate of not interfering. He wondered how Trystan had justified his actions. "If I'm correct, his house is distant enough from town that we shouldn't be noticed immediately."

"Trystan is no longer there," she reminded him. "If he had servants, they could report our presence."

"And persuading servants to stay silent is a problem for you?" He lifted his eyebrows and gazed at her quizzically.

"No, it's not a problem," she agreed. "I simply don't like playing with the minds of Others." Coolly, she handed him back the reins.

"It's better than hacking off their heads," he informed her.

And he regretted the sarcasm as soon as it left his tongue.

He remembered the horror of the king's head rolling in Paris. Hacking off heads had become the popular new sport in France. Anyone without documentation—as they were—was considered a threat to the new republic.

And now he was taking Lis to the very town from which Trystan and his family had fled to avoid capture by the Tribunal's spies.

# Thirteen

Twilight settled over the coast as Lissandra guided the mare down the path that Murdoch had indicated led to Trystan's home—right before he'd abruptly drawn his sword, leapt from the cart, and disappeared to scout the area.

She took in great lungfuls of sea air and longed for the warm shores of home, where one had no reason to suspect danger around every bush.

As one of Aelynn's leading citizens, Trystan would have a heated bath even in his Other World home. That was all she required right now. A bath and a bed. She was no warrior, prepared to trek across the countryside night and day, living on the edge of terror.

Like Murdoch.

If nothing else proved the differences between them, his appearance as he emerged from the hedgerow did. Now that he had his weapons, his dangerous energies were no longer banked. He even looked larger and more superhuman, although all he wore was a muslin shirt, cotton trousers, and makeshift sandals. He'd be formidable in the full dress she'd seen on other men here. He showed no sign of the stress she felt.

Wordlessly, he took the horse's bridle and led the cart into the yard. "The house is empty. Trystan has left it guarded by an Aelynn barrier. We should be safe enough." He began unbuckling the horse's harness.

"Trystan shouldn't be able to keep up a barrier for any length of time, this far from home," she protested, climbing down from the cart without his aid.

"Tell that to our Guardian when you see him," Murdoch replied in the familiar tone with which he'd always referred to the man who had once been his rival for Lissandra's hand. "I've a little of his ability and have strengthened the barrier. Maybe that's what he hopes will happen—that someone will renew it regularly. It's more pure energy than his moon shield around the island."

The gray stone house loomed tall against the western sky. It wasn't a pretty house, although someone had planted climbing roses along the walls to brighten it. The Guardian's energy shield shimmered slightly in the slanting sunlight. Normally, it couldn't be seen at all.

"I didn't realize he could create a shield to divert strangers," she mused aloud.

"If Ian was here, they would have worked on it together. Ian has the knowledge, if not the full extent of Trystan's ability."

There was so much she didn't know—about the Outside World, about her own brother.

"We don't need these things on Aelynn," Murdoch reminded her. "We learn and grow from our experiences here."

Which said it all—Murdoch had grown apart from her here. Once he understood the extent of her ignorance, would he still desire her?

Foolish question. The *desire* part had been with them since adolescence. If all she'd wanted was their physical connection, she could have had it at any time. Perhaps she should settle for mere physical coupling, but the shackles of amacara bonding held her back—for both their sakes.

They fed and watered the loyal mare before advancing on the silent house from the rear. Aelynn people went in and out of one another's homes with regularity. Even the hearth witches and hedge wizards wandered freely through the abodes of the more skilled classes. For that reason, it did not seem extraordinary to enter Trystan's home uninvited.

But for all that, this Other World house was strange to Lissandra. Aelynn houses did not have towering walls of thick stone, or floors of rooms built one on top of another. They entered through the kitchen, and Lissandra gazed around Trystan and Mariel's low-ceilinged room with interest, identifying familiar objects like fireplaces, kettles, and cupboards, before stepping into the airless, dark chambers beyond.

More comfortable with his surroundings, Murdoch lit candles and lanterns and set a fire to burn merrily in the kitchen grate. By the time Lissandra followed him to the larger rooms, they did not seem so gloomy. The sea wind beat against the glass, blowing up a storm, and she was grateful for the shelter.

"Mariel told me this was once her father's house," she said, just to hear a voice in the stale air.

"Her mother was a Crossbreed with a large dowry." Murdoch closed the draperies so the lantern light wouldn't be visible when the sun dipped below the horizon. "I thought it interesting that her mother seemed to have a form of Sight. Either there is a stray strain of that gift in our blood, or she is related to your family."

Lissandra had thought the same. That Murdoch's Sight equaled Ian's seemed to indicate that the gods chose whom they willed without consideration of family name—although most Aelynners would disagree with her theory. Perhaps they *all* possessed some degree of all talents but through family tradition acknowledged and honed only one or two.

"I'm glad Trystan and his family escaped before the Tribunal established a strong footing here," he continued. "Mariel's father was an aristocrat, and her brother-in-law is on the losing side of politics in Paris these days. I trust he had the sense to leave the country with Trystan."

"Trystan's in-laws were with him when he left." She longed to stand beside Murdoch in the glow of his lantern but resisted. She looked around for a hall that might lead to the bath.

He nodded toward the front entrance. "Try taking those stairs. I sense water below us."

"There's an ocean below the cliff—of course you sense water. Have you been here before?"

"I've not been inside." He followed her to the stairs, holding up his lantern. "I know you will not believe me, but just before I was waylaid in the village, I was on my way to warn Trystan that the Tribunal was sending soldiers here."

"I have no reason not to believe you. Trystan was once your friend." She lifted her skirt and followed the stone stairs down. "The warning had reached Trystan when I arrived. Perhaps your escaped prisoners carried it."

"I'd like to believe they made it here safely after all the trouble I took to get them out." Murdoch held up the lantern at the bottom of the stairs. "It's a warren down here."

Lissandra followed her nose and found the bathing room.

They stood in the doorway and admired Trystan's grotto. The old cellar room had been transformed into a wonder of limestone tile the sandy color of the beach below, with a bathing pool that reflected the ocean's blues. The corners had been walled off to form an octagonal room, and padded benches and Roman niches holding oil lamps had been built into them.

"Trystan never struck me as a sybarite," Murdoch said as he turned the spigot of a dolphin fountain and steaming water poured from the sea creature's mouth.

"Trystan has three children and a fourth on the way. I think he's found someone to share his secret sensuality." Lissandra supposed she ought to be embarrassed to say such a thought aloud, but she envied Trystan's relationship with Mariel.

Slipping off her shoe, she tested the warm water with her toe. "It's perfect. Almost like the hot spring at home."

"Food first, while the tub fills." Murdoch caught her elbow to steer her from temptation.

So many temptations... food, the lovely bath, the firm grip of Murdoch's hand, the combination of all three...

Panicking at the strength of her desire, she jerked free. "I'm not hungry. Leave me here." She wanted him gone—now—before she was foolish enough to let down her shield and act on the lust simmering between them. If he so much as looked at her wrong...

"Don't be foolish. You need food, and the bath takes time—"

She whirled and glared at him. "Don't start telling me what to do, LeDroit. I found you on my own, and I can leave you anytime I want. I don't need you to take care of me. I don't need *anyone* to take care of me, and it's time people realized that."

He stared at her, as he had every right to do. She should have said those things long, long ago. She wasn't the fair-haired princess who must be sheltered from reality. She was simply a woman who wanted her own life, without everyone hovering.

"We *want* to take care of you," he said flatly. "We cherish and worship you and would lay down our lives for you. And you walk on our backs as if we were doormats."

Tears rimmed her eyes, but with head held high, she would not let them fall. "I thought you, of all people, would understand. Go upstairs, Murdoch. Leave me be."

Murdoch left. It was either leave or take her in his arms and ravish her, and she would no doubt neuter him if he tried the latter, no matter how much they both wanted—*needed*—the physical joining. It was becoming increasingly difficult to ignore the craving, but he summoned his will and turned his thoughts elsewhere.

What was he failing to understand? Lis had everything anyone could ever want. Everything *he* had ever wanted. Was he supposed to feel *sorry* for her?

There was no understanding women, and he had too many puzzles of his own without starting on hers.

Murdoch tried not to think of Lis undressing and stepping naked into the steaming water. He was walking around in a permanent state of arousal as it was. Instead of food, perhaps he ought to look for a woman.

But the woman he wanted was just below, and no substitute would suffice. Grumbling, still puzzling over her words despite his vow not to, he searched Trystan's larder for aged cheese and smoked meats. He munched on those while taking a large chopping knife and relieving his frustration by whacking into mincemeat vegetables he'd found in the root cellar. He'd learned to cook over campfires these past years. This was a feast compared with what he'd eaten then.

Maybe he should have accumulated wealth instead of whatever in hell he thought he'd been doing lately. An expensive fortress like this one would make an excellent safe house for transporting those who would avoid the guillotine. . . .

The soup was bubbling by the time a lilac scent indicated Lissandra's approach. Mariel must have left her bath powders behind.

Murdoch tried to rein in his lust as he had these past days, but that had been before he'd revealed his weakness. Before he'd blasted the barriers in his head. He'd been a fool as a youth to deny them the final bond of lovemaking for the sake of a few words spoken over an altar.

At the time, he thought he'd been *protecting* her.

He rolled his eyes as her earlier words returned. She hadn't wanted his protection. She'd once wanted him to court her, to make love to her. She had seen his refusal to do so without vows as a form of blackmail, an effort to bind her to him and claim his right as Council Leader.

And maybe she'd been half-right.

Examining his behavior from the distance of time was a damned painful business. He glanced up at her entrance. She'd washed her hair and bound it tightly in a braid but donned only her lightweight Aelynn garb. He closed his eyes against the strong image of his hand cupping her unfettered breast and gestured at the table with his knife. "I've set out bowls. Help yourself."

"Have you eaten?" she asked stiffly.

Sensing her discomfort with the sexual tension between them, Murdoch set down his knife. "Not yet. I think I will bathe first, too." He kept the table between them until he left the room.

He felt as if he were ripping his soul into a hundred different puzzle bits and now had to piece himself back together again in a different order before he could know how to act.

# Fourteen

Having barely tasted a bite of Murdoch's meal, Lissandra cleaned up the mess he'd made of the kitchen, then wandered through the house rather than wait for him to return from his bath. Upstairs, she paused to admire the nursery. If she'd married, would she have babies now?

She fought the itch under her skin that was her awareness of Murdoch in the bath, simmering with desire—for her.

Growing up surrounded by an island full of powerful, bullheaded males, she ought to be accustomed to their blustering lusts. But Murdoch's acute intellect and overt sexuality made him more desirable than any male she knew. She was amazed he didn't terrify mere mortals. He must use his illusions to hide his considerable . . . virility.

If she wanted to discover who she really was, what she was truly meant to be, she had to be honest. Everything she'd ever learned told her that the gods intended Murdoch to be her amacara. She didn't think there could be any other reason for her heightened awareness of him to the exclusion of all other men.

But she could not submit to an eternal bond with an unpredictable menace. Perhaps the gods meant for her to suffer. Two strong, independent-minded individuals would likely kill each other with their passions if they did not agree. Murdoch's warlike temper and her need to avoid conflict would put them constantly at odds.

Other Worlders prized virginity in their spiritual leaders. Perhaps she should learn from them.

She ran her fingers along the rocking cradle that loving hands had fashioned for Mariel's babies, and her own womb ached at the lack. She'd never given real thought to children except as the Olympus heirs Aelynn required. If she wasn't meant to be Oracle, would her children matter to anyone but herself? Would she still want them?

How could she consider children when she hadn't experienced lovemaking? She simply knew that she felt empty and unfulfilled, but that could be because she no longer felt needed or valuable to anyone. She had sufficient understanding to recognize that children shouldn't be used to fill her own lack.

Impatient with useless fantasies, she chose the nursery cot so much like her own, and began preparing for bed. How could she even think of touching Murdoch's emotions to help him stabilize his erratic powers when an entire three floors between them didn't smother their smoldering desire? Just because she couldn't hear Murdoch roaming the house didn't mean she wasn't aware of him. She'd been aware of him for four years when he hadn't even been in the same country.

She knew when he hesitated outside the nursery door. She held her breath, uncertain whether to will him to come in or to go away.

They both hesitated. This was *ridiculous*. They were adults. Adolescent desire shouldn't prevent them from carrying out the wishes of the gods.

She opened the door and nearly slammed it shut again.

Freshly shaved and no longer scruffy, shirtless and wearing short Aelynn trousers he must have borrowed from Trystan's dresser, barefoot, with his thick hair hanging sleek and wet down his bare back, Murdoch stood before her. He was the childhood friend she desperately missed, the lover she'd never had, the man she wanted beyond all reason. He propped his hands on either side of the doorjamb as if sensing she would run, and his muscles rippled beneath her gaze. The hair under his arms and down the center of his chest was as slick and dark as that on his head. She craved the right to touch and explore. . . .

"What do you want to do with me?" he snarled, flinging their dilemma in her face.

Now, there was a question she didn't dare answer.

The blue spirit light on his ring wavered as if trying to send her a message that she couldn't interpret.

"I want to help you," she whispered. That was about as daring as she could be in the face of his blatant masculinity. If that was disappointment in his eyes, so be it. She could either help him or make love with him but not both at the same time. Helping had to take priority.

"How?" He straightened now that she'd voiced her preference.

Just his act of straightening to his full height forced her to step back. She gestured at the nursery. "This is hardly the place."

He glanced over her shoulder. "That depends on what you have in mind."

He scrambled her wits so thoroughly she could not think straight. Of course, she had lovemaking on her mind, and so did he, but that wasn't what he needed now. He needed to learn how to tame his dangerously unpredictable powers. She tightened her fingers into her palms and nodded. "Then take a seat in the rocking chair. I need to See into your head first."

He shot her a doubtful look, carefully eased past her, and lowered himself into the rocker as if it were a chair of execution. "Explain," he commanded.

"You have some Healing ability." Feeling a little more assured now that he was seated and not looming over her, she stood behind him, held her hands above his damp hair, and closed her eyes. "You must know how it feels to sense blood vessels and ligaments and so forth."

"I know a broken bone when I see one," he agreed, spine rigid, clenching the rocker arms.

"I have trained myself to See even deeper, to smaller parts. The medical texts are muddled. Some call them humors, I suppose, but the more scientific texts in the Aelynn library call them nerves and say they come in motion and sensory forms."

"Nerves," he said flatly. "Like puppet strings that pull our limbs."

"The motion ones, yes." She circled his head with her hands, and he almost imperceptibly relaxed. "Aristotle claimed they originate in the heart, but dissections show their source is in the brain. And that's how I sense them, originating in our heads, although I cannot prove that the heart doesn't affect them."

"And the sensory ones?"

"Those are the puzzle. I wish I could work on Other World heads a few times so I could understand the differences between ours and theirs." Absorbed in the sensations of the energies pulsing in Murdoch's mind and talking to someone who understood, she forgot to be re-

served. "For instance, I sense you have"—she hesitated,
trying to think of a descriptive word as she pressed her
fingers to a spot on the right of his crown—"more heat,
more pulsations here than in the rest of your brain. The
area is highly complex, more so than in that of a hedge
wizard I examined after he was hit by a falling coconut.
This part of Ian's brain is also very active."

"You've done this to Ian?"

"Once. He becomes impatient. Mariel and Chantal
have allowed me to examine them, but they're Cross-
breeds and female. The brains of men and women do
not seem to work alike."

He snorted with what almost sounded like laughter. "I think I've observed that." She snapped her finger against his skull in retaliation, and he chuckled. "I
wouldn't want it any other way," he assured her.

"I should hope not. Men are amazingly simpleminded, actually." This time, she laid her palm directly
on that part of his skull where she sensed the most energy. "Energy pulses back and forth in a woman's mind
faster than I can follow, but men"—she shrugged and
placed her other palm on the other side of his skull—
"think one thing at a time. And your thoughts right now
aren't on scientific observation. That's over here." She
knuckled the left side of his head.

"You don't want to know the path of my thoughts,"
he warned. "You see nothing broken?"

She didn't need to observe the way his body coiled
and tautened like a panther prepared to pounce to know
he feared her reply.

"Not broken," she agreed. "But as Benedetti said,
'The pathways of the senses are distributed like the roots
and fibers of a tree.' I would have to follow all the paths,
and even then, it is difficult to know if they are twisted

the wrong way or connected improperly, because I don't have enough experience."

"Or the right teachers." Murdoch rose abruptly from the chair, turning to catch the arms and lean toward her. The colors of a nighttime storm swirled in his eyes, flashing lightning much as the storm brewing outside the walls. "I would have to bed you for you to know all of me."

"I would have to bed many men, then, to compare." Summoning all the dignity she could find, Lissandra walked out in search of another chamber, leaving him to simmer alone.

"I thought of a new way to study your mind. Why must we leave so soon?" Lissandra said in frustration when she came downstairs the next morning to discover Murdoch already dressed in borrowed clothing. He wasn't as barrel-chested as Trystan, so the frock coat hung loosely from his wide shoulders. Still, she admired the fall of white lace against his dark throat and the borrowed boots reaching his knees. He was as handsome and elegant in the clothing as she'd anticipated, and she dearly longed for a husbandly kiss, even though she knew the danger.

He'd buckled on sword and rapier as if he was expecting trouble. Perhaps he meant to hold her at bay by blade point.

She'd hoped they could play house here while she learned more about his headaches, pretend they were truly man and wife and do normal things like cook meals and watch the roiling sea outside the windows. But Murdoch's restless energies weren't suited to domesticity.

"France isn't safe," he said. "It's imperative that we leave before we attract notice. You're protected here until I find a ship." He was paying more attention to his weapons than to her. The lust they'd denied last night pulsed almost visibly between them this morning—he was running from it.

That was the penalty for letting him get too close, she knew. Men hated rejection. Fine, then, two could play that game. She would pretend he was a block of wood instead of a man who wanted her. "I have no grand desire to come looking for you a second time should you end up in trouble or decide to go on without me," she said nonchalantly, removing a straw hat from a hook.

She adjusted the brim over her distinctive silver-blond hair. Mariel's dresses fit her well enough. The outfit created the illusion of propriety, but perhaps she ought to create an illusion of invisibility to force the damned man to recognize that she didn't need to be sheltered like a helpless babe—from him or anyone else.

"Even in a harbor town, they're suspicious of strangers," Murdoch argued. "They'll ask for our documentation, and if we can't provide any, they'll think we're émigré spies."

"Then perhaps we should wait for evening instead of parading around in daylight." Satisfied with her image in the small wall mirror, she adjusted her borrowed shawl, picked up her bag, and faced the kitchen door where Murdoch blocked her path.

The heated hunger in his eyes shot straight to her damnable desires. In retaliation, she gave him a syrupy come-hither look and stepped forward until her breasts nearly brushed his coat—forcing him to back off or grab her. For now, he stepped back.

"Why don't we just introduce ourselves to the local surveillance committee and ask them to escort us to the nearest prison?" he countered, still not opening the door, although the steam in his eyes ought to scald.

"And how many men do you want me to neuter in self-defense?" she asked serenely, deciding a reminder of what she could do to him ought to deflate some of his male arrogance. "I have done this once on my own. Do you think that your unreliable energy can do it better?"

Murdoch growled in exasperation and flung open the door. "I have lived here for four years without your help. I don't need a nanny."

"A leash and collar, perhaps." Stepping into the fresh morning, she inhaled salt air, much as a starving person gulped food. The fresh air did not cool the heat between them, however.

"Why am I so blessed as to be the one you practice your independence on?" Murdoch replied, and strode briskly toward the stable.

"I thought perhaps you hadn't been tortured enough," she offered, taking comfort in knowing she affected him as much as he did her.

A sudden rush of wind tossing tree branches reminded her that he was still Murdoch, ruthless and unsettling. "Or maybe I've been sent to teach you restraint," she amended.

He swung abruptly around, caught her in his powerful arms, drew her hard against him, and shut her mouth with his.

Lissandra grabbed his shoulders to steady herself, then melted into the fire that consumed her from the inside out.

His muscles rippled beneath her fingers where she clung to him. Her breasts were crushed against the unforgiving wall of his chest. His hands slid to cup her buttocks and lifted her more fully against him. And she gasped at the extent of his arousal. And hers.

She'd felt safe teasing him in daylight. She'd been wrong.

She wrapped her arms around his broad shoulders, clinging as she'd wanted to do all her life. His tongue plundered her mouth, and his breath filled her lungs more sweetly than sea air. She became so much a part of him that she no longer needed her legs to support her.

Molten heat inundated them, and in some distant part of her mind, Lissandra recognized Murdoch as the embodiment of Aelynn's volcano—hot, dangerous, and unpredictable. Why had she never seen that?

And like the volcano's fire, he fed on air—and that was her, cool, formless, and consumable, fanning the flames higher.

Overwhelmed, she returned his kiss with regret as well as desire. She *wanted* to be devoured by him. But she could not let herself be consumed. For Aelynn's sake, she had to be strong, stronger than Murdoch—and she could not be if she was bound to a man who weakened her will and tempted her from her duties.

Sensing the change in her mood, Murdoch carried his kisses to her cheek and hair and lowered her to her feet again. He held her face between both his hands and kissed her with desperation, and when she still withdrew, he bent his brow to rest against the top of her head.

"I dreamed of you every night that we were apart. I burn for you every day. To have you here and not be able to touch you is like a whip flaying my soul," he muttered.

"The French must have taught you how to flatter," she retorted, stepping backward and nearly falling to her weak knees. "I am more easily won by action than words."

And that was half a lie. She knew the words had been dragged out of him. Murdoch seldom said what he thought and never willingly admitted weakness. That he did so now showed he was as frantic as she to satiate the desire between them and would go to any lengths to have her in his bed—except he knew as well as she that they could do neither.

"Stay here," he ordered. "Let me attempt Mariel's feat of swimming beyond the English barricade. I'll send Waylan back for you. You've done what you could. The rest is up to me."

Lissandra considered his request. He was no doubt right. She'd accomplished what she'd set out to do, found the man the gods had chosen. If she couldn't help him without falling into his bed, then she could do no more.

Her lips burned and her breasts ached, and she was in no state for rational thought. Murdoch had the ability to reduce her to nothing but animal instinct, and it frightened her.

"I can't let you out of my sight," she admitted. "I'm terrified I'll lose you again." She nodded at his glowing ring. "The gods are telling us something, but I can't interpret their message."

"The ring does not glow as much now. Perhaps you are wrong and the gods do not want me now that they know me better."

Which frightened her even more. If Murdoch wasn't the next Oracle, would Aelynn, left leaderless, fall into ashes and be destroyed, its population left to starve or scatter to the winds?

She tried not to think it, but the possibility was there, lurking in the back of her mind—did it mean her fears were well-founded and the only way Murdoch could control his gifts was through her? That she must sacrifice her freedom totally to become no more than his servant?

As she had been her mother's. The gods surely wouldn't do that to her.

"I asked for guidance last night," she admitted, refusing to voice her worst fears, "but I'm still only shown clouds of turbulence. Our paths are unclear."

"Blood, violence, war," he said curtly, striding toward the stable once again. "I See no peace in our future."

"What do I tell our people?" she whispered, distraught.

"To stockpile what food they can and prepare to live like the rest of the world." His voice was gruff as he bridled the mare, though regret tinged his warning. "Providing we survive this forsaken place to tell anyone anything." Relenting, he helped her into the cart.

They rode boldly into town, appearing on the surface like any poor farmer and his wife dressed in their Sunday finest, with little worth stealing. They carried Lis's bag, disguising it to look innocuous. People glanced their way, but Aelynn illusions deflected the interest of onlookers and reduced any speculation. Passersby returned to hurrying about their business.

It was only when they used their superhuman skills that they were in real danger.

"You do this well," Lissandra said quietly, hanging on to her hat as they approached the windy harbor.

"I developed a talent for mind manipulation after I saw Ian last. I don't even need my sword to concentrate on the illusion."

"Extraordinary. You must have the ability to absorb and mimic the talents of others. I had no idea. . . ." But then, she knew so very little beyond her own limited interests. She should have worked with Ian and Murdoch more when they were growing up, but they'd been older and preferred swordplay and staring at stars, and she'd wanted to play dolls. Perhaps it wasn't just her that he needed, but all Aelynners. "I can't even tell if my illusion is actually turning people away or if they wouldn't have noticed me anyway."

Murdoch snorted. "Any man who doesn't notice a woman like you would have to be blind. You're succeeding very well in your concealment. I'd say you've had practice, if I did not remember otherwise."

"I never had to hide from you," she said primly, watching the boats bobbing in the harbor, hoping to see a familiar one.

"You had to hide from others? Who?" As his mind turned to the possibility that she referred to suitors like him, he demanded, "Why? What did they do to you?"

She gifted him with a look of scorn. "Use your head instead of your temper. It's not difficult to figure out why I might hide from others."

She had used an illusion of cold efficiency to hide her inadequacy from everyone, including her mother, but she let Murdoch brood over his competition while she searched their surroundings. Trystan and Mariel had lived safely in this town for years. Could she do as well here?

It seemed so alien. The wind blew too hard. The twisted, gnarled trees gave evidence of the harshness of winter storms. The colorful flowers were pretty, but they would not last through the cold.

Lissandra didn't know why she considered such a thing anyway. Her duty was to Aelynn, even if the gods rejected her as Oracle. Even she could acknowledge she would be an inferior Oracle. The admission tugged a smile out of her.

"What do you have to smile about?" Dragged from his surly contemplations, Murdoch guided the cart into a stable yard.

"I was trying to imagine standing in front of the Council, telling them they must learn to preserve food and build warships. Chantal's father would outshout me, declaring that what we need is peace and equality. Old Arnold would start yelling that we need not fix what isn't broken. And I would be left no choice but to mentally swat them all or walk out."

Murdoch choked on what might have been laughter. "Agreed, you were never meant to be Council Leader. That doesn't mean you can't be Oracle." He handed the reins to a stableboy along with a small coin.

"An Oracle should be able to See the sacred chalice, predict the approach of danger, give comfort in times of trouble. I'm more likely to be delivering a breech birth or reading a medical text."

That was who she really was, a mere midwife and a good student, with no pretensions of glory. But her name alone gave a semblance of authority, and her illusion of dignified omniscience had sustained it. People often preferred illusion to reality.

She shuddered, realizing that was what Dylys had done—given everyone an illusion of security. Shaken, she had to force herself to keep up with the conversation.

"If you waste time hiding, as you say, people learn to overlook you. Or to avoid you." Murdoch caught her elbow and led her down the cobbled street to the harbor. "I have watched you go about with your don't-touch-me princess air. You have a way of looking at men that reduces them to ashes. Although I wouldn't precisely call that hiding."

"I suppose I could have welcomed all male overtures as you did female ones," she responded with sarcasm.

He clenched her elbow tighter, and Lissandra glanced around with curiosity to see if the roof blew off any buildings. Apparently, he was managing his temper. She ought to be more careful about how she riled him, but she was still testing her wings. And his, she admitted.

"It's different for men," he finally grumbled.

She debated shoving him down the flight of stone steps to the pebbly beach, decided that would set a bad example, and gave him a mental swat instead.

He retaliated with a vision memory of both of them naked in the grotto at home. His hair and face were dripping, and he stood up to his hips in water, fully aroused. She remembered that moment. She'd just turned eighteen, he was twenty-four, and he'd asked her to marry him. She'd refused, and he'd sailed out of her life. . . .

She jerked her arm away and walked faster, although every particle of her burned with lust. How could anyone think while aroused like this?

He barely broke stride to keep up with her. "Most women don't require that men be their equals or more, but you do. You never knew a man besides me who was your match or better."

"And you did?" Scorn dripped from her tongue.

"Find a man or a match?"

She didn't acknowledge his wickedly bad wit because he was right. *She* was the only match for him. She gazed over the line of derelict fishing boats. "They don't appear seaworthy."

"The sound ones are out fishing and earning a living. We need to find the harbormaster. Play dumb for a change, will you?" He grabbed her elbow again and started down the cobbled walk.

"*Oui, oui, citoyen,*" she mocked in her bad French.

"On second thought, don't speak a word."

"Overbearing, arrogant, domineering . . . ," she whispered under her breath while searching for more telling adjectives.

"For good reason," he grunted in an undertone as they approached a self-important-looking man wearing a blue uniform with brass buttons.

Lissandra adopted an insipid smile and steered the man's mind to Murdoch and away from her. Child's play.

If she concentrated hard, she could translate their rapid French—more Breton than French, she gathered—but she didn't doubt Murdoch's ability to talk birds from a tree or ships from a harbormaster. Her task was to observe their surroundings and watch their backs.

So she knew before he did that an Aelynner was waiting for them around the corner.

# *Fifteen*

Acknowledging Lis's tug on his arm by squeezing her hand, Murdoch continued his inquiry about hiring a small boat, while opening his awareness more fully to his surroundings.

His ability to sense the presence of other life-forms was second nature. Unfortunately, in a town filled with creatures, large and small, the skill wasn't entirely useful or practical.

He'd obtained as much information as he could from the harbormaster, and turned away before he found what Lissandra had warned him of—a living creature with no discernible emotions in the alley. Even rats cast images of food or vibrations of hunger. Trained Aelynners did not.

His first instinct was to walk directly toward the alley and see who lurked there. Only a few Aelynners possessed his and Lissandra's sensitivity to emotions. Most would not realize he could sense their presence from their shielding. Chances were excellent, however, that an Aelynner could recognize someone as visible and powerful as an Olympus.

Ignoring the instinct to confront the lurker, heeding the rational thought to get Lis to safety, Murdoch steered her back up the hill in the opposite direction of the alley.

"We must see who it is!" she whispered, jerking her arm free of his hold.

"They must not see who *you* are," he corrected. "Don't you realize that, like Helen of Troy, you could launch wars? All Aelynn would rise up in arms should anyone harm you. What if this is the same person who was with the committee the other night? Let's not give Ian and company failure of the heart because you've been taken hostage as the priest was."

"But what if it's someone who is stranded here like us? We cannot abandon him."

"This is a village. I'll find him easily enough. Do you have any money on you?"

"A few coins in my pocket. More in my hem. What do you mean to do?"

"Assuming you won't return to the house, I'll hire a private room at the inn where you can wait while I look for our spy."

He willed her to understand without his having to explain what a valuable hostage she'd be for anyone who wished Aelynn harm—or who simply wanted the use of their strength for some unfathomable reason. He'd rather believe his fellow Aelynners were better than that, but he'd lived in the real world too long not to be distrustful.

To his relief, she didn't argue. "No Aelynner of your ability would challenge you unless they thought you were causing me harm," she reluctantly agreed, "and anyone less would have to be mad to confront you. It is what I don't know or understand that I fear most."

"That is wise. What we don't know can kill us. It will be easier for me if I know you're safe." He took one of the coins she slipped to him and talked to the innkeeper, who showed them to an empty chamber with a small table and chairs beside a cold fireplace.

"Don't take too long," she warned.

Knowing she cared enough to worry about his sorry hide warmed the hollow space where his heart should be. He brushed a kiss of affection across her brow, revealing his weakness, before he turned and left her there.

Hurrying back to the port, fretting over Lis's safety while studying alleyways for the blankness of the person he sought, Murdoch almost didn't hear the childish cry of "Monsieur LeDroit! Stop, please!"

Only the rattling of an empty milk pail caught and held his attention. He spun on his heel in time to catch both pail and child as they tumbled down the hill toward him.

Filthy gold curls spilled from a torn bonnet, and small fingers clutched his coat sleeves as he tried to release her once he had her standing upright.

He recognized the child he'd tried to rescue, along with her father and the other prisoners, on the fateful day he'd nearly burned down a village. After what he'd done, he was amazed she dared approach him. "Amelie, what are you doing here?"

"Monsieur, *please*," she begged in a husky whisper. "Papa is ill and the boat left without us. Help us, please."

He couldn't ignore a child's cry. "Where is your papa?" he asked. Pierre must be near death's door for the others to have left him behind.

Amelie tugged his hand and led him down a dark side street of huddled medieval buildings that Murdoch recognized as the kind that housed the owners in cramped apartments above their ground-floor shops. This wasn't the squalor of a city slum, but the humble abodes of simple artisans.

He followed her down a bleak alley between a

shoemaker's shop and the ovens of a bakery. A crude wooden lean-to had been erected behind the shop to protect crates of leather and other supplies of the trade. Between the crates a haggard man rested on a dirty blanket, an awl in one hand, a shoe in the other. His eyes were closed as he leaned against a barrel, and Murdoch felt the man's extreme exhaustion, a deep desire to die, and an even stronger love that kept him alive.

The intensity of that love almost bowled Murdoch over.

"*Citoyen* Durand, we meet again," Murdoch said softly, so as not to startle the man.

Pierre opened his eyes and looked up at Murdoch with the child clinging to his arm. "Monsieur LeDroit, you lived. That is good."

"The priest told me you saved my life by throwing me in the cart and fleeing the fire. I owe you," Murdoch told him. "But why did you not set sail with the others?"

"I lacked the coin," Durand said with a bleak smile. "I have found work here, and no one asks for my papers. We would not be alive if it weren't for you."

If the Tribunal's representatives had reached Pouchay, they would be asking for the shoemaker's papers soon enough. Inevitably, if he lived, he'd be returned to prison.

"I believe I made a promise to take you to England, and I failed you." That these two suffered because of him gnawed at his pride. The strong and wicked would always survive, but the innocents who shed light—and love—on the world often needed aid.

The shoemaker focused his glassy gaze on him. "I doubt that I could endure the journey, but Amelie . . . ," he said in his poor English, before his voice trailed off in a plea.

The child fell to her knees beside her father and flung her arms around his neck. Huge blue eyes turned up to Murdoch's as if he were truly the paragon the village had called him. He knew nothing about children or their ages, but he assumed this one couldn't be much more than six. She didn't have to speak a word. The emotions of Outsiders were easy to read.

"I've hired a vessel," Murdoch said carefully. "There should be room for both of you."

That was a huge lie. The harbormaster had told him little except when the fishing boats would return and which had the most reliable sailors. But he knew Lis would scratch his eyes out if he left these two here to die. And she would know without his telling her. She couldn't read his mind, but she knew his heart inside and out.

She was his conscience.

"If you would just take Amelie, please." Durand laid his stained and calloused hand on his daughter's head. "She's no trouble. I have a cousin in London...."

Murdoch wasn't a man for argument or explanation. Action was simpler. Without further ado, he crouched down, lifted the nearly weightless man in his arms, and jerked his head at the child. "Come along. My wife will wish to meet you."

*His wife.* Under the circumstances, he couldn't have said less, but the phrase came naturally. He was a man without a home, but in his mind, Lis was his and always would be. After four years away and every reason to erase the arrogant princess from his thoughts, his feelings for her hadn't changed. He would have to be a coward or a fool to pretend he could ever want another.

Durand was too weak to struggle, and Murdoch ignored his protests as he carried the ill man down the street and through the front door of the inn, causing heads to turn. He made his way back to Lis, the child clutching the leg of his borrowed breeches.

Lis had the door open and was ordering hot water before he even came within knocking distance. Although the shoemaker was too weak to think straight, the child was clearly generating enough emotion for Lis to notice. She might fool others with her placid ice-princess air, but Murdoch knew she was a Healer at heart.

"Find them clean clothes. I'll need the strongest alcohol you can find," Lissandra ordered as if she were a general and he, her lieutenant. "Ask the innkeeper for blankets. We need a larger cart to take them to Trystan's. They would both benefit from his bathing pool."

She spoke in Aelynn's language. Both father and child stared at her in bewilderment. Murdoch knew how they felt. He had to distinguish between the Olympian commanding general and the Healer. Lis would never be an easy woman to understand. He carefully laid the shoemaker on the floor by the fireplace. "We can't linger past the evening tide."

"You brought them here. You can't very well argue about the danger now."

He could, and he would, but not until the Healer had a chance to work her magic. "Don't make me fight you," he warned, drawing off his coat, and covering the shoemaker.

"If it is me that you worry about, know that I can Heal with one hand and still lash a man into bacon strips with the other. Fetch the cart," she ordered in that imperious manner he remembered well—there was much of her mother in her.

"You must Heal them quickly, *mi ama*," Murdoch said harshly, not allowing her the upper hand in this. "We're leaving tonight."

That neither of them mentioned his choice of endearment acknowledged what they both knew and continued to deny—despite their differences, they were bound to each other by more than circumstance.

The trouble began when Murdoch returned to town in Trystan's farm cart. Lis had him thinking like a peaceful Aelynner instead of the wary warrior he'd been. He knew the horse was a coveted asset and a temptation, the large, comfortable cart even more so. And without Lissandra beside him to add her mental manipulation, he failed to disguise them adequately.

Openly wearing his weapons was another invitation for trouble.

A soldier stopped him on the edge of town, stepping out before Murdoch could react. "Your papers, *citoyen*," the lad demanded, holding his sword at rest and his hand out.

Having no documentation approved by the Tribunal for his presence in this corner of France would land him in prison. Stoically, Murdoch bit his tongue to tamp down any violent reaction, and sought a means of solving the problem without blasting anyone to purgatory.

It was too late to attempt mind manipulation. He could call down the wind or attempt a small earthquake, but the result would alarm Lis. With someone else to worry about besides himself, he must act with caution first.

Lips tightening at being reduced to this powerlessness, Murdoch mimicked reaching for a coat pocket that wasn't there, and frowned. "*Mon Dieu*, I was in such a hurry, I've forgotten my coat," he exclaimed. "My wife is taken ill, and I've come for her cousins. If you will come with me, they can vouch for me. My humblest pardons, *citoyen*, for the inconvenience."

The fresh-faced boy frowned. "I am not supposed
to leave my post. You must wait here while I send for
someone—"

Murdoch produced a coin and held it out. "It is all I
have. Hold on to it, and I will bring back the cousins to
vouch for me in exchange, if you will let me pass. My
wife is very ill, you understand. I must hurry."

The lad looked confused, as he was meant to be.
Wishing he'd practiced more of Ian's mind tricks, Murdoch tried nudging the young soldier to agree. The lad
wanted the coin far more than the documents, and curtly,
he nodded and stepped back.

"Just this once, *citoyen*. Next time, have your papers."

Clinging to his illusion of humility, Murdoch hurried
the mare down the cobbled street.

The next incident occurred when he drove the cart
down the backstreet behind the inn to the stable. Climbing down to hand the reins to the stableboy, Murdoch
was confronted by two older and more battle-hardened
soldiers emerging from a stall to one side, as if they'd
been expecting him. Was the Aelynner he hadn't found
involved in this harassment? His suspicion was aroused,
but there was little he could do about it.

His hand went to the sword on his hip before he remembered he was posing as a simple peasant and the
weapon was supposed to be hidden by illusion.

"Your passport, *citoyen*," the mustached officer commanded.

Murdoch sensed that humility would only get him
thrown into prison this time. These two had no compassion. Hunting aristocratic spies who would endanger
their revolutionary independence, they bristled with
mistrust.

With his weapons momentarily concealed on the far

side of the cart, Murdoch wished he could lie as swiftly as he could run, but his thoughts scattered like leaves in a breeze. Only the knowledge that Lis waited for him prevented him from drawing his rapier.

"Let me buy you a drink while the innkeeper fetches my coat," he suggested, boldly assuming the air of a man of authority and swaggering from behind the cart, letting the gold hilt of his sword flash in the sun.

Their misgivings lightened at his perceived honesty, but that would last only so long as it took for them to realize he had no papers. Murdoch wished he hadn't led them to Lis and her patients. It was much simpler when he was alone.

He glanced up at the sky, but there wasn't even a hint of a cloud. Where was a good storm when he needed one? Maybe he should irritate the duo until they angered him enough to raise thunderheads.

Using reason instead of temper wasn't working so well.

It worked even less well when he heard Lis scream an angry obscenity just as they entered the inn.

# Sixteen

Looking for a servant, Lissandra hadn't paid enough attention to the muddled wits of the drunken sailor staggering down the hall—until he grabbed her from behind and squeezed her breast. She yelped in surprise and dropped the pretty painted bowl of water she'd been holding, then cursed herself for letting down her guard in her haste to be useful.

Recovering from her surprise, she reacted as Ian had taught her by screaming to attract attention. Directing her elbow backward with all her considerable strength, she connected with the lout's soft midsection and was rewarded with an *oomph* of pain. Pulling from his clumsy grasp, she swung around in a swirl of skirts, and dug her fingers into his wrist. She focused her mind on the fragile bones beneath her grasp and snapped one.

Her assailant's wail shook the walls. Or, more likely, unless the area was prone to earthquakes, Murdoch had heard her screams and caused the walls to vibrate with his rage.

She refused to let the thought distract her from teaching the villain a lesson. She increased the pressure of her fingers, and the drunk bellowed in agony and dropped to his knees. Her gown and the floor were soaked, and she considered rubbing her assailant's face in the wet filth of the floor as extra measure. She was resisting that impulse when Murdoch burst into the hall, followed by two uniformed soldiers and the innkeeper.

"She's murdering me!" the stout sailor cried in hopes of rescue from his fellow men.

The floor stopped shaking, and Lissandra appreciated that Murdoch was able to control himself once he saw she had the situation in hand. In fact, the insufferable superman appeared to be biting back a grin.

"This churl assaulted me," she said in the tone of command she'd heard her mother use. "I wish to press charges before he hurts some other helpless innocent."

"That is not possible," the innkeeper protested in an accusatory tone that insinuated Lissandra had brought this on herself. "I run a decent inn. Such things do not happen here!"

Perhaps she *was* to blame, if being female was all that was required to be accosted by strangers. Lissandra considered twisting the pompous innkeeper's nose, but Murdoch took care of the offensive man for her. His rapier was under the innkeeper's chin before any could notice he'd even removed it from his belt.

"You will apologize profusely to my wife for the assault on her person under your roof," he said in a tone of cold command that would curdle the blood of any who truly knew him.

The innkeeper stammered, and Murdoch's grim expression grew more fierce. A knife appeared in his other hand, pressing to the man's belly.

"I apologize, madame, monsieur," the innkeeper whispered, stepping backward until he bumped into the soldiers behind him.

"I did nothing, nothing, I say!" her assailant cried. "Make her release me!"

In a swirl and flash of silver, Murdoch spun to neatly slice her attacker's shirt from his back and trousers from their binding. Releasing the man's wrist, Lissandra swallowed an inappropriate laugh at the sight of his fat white rump before turning her attention to the astonished soldiers. She appreciated that Murdoch did not draw blood, but she could find more productive uses for the belligerent instincts of the men with him. She mentally nudged their thoughts into more suitable patterns.

The soldiers looked from her to the burly sailor on the floor. "The lady does not appear to need help," the clean-shaven officer said snidely, no doubt wondering whether he'd be able to bring such a large man to his knees—and keep him there.

"I don't recognize him," the mustached officer decided, lifting her attacker by his neckcloth—the only whole garment left on him. "We'd better take him in for questioning."

The younger soldier looked confused, glancing from Murdoch to their new prisoner. With his fury discharged, Murdoch jovially pounded the man's back and shoved him after his companion. "I will be down directly to press charges," he said in his impeccable French. "It is a scandal and a shame the way these foreigners think they can assault our women. I wager he's the émigré spy you've been looking for. My wife is the honey that ever catches flies."

The innkeeper's gaze darted nervously from Lissandra to Murdoch to their ill patient wrapped in blankets in the chamber behind them. She ought to feel sympathy for his confusion, but he was broadcasting concern only for himself, and she wasn't feeling generous.

Returning to the small parlor, Lissandra pressed a reassuring finger to Amelie's nose to make the terrified child smile in trembling relief, then knelt to cradle

Pierre Durand's head so she could help him drink the herbal tea she'd prepared. "All is well. We'll take you home now."

Still struggling with his volatile emotions, Murdoch offered the innkeeper a coin to quiet his protests and sent him away.

"I think I've reduced the infection and balanced his energies so that it will be safe for him to travel in the cart," Lissandra said, hoping she could distract Murdoch from his desire to fling her on a ship and sail away. "And Amelie mostly needs nourishment. A few good meals and a bath, and she'll be fine."

She thought it was a good sign that Murdoch had conceded to fetch the cart and take them back to Trystan's house. He wouldn't renege on that agreement, although she assumed the soldiers who had tagged behind him were an ominous portent.

Instead of speaking his thoughts, Murdoch turned to the child. "I think, back at the house, I saw some pretty gowns lying around, looking lonely," he said in an almost genial tone, while he lifted Durand from the floor. "I believe they might be just your size."

If Murdoch hadn't already stolen her heart, Lissandra would have handed it to him there and then. The promise of pretty clothes easily diverted the child's attention while his voice covered up Durand's moan of pain.

Murdoch had always been kind to Lissandra as a child, but she had assumed that was part of their rapport. No matter how tense their relationship became over the years, they'd always danced around each other like two expert swordsmen feinting without actually fighting.

Perhaps, if they were ever to get beyond their polite surfaces to the truth, it was time to quit parrying and engage weapons.

They tucked Pierre in the back of Trystan's cart as best as they could and listened to Amelie's happy chatter while they drove out of town.

They blended their illusions to disguise the cart without discussing it. Murdoch touched his brown fingers to Lissandra's when they passed the puzzled young soldier on the outskirts of the village, letting her know she need do no more.

And they both simmered in different kinds of frustration as they returned to Trystan's comfortable house, which they'd thought never to see again.

"Baths first," she murmured after Murdoch unhitched the horse and lifted their unconscious patient from the cart. "They have fleas."

"I'll not have you bathing a stranger," he grumbled in a low tone. Even though they spoke in their language, he tried not to disturb the child, who was warily studying her new surroundings.

Lissandra was not unfamiliar or uncomfortable with naked men, and Murdoch knew it. He was simply being jealously stubborn. "Male anatomy does not differ with name or familiarity of the individual," she argued. "Pierre cannot travel until we remove the infection and he regains his strength. The heat of the bath is the best way I know."

"Then add your herbs and incense and leave me with him," Murdoch insisted while she opened the kitchen door to let him pass with his unconscious burden.

"You are being deliberately thickheaded about this. The infection is in his lungs. I must find it and apply my energies there."

"And exhaust yourself in the process. I have some of your ability. Let me use it." Murdoch's jaw was rigid with obstinacy.

She opened her mouth to argue, then shut it again. Murdoch was being his usual domineering self, expecting everyone to obey his commands. She'd never seen anyone win against him, except her parents. And occasionally Ian. She certainly never had.

"If you can't Heal him, our departure will be delayed," she reminded him.

"I'll Heal him." Now that he had his way, he strode through the house as if he owned it.

Swatting the thickheaded man with a brick might help, but she had better things to do. Carrying her bag in one hand, taking Amelie's in the other, she made a game of racing the child down the stairs to the bath.

"Amelie is sound asleep in the nursery. How does your friend fare?" Lis stopped in the doorway of the bathing room, looking to Murdoch like an ethereal goddess.

The scene at the inn had certainly proved she wasn't delicate. His heart had almost stopped in his chest when he'd seen the size of her assailant. And she had brought the man down with no more than a supercilious lift of an eyebrow and a flick of her wrist.

Murdoch could tell when she was annoyed with him. Lis thought Healing was her territory, but he'd been in this world long enough to know men here did not accept female physicians. Her temper aggravated his, sparking flares inside him just by her existence. He was equally annoyed that she had been right—she could have healed Durand faster. And they'd lost the opportunity to leave tonight.

"Pierre is breathing easier," was all he said.

"Can you tell if the infection is gone?" She stayed in the shadows, not reacting to his irritation. He'd lit only one candle, so she was nearly invisible to his eyes, but not to his other senses. She smelled of lavender, and the air hummed with her feminine desire—another reason his nerves were on edge. He reacted like a tomcat to a female in heat.

He growled under his breath but tried not to disturb the shoemaker, who had drifted into sleep. "I sense a hot spot on the left side."

"Maybe if he is stronger tomorrow night, you can cure him then."

"We are not staying another night." He placed his hands on Durand's shoulders and tried to focus his mind again on the sensation he only dimly recognized. He'd learned to use the spin of his sword to gather his energies. Without it, his scattered abilities were of little more use than pebbles flung into a pond. He was afraid that if he heaved a stone, he'd inundate them all.

"Concentrate your energy on your thumbs," she suggested. "Perhaps just the left one. Pour all your strength through that point and see if you can direct it better."

"Go to bed," he ordered. "I can do this."

"It is not what you're trained to do."

"I wasn't trained to cook, but I'd starve if I didn't. Now go away; you're distracting me."

To his intense annoyance, she obeyed, slipping silently away as she often did when confronted with his damnable temper, leaving him alone with his ugly thoughts and frustrations. He could conceal his anger from the rest of the world, but not Lis. He jammed his thumb against the pressure point above Durand's shoulder blades, focused all his energy into it, and nearly sizzled his patient's lungs.

Durand woke, coughing and gulping the incense-laden air.

"With due respect, monsieur, you're no physician," Durand told him.

"True, but you'll feel better shortly. It is time you got some sleep. Let me help you out."

Their patient was recovered sufficiently to don a robe and limp from the cellar up to the servant's room behind the kitchen. To ask him to climb another flight of stairs to the guest chambers would have meant trying his strength.

Gratitude and bewilderment rolled off Durand in waves, but Murdoch brusquely settled him into bed, set a small fire in the grate even though the night was warm, and left him sleeping.

He hadn't tried to Heal anyone since adolescence, perhaps because he had seen no purpose in competing with Lis's superior ability.

He didn't like some of the insights he had gained since her arrival.

Insight didn't ease the need to gnash his teeth as he sensed the evening tide ebbing. They should be on a ship right this minute, sailing away from this dangerous land.

He didn't know why the soldiers had been waiting for him at the inn, but it would be only a matter of time before they came looking again.

# Seventeen

Lissandra checked on the sleeping child in the nursery a half dozen times, even though she would have known instantly had Amelie awakened. She needed an outlet for her restless energy, and walking the floor had grown tiresome.

Returning to her own chamber, she prepared for bed, beating the dirt from the gown she'd worn that day. She didn't take off the fine linen she'd worn under the gown. At home, she slept nude, but Aelynn was a tropical climate. The weather here was too uncertain, even in summer. Or so she told herself.

Mostly, she felt too vulnerable to be naked while Murdoch was building up a cloud of anger, frustration, and sexual hunger that would surely burst like a volcano should they meet in the hall. And she kept walking the hall.

Too many thoughts and fears and desires raced through her for her to settle down. She paced the floor of the room she'd taken after giving Amelie the nursery.

She knew when Murdoch led Pierre up the stairs from the bath. She should go down and help them. Normally, she would have.

But she feared ... What did she fear? Not Murdoch, not really. He might back off and slam the door, or ride off into the night, or do any of a number of things to put distance between them. But he wouldn't lay a hand to her.

And she wanted him to.

She feared herself.

She heard Murdoch climbing to the second story and froze, trying not to make a sound, knowing it was useless. Murdoch could hear her breathing if he put his mind to it.

He opened her door and walked in.

He filled the doorway, looking as if his head would brush the low ceiling if he held it any higher. He'd shed his coat and waistcoat. The unfastened neckties of his wet linen framed the brown column of his throat. She couldn't mistake the breadth and strength of the muscles of his shoulders or the tautness of his flat abdomen.

His eyes held her pinned. They flared with fires of lust, and she felt their heat all the way down to her toes.

"I am riding into town to find a ship willing to take us on the morning tide."

"Fine, then," she said with icy pride. "Ride off and leave me behind again." Embarrassed at her retreat into childish behavior, as if she were still a needy adolescent and he the adult, she hugged herself and glanced away. She didn't know what she'd expected. Murdoch knew better than to make love to her. So he was putting distance between them. She understood. She simply expected more than he could give. Foolish of her.

"I'm not leaving you." He held his temper by curling his fingers into fists. "I'll be back before dawn."

"Maybe it's better if you don't come back." She couldn't contain her frustration any longer. She threw the challenge that preyed on her mind.

"Do you think I have a choice?" he asked, visibly

controlling his temper. "You're the one who always treats me as if I'm a dangerous poison you wish to experiment with." Without further explanation, he turned on his heel and walked away.

"I won't let you run out on me again!" The tensions of the day had melted the icy shield that had confined her, until it could no longer withstand her pent-up rage and despair. Lissandra raced after him. "I will no longer tolerate your disappearing every time we disagree." The fury spilled from her tongue.

He took the back stairs two at a time. "You're a fine one to talk," he called back at her. "You're the expert at avoidance. Why argue when you could hide behind your mother's skirts? Who will hide you now?"

"Do you think I like avoiding argument?" she cried, wishing she could catch up with him and hit him over the head. *Hard.* But he was walking too fast, crossing the kitchen and heading for the door more swiftly than she could dodge tables and chairs to follow. "What choice do you leave me? I can risk you raising a cyclone, or I can watch you sail away!"

When he didn't reply but slammed out of the kitchen, she threw the door open and raced into the windy night after him. Her hair tore loose of its pins to slap her in the face.

"You want a confrontation?" she cried over the pounding of the surf on the rocks below. "Why don't you tell me the *truth* about how my father died?"

Murdoch whirled around, his normally composed features contorted into a mask of anguish. "You think I don't regret that night? I have nightmares recalling how you looked at me when you ran to him and wailed your grief. If only I could wipe that scene from my mind!"

Lightning flashed. Lissandra glanced at it warily, and

Murdoch said something acerbic that the wind carried away. Swinging around again, he hastened down the rocky path to the beach rather than to the stable—where he might set the straw on fire with his fury.

Tears filled her eyes, and she raced after him. "How was I supposed to look on you?" she cried. "I saw everything! I told Mother I didn't, but I did. I saw the two of you talking, yelling. Then he pounded you on the shoulder, and you raised your arms in a rage while he walked away. And I knew you were going to leave, that he'd driven you off again."

She stumbled over her feet in the dark, searching for the path Murdoch followed so easily. She might as well be shouting into the wind. She should turn back, forget she'd ever found him. . . .

She wouldn't repeat the pattern of the past. Not this time. No more hiding or walking away from a fight— even if Murdoch blew France to the moon.

She flung a rock at his back, and although it merely glanced off his sore shoulder and thunked on the path, it made him turn and look. A bolt of lightning cracked across the black night sky. "You called down lightning then, too!" she shouted. "Just like now. Can you deny that?"

"No." He turned his back on her again and continued down the path. "I deny nothing. You have every right to scorn me."

Perversely, now that he'd agreed with her, she didn't want to scorn him. "That's giving up!" she screamed after him. "I thought you a better man than that! I thought you a man who would fight for what he believes! Instead, I discover you *prefer* running away."

He disappeared around a boulder. She was terrified he would disappear entirely, and ran down the pebbly path as quickly as she dared, slipping and sliding on her sandals, the gravel tearing at her feet. She nearly ran into him at the bottom.

He grabbed her shoulders and shook her before she could catch her breath. "Do you want me to make the skies weep?" he asked in a voice that pierced her heart for all that wasn't said. "Don't you think I loved Luther as much as you did? He was the only father I ever knew, and I *killed* him!"

Stunned, Lissandra fell against Murdoch's chest and wrapped her arms around him; whether in consolation or despair, she couldn't say. She simply knew she had to hang on while the wind whipped their clothes and hair and the surf pounded at their feet.

"If you loved him, how could you fight with him?" She was weeping into his shoulder. She beat him with her fist when he tried to smooth her hair.

He settled for holding her closer. His voice was inside her heart as much as in her ear when he replied, "It was an accident. He'd just granted my fondest wish, and then he announced that Trystan was to be your suitor."

"Your fondest wish?" She shoved away, trying to read his eyes in the flashes of lightning—but as always, Murdoch's expression remained dark, mysterious, and unreadable.

The wind whipped his hair across his sharp cheekbones, and his lips formed a thin, forbidding line before he relented. "He'd told me that if I would stay and take a place in the Council and behave civilly, he would let me court you."

The words struck Lissandra with the force of an earthquake. She shoved out of his arms, fell backward, and caught herself on a black rock. She waited for the earth to quit moving before she realized Murdoch had released his unspoken grief by turning the tide high, and it shifted the sand beneath her feet.

"How can I believe you? Why would my father lie to you?" she screamed over the wind. "Challenge all Ae-lynn if you must, but please, please, don't lie to me."

Black water swirled around their ankles. Murdoch touched her jaw. She would have shaken off his rough caress, but the white-hot blast of his pain stunned her senseless.

Her knees gave way, and she crumpled toward the sand until Murdoch caught her and set her on the slippery rock. He said nothing, simply let her feel what he felt—

*His shields were down.*

No wonder he hadn't wanted to let her inside his head or his heart. She couldn't survive the onslaught of horror and guilt that consumed him. She didn't have enough fortitude. Frantically, she shut him out, but she dug her fingers into his hard shoulders so he could not back away. If she could Heal him with her touch, she would, but the black hole eating at his soul wasn't curable—not by her.

"Tell me," she commanded. "Use words."

And for the first time in memory, he obeyed.

"Do you have any idea how long I'd waited for his permission to court you?" he asked. "I have known you were my future, my life, since I was barely old enough to know what such a bond meant. I told your parents we were meant to be, and they were horrified. Very polite, but horrified. They insisted I give you time. And I did. I honored their wishes and sailed off to make my fortune so I could prove myself worthy. But by that night . . ."

He shuddered, and she had to clench her jaw to remain rigidly disbelieving. Here was the man she'd desired all her life telling her that he'd wanted her, too, but he'd waited for her father's *permission* to court her? The most powerful man she knew, and he'd *asked* to court her, instead of simply taking what he wanted?

When she said nothing, Murdoch continued. "By the time you turned twenty-one, your father had to admit that you would look at no one else, and he agreed—with conditions. Selfish, arrogant beast that I was, I had no doubt that I could pass his test, and I was ecstatic at his agreement. I threw up my arms, not in anger, but to release the energy of my joy into the sky. I wanted to light the night with bonfires, declare my intentions to the world. But I could not, not until I proved myself.

"I had already set up the fireworks to celebrate my homecoming. And Luther gave me more reason to rejoice, even if he did not mean to publicly announce his approval. But he . . ." Murdoch tensed, searching for words he'd said to himself over and over, excuses that no longer rang true even in his own ears. But this was Lissandra. She deserved to know the full extent of his culpability.

"I was focused on the fireworks, waiting for any word or phrase in his speech that would justify releasing my elation with a spectacle."

He held himself rigid and spoke coldly. "Instead, Luther named Trystan Guardian and all but offered him your hand. I knew it for the challenge it was, a test to see how I would react, and I tried to control my rage."

He released Lis and stepped back, trying to spare her his dark guilt. "But in my joy, I'd already focused on the fireworks, and I couldn't redirect my focus fast enough. I lost control, as usual, brought down lightning, and killed him."

He bent his head and walked toward the ocean. If he was lucky for once in his life, he would drown before he had to see Lissandra's disillusion with the hero she'd invented in her mind. The white knight that he would never be.

# Eighteen

Murdoch waded into the water. Whitecaps had formed on a tide that should have been pulling back to sea. Clouds scudded across the moon. No matter how far he swam, he doubted he would drown. More likely, he would accidentally raise a cyclone and wipe out a village. And she wanted him to stop running away?

He lived in terror of accidentally killing Lis as he'd killed her father.

Before he could dive, a wave he hadn't called forth curled from the depths to slap him in the chest. He staggered, caught off-balance.

An abnormal gust of wind hit him from behind. The powerful blast of air cast him face forward into the pounding surf. He broke his fall by bracing his arms in the gravelly sand and coughed up a lungful of water as the tide swiftly withdrew—unnaturally so. *And he wasn't doing it.* He could swear he wasn't.

Waves crashed over his head, drenching him, dragging him far from shore, nearly drowning him with their powerful undertow. He opened up his mind, seeking his tormentor, verifying he hadn't gone mad and done this to himself. *Lis!* Her fury and tears swept through him as powerfully as the ocean's tide. The damn woman could drown him—and he didn't have the skill or strength to stop her.

Humbled by that realization, he fought the force of the undertow, unwilling to die so ignobly. Was she even aware of what she was doing?

The tide abruptly receded, as it should, as if the bizarre tempest had passed on. Stunned nearly senseless, floating on the eddying current, Murdoch thought perhaps he'd just rest there a little longer rather than stand up and face Lis's wrenching disillusionment.

"You turned your back on me and your friends and your home, for what?" a haunted voice cried over his head, beyond the water frothing in his ears. *Lissandra.*

Shoving up on his elbows, he shook his head, and his wet hair smacked him in the face.

"I became what you made of me," he growled, climbing to his knees and pushing his hair back. He ought to face her, but the pull of the dark sea was strong. "Your parents turned me into a freak who should never have been born. I became a man without a home, a mercenary for hire, a warrior without a cause. Not one of my so-called friends came to my aid when I was banished."

This time, she slapped him with her mind, nearly tumbling him back into the waves.

Stunned that she would actually try to drown him, Murdoch clambered to his feet and swung around to take her blows like a man. He couldn't strike back. He would never raise a hand to her.

"You did what you always do," she replied scornfully, her voice rising above the roar of waves crashing against the rocks. "You went your own way, ignored the gods, followed your own misguided goals, *forgetting those who loved you*," she added with anguish. "You did what *you* wanted instead of what was best for all. You thought of no one but yourself."

This time, the mental blow came from in front of him, staggering him backward. Spinning dizzily, Murdoch flung himself forward by sheer strength of will, catching Lissandra by surprise as he crashed into her and dragged her down with him to the sand. He wrapped his fingers in her windswept hair and forced her to look him in the eye.

Her gaze flashed with a fury and pain she never showed the world. This was what she hid from others. *Expressing* passion had been trained out of her, but not passion itself. Her agony circled their heads, battering the wind and water around them but nowhere else. Lissandra had no trouble with control.

She was a living definition of restraint—

"That's why the gods struck me down," Murdoch cried over the noise, shaking her shoulders to force her to listen.

Still wrapped in anguish, she stared at him uncomprehendingly.

*"The gods struck me down."* His voice was harsh with strain as he related the moment he'd tried to deny. "As we were escaping the brigands, the blue spirit ball arced out of the sky at the very same moment that the scoundrels shot me. Instead of dying, I was knocked to the ground, unconscious. Later, I remembered only the fire I had accidentally set. *I should be dead.*"

The wind died to a normal breeze. Eyes wide with wonder, Lissandra shook her head. "No, you should be Oracle."

He stared at her, feeling his shirt plastered to his back and water running off his nose. The idea that the gods were real and had chosen a misfit like him for Oracle instead of killing him for his sins was so ludicrous that he couldn't absorb it. Not while he had Lis beneath him, and his brain departed his head. If he accepted that the gods were real and he was Oracle ... *could he also have Lis?*

Apparently oblivious to the cold and wet, she slid her arms around his shoulders as if in answer to his question. She lifted her tempting lips, and even thunderstruck as he was, he could do no more than obey the call of nature. He leaned forward and captured her mouth with his.

It could be no other way. Out here, where the gods could watch over them and their wild instincts could fly free, they came together with a freedom they'd never dared elsewhere.

If he believed in the gods ... she was his. He desperately wanted to believe again.

Murdoch sank into the sweet bliss of Lissandra's mouth as if he were coming home at last. Releasing all his carefully manufactured restraint, he crushed her against his chest, possessed her with his tongue, and relished the joy with which she returned his kiss.

He didn't want her to pull away this time. He wanted *his* Lis, the loving woman, not the imitation Dylys who sought to teach him lessons.

They were soaked to the skin, but steam rose everywhere he touched her. Moonlight illuminated the rapture on her face as he stroked her stiff spine until it softened, and he covered her cheeks with beard-stubbled kisses. That she could forgive him ...

He drew in air and tried to be reasonable, but his head was spinning too hard.

"Don't," she warned before he could speak a word. "Don't run away without explanation again. That is what I cannot forgive."

He filled his fists with her hair and stared down into her glistening eyes. "I have only ever wanted what was best for you."

She nodded. "I know. But understand that even I don't know what that is, and I cannot expect you to know it either. We have been denying the gods instead of listening to our hearts."

She leaned forward and bit his lip, then licked the hurt with her tongue. The hard points of her nipples pressed into his chest through their wet linen, pillowed by her lush breasts, and a surge of lust nearly had him pushing her into the sand so he could cover her right there and then. Only a restraint as strong as his arms prevented him from doing so.

His loins burned with desire. The woman he'd wanted his entire life was his for the taking. She was telling him that the price was his independence.

He'd had complete autonomy for four years. It wasn't all he'd hoped it would be, not without Lis. Melding his lips to hers, Murdoch pushed her back into the wet sand, cradling her head in his hands as his tongue plundered her mouth, possessing it as he meant to possess all the rest of her. She dug her fingers into his hair and gave him full access.

This time, he would not run away from temptation. If this was what she wanted, he would not protect her from their tempestuous passions. He had learned his lesson.

He ripped her soaked linen and filled his palms with the luxurious heat of her breasts. He pressed his groin against the juncture of her legs, rubbing to relieve the pressure while he leaned over to lick and suckle and claim.

She bucked beneath him, coming up off the ground

with passionate cries that were more music to his ears than the crash of surf on rocks. The tide continued its retreat, leaving them untouched.

He didn't want their first time to be so crude, but the gods would have to pick him up by the scruff of the neck and fling him into the cold sea before he could stop now. With Lis in his arms, it was a simple matter to will the wind to warm her bare flesh. He tore off his shirt and made a bed for her on the softest sand.

Lissandra pushed up and found his nipple and sucked until he groaned and pushed her down again. There would ever be this struggle for dominance between them. Only now, freed of restraint by her words, he relished the challenge.

"Do you want vows?" he asked. "I'll give you all you ask and more."

She cupped his face between her slender hands and shook her head. "I want vows when we're home again, on the altar before the gods. Tonight is just for us."

She was wise not to permanently bond them, but Murdoch knew she was his future, no matter what. He kissed her in gentle acceptance and let his body speak the rest.

Lissandra finally surrendered to the need within her, to the accelerating desire between them that they'd fought for so long. At the insistence of Murdoch's large hand, she yielded all her defenses, spreading her legs and raising her hips. She sighed and shivered at the exciting shock waves of the intrusion of rough male fingers against her sensitive femininity.

He was being gentle with her, but she did not need gentleness. Desire poured hot and strong through her womb. She opened for his fingers, wept at his stroking, and clung to the bulging strength of his upper arms while her inner muscles spasmed under his hand.

She had wanted this for too long to retreat into maidenly reluctance. She nipped at his arms, urging him to hurry.

He tugged off his breeches, flinging them aside while she lay there and admired his beauty. She had no more fear of his male weapon than she did of his sword. She knew she was made to fit him as no other could.

Her only fear was of their growing physical bond, but that could not be helped. The gods seldom granted children to Oracles unless they were mated in the sacred temple, so it was not that permanence she feared. It was the irrevocable bond of amacara that they risked.

And still she surrendered, reveling in the ecstasy of Murdoch's big hands caressing her breasts as if she'd gifted him with his heart's desire. That she could please him in this manner thrilled her as much as his touch did. His hungry kiss lavished her skin with burning brands. If he was the volcano, she was the lava that spilled through him. They could no more be separated than moon and sky. They were already bound, vows or no vows.

She arched her hips and urged him on.

With a groan, he pressed his forehead to hers. "Aelynn give me strength," he prayed.

"Aelynn gave you more strength than you deserve." She wrapped her legs around his hips and felt a rush of pleasure when the tip of his maleness slid into her cleft.

"I just hope Aelynn gives me enough strength to remember you are as strong as I am," he said against her mouth—before he took advantage of her position to plunge his hips downward, filling her in a single thrust.

Lissandra cried out her pain and triumph as Murdoch's thick maleness seared through tender tissue, invading and conquering and making her feel like the frail wisp he feared she might be. He stilled, giving her time to adjust to the initial sting and fullness, but she'd waited far too long to let a little pain stop her. She wanted him with every particle of her mind and body. For now, it was her body that ruled.

She lifted her hips and gasped as he angled deeper. He abruptly withdrew until she was empty and tingling with the need for more.

"Please," she begged, rubbing her hands over the tensed muscles of his back, squeezing her legs to urge him on.

He obliged with alacrity.

The waves were akin to liquid smoke curling around their bodies as they came together. A gull called in the distance, echoing their cries. The moon bathed them in silver, and the magic of their memories wafted the jasmine scent of home upon the breeze.

The pressure in Lissandra's womb was too great. She feared she would come apart and never be whole again if he did not relieve the ache soon. She tried to force him to hurry, but Murdoch merely kissed her nose and adjusted their positions until he rubbed against the wall of her womb.

And then he caressed between her legs with his thumb, and the pressure exploded. She bucked and cried and came apart in his hands, and spasmed again when he shouted his joy and plunged so deep she could see the moon and stars with her eyes closed. Saw them through *his* eyes.

His shields were down.

The shock and wonder of their mental joining was lost in the sensation of their physical completion.

The hot fluid of his seed spilled deep inside her, lubricating his thrusts, encouraging her muscles to clench and relax until he'd wrung every ounce of pleasure from her and drained her to limpness.

"I was your first," he murmured in wonder, holding himself up to prevent crushing her into the sand where she lay languid beneath him.

"Did you think I would take another and allow you to destroy the island with your jealousy?" she murmured in return.

He chuckled, and finally, after all the years of denial, they relaxed together, as one.

# Nineteen

Feeling strangely at peace with himself despite fearing he'd committed an irrevocable sin, Murdoch wrapped Lis in his shirt and carried her back to the house.

The brief glimpse of the glory of Lis with her shields down was as close to heaven as he'd ever hoped to experience. It was probably best that they both retreat behind their emotional barriers before he started believing in her amazing confidence in him.

Lis laid her head on his shoulder as if she were a docile, newly ravished maiden, but Murdoch knew now that she possessed a hard core of strength and volatile passion—and he stood in awe of what she concealed behind her starchy demeanor.

She'd raised the tide with her mind, and slapped *him* down—the strongest man on Aelynn—thereby preventing him from destroying himself or possibly others.

She might not wish to wield her warrior strength as he did, but she was his equal, his match, his mate.

He still had difficulty grasping the concept of his sometimes gentle, often imperturbable Lissy summoning the rage to knock him over. Even her powerful brother had done no more than bring him to his knees, and that had been with sword and staff.

Murdoch supposed he'd always known her strength, but she'd never used it in anger or with reckless zeal—as he had.

She'd knocked him flat in more ways than one.

"What am I going to do with you?" he murmured against her hair as they ascended the stairs to the room he'd claimed for the night.

"Listen to me?" she asked drily.

He snorted. "And hear you tell me again that I should be Oracle? Have you no more rational reason why the gods did not let me die?"

"I'm sure the opportunity to die will arise again if you do not follow their commands. As long as your ring glows with their light, though, you can be assured they have not forgotten you."

Unwillingly, he glanced at his ring. The blue light was barely visible. Lis had said earlier that meant he'd accepted the gods instead of fighting them. Right this minute, he could almost agree. If the gods meant for him to have Lis, he was in complete accord with their wisdom. But if they meant for him to be Oracle, the gods were crazed. His ring flared hotter.

"We should bathe," Lis demurred as he laid her on the clean sheets of his bed. "I am covered head to toe in sand."

"Do you think I have waited for you all these years to let you out of my bed so easily? What if you changed your mind while bathing?" He preferred to deal with the here and now and not the might-be's and could-be's over which he had no control.

He climbed on top of her, straddling her legs. Her eyes widened as she noted the extent of his arousal. He needed to be inside her again. He waited for her to feel and accept the desire that was coursing between them.

"I need to consult my spirit guide," she whispered, half in protest. "We must See what the gods intend."

"You consult. I'll proceed." When it came to Lis, he was incredibly focused. He leaned over and caught her nipple between his teeth. She writhed beneath him, whether to fight him off or part her legs wasn't easily ascertained.

Just to prove he was in charge, Murdoch flipped her over on her stomach and pressed his arousal against her buttocks. She instantly quit squirming.

He raised her up enough to stroke between her legs until she buried her moans in the pillow. He teased her breasts until they were swollen in his hands, pressed his kisses down her spine, then pushed her to her knees in a position of supplication. He heard her strangled cry as he kissed and licked along the line separating her rounded buttocks. Then the bond between them became too strong to deny.

He was no more in charge than she was—just more experienced, for now.

He sent Healing energy to the soft tissues he'd bruised earlier in the evening, then inserted the tip of his erection into her welcoming moisture.

Gently, he pushed deeper, stroking back and forth until she surrendered. With a moan of pure lust, she thrust backward, plunging him deep inside her, where he needed to be to make her fully, irrevocably his.

He held her as she climaxed, keeping his rod straight and strong until he'd wrung the last tremor from her, and then he pushed deeper still. The rush of power to his loins emptied him of all except the exploding joy and acceptance of finding his mate. Together, they collapsed in a tangle of limbs, sweaty and satiated.

He felt the heat and bruising of her newly ravished

body as if they were his own. As before, her mind was fully open to him, and he was too exhausted to take advantage by tiptoeing through her thoughts or feelings. Maybe someday, in the future, they would grow accustomed to this joining and learn to explore each other in new ways. Not now. The physical exploration was too demanding.

Falling to one side, Murdoch tugged her with him, cradling his Lis in his arms as they both drifted into a satisfied sleep.

*Gleaming silver, glittering with precious gems, the Chalice of Plenty illumined the shadowed chamber with the holy light of the gods. On an altar consecrated in the dark ages of forgotten time, the sacred object beckoned, promising answers, promising ease and plenty.*

*A fair hand reached. . . . The incandescent light flared brighter, hotter, preventing touch.*

*Another hand stretched through the darkness, a bronzed male hand with a black pearl and onyx ring rimmed in blue light.*

*Fireworks exploded across the night sky. Red, yellow, blue stars illuminated the rocky cavern.*

*And when the stars blinked out, the chamber fell dark. The sacred chalice was gone.*

With the first light of dawn, Lissandra discarded the uncomfortable remnants of the dream in her head and woke to a heated male body warming her backside.

She and Murdoch had tested the strength of their wills on each other since childhood. She knew his mind as well as her own, and she felt his equal in most things, but she'd never fully appreciated how much larger he was than she. She fit into the shelter of his long, broad body with room to spare. Everywhere he touched her, he was hard. *Everywhere.*

She smiled like a cat with cream, rolled to her back, and let her fingers glide through the soft hair of his broad chest, down to his taut abdomen. He was awake. He could never fool her about that.

"I dreamed of the chalice last night." He cupped her breast as casually as if he spoke of their next meal.

Startled, Lissandra tore her gaze from the fascinating prize below his waist and met the concern in his eyes. "So did I."

Taking advantage of her momentary distraction, Murdoch straddled her hips and began planting swift, tickling kisses to sensitive zones he'd discovered the prior night. "What did you see in your dream?"

As if she could think while the musky scent of him made her head spin. She wrapped her fingers in his satiny hair, but forgot to halt him when his mouth found her breast. "You have the unfair advantage of experience," she complained. "Either talk or do this. I cannot do both."

"Good. I want you thinking only of me when we're together."

And he made certain to give her something worth thinking about as he taught her how to use the passion of which she was capable. Lissandra surrendered to his lessons with the eagerness of a dedicated student. When they reached the pinnacle of bliss, she deliberately held her eyes open and enjoyed the grimace of ecstasy that softened Murdoch's sharp features as she used the final throes of her orgasm to push him to the brink and over.

Opening her mind as well as her eyes, she allowed him to see the vision of her dream.

Startled by her mental intrusion, he collapsed on top

of her. With his maleness still firmly embedded in her, he braced his weight on his forearms and touched his forehead to hers. "How do you do that?"

"Make you come?" she asked demurely, wriggling until he shifted his heavy weight to a more comfortable position.

"I wager with enough experience you can accomplish that with just a look," he said drily, rolling off her and back to the bed. "It's your ability to play around inside my head that frightens me. You just *showed* me your dream."

"That will teach you to think you are more powerful than everyone. I cannot plant images unless your shields are down, but there are several of us with the ability to insert impressions into open minds. You would be more careful in your lovemaking if you'd spent more time on Aelynn and less with untalented Other World women."

"I didn't dare test your green-eyed monster by lying with Aelynn women. I feared you would turn me into a toad." He caught her hand and squeezed it. "I can't decide if your ability to play with my mind is good or bad. For now, it's convenient. My dream was the same."

"The gods are telling us to seek the holy chalice in a cave?" Lissandra tried not to sound too excited. She hadn't expected to accomplish what others had failed to do, but if in some extraordinary manner she and Murdoch *together* could retrieve the Chalice of Plenty . . . *it could save Aelynn*. Hope and joy swelled within her.

"I recognized the surroundings in our dream—a tunnel, not a cave, and a sacred tunnel at that." He lay still, studying the vision they both held in their heads. "If that's where it is, there's no wonder that we could not sense its hiding place."

She felt him abruptly shut down his thoughts. She refused to release his hand when he tried to sit up. "What?" she demanded. "What are you thinking?"

"That it's too convenient. Someone planned this."

"Planned what?" She sat up, dragging the sheet across her breasts, not out of modesty, but because she wanted Murdoch to focus on this crucial discussion.

"If the dream is true, the chalice is still in England, near where Ian lives," he said curtly, pulling loose from her grasp and locating his still-damp and salt-encrusted trousers on the floor. He threw them aside in disgust.

"And?" she encouraged.

"Ian knew the Chalice of Plenty had gone to England. I tried to Find it for him, but it vanished from all our senses. It appears to be sentient, or at least guided by the gods. At the time, I believed the gods had deemed me unfit to touch a sacred chalice."

"Ian was furious when you abandoned the search."

Comfortable in his nudity, Murdoch sat on the bed's edge and gazed down at her. She was all too aware of how wanton she must appear with her hair spilling across the linen and her face still flushed from their lovemaking. When he looked at her like that, she forgot all argument.

"We have time to idle before the fishing boats return this evening," he said without expression, dismissing their talk of dreams.

She couldn't tell whether mischief or seduction was behind the blue intensity of his dark gaze. "Time for what? We cannot spend it in bed," she reminded him. She had to make him talk, but when he looked at her like that . . . talk was far from her mind.

"You have an Other Worlder as patient," he agreed, grimacing. "Still, if you wish to discover where my mind differs from others . . ."

She widened her eyes at his easy acceptance. "You will let me compare your brains?"

"If it will help you understand how our minds function." He stood and padded across the room to search the wardrobe.

"You said that to distract me." She flung a pillow after him. "If you want knowledge of why your gifts go astray, then I will give you what I can, but that doesn't deny the fact that without the chalice, Aelynn is at grave risk. And without an Oracle, all is lost. We *need* you."

"Aelynn is one very tiny part of a much larger world. The chalice didn't mean for me to find it, so I returned to France to a more useful occupation of aiding those who'd been unjustly imprisoned. Why would the chalice be any more inclined to fall in my hands now than it was before?"

Their impending disagreement was interrupted by the sound of a child's bare feet running down the hall and cries of, "Papa, Papa, where are you?"

The day was upon them.

"Pierre is well enough to travel," Murdoch warned, trying on a pair of Trystan's trousers.

Lissandra opened her senses to their patient downstairs. "He seems to be, although it would be better if he rested for a while longer. He needs to recover his strength."

"You can work on him once we're safely gone from here."

"I don't take orders from you," she reminded him, wrapping herself in a sheet to go in search of clothing.

"That could be a problem if I'm the Oracle as you claim," he called after her.

# Twenty

Murdoch watched as Lissandra happily arranged a lounge chair in the summer sun, then settled Pierre into it, and tucked a blanket around him. She'd found Amelie a pretty gown and a doll to play with and set her to making a daisy chain. Leaning against an apple tree, Murdoch waited with interest to see if Lis would make a doll of him and arrange him in her playhouse, too. He'd once considered her as domineering as her mother for this habit of pushing people into the place she assigned them, but back then, she'd been wearing her illusion of authority. Now he could see that she was just Lis, a woman who enjoyed Healing and wanted to study people in order to become better at it.

With this new perspective, he recognized that the Oracle's daughter needed people to care for as much as he needed air to breathe.

"Have a seat. I can't reach you when you loom over me like that." She shooed him from the shade into the sun where she'd set a kitchen chair next to Pierre.

"What type of experiment is this, Madame LeDroit?" Pierre asked, stretching his thin frame on the cushions and turning his face gratefully to the sun.

Murdoch jerked uneasily at the sound of his plebeian surname being attached to his noble Lis, but she seemed blithely unaware of the disparity. He leaned against the chairback and sprawled his—Trystan's—boots in front of him. Trystan had clodhoppers for feet, but with the padding he'd added, the boots worked well enough.

"There is a Dr. Gall in Germany who believes the shape of our skulls reflects the areas of interest in our brain." Lissandra measured her fingers across Pierre's hair.

Murdoch knew she was giving the shoemaker an explanation that would make sense to his Other World mind, but he didn't know if she was making up the doctor and his beliefs. He examined a scuff on the toe of his boot and tried to school his impatience. When was the last time he'd simply sat in the sun and enjoyed the laugh of a child and a pretty woman's touch?

His soul ached for the peace this moment offered.

Satisfied with her measurements of Pierre, Lis turned to him. Her hand grazed his hair gently, and he could feel her soothing energy. She had Healing in her touch, a heat that drew off his ill humors and bathed him in relaxation. He could almost imagine falling asleep under her ministrations. He leaned his head back to smile up at her, and she smiled back, wickedly pulling both the strings of his heart and the thread of amacara that bound them. His reproductive organ jerked to attention.

"You're playing with fire," he reminded her.

She laughed. "And so I am, Lord Volcano. Close your eyes and think pleasant thoughts."

He thought of her pearly pink nipples jutting from the frost-colored cascade of hair tumbling over her golden breasts.

Lis tugged his hair, jarring him from the pleasant image. "Your shield is too easy to breach like this. You'll embarrass me."

Murdoch grinned wickedly, not in the least displeased. "Get used to it."

With a sigh of exasperation, she returned to Pierre and asked him to think of something pleasant. Then she asked him to think of something that made him angry. Murdoch raised his eyebrows when she jerked her hands away from Pierre's head as if she'd been burned.

He noticed she was reluctant to ask *him* to think of something unpleasant when she returned her hands to his skull. "Can you feel what he's thinking?" he asked in an undertone.

"I don't have as strong an ability to read a jumble of thoughts as Ian does," she acknowledged, "but I can feel the pain of his ordeal."

"Then it may be best if you do not touch me again." He started to stand up, but she shoved him back into the chair.

"I am only beginning to sense the differences," she scolded. "This isn't an easy task. Try thinking of something not too bad. Imagine you're hammering your thumb."

He nodded in appreciation of her wisdom. "Pain isn't as apt to make me angry." He summoned the image of smashing his thumb and winced.

"I think I see it," she said with excitement, keeping her voice to a whisper. "It's a very different sensation from Monsieur Durand's. How extraordinary! You have an intensity here"—she touched her finger to the front of his skull—"that connects with your motor skills here." She touched another part of his head. "You do not simply feel pain. You react to it."

"Like a skunk throws scent when frightened," he said in scorn.

She thumped his head with her knuckles. "Do not underestimate the power of self-preservation."

He glanced over at their guest, who had fallen asleep. "But now you would have to compare me with others of our kind before you can see if my brain is different from theirs."

"Oh, certainly. And it would take many tests to develop a theory. But it's a very good start, don't you think?"

Only if they had a hundred years or so. Murdoch wished he believed they had even a year together ahead of them, but though he was a dreamer, he wasn't a fool.

"The stranger is here," Lis murmured that evening as Murdoch helped Pierre down the long flight of stone stairs to the harbor dock. There was no hope of disguising their activity in the red glow of the summer sun setting over the Channel.

Murdoch didn't have to ask whom she was talking about. While waiting for the tide to turn, they'd both kept their senses open for the silent Aelynner who was lurking about Pouchay. They could linger no longer. The ship they'd hired awaited them.

An Aelynner who did not greet them directly was not a friend. Out of caution, Murdoch had to assume they'd been followed from the village. Lis wouldn't care. She'd insist all Aelynners should be rescued, regardless of who they were. He'd feel safer if he knew with whom he was dealing.

"Get the child aboard," he ordered, scanning the nearly empty dock below.

He was aware of the limits of his energy. Even if he thought he could successfully raise a fog on a dry summer evening without causing a hurricane in doing so, he would expend more vital forces than he could afford. He didn't want to be crippled and nauseous if they had to run a Channel blockade later.

Lis shot Murdoch a look that said she obeyed only because she agreed, then took Amelie's hand and ran lightly down the stairs to the dock.

Her quiet determination concealed as much willful bullheadedness as he could claim. If she really thought they had a chance of finding the holy chalice, they needed to agree on who was leading this expedition. First, they had to make it out of France alive.

"If you can go faster without me, then go," Pierre urged. He attempted to pick up speed, but his weak legs barely held him up.

Murdoch ignored the admonition and helped him down the last steps.

The burly captain of the hired ship hurried to the rail to help load their last passenger. "We should have waited for a dark tide," the sailor muttered as he grasped Pierre's arm. "I don't like that we can be seen."

"I don't like that the committee is allowed to watch," Murdoch retorted. "When you return with your hold full of cheap grain and English cotton, you'll be a hero."

The captain ceased grumbling. He'd known the risk before he'd accepted the task. And Murdoch had paid him well for concealing the refugees. Wealth couldn't be had without risk.

Instead of marching boldly along the harbor road, the soldiers Murdoch had feared arrived stealthily, through the shadows of the rocks along the gravel beach. He heard them before they could see him. He gave Pierre the final boost that lifted him over the railing and onto the ship. The captain grabbed his invalid passenger and hauled him toward the cabin, shouting at his crew to weigh anchor and raise the sails.

Murdoch could have joined the others aboard with a single bound, but he wanted to know who was watching, unseen, concealed by the soldiers' approach. Were the soldiers oblivious to the lurker's appearance, or hiding him?

Coming around the bend and finally seeing Murdoch, the scarred sergeant who had trapped him in the stable the previous day shouted, "Halt!"

The sergeant led two foot soldiers in their plain blue uniforms, but none of the three was the Aelynner that Murdoch sought. "We have business in Le Havre," he informed the Guards, leaping from the planks to the shore while reaching for the forged documents for which he'd spent the last of Lis's coins. Lis still had the rest of her pearls, but he wouldn't waste them on this crew. They were likely to let him rot in prison in hopes of prying more valuables out of him.

The sergeant grabbed the papers, and held them upside down while pretending to peruse them. Many of these conscripted, untrained soldiers protecting France's shores couldn't read.

"It lacks a seal," the sergeant decided. "You must come with us."

*Not bloody likely.* Still conserving his energy, Murdoch raised the wind just enough to blow off their useless but costly bicornes.

The youngest soldier chased the hats down the beach, while the older two pulled their sabers. With the rising wind, the surf slammed harder against the rock wall, wetting their boots.

"The tide is going out, gentlemen," Murdoch said in a tone of regret. "I do not have time to accompany you. I will be happy to obtain the proper seal when we return." He made a gallant bow, then righted himself—with rapier in hand.

The sergeant didn't have time to properly engage his weapon before Murdoch used his rapier point to strike the saber from his opponent's grasp, sending it flipping and twisting into the deeper water. "I regret the misunderstanding," he said in amusement.

That he was amused instead of furious was Lis's doing. How could he be angry or frustrated when he'd recently been granted all he could desire?

The remaining armed soldier raised his musket to his shoulder. Quelling a smirk, Murdoch nicked the man's wrist before he could lower the weapon into position. The soldier yelped and almost lost his grip.

Using his rapier as focus, Murdoch set fire to the musket's gunpowder. The ancient weapon blew apart, scorching the soldier's coat sleeve and tumbling him backward into the wall.

Even Lis couldn't complain that he'd revealed his gifts, he thought smugly. Muskets exploded all the time.

In the meantime, the weaponless soldiers wouldn't waste their lives by attacking an armed and skilled swordsman. As the third soldier returned at a run with the wind-tossed bicornes, Murdoch tipped the edge of his blade to his own hat in acknowledgment. "Until we meet again, gentlemen."

He splashed through the surf, vaulted back to the dock, and leapt across the growing gap to the ship's deck just as the wind he'd raised caught the canvas. It would be a race to see whether the ship escaped before the last two muskets were brought to bear.

"He's still hiding in the rocks," Lissandra murmured, appearing beside him as silently as a wisp of smoke, referring to the hidden Aelynner.

Murdoch dragged her back against the cabin wall, placing himself between her and the musket fire. He'd given the man every chance to leap on board. In his opinion, any Aelynner who was cowardly enough to fear these soldiers wasn't worth saving.

But Lis's concern touched a soft spot he hadn't known he harbored. He grimaced and extended his energy to heat the tide and cool the night air. As the sun burned orange and red and dipped into the water, Murdoch created a fine mist that swept over the shore, drenching the beach in early dusk, and providing concealment to any who might be slipping along the water's edge.

Despite the mist, the soldiers took aim at the bow where he and Lis stood.

His keen hearing caught a splash that wasn't surf. The sloop lurched to starboard, on the side away from land. The soldiers aiming their muskets noticed nothing unusual. Murdoch didn't know if Lis did.

As the first shot fired over the bow, Murdoch caught Lis's eye. She nodded, and together, they dived for cover while filling the sails with air.

Lissandra waited for Murdoch to comment on the feat they'd just accomplished. She was still astounded that they'd understood each other's needs and shared their strengths with such coordination.

Instead, Murdoch stalked grimly toward the small cabin below the mainmast.

The shots fired over the bow ceased as the ship slipped into the mist. The sun was already setting, obscuring the horizon.

"I'm not sure I like this world," she said aloud, just to disturb the walking thunderhead beside her.

"You don't belong in it," Murdoch agreed. "Trystan can take you home once we reach England."

"Once we find the sacred chalice," she corrected, reminding him of their mutual vision and goal. The shared dream of security and plenty just within their reach had to mean something—although she disliked the part where the chalice wouldn't let her touch it.

The reason for Murdoch's testiness rose from among the water barrels, soaked and dripping, interrupting any further disagreement. Murdoch must have heard the newcomer arrive. If he would not communicate, she must learn to read the blasted man's mind to grasp his moods.

"Monsieur, mademoiselle." Of average height but built sturdily, the intruder made a squishy bow. The lack of hat revealing his graying hair diluted the gallantry. "I fear I am a stowaway."

"You will be shark bait shortly if you endanger any of us." Murdoch caught the man by his elbow and dragged him into the cabin where their companions waited.

Lissandra knew from his mental shields that the stranger was the countryman they'd been seeking. But unlike Murdoch, she did not instantly assume that he was the village man who'd aided the committee. She had learned not to make hasty judgments. Besides, on the sea, neither she nor Murdoch had reason to fear him. He would, indeed, be shark bait if he caused harm.

She struggled to determine the stowaway's identity. On an island of only a few thousand people, she'd met them all at some time. But this one had made no impression on her memory.

She checked his ring in the pale light of the cabin's lantern and recognized the family crest. "A Minutor," she said cautiously. "I regret I do not recall your full name."

The newcomer bowed again and replied in their Aelynn language, "I go by Guillaume Badeaux these days. I have not seen our home since childhood."

Which would have been before her birth, if she judged his age correctly. How many other Aelynners of whom she knew nothing resided in the Other World? Had her mother left a list?

Their patient, Pierre, lay sprawled on the floor, his back resting against the wooden bulwark while Amelie helped bring a cup of water to his lips. Lissandra sensed that Pierre was perfectly capable of holding the cup but allowed his daughter to feel needed. She liked these two immensely and was glad Murdoch had rescued them.

The Minutor—alias Badeaux—she was less certain about. He gave off no clues to his character. A Minutor who never returned home was not unusual. Miners hated the sea.

"Why are you following us?" Murdoch demanded, kneeling to test Pierre's pulse.

"I only seek safe passage to England, monsieur," the stranger said with a Gallic shrug.

"Why would a Minutor be on the coast?" Murdoch turned an accusing glare on their countryman. "There is little mining in these regions."

There was little mining on Aelynn as well, which was why there were so few miners—Minutors. Lissandra knew very little about the family that had explored the island's volcano, expanded the caves and grottoes for public use, then migrated to other countries in search of gold and valuables of more use in the Other World than on Aelynn. Perhaps that was why she couldn't judge this man's guilt or innocence.

"We settled in Strasbourg, France, near the coal mines," Guillaume responded. "You understand, the sea, she is not good for us."

"Your kind are earthbound and don't sail," Murdoch said bluntly.

"We all do what we must," Guillaume said with stoicism. "I had wealth and thus have become suspect during these turbulent times." His face hardened momentarily before he forced it into a bland mask. "I returned from a business journey to discover the Tribunal had imprisoned my wife and family. They died of dysentery before I could rescue them."

He said the last in French so that Pierre could understand.

"I am so sorry," Lissandra murmured into the ensuing silence. "This is a harsh world."

Pierre murmured a Catholic prayer for lost souls, while Lissandra offered silent entreaties to Aelynn.

Murdoch, being Murdoch, glared at the stranger. "You will forgive me if we don't trust a man who does not come forward and greet his countrymen openly," he said with his usual bluntness. "Where have you been this past week?"

"Me, monsieur?" the miner asked in surprise. "Why, here, seeking transport from the mad place that was once my home."

Despite his expert shielding, Lis knew the miner was lying.

# Twenty-one

"You are an Olympus, the Oracle's daughter?" Badeaux came to stand beside her as Lissandra waited at the rail, searching the night-darkened horizon for thoughts and emotions that might reveal the location of sailors on distant ships. With no understanding of why he had lied earlier, she still could not convict the miner of wrongdoing.

She nodded at the man's assumption but did not reveal that her mother had died. She had to believe her mother's spirit was watching over her, and thus Dylys lived in her heart. To imagine otherwise would cripple her with sorrow.

"Then you have the power to right the wrongs of the Revolution," Badeaux said in an urgent whisper. "The radicals in Paris declare war on all the world. They will destroy Aelynn as they have destroyed my family and the best of France."

"We have no right to interfere in the Other World except to correct those mishaps that an Aelynner might have caused." She parroted her mother's assertion without mentioning her own doubts.

"That is insane," Badeaux responded harshly. "They are murdering innocent women and children. What could that poor shoemaker and his young child have done to justify their imprisonment? How can you witness such injustice and not act to stop it?"

"The leaders of France believe they are right," she said, reacting not to his anger but to his anguish, "just as the leaders of Aelynn believe in their way of doing things. Who is to argue which of us is better, smarter, or more capable? It is not my place to judge others."

"Then what is the purpose of an almighty Oracle if not to judge and rule?" he cried.

That was a question she often asked herself, but she had no answer.

As if they'd called his name, Murdoch appeared out of the darkness. "Does he disturb you?"

"No more so than my own thoughts do," she acknowledged. She supposed she ought to resent Murdoch's protectiveness. But just knowing that the madly independent, elusive Murdoch *wanted* to take care of her filled her empty heart. Still, he ought to be guiding the ship, not bothering with this damaged man. That was her task.

Despite her declaration, Murdoch deftly inserted himself between her and the miner, leaning against the rail and crossing his arms. "Tell me where you stayed this past week." Were it not for his hostile tone, the question could have been an innocuous pleasantry.

"I hid from the soldiers," the miner said, stepping back in puzzlement at Murdoch's tone.

"He is ill," Lissandra murmured to Murdoch. "His mental shields have somehow corrupted his mind. Let me work with him."

"I don't want him anywhere near you," Murdoch grumbled. "I can't watch out for you, the English, this ship, and him all at once."

Lissandra nearly laughed. "I thought divided attention was your specialty. Go; I'll be fine. A mere miner is no threat to me."

"Aelynners could lead an army and a navy!" Obsessed with his topic, Badeaux continued his argument as if they were listening to him. "We have Greek fire! I heard it was used not so long ago."

Lissandra raised an eyebrow at Murdoch. He was the one who had unleashed that horrifying formula for setting fire to water, and he'd nearly set Pouchay aflame because of his erratic inability to control the results. Trystan still held a grudge against him for that error.

"That was a mistake that will not be repeated," Murdoch said. "As Lissandra says, no one has invited us to be judges for their disputes. We can do no more than defend what's ours."

"What if the world asks you to help?" Badeaux demanded, balling his fists with rage at their refusal. "Can you allow a rebellious rabble to destroy entire civilizations?"

"The world does not know of our existence," Lissandra reminded him. "And it must remain that way. We are too few and our sacred treasures too important to risk." The loss of the precious chalice had proved the importance of keeping Aelynn untouched and unknown.

To Lis's surprise, Badeaux leapt past Murdoch to grab her arms and shake her. "You're an Olympus; you can tell the world! Go to London, pledge your allegiance, offer your aid!"

Before she could give thought to freeing herself from the grieving man's grip, Murdoch caught Badeaux by his neckcloth, lifted the burly miner from his feet, and held him out over the ship's railing and the lapping waves below.

"*Never* lay a hand on the lady," he said in an ominously detached voice.

But it wasn't Murdoch that terrified Badeaux. The miner struggled to right himself while staring in terror into the Channel's churning depths. "There are sharks down there!"

"And I'll feed you to them if you don't leave the lady alone." Although Murdoch strained to subdue his anger, his energy escaped to whip the sails with a gust of wind. Breakers crashed against the bow, causing the ship to lurch in a sudden towering swell.

This time it was Lissandra who laid a reassuring hand on Murdoch's shoulder. "Judge and executioner," she murmured. "Do you claim the right of Oracle?"

The wind calmed as suddenly as it had risen, and the waves flattened. With disgust, Murdoch returned his adversary's feet to the deck. "I will not have you sully her with Other World corruption."

"I meant nothing by it," Badeaux protested, raising his hands in surrender. "My grief overcomes me. I apologize."

"Stay away from the lady. Keep to the other side of the ship," Murdoch ordered. Gripping Lissandra's elbow, Murdoch practically dragged her toward the cabin.

"He is telling the truth," she argued in a whisper. "He is destroyed by his anguish."

"He's too polluted by the muddy views of Others to think as an Aelynner should. Until we have time to question—or Heal—him, stay in the cabin, where it's safe."

With exasperation, Lissandra shook off his grasp. "I thank you for your concern, but you will remember that I am not a vaporous lady who cringes at the sound of raised voices."

"He could have cast you overboard. Do you know if you can swim like a mermaid? You've lived too sheltered a life to know what you can or cannot do."

"True, but I would not have rocked the ship with my wrath either." Refusing to enter the cabin, she studied Murdoch's grim expression in the moonlight. "The wind stopped without causing harm. You seem to be gaining better control. Is it deliberate?"

He shoved his fingers through his hair in a gesture of frustration that she knew and loved. With everyone else, Murdoch simply acted, and not always with thought or consideration. With her, he was forced to pull back and think. She liked having that tiny bit of influence.

"Some of your restraint seems to be brushing off on me," was all he could say.

She raised her eyebrows in surprise, then, still refusing to enter the cabin, strolled around to the aft rail, admiring the stars. She glanced toward the wheel and saw that Murdoch had left one of the crew to steer the ship while the captain grabbed a nap.

"Would you at least get some rest?" he asked gruffly, following her.

"When you do. You must accept that I am as responsible for these people as you are."

Lissandra bit back a smile as Murdoch struggled with that observation. He'd always taken the weight of the world on his shoulders, believing he was the only one who could do anything the way it was meant to be done.

"You are half my size and like a reed in the wind!" he said. "You can't know what lies ahead or how it will test you. Give me some credit for my experience and greater strength."

"I do give you credit, but you must give me equal respect for my intelligence and the ability to know my limits."

"I'm reaching my limits now," he growled, hauling her into the shadows outside the cabin.

He did not give her time to respond but rubbed his scratchy jaw against her smooth cheek, then nibbled her ear while his hand aroused unspeakably pleasurable sensations in her breast.

Lissandra gasped and arched her neck to accommodate the erotic kisses trailing down to her nape and on to the hollow of her throat. He could have taken her right there, and she would not have objected. Could not.

"We must deal with this sometime," he muttered, pushing her breasts up with his hands and leaning down to kiss the curves rising above her bodice. "If you must apply your sharp wit anywhere, apply it to how we can survive with this constant craving."

"We will stay busy. We will think of others." She stifled another gasp as he nibbled at her nipples through her linen shift. She caught his shoulders and shoved him away.

He staggered back a half step and lifted his dark head to rest against her lighter one. His fingers still dug into her arms. "You make me feel like a slavering animal."

"I can't even summon my spirit guide while thinking of what we've done together. It's too embarrassing."

He laughed curtly. "You have no idea what I imagine doing to you when we are alone. How am I supposed to stay composed and think straight?"

"Are you saying we made a mistake?" she asked. "Should we have stayed apart?"

"No!" He relaxed his grip and stroked the bruise he'd created. "If we can't muddle through this, no one can. You say I must stay focused, so I will concentrate on one goal at a time. Reaching England safely comes first."

She took a deep breath, filling her lungs with good, clean salt air. "Then reclaim the wheel. There is a ship to starboard."

He released her instantly and ran for the foredeck to take over the steering.

The moon hid behind a bank of clouds. Lissandra lingered in the dark, calming her racing pulse by listening for clear thoughts among the distant emotions of hundreds of souls. The foreign ship was too far away to distinguish anything more than vague fears and hungers and boredom, the essential elements of humankind.

She leaned against the cabin wall and waited to see what Murdoch would do and how she might help. She did not fool herself into believing a domineering male would *ask* for her help. Giving him aid was something she must learn to do on her own.

Not that the obstinate man would appreciate it.

The unpredictable Channel winds flapped the canvas above her head. Since the small fishing vessel bore no running lights or flag, they would be identified as smugglers, if naught else.

Although she could not yet see the ship, their own craft was sailing right into its path. She could discern fleeting words, enough to know the crew was French. The frigate was no longer off their starboard bow but on a collision course with their midship deck.

The words that reached her now were not in someone's heart but shouted, carrying faintly over the night air. *"Ship to port!"* She could easily translate the French.

Despite the night and cloud cover, they'd been seen.

Closing her eyes and praying, Lissandra splayed her fingers against the walls of the wooden cabin to steady herself—

And realized they were sailing directly into the path of a second ship.

# Twenty-two

Standing at the helm, Murdoch sensed the second ship shortly after Lis did. He swore in three languages and with a few phrases he made up on his own. Two vessels at once! How large? What flag did the new one fly?

Had he possessed an Aelynn schooner, Murdoch could have sailed circles around both bulky vessels, but this fat fishing sloop had only one mast and little velocity.

At this wind speed, he had just minutes before they would be trapped between the two warships. Not possessing Aelynn hearing, his crew hadn't heard the faint warning cry from the frigate's crow's nest. They continued about their normal business.

If his men couldn't see either vessel, then the distance between them was too great for the cannoneers to target their tiny sloop. But sound carried at sea. If he started shouting commands to his three-man crew, the other vessels would pin down their location—preventing collision perhaps, but risking capture.

Murdoch groaned as Lissandra laid a hand on his shoulder. "Get inside," he said. "I don't have time for distractions."

"I know as much as you do about what is out there. I am not as adept at steering or raising sail, but I can pass on orders."

Despite his raging desire to wrap Lis in cotton batting and stow her safely in a barrel somewhere, the risk was higher without her aid.

"Fetch the mate, the man over there in a striped shirt." He nodded at the sailor at the jibboom, alert but unaware of impending disaster.

Traversing the bobbing deck as if she'd lived on a ship all her life, she obeyed his command without argument.

Needing to think of others instead of just himself hindered Murdoch's natural instinct to react swiftly. He had to plot and plan and calculate risks and results. By the time the first mate had taken the wheel from him, Murdoch's strained patience had raised the first drifts of fog and mist—which did not necessarily improve the situation.

The farthest ship was British; he could hear the crew more clearly now. They could be caught in the midst of a naval battle!

"Wake the captain," he ordered next, trusting Lis to obey before he strode off to give quiet orders to the rest of the crew.

He could sense the English vessel looming off their forward bow. From the sheer enormity of sensation bearing down on them, he had to assume it was a galleon. A galleon! Their tiny sloop could be no more than flotsam when viewed from the height of those decks.

A sliver of moonlight peeked from behind the clouds, illuminating the silhouette of the French frigate bearing down on them from the north.

Murdoch set the rest of the crew to hauling canvas to the course he'd set. Finally seeing their danger, they came alive, muttering curses. The French ship slowly came about, readying its cannon in preparation for ordering the sloop to present its colors. Neither his crew nor the frigate was aware of the galleon approaching. Maneuvering between the two enormous vessels without colliding, or one blowing up the other, might take more skill and concentration than Murdoch possessed.

He had stationed himself against the cabin wall to gather his energy and call on all his senses when Lis returned with the captain and awaited his next command.

In that moment, when his brilliantly relentless Lissy stood still without making a single suggestion, Murdoch was struck with the realization that she was *accustomed* to taking orders, that she'd obeyed her demanding mother all her life. No wonder she smacked him every time he tried to tell her what to do. In some ways, he'd been on his own since the day he was born. Lis had never been on her own and now struggled to learn how, and he wasn't helping.

It was a revelation and a dilemma he didn't have time to ponder. He commanded the captain to change course to the one he'd chosen, and when the man tried to argue, Murdoch used what little mind manipulation he could, along with the promise of an extra pearl.

Then he turned to Lis. "Can you keep our crew and passengers calm while I do what I must?" he asked as the small sloop rose and fell on the currents.

At least he hadn't raised a cyclone. Yet. His mind was too busy.

She didn't frown at his suggestion, although she had to know that whatever he intended could create a dangerously unpredictable situation. "I may need to touch the ones who panic."

He'd rather lash her to the mainmast than let her roam this fragile vessel while waves splashed a slippery deck. Murdoch ground his teeth and nodded, forcing himself to trust her instincts instead of telling her what

to do. Still, knowing her selflessness, he couldn't hold
back a warning. "Keep in mind, you are more valuable
than anyone else aboard."

Her clear blue eyes pierced him as if she would drill
through his skull and implant her opinion like a flag
bearer stakes his claim.

"We will see," she said, gliding off before he could
respond.

Cursing, Murdoch watched the crew change sail to
catch the direction of the wind he meant to create. Surprise would be his best strategy.

"Ahoy there!" came the cry they all feared. The French
frigate loomed to starboard, blocking the moon's light.
Cannoneers aimed their weapons. Armed soldiers stood
on a deck high above them, waiting for orders to shoot
if the sloop didn't drop anchor and trim sails.

Which Murdoch had no intention of doing.

Painfully aware of Lissandra slipping from man to
man, reassuring them, encouraging the captain to hold
tight to the inexplicable course he'd ordered, Murdoch braced his back against the cabin, spread his legs
to steady himself, then held his hands to his temples to
concentrate with more force than he'd ever applied before in his perilous life. He needed to change the wind's
direction, circle it from west-blowing—

A burst of fresh southerly wind billowed the sails of
the frigate. With its canvas set to heel into a westward
breeze, the French ship lurched in the sudden shift, its
heavy weight abruptly tilting northward, away from the
sloop. Surprised shouts and confusion filled the air as
soldiers slid backward and cannonballs rolled loose.

With their canvas already prepared to catch the wind
shift, the small sloop sailed into the frigate's shadow,
well to the north of the larger, slower galleon bearing

down on their forward bow. As Murdoch had planned, they now sailed the strait between the two vessels.

Muskets fired through their sails. Still unaware of the galleon's approach, the frigate's disorganized officers shouted furiously, directing cannon to new placements. Should the two great ships see each other . . . men would die, and the sloop would be caught in the cross fire.

"Lissy, get inside," Murdoch shouted as one wild cannonball overshot the bow and splashed into the water beyond them.

Damn it, that would alert the British!

Lis touched the elbow of the youngest sailor, who was giving off mental shrieks. The boy quieted. Then, to Murdoch's relief, Lis ducked inside the low cabin. He could feel her resting her hand against the wall behind him, as if to steady him. Amazing.

"Helm alee!" he shouted. Now that firing had ensued, he no longer cared if the French heard him. As the captain steered their dangerous course, catching the wind and speeding past the foundering frigate, Murdoch cried, "Galleon to port!" in a voice that thundered above the shouts of the frigate's officers and the explosion of gunpowder.

With the hell stench of sulfur, more cannonballs shot through the rigging, coming ever closer to splintering the deck. Murdoch didn't dare attempt to misdirect the balls for fear they'd crash through the sloop instead of into the water. If ever he needed to control his unpredictable abilities, it was now.

A fog might hide them, but it would also disguise the galleon bearing down on the frigate. Neither ship understood its danger yet.

"Galleon to port!" he thundered again, in clear French. Finally, he heard the cry picked up aboard the

frigate. He trusted that someone over there would recognize the peril of firing on a British man-of-war, even if
all they could discern was the galleon's running lights.

Another ball crashed through the railing before the
frigate's officers could halt their gunmen. The French
crew was already in the rigging, correcting its course for
the southerly wind. Straining with all his might, Murdoch
held the breeze steady, drawing on Lis's more reliable
energy. With care, he filled the sloop's sail long enough
to let it tack past the barricade, guiding it through the
rapidly narrowing gap.

The horror of his crew was palpable as the galleon's
menacing bow emerged through the mists. One strong
burst of wind in the wrong direction and they could be
crushed between the massive vessels.

The galleon's crew was too engaged in trying to correct its course to bother shooting at a fishing sloop. The
abrupt wind change had caught the crew by surprise as
much as it had the frigate's officers. Murdoch pressed
his temples and continued to hold steady, drawing on
the currents circulating in the air, keeping a chart in his
head of their position, attempting to navigate the water's natural current below them.

His head might explode if he lost even one bearing
and had to find it again.

Behind him, Lissandra calmly let her energy flow. He
feared sapping her, but he couldn't afford to reject any
offer of aid. Too many lives were at stake.

The instant the sloop slipped free of the galleon into
open water, Murdoch staggered and gladly dropped
his concentration, letting the wind and water return to
their normal courses. With canvas newly set to catch the
southerly current, the frigate lurched again with the new
wind change, widening the gap between the two battle-

ships. Still in the process of having its massive rigging reset, the galleon blew eastward, easily diverted from the collision.

With a slight tack of its limited canvas, the sloop steadily maintained its westward path, sliding into the Channel's fog and disappearing from the frigate's sight.

Temples throbbing, Murdoch slid down the wall, utterly depleted.

The crew didn't disguise their disgust when they dropped Murdoch in the cabin, thinking that their large gentleman passenger was frozen in fear. It had taken three of them to carry Murdoch's prone form out of harm's way.

"What's wrong with him?" Amelie asked worriedly, hovering near his hammock.

"Inflated self-importance," Lissandra answered with a smile. This time, she had a better understanding of the forces that ripped through Murdoch's powerful mind, so she did not worry quite so much. Energy depletion could be treated with time.

His erratic and volatile reactions were a different danger, but tonight he'd kept them under masterful control. She applied a soothing compress to his brow and began the task of pulling off his overlarge boots and stockings.

Apparently lost in his own surly thoughts, Badeaux guzzled ale to drown his grief, unaware of, or unconcerned by, the danger they'd just escaped. Pierre had comforted his daughter through the gunfire, but he was too weak to be of much further use. Amelie, on the other hand, was a ball of energy and willing to run in circles upon request.

"Did Monsieur LeDroit get shot?" she asked.

"Not that I can see. He has headaches. They are simi-

lar to what the ancient Greeks called *hemikrania*. He
will recover if we keep the room dark and quiet and let
him relax."

Lissandra had studied all the ancient medical texts
in Aelynn's vast library. She doubted any physician had
studied a man of Murdoch's unique abilities, but the
symptoms he suffered were similar to those described
in Greek treatises about migraines, although Murdoch's
seemed related to energy exertion and not noise or
light. She held her palm to the side of his head, felt the
fiery heat of his distended blood vessels, and carefully
applied her Healing energy.

Interfering with the brain was dangerous, she knew,
but the arteries had to be reduced to their normal size
before his agony would retreat. She feared too much
overexertion could burst a vessel and cripple his brilliant mind.

She would have the rest of the night and the next
day to ponder all the ramifications of an Oracle with a
crippled mind. No wonder he had resisted training. To
focus his energies inward as she and Ian did so naturally
caused Murdoch excruciating pain. As a child, he must
have learned to protect himself by diverting his energies
elsewhere. Anywhere. And no one had known to teach
him otherwise. Instead, he'd been condemned as an unreliable troublemaker.

She kissed his brow, placed her fingers at the pulse
point of his throat, and let him relax.

England—and the precious chalice—awaited them,
the magical chalice with the power to solve Aelynn's
problems, return Murdoch to his home, and—with the
will of the gods—raise him to the rank of Oracle. She
had no idea what pitfalls might lie in their path.

She did know that once they reached her brother's

home, if Trystan and Mariel still resided there, a battle of giants was inevitable.

Murdoch and Trystan had ever been rivals for her hand and for Council leadership. And Trystan had never forgiven Murdoch for unleashing the Greek fire that had nearly burned Trystan's ship and Mariel's home. The nature of Aelynn men would require a physical resolution.

The image of Trystan and Murdoch thundering the earth to throttle each other like two mighty gladiators fighting to the death gave her cold shudders—and made her doubt her wisdom in choosing this course of action.

# Twenty-three

Murdoch woke to a child's laughter and the scent of tropical flowers overriding the stench of fish and salt water. Feeling more peaceful than he could ever remember being, wondering whether he was dead, he almost allowed the rocking of the waves to lull him back to sleep.

The cry of "*Land ho!*" jerked him wide-awake.

Placing a hand to his head to verify it would stay on his neck, he threw his legs over the side of the hammock. Balancing precariously with his feet on the deck, he sat up.

Instantly, Lissandra was beside him, her skirt brushing his knee as she offered him a mug of coffee. He didn't dare meet her eyes until he'd swallowed half a cup of the thick brew.

Once assured he was in full possession of his faculties, afraid he looked as if he'd been afflicted with the wrath of the gods, he gazed ruefully into her smile. "I am not my best in the mornings."

She laughed, and her entire face brightened. It occurred to him that he could wake to the music of Lis's laughter more willingly than to the sun rising at dawn.

"It is late afternoon, and your captain is arguing with our Minutor over the safest port for landing."

Murdoch frowned, still not trusting the miner, but they were surrounded by water. Surely he could not cause trouble . . . yet. Murdoch preferred to enjoy Lis's laughter for now.

She looked like the angels he had seen in churches, blissful and innocent, although he knew that beatific look hid a sharp mind. He didn't deserve her admiration, but he would bask in it for as long as he was able. At least he had managed not to kill anyone last night. Not that he knew of.

"I ordered the captain to steer a course up Cornwall's west coast," he said. "How long was I out?"

"You've been unconscious all night and half the day, but I helped you sleep. It was not until they began arguing that I let you wake."

He rubbed his temple, felt no lingering pain, and nodded at her decision. "If this happens often, it could become awkward. I can't allow you to decide when to turn me on and off."

She laughed again. "If it were that easy, it would be most amusing to have you for a puppet. But you collapse of your own accord and wake when you wish. I just help you relax."

He rubbed his whiskered jaw and didn't let his relief show. "Fair enough. I still think we should feed our Minutor to the sharks."

"If we cannot prove him guilty of any crimes, we will have to free him. Do not take too long with your ablutions, please. Tempers are flaring."

Lis had left a washbasin of water, a comb, and bread and cheese on the tray along with the coffee. Murdoch made himself as presentable as he was able, grateful that their patients were taking the fresh sea air and had left him alone. The food and coffee revived him.

He didn't take time to shave. He needed to be on deck to guide the ship. Once they reached Bridgwater Bay, they would have to wait until high tide to slip into the mouth of the Parrett River. He and Ian had marked the channels two years ago when Ian had first bought his property. It took expert timing of the tides and knowledge of the currents over the mudflats to reach the place Murdoch had in mind. His keener senses would make him better at the job than the captain.

Once upon a time it must have been possible to sail right up to Glastonbury, but time and tide had changed that. Now flatland dotted with livestock filled the old bay. Still, Ian had chosen his estate wisely for Aelynn purposes. Their knowledge of tides and ability to See what Others could not would allow their swift ships to slip unnoticed up the nearly invisible waterways.

Pierre and Amelie greeted Murdoch as he strolled down the deck. Unaware of Murdoch's extraordinary role in running yesterday's blockade, the crew barely acknowledged his existence. He would have resented that when he was younger but now shrugged it off. He no longer required adulation.

For once, he felt easy inside his skin. If he turned his mind to the problems they faced, anger and frustration would knot him up inside, so he chose to enjoy the sun and the breeze and the brisk sail up the coast. The damned elusive chalice was a problem for another day. For now, he hoped they could reach the farmhouse tonight where he could have Lis to himself.

He kissed her cheek in view of all, claiming her as his own, and she didn't reject his assertion. With the wind billowing his shirtsleeves, he took over the wheel with the assurance of a man who had everything he wanted. For now.

*    *    *

Letting her hair blow back from her face, Lissandra admired the way Murdoch steered them through the murky waters of the estuary even though night had fallen and visibility was limited. Barefoot, unshaven, his queued hair blowing in the wind, he looked like a pirate. Wearing Trystan's breeches and the shirt she'd made for him, he commanded the wheel as if he had the world at his fingertips.

She opened her senses to the dark landscape. She heard the crew grumble that they would run ashore, that there was no wealthy port filled with food and women here, but she understood Murdoch's course. Ian had told her of the land he'd purchased in England, an estate where his wife's horses could run free, a haven the same distance north of Aelynn as Trystan's Breton home was to the south. From Aelynn, on swift Aelynn ships, they could reach either destination in a day.

Under Murdoch's uncanny guidance, the fishing sloop slid down an invisible river channel hidden by willows and reeds. Sleeping ducks and geese flew up in surprise. Small animals onshore splashed into the cover of water. Murdoch gestured for the anchor to be lowered even before she saw the dock.

The shoemaker limped up to stand beside her, puzzled at the silent English countryside. "Are we near London?"

"No, on the other side of the country, but I understand England is not so large a place as France. You may rest here with us until you are strong enough to make the journey. The fresh sea air will be better for your recovering lungs than the coal smoke of the city."

"We cannot take advantage of your extreme kindness any longer," he protested. "We owe you far too much already."

"You owe it to your daughter to be as healthy as you can be," she reminded him. "There is a town not far from my brother's home. Perhaps you might prefer the coast to London and whoever awaits you there. Take time to consider your choices."

Pierre did not know to shield his emotions from her, but Lissandra politely shut them out. She already knew he hoped to find relatives in London, that he wondered if the sloop might go there next. In that, she couldn't help him. He had to make his own decisions.

While Murdoch consulted with the crew, and paid the captain the remainder of the fare for their safe journey, Lissandra returned to the cabin to fetch her bag.

After all they'd been through, she longed for the familiarity of home. At the same time, her blood raced in expectation of the possibilities that lay ahead. She and Murdoch had shared the same dream of the chalice. Deep down in her heart, she prayed that meant the holy relic had accepted Aelynn's leader and was ready for the true Oracle to take it home.

But most of all, right this minute, she hoped there was a bed nearby that she and Murdoch could share. She'd had far too little time to experience the pleasures of their bodies, and knowing the uncertainty of the future, she considered wasted every hour they spent apart.

Responding to the tug of Lissandra's desire, Murdoch appeared silently at her side, and took the bag from her hand. "This is all Ian's land. He lets most of it to tenants. There is a tenant farmhouse on a slight rise not far from here. It is not much, but the couple who live there are accustomed to receiving late arrivals."

"What about our passengers?" she whispered. "Will the crew take them elsewhere?"

"I would like to truss up our Minutor and heave him

into the river, but I cannot in all good conscience do that. He's sticking to his story, claiming he traveled straight from his home to Pouchay and knows nothing of a priest or soldiers. He wants to get off now."

"It's possible," she murmured thoughtfully. "Or, since he does not reek of guilt, he may believe whatever he's done was in the cause of the justice he seeks."

Murdoch, who had sought justice in France, and in so doing had set fire to water and nearly killed Ian, knew how misguided the search for justice could become. Wounded creatures of any sort were inherently dangerous.

"We can watch the Minutor now that we recognize his shield. There are minerals in the distant hills, so we can hope he will leave us. As you say, I'm in no position to judge him. Our shoemaker has agreed to disembark also. Unless the farm couple already has guests, there will be room for all. In the morning, we can take other transportation to Ian's home."

Lissandra accepted the wisdom of his decisions.

At her silence, he hugged her close, and she leaned her head against his shoulder. The beat of her heart accelerated with expectation, and Murdoch chuckled and pressed a kiss to the top of her head. The intimacy of the gesture heated her all over.

"Soon," he murmured.

"Soon isn't fast enough," she whispered back.

But it would have to do. The crew assisted their passengers to land, eager to prepare for the turn of the tide rather than be stranded in mud. Frogs croaked in the reeds. Odd plops in the water spoke of nocturnal creatures going about their usual business. Lissandra sensed this was sacred land, blessed by the gods long ago, as mystical as the home she'd left behind but in ways she did not yet comprehend. Ian had chosen well.

The city dwellers stared up at the starlit sky and the Stygian countryside and huddled together on the newly constructed dock. Apparently frozen in his angry thoughts, Badeaux merely waited for direction.

"It's not far," Murdoch reassured the company. He led the way down a boardwalk built over water overhung with willows.

Lissandra lifted Amelie as if she were a toddler. The child clung to her neck and stared around her with wide-eyed wonder.

"Are there other children here?" she whispered. "Will they like me?"

The child's fears echoed Lissandra's own. "They will like you very much once you learn to speak English as they do. You will need to learn lots of new words."

"Papa studied English. He can teach me," Amelie replied proudly. "I already know 'How are you?' and 'I am fine.'" She parroted the phrases in English with a charming accent.

"That is excellent. I think you will like your new home."

Lissandra swallowed a lump in her throat and prayed she spoke the truth, for unless they found the chalice, Murdoch, like Ian, might end up living here, and she would have to sail home alone.

"I wish I understood the will of the gods in matching an amazing woman like you to a scoundrel like me," Murdoch murmured.

In the privacy of their farmhouse bedroom, he slid Lissandra's sleeve off her shoulder and pressed a warm kiss to the flesh he bared.

"You are not a scoundrel," Lissandra murmured, running her hands into his hair and releasing the tie that held it back. Every particle of her thrilled in expectation of these next minutes, hours, and she could barely think to speak the words. She flattened her hands against the solid muscle of his chest to feel his heart pound in tandem with hers. "The gods have given you handicaps to keep you humble."

"Now I am to be a *humble* Oracle? You ask the impossible." He laughed and pressed eager kisses to her throat. "I don't believe the gods have succeeded in teaching me humility."

"No, but there is always hope for the future." As her gown slid to the floor under Murdoch's capable hands, she wrapped her arms around his neck and let him carry her to the tidy bed in their attic room. Tomorrow, she would fear the future. Not tonight.

"You make a most imaginative priestess if you See a wretch like me as a holy man."

Below them, their company prayed and slept and worried. But for now, they did not need her attention, and for this brief reprieve from responsibility, she thanked Aelynn. "I only interpret as I've been taught."

"I would that we could do this in the temple. You deserve the blessings of the spirits," Murdoch murmured as he climbed in bed beside her, not releasing his grip on her until she was under him.

By the light of a single candle, she watched him tug his shirt over his head as he knelt over her. Shadows danced along the bronzed planes of his wide chest and the narrow line of curls that disappeared into the band of his trousers. She had seen him like this many times, and each time was new and even more exciting.

"Our time must come." She spoke her beliefs, not

her thoughts. If she had to think about it, hopelessness would wash over her. "For all we know, we will tire of each other."

Murdoch laughed. "Not in this lifetime." Propping his hands on either side of her head, he leaned over and plied her mouth with kisses as deep and fiery as the volcano of home.

She thrilled at the certainty of his pledge and surrendered to his lovemaking with all the joy she possessed. With Murdoch's confidence to shield her, she could be as free and irresponsible as she liked. If he stayed with her for long, he would have her dancing in the moonlight like a child again.

The rest of their clothing fell swiftly to the floor. The need was too strong in them to linger over loving caresses. Lissandra arched her hips into Murdoch's, demanding satisfaction when he suckled at her breast. He licked her nipple, and she nearly wrestled him to the bed to get what she wanted. She'd been patient much too long.

Laughing, he rolled over, placing her on top of him. "My queen, I am yours. Do with me as you will."

And she did. Without shyness or hesitation, she positioned herself over his erect phallus and sank down until she was filled to bursting. His groans of pleasure and desire urged her on.

When she did not move at the rate he desired, Murdoch rolled over again, thrusting deep and high as soon as her backside hit the sheet.

Even in their mating, they competed, but it was a wonderful competition, an encouragement to spread their wings and soar beyond their normal bounds. As she reached the heights, Lissandra dug her fingers into the sheets, clung to Murdoch's pumping hips with her legs, and let her spirit fly free. She closed her eyes at the wondrous liberation of their bodies exploding together. Stars spun behind her lids and the universe was hers for the taking.

In the climactic moment of release, she escaped outside herself and discovered her spirit guide waving with delight. A burst of gold dust showered from her guide's hand, and—

Liquid lightning seared her womb.

Inhaling sharply at the strange sensation, Lissandra tumbled back to earth, only to have Murdoch catch her in ethereal arms, slowing her fall. He stared at her with the same startled wonder she was experiencing as they floated into their bodies, firmly grounded on the mattress. She felt him inside her and out, knew the strength of his muscled arms, the potency of his maleness, the immensity of his spirit.

The tenderness in his midnight eyes brought her to tears.

Not until he kissed away the moisture running down her cheeks did she fully comprehend that she had returned to the real world.

And that a child now formed in her womb, a miracle child, one not conceived at the altar of the gods as expected—and yet powerful enough to make its presence known at the moment of conception.

# Twenty-four

The vision with which Lissandra had gifted him filled Murdoch with such joy and fear that he contemplated never moving again. Nevermore would he view sex as a mere physical release. It was a gift of the gods as surely as his ability to steer the wind.

A child? Had they actually created a child? Or had this just been a vision of the future? A future he scarcely dared hope to see.

"Your spirit guide has an unholy sense of humor," Murdoch grumbled, unable to shift from between Lissandra's legs, although he knew his heavy weight must be crushing her.

He was frozen between his own selfish elation and his fear that a child would force Lis to return to Aelynn—where he couldn't follow. Until that moment, he'd not allowed himself to think of the future and what it might bring. *He didn't want to lose Lis again.*

"Then I did not dream or imagine that." She lay there thoughtfully, not crying out in shock or protest over what had just happened. *Shouldn't* have happened, if all they'd been taught was right. Only after their union in the temple should they be blessed with a gifted child.

"We shared a dream before," he stupidly reminded

her, still groping for the sense of their shared vision, and too confused to believe in miracles.

The blood had not yet returned to his brain and was pooling stronger in his loins. He wanted Lis again. He leaned to one side so he could splay his hand over the silky softness of her flat abdomen. "A child is far beyond anything I dared dream. Can it be true?"

"Baby Murdoch." Her lips turned upward. "A miniature you."

"The gods forbid such a disaster," he said with feeling. Still, he swelled with pride that Lis did not regret the possibility of a son like him. "Rather hope for another you." Another Lis would be a blessing he could truly take delight in. He discovered a sudden overpowering desire for his child to live and breathe in his world, a child fashioned out of the best of both its parents.

An entirely new future widened before him, one he could no longer reject or ignore.

The immense responsibility of a child ought to be overwhelming, but chuckleheaded joy prevented him from seeing any dark side. He turned and ran his hand from Lis's abdomen to her breast and attempted to show her how he felt. "I ought to regret that I have placed the burden of a new life on you, but I know I can trust you to do what is best for it, and I'm proud to bursting that you will carry it for me."

Tears streaked her cheeks, and Murdoch ached in helplessness that he'd put them there, that he couldn't honestly reassure her that the future would be perfect. He kissed her softly, wrapped her in his arms when she sobbed, and did not mind when she fell asleep on his shoulder.

Now he had two precious treasures to guard. He was no longer a free man but chained to the mundane like all others. He tried not to panic at the possibility of failing them.

After years without any ties, he would need time to adjust to this new bond. Despite his brave words, he feared his heart was too hard and his spirit too calloused to open up and let in the light that Lis and a child would require.

Just as Lis had forced him to think about the future, he would have to *care* again.

"They're such beautiful creatures." Riding through the morning mist, Lissandra patted the proud neck of the bay mare they had found stabled at the farmhouse. She'd never ridden a horse before, but she'd found that connecting with the animal's mind was amazingly simple.

Ahead, the marsh flats spread as far as the eye could see. Willows dipped into rivulets. Egrets took flight in splashes of white. A humid breeze spread thin gray clouds overhead. This land had an exotic beauty all its own.

*I carry a child who will inherit the spirit of this land.* She shook her head in disbelief at the enormity of what they'd done. "I see why Ian has become so enamored of horses," she continued, rather than sink into silent contemplation as Murdoch had evidently done.

They'd made love again when they'd woken. The sexual bond between them was stronger than ever, but no longer as immediately demanding.

She was grateful for that. They would have burned to cinders quickly otherwise. She had observed enough to know that once a man achieved sexual satiation, he often turned his eyes to new territory to conquer, but she didn't sense this desire in Murdoch. She did, however, sense that the child had renewed his determination to shelter her as if she were fragile porcelain.

Which was why she had insisted on riding the mare rather than traveling in the cart with the others. Much as she enjoyed the feminine thrill of a man's attention, especially that of a warrior like Murdoch whose inner vision roamed so far that he could not see the nose on his face, she knew it was selfish to demand his attention when she was perfectly capable of caring for herself.

"Ian uses the speed of the animals to focus his Sight," Murdoch said gruffly, studying her seat and the harness for the hundredth time, as if they'd come loose if he did not. "I've seen him fly across these flats as if he would take wing."

And she'd left her brother trapped by duty on the island, unable to take solace in the open space of his new home. Ian was a saint among men who would look after Aelynn even better than she, but he needed freedom to enhance his gifts. She was being shamelessly selfish to stay here.

"Riding does not help you concentrate on your vision as it does Ian?" she inquired.

"No. My sword is the best element for focus I have found."

She understood his curtness. People avoided madmen waving swords in the streets. It made sense to live in a country at war, where his gifts could be better employed.

And it followed that he would never fit in on an island at peace. Was she horribly wrong about the gods' intent? "I have often wished I could point a sword at the Council and raise the roof over their heads to get their attention," she mused.

He sent her a look of disbelief at the path of her wayward thoughts. "They would probably run for their lives should you produce a sword." He returned her to more pragmatic matters. "That's the estate, up ahead." He nodded toward a rise of land.

They'd left the farm cart carrying their guests some distance behind. Lissandra had lost track of the miles from the coast to this inland country. She knew only that it took longer to arrive here than it did to traverse Aelynn from one side of the island to the other on foot. Horses made it possible to travel much longer distances.

She studied Ian's new home with equal parts wariness and eagerness. That her brother had found a place to live far from the shores of paradise was a matter of much wonder to her.

At first sight, she thought it a larger version of their island cottages. Whitewashed walls sprawled along the ridge, glistening in the sun. Instead of thatch, the roof had slate tiles, but that seemed sensible in this less tropical weather, as were the windows. At home, shutters were all they needed.

"Will Chantal's family be overwhelmed by so many guests when they are already entertaining Trystan and his family?" Lissandra asked.

"Chantal's sister-in-law, Pauline, is a Parisian who loves company. Her children and Trystan and Mariel's offspring will be delighted to have a new playmate. I believe Pauline's brother, the priest, remained in Ireland after the chalice escaped him. Mariel's family . . ." Murdoch shrugged eloquently. "They are plainspoken Bretons. The political arguments are intense."

"It's hard to imagine my brother living in such worldly company as Chantal's family, or in any company at all. He has ever preferred solitude."

"He has not been here since the arrival of Trystan

and his in-laws," Murdoch reminded her. "You will understand better why Ian chose this home once you know more of this area."

"It is a sacred place," she acknowledged. "I realized that as soon as we arrived. It was once an island, much as Aelynn is. The water is all around, even when it cannot be seen. The gods live here, although they have not been worshipped for a long time."

He shot her a look of appreciation. "I should never underestimate you. And I always do. Why is that?"

"Because I am female, and you are accustomed to thinking brute strength is all that matters. It was the same when we were children. I wanted to play with babies. You wanted to play with ships and swords. But without babies, there would be no ships or swords."

He let that sink in while they rode closer.

"I hope you do not resent that you must play with my baby," Murdoch said, intruding on her study of the house.

She heard his concern—for her. She wanted to wilt in relief that he understood her apprehension. "It is not what I anticipated," she murmured. "I'm both overjoyed and frightened. I must trust the gods' wisdom in believing I'm strong enough to bear the responsibility of a gifted child conceived without the altar, one with parents as willful as we are."

"I begin to think the gods are mad old goats who meddle where they shouldn't," he complained. His ring glowed brighter, and he turned the stone around to hide the light. "You have only just learned what it is to be on your own. Now you are weighed down with responsibility once again."

"My parents are dead. Ian wishes to live here." She gestured at the enormous manor. The gabled front had looked welcoming, but extending behind the modest front were long wings on either side. She was grateful the house had only two floors, but its size was still daunting. "That leaves the safekeeping of an entire island to me. I don't think one babe will add significantly to that burden. In fact, having a child to love will give me more to live for."

The knowledge that she needed a spouse with whom to share her burdens loomed between them. Murdoch still had insufficient control of his destructive gifts to be confined to a peaceful island—a dilemma neither of them had yet solved.

"The garden is lovely," Lissandra exclaimed in surprise as a glimpse of a rose-strewn wall came into view, diverting her attention.

And that was where they left the matter, because along with the garden, the couple occupying it appeared.

Despite her awareness of the simmering animosity between Trystan and Murdoch, Lissandra wasn't prepared for the swiftness of their reactions. Within seconds of seeing each other, they were standing in the rose garden, weapons drawn, muscles flexing. And she hadn't even figured out how to dismount! Trystan seemed bent on cutting her off from Murdoch, and Murdoch seemed intent on cutting Trystan off at the knees in self-defense.

Surely Trystan did not think Murdoch had harmed her? She ought to clout him for his presumption.

She glanced at Mariel for aid, but the Breton mermaid merely rested her hand on her expanded waistline and watched the impending battle with interest. Since Lissandra had always fostered an Olympic attitude of omnipotence, Mariel had no idea that a would-be Oracle couldn't do anything that she wanted. Perhaps that omnipotent image was another facet of her life that must change now that she was not expected to be Oracle.

"You must be mad to bring Lissandra here," Trystan stated, holding his saber in both hands and prepared to strike the instant Murdoch did. "Did you think to hold her for ransom?"

Aware of the farm cart rapidly approaching with Other Worlders who did not understand Aelynn ways, Lissandra sighed with impatience. Trystan was too arrogant to entirely close his mind to her. She'd never taken advantage of his insolence in the past, but this time, she mentally swatted him. *Hard.*

"Stop that," she demanded so he knew with whom she was dealing.

Startled, the golden giant almost dropped his sword but didn't dare swerve to face her while he had Murdoch in his sights. "You do not understand his menace," Trystan protested. "He is safe only when bound in chains."

At ease in billowing shirtsleeves and loose trousers, Murdoch snorted and produced his rapier. With a weapon in each hand, he was beyond formidable. Broader and taller than Murdoch, Trystan was hampered by his formal frock coat and tight doeskin breeches. As usual, Murdoch did not speak his thoughts, but began circling his opponent, searching for a weak spot.

Which meant Lissandra had to speak for him. She ought to swat him as well, but she knew she'd only distract him into a mocking smile, which would no doubt infuriate Trystan further. *Men!*

"There is a reason I dislike being a leader," she complained, searching for a bench or something of equal height to help her dismount. "I cannot reason with male absurdity. You know perfectly well that if I wanted Murdoch in chains, he would be in chains. It would be so much simpler if I could just pull a sword and give each of you a sample of your own foolishness."

With a nod, Mariel indicated a stepping block. "It's equally easy and more amusing to watch them hack off each other's heads, as Chantal so politely says. Will they have the sense to stop before then?"

"In this case, most likely, no." Lissandra unwrapped the skirt of her island attire from the saddle and stepped down just as the farm cart pulled up to the gate. The driver hastily halted his mule at sight of the confrontation in the garden.

Now that Lissandra had moved out of their path, the two men began testing each other. Their weapons flashed in the sunlight with each graceful movement. In moments, they would spin them faster than the Other World eye could see—and their audience would faint dead away.

"Trystan may be larger, but he is a diplomat, not a warrior, so he will most likely fare worst," Lissandra reminded her hostess. "I recommend that you call him off while I take Murdoch down."

At her cool assessment and improbable solution, Lissandra sensed the startlement of everyone from Mariel and their onlookers to the two combatants. With the advantage of surprise, and for the benefit of their non-Aelynn guests, she strode with regal authority and no hesitation between the two large oafs and their swinging swords.

When they had no choice except to stop, she kicked Murdoch's shin, mentally swatted him, then gave him a shove backward into the yews. Caught unprepared, he yelped in surprise—but not for long. From the depths of the greenery, he grinned back at her so widely that Lissandra had to stop herself from swiping his sword and pounding him into the ground with it.

Behind her, Mariel sensibly launched her clumsy weight into her husband's long arms, forcing Trystan to drop his weapon to catch her.

"I like this diversion," Mariel cried, clinging to her husband's neck so he couldn't set her aside. "Can we do it again?"

# Twenty-five

Murdoch set his tiny teacup on the delicate table beside his equally frail chair and glared at his empty palms, trying to figure out what to do with them while the women chatted and the chalice awaited. He needed to be doing something—like challenging a still-simmering Trystan.

He was fully confident that he could defeat Trystan in battle. He had done so before and had more experience now; meanwhile Trystan had been living the peaceful life of diplomacy.

What Murdoch doubted was his own patience to deal with the protocol of forcing Trystan to see that— impossible as it might seem—the Oracle's daughter had chosen him for a mate, even though he was the most unsuitable man in the known universe.

Life was much simpler when its challenges were met with the sharp edge of a blade.

Crushing china didn't seem practical, but if he let his tension build, he might shatter the entire table. Or set fire to the draperies. He needed *action*. Although the confounded tight breeches and frock coat he'd been forced to wear for this charade didn't allow for much movement.

Following Lis's example, he'd left the subject of the

chalice unspoken. Trystan and Mariel possessed few
Finding abilities. Their gifts for protecting the island
were too valuable to risk either of them on what could
easily be a dangerous mission. So everyone sat about
sipping tea as if he and Lis were here for a mere social call. Murdoch clenched his teeth, nearly crushed the
delicate cup in his big hand, and tried to ignore Trystan's
glare.

"Your Parisian shoemaker would fare better in London where the crazed *ton* are desperate for the latest
French fashions," Mariel said over the tea table.

Even Murdoch could see that pregnancy suited his
hostess. She possessed the complacent beauty of a Ma-
donna, which made him even more uncomfortable.
Would Lis look like that in another few months? Would
he even be by her side to watch her grow round with his
child? He didn't know whether to look proudly at Lis
the way Trystan looked at his wife, or pretend he was
his usual surly self. Hell, he didn't know himself at all
these days.

Pauline, Chantal's sister-in-law and their émigré hostess in the absence of Ian and Chantal, had taken their
guests in hand, showing them to bedchambers where
they could freshen or change their clothing, and had
introduced Amelie to the nursery crowd. As an Other
Worlder, Pauline had no interest in this discussion. Or
nondiscussion. She'd not returned to entertain them but
apparently joined Mariel's Other World sister, Francine,
in more prosaic household tasks.

Lis sipped from her cup as if she'd done so all her
life. "Pierre's lungs need to fully heal before he travels
again. I don't think he will accept our charity much longer, however. He would prefer to be useful. Is there a
town nearby?"

"Glastonbury is not far. It's little more than a village, though." Refusing to sit, Trystan paced the far end of the room in front of the cold fireplace.

Lissandra outranked all of them. If she chose to discuss her Other World patient rather than why they had come here, they must all natter aimlessly. Murdoch thought he might explode.

Perhaps he could focus on shattering the crystal candelabra. If he narrowed his eyes, placed his hands on his knees, and pointed his fingers in the direction of the dangling crystal . . .

The prisms started to chatter. Across the room, Lissandra cast him a mocking look. The damned woman was daring him to behave and keep his excess energy under control.

Murdoch rose abruptly from the bent-legged chair. "Why don't I take our shoemaker and Minutor into town while the three of you catch up on your gossip?" He didn't bother hiding his sarcasm. They all knew he had no more place in this proper drawing room than he did on Aelynn. He belonged on a battlefield, where killing was necessary. His borrowed cravat was about to choke him.

"I don't think you'll find the chalice without me," Lissandra said complacently, returning her gaze to a book Mariel had been showing her.

Trystan stopped pacing. Mariel nearly dropped the book in surprise at this casual mention of the holy relic that had been lost years ago—and the suggestion that the renegade and the Oracle's daughter would be working together to retrieve it.

Murdoch almost laughed. His Lis had blasted the conversation wide-open without need of his assistance. Their hosts stared at her as if she'd lost her mind; then they turned warily to him.

Trystan's eyes narrowed first as he brilliantly recognized the unnatural affinity between the outcast and the Oracle's daughter. Murdoch offered a sardonic smile, daring the Guardian to ask if he and Lis were sharing a bed. He could not brag, "The lady is mine," since he had no legal claim to her. But men understood these things.

Trystan's big hands balled into fists.

"Prepare to fling yourself at your husband, please," Lis warned Mariel, still without looking up. "Even if I am not anointed Oracle, I'm free to do as I please. It's difficult enough to teach that to Murdoch. I'd rather not have to force our arrogant Guardian to accept it as well."

Murdoch did not relax his defenses until Mariel considered all that had not been said, then smiled up at her giant of a husband. "I don't think Ian would appreciate having his lovely home wrecked by two territorial curs with no homes of their own. Sit down. I'm sure Lissandra will explain in her own time, in her own way."

Since the Oracle's daughter wasn't accustomed to explaining herself at all, and was currently displaying the unruffled detachment she'd learned at her mother's knee, Murdoch doubted that, but he wouldn't be the one to correct his hostess. "It will be easier for all if I am not here while you talk. Let me take our guests into town."

He couldn't believe he was even asking. He ought to simply walk out and do as he thought best, as he'd always done.

But what he'd always done hadn't worked out well. So he stood there stupidly waiting for approval. The crystals still chattered, but at least he hadn't rumbled the foundations. Yet.

Lis's lips turned up and her eyes sparkled as she finally regarded him over the top of the book. "It will get easier, I promise," she said, as if she'd read his mind.

Or his emotions. His Lissy was astonishingly good at that, even when she seemed not to notice anything at all. She understood him too well, as he did her. The knowledge that others didn't recognize the passionate nature beneath Lis's apparent indifference eased his irascible temper.

Trystan and Mariel glanced back and forth between them with the appalled fascination with which one watches a shipwreck. The unpredictable warrior banished from Aelynn and the dutiful daughter who would never desert her home did not appear to be the best of matches.

"I am trying to be civilized," Murdoch reminded his gloating mate. "I have yet to punch Trystan in the nose, although he's crying out for it."

"And I appreciate how hard you are trying," Lis conceded. "But you do it for my sake and not for anyone else. So if you take our guests into town without me, I fear you'll revert to your normal behavior and thwack Guillaume against a tree."

"What if Trystan and I both take our guests into town and thwack our Minutor against a tree?" Murdoch suggested hopefully.

Mariel burst out laughing.

Even Trystan's mouth twitched.

For a very brief moment, Murdoch almost enjoyed himself. If he didn't think of the burdens being heaped on his head, he might conceivably learn some form of polite behavior.

"Did you consider that the gods may have sent us an Aelynner with earth skills, who is knowledgeable in tunnels and mines, for a purpose?" Lis suggested before Murdoch could raise another objection.

He glared at her. "You are too damned perceptive and willing to be reasonable." He grabbed a tiny sandwich off the tray and began pacing in front of the floor-to-ceiling windows.

"I appreciate your prevention of brawls in the salon and thwacking of guests against trees," Mariel said to Lissandra with a giggle, "but I think you need to explain what this is about. You have evidently harnessed a wild stallion, but I fear he will rip through your bridle soon."

"Murdoch has somehow convinced Lissandra that they can find the Chalice of Plenty," Trystan surmised, stopping his pacing to take a seat next to his wife on the silk settee.

Mariel's giggles dissolved into a worried frown. It was she who had first set the chalice free upon the world, and her guilt fretted her. At the time, she had thought it no more than an ugly bauble she could sell to feed her family. Since then, Ian had decided the chalice had chosen Mariel, and not the other way around, but the deterioration of Aelynn since the chalice's loss could not be easily dismissed.

Murdoch hastened to reassure her. "The Chalice of Plenty has its own purpose here. It has provided for Aelynn for centuries, and we must trust it continues to do so now, although not in the normal manner, since these times are not normal."

Lis's eyes widened. "That's true. It last escaped during the plague in Europe, well over a hundred years ago. At the time, our sailors chased it through ports that had no disease, thus preventing them from bringing the epidemic home."

"If we had annals of that time, we might also note that the chalice found amacara matches with Healers or others who helped stem the disease in some manner." Murdoch shrugged in response to their stares. "It seems to bring unusual people together, does it not?"

Since Trystan and Mariel had been brought together because of the cup, and two people with more different backgrounds could not be found, they had to agree. The same was true of Ian and Chantal. Murdoch and Lis had similar backgrounds, perhaps, but they were still oceans apart in everything else. Yet they were finally together, at least partly because of the chalice.

"Ian lived here for two years, searching for the blasted thing," Trystan reminded them. "If he couldn't find it, what makes you think you can?"

Murdoch waited for Lis to explain. Provokingly, she watched him in anticipation, as if he had the words to clarify without revealing the lovemaking that had produced their mutual vision. Fine Oracle he'd make when he couldn't explain something so elemental.

"We've both Seen the chalice," he finally said. "In the same place, a tunnel beneath the earth, on a pagan altar."

"Glastonbury Tor," Trystan and Mariel guessed at once.

Lis looked questioningly at Murdoch.

"The tor is the site of several ancient temples," he told her. "The hill beneath it is said to be riddled with tunnels, perhaps leading to more altars of the old gods."

"And if Aelynn and the pure of heart like Chantal are able to shield the chalice's vibrations from our Finding senses, then a sacred altar might do the same?" Lis asked, comprehending immediately.

"Exactly, although how the chalice got there, we may never know," Murdoch said, hoping she would let him escape this stifling parlor and ride to the tor to start the search.

Lis smiled in delight. "Then the chalice may be waiting for our next Oracle to take it home, rather like Arthur and the sword in the tales of old."

For a conversation stopper, that had to rank right up there with "The world is on fire."

"Oracle?" Trystan shouted. "You're saying *Murdoch* is the Oracle? Devil take it, Lissandra, I knew we should have bound and gagged you when you insisted on getting off the ship in France, but if I'd had any idea it was this renegade you were seeking . . ."

Murdoch sank down on a long sofa, swung his legs over the arm, covered his eyes with his coat sleeve, and waited for the roof to collapse and smother him. This argument could last well into the night, and he didn't think he had the patience to hold back his energy much longer.

Lissandra watched from the window of her darkened bedchamber as Murdoch and Trystan slashed at each other with rapiers in the lantern-lit courtyard. Dueling was the manner in which Aelynn men had released their irritation and settled their disputes for centuries.

She no longer sensed hostility from either man. Trystan and Mariel were highly doubtful but willing to consider her theory that Murdoch was the next Oracle. And their acceptance of what Murdoch couldn't believe had exacerbated his frustration. His energy simply needed to be released in some controlled activity.

Which was why he was out there now, attacking Trystan with great zeal. Trystan would no more harm a possible Oracle than he would harm her. Which must be frustrating Murdoch even more as Trystan defended himself but refused to fight back.

How could such a volatile man also be the steadfast, reasonable Oracle the island needed? Simply stifling his excess energy wasn't sufficient, which was what Murdoch was trying to tell her with this exhibition.

The men had stripped to loose trousers and fought in bare torsos and feet, as they often did at home. Blades whirled with uncanny speed, halting only when one caught the other and sought leverage. Trystan was a big man, heavily muscled through the chest and shoulders. Murdoch was lean and strong, like a fine-honed dirk. Both were deadly.

The combatants had worked up a glistening sweat, but Lissandra suspected most of their energy was consumed in not killing each other. A dozen times Murdoch had leapt backward to prevent his blade from slipping under Trystan's guard and nicking flesh. She hoped their Other World guests weren't watching.

Even though the shoemaker and his daughter weren't Aelynners, her concern for them was as strong as if they were. In some way, she understood that saving these two courageous innocents had redeemed Murdoch's soul. They deserved the best care she could provide. Badeaux, on the other hand—she glanced at far windows, sensing him nearby—could not be denied her aid simply because she didn't trust him.

Murdoch, of course, didn't agree that she should be here at all, much less tending Others. They would always disagree on many subjects. The puzzle was how to deal with their disagreements. She couldn't physically battle him as Trystan did now. She didn't have any authority that he would respect. The solution required patience and understanding and *communication*, not virtues either of them possessed in great quantity.

But they had other virtues that might work as well, if applied correctly. Smiling with mischief, Lissandra let her lusty admiration of Murdoch's physical grace flow into the universe. The connection between them was instantaneous.

Sculpted chest heaving, Murdoch focused his attention upward, causing Trystan's rapier to nearly pierce his ear. With an abrupt twist, Trystan withdrew his thrust, then followed Murdoch's gaze, and let his sword arm fall to his side.

Discovering where his opponent's attention had wandered, Trystan grinned, saluted Lissandra with his weapon, and sauntered off.

Heeding her desire, Murdoch lowered his weapons, strode across the courtyard, and took the steps two at a time. She had no illusion that he would come directly to her, though. He would find the bath first. He would always do what he thought best, regardless of her opinion. That was how the gods had made him, and she couldn't undo it, nor did she want to. The best she could hope to do was persuade him to see her side.

To that purpose, Lissandra left her room for the bathing chamber below.

They *communicated* much better when enthralled by lust, and possessed far more patience and understanding in the languor of satiation.

She could think of no better way of insisting that he take her down into the tunnels with him.

# Twenty-six

The next morning, Murdoch rode beside the open-air carriage carrying Lis and their guests. He still wasn't entirely certain how he'd been talked into this expedition, if *talked* was the correct word. He and Lis hadn't discussed much last night in the tub. He'd turn into a sybarite if she plied her wiles any more thoroughly, and right now, he was so physically satisfied that he might let her.

He could not afford such luxury, and neither could she. They were not ordinary people, and they could not expect ordinary lives. It was foolishness even to consider it, so he turned his attention back to the task at hand—riding into Glastonbury in hopes of finding the chalice.

Amelie bounced up and down in the carriage, pointing out cows and sheep and repeating the English words for everything she saw. Her time in the nursery with the other children had been well spent.

Guillaume the Minutor scanned the flat lowlands through narrowed eyes. The hill of Glastonbury Tor rising above the fields in the distance seemed to have caught his interest. Like all Aelynners, he could not speak of their home in front of Other Worlders, but the tor bore some resemblance to Aelynn's volcano. Except the volcano had never been terraced all the way to the top, as this hill must once have been, if the paths circling upward were any indication. And Aelynn possessed no imposing stone tower to cap the peak as this one did.

Murdoch studied the grassy ridges circling the tor's side, and felt the pull of the earth. The hill hid secrets.

Not as comfortable with horses as he was with ships, Trystan rode an older gelding on the far side of the carriage, acting as tour guide, although he'd been here for only a few weeks. Suffering morning sickness, Mariel had stayed home. Murdoch missed the comfortable barrier she provided between him and her Guardian husband.

But so far, despite his tension, he hadn't lost his temper, shaken any hills, or set any fires. He probably had Lis's calming effect to thank for that. She could easily set him to vibrating with rage, but in his desire to protect her, her presence always forced him to think first and act second. An interesting concept for a warrior who'd been trained otherwise.

"There are not many people here," Pierre said in disappointment.

A fact for which Murdoch was grateful, but he could see the man's point. "Villagers need shoes as much as city dwellers do. If they have no shoemaker, then they need you more than a city filled with shoemakers."

"Boots are important here," Trystan said helpfully. "Can you make boots?"

"Of course, but it takes leather, and that is expensive."

"They have a tannery," Trystan informed him. "Perhaps a deal could be worked out."

Murdoch left them to discuss the practicalities of commerce while he studied the fascinating tor looming hundreds of feet above the village. His earth skills could not compare with a Minutor's. He did not know one ore from another. But he sensed the limestone waterways channeling through the ground. He could not sense the chalice, but if the dream spoke truth, it sat on an altar that might conceal its vibrations.

If the chalice was there.

If the chalice wasn't there, then Murdoch's one feeble hope of keeping Lis was lost.

He'd have to return to France and hope he could find some means of leading the French out of their bloody pursuits before they destroyed half of Europe.

After four years, he no longer possessed the arrogance to think he could do so alone.

That should bother him, but he hoped it meant he'd gained some wisdom. Much to his chagrin, he was starting to realize he needed the aid of others like him to channel his energy.

He wouldn't have that aid if he lost Lissandra and his home.

With that burden eating at his heart, Murdoch scanned the village as they entered it, and looked for some means of discarding his traveling companions so he could explore the tor and learn its dangers before deciding on a course of action. If he'd learned anything from experience, it was that nothing worth having could be had easily. He did not delude himself into believing the chalice would fall miraculously into his hands.

The carriage halted in front of a tavern. Trystan politely dismounted to help Lis out of the vehicle while Murdoch let his horse prance in the street.

"I want to explore the land," he said, backing the horse away from the company.

Guillaume the Minutor scowled. "There is no gold, or even coal, in yon hill. The land is worthless. But I'd like to see more of those hills to the north. The view would be better from the top of the tor."

"Another time," Trystan said smoothly. "Amelie is too young for such a walk. Perhaps you would be interested in the ancient abbey? The buildings are mostly destroyed, but the grounds are just down the street."

Despite Lis's suggestion that the Minutor might be of help in their search, Murdoch preferred leaving him behind. He mentally tipped his hat to Trystan for keeping the scoundrel in hand. He couldn't physically tip it, since he'd not found a hat to suit him in Ian's meager wardrobe. After years of brightly colored uniforms and gold braid, he considered the dull brown frock coat he'd borrowed far too ascetic to alleviate the annoyance of its confinement.

Lissandra wore her Aelynn clothing under a cloak suitable for this cooler British climate. The morning mist saturated cloth and hair alike. Without the mantle, she'd be soaked and nearly naked. Murdoch hugged that image to himself.

Feeling the tug of his lust, she glowered at him, and he grinned back. He made a gesture to indicate that he was leaving. He threw up a mind shield to prevent her from knocking him from his horse with a mental blow of retaliation. Beneath her glacial exterior, his Lis had a temper as fiery as his.

He would not risk her health and well-being and that of his child. *His child.* May the heavens preserve him. He'd never once thought of himself as a father.

After bowing his farewell, he steered his horse down the street past the abbey, following the magnetic draw of the earth ahead. The power in this place was incredible, possibly even more so than on Aelynn. He and Ian had toured the tor with fascination when they'd first arrived here two years ago. He knew where to find the lane that would lead him to the top. He knew how to find the Chalice Well at the bottom. The old name rang prophetic.

He didn't know how the chalice could have arrived here. In his previous search, he'd learned that the priest who'd carried the chalice from France had donated it to a university in Ireland in exchange for a position on the staff, and the school had passed it on to a cathedral in Dublin, where it had disappeared. At that point, Murdoch had abandoned the fruitless search. It was evident to him that the sacred object had a will of its own, and that will was rejecting him. So he'd returned to France, assuming Ian or Chantal was more apt to locate a holy relic than he was. Shortly thereafter, the chalice had vanished from their Finding abilities entirely.

What, by all that was sane, made him think he could uncover it now?

He'd barely reached the Chalice Well at the foot of the tor when he heard the beat of horse's hooves behind him. He knew who followed without need of opening his mind.

Stoically, Murdoch turned his mount to wait for Lis to catch up. She'd bound her hair in ribbons and braids, and they streamed behind her, catching the mist with the ethereal sparkle of a fairy crown. Trystan had evidently surrendered his horse to her command. It was Murdoch's own fault for showing her how simple it was to ride the animals.

"You know the history here?" she demanded the moment she was within hearing.

"I do." And he hadn't been about to inform her and excite her more. Curse Trystan or Mariel for relating the stories about Glastonbury and the Holy Grail. Some

believed the Christian tales of Joseph of Arimathea
burying the chalice from the Last Supper—the Holy
Grail—in Glastonbury. Others believed that the Arthurian legends of Merlin and the king-making sword in the
stone were connected to this primitive place of worship.
And those were just the more recent tales.

Murdoch swung his horse back to look past the well
to the mysterious hill rising above them. It was difficult
to see the terracing through the trees and hedgerows
from this angle, but he'd walked them. They resembled
a giant labyrinth spiraling up the sides of the hill.

"The Chalice of Plenty could have *originated* here!"
Lis kicked her mount over to a fallen stone that may
have once marked the entrance to the spiritual labyrinth
ringing the hill. "Perhaps it has come home."

"That's one theory," Murdoch replied noncommittally.
"Legends of golden giants walking the earth, preaching
of the stars, and teaching healing can be heard in many
places. That does not mean that they were our ancestors any more than it means they are ghosts or fairies or
saints, or that they actually carried sacred vessels."

They both knew he lied. They were as bound to this
earth as they were to each other. He understood entirely
why Ian had chosen to settle here. Ian's astral power
would be enhanced here, and he would feel closer to the
gods he worshipped.

Murdoch's earth gifts were darker and more connected to Brittany, but they were not so different. He
wished their ancestors had kept better records. Ancient
Aelynners may have collected a voluminous library of
scientific texts, but their skills had always been of a practical nature, aimed at survival and guarding their treasures. Storytelling accomplished neither.

"If the tales are true, then the chalice has wandered

frequently," Lis argued. "It's also a part of Other World religion, as my mother told us. I believe our gods are similar to the Christian saints and their God, just differently named. What if the chalice is meant to stay here?"

"I have no idea what that will mean to Aelynn," he said curtly.

He had an excellent idea what that would mean to him. He couldn't even dream of going home without it.

Lissandra gazed up at the magnificent tor. The hill radiated a different energy from Aelynn's. Until recently, the volcano had always been peaceful and reassuringly solid, but the tor was not peaceful. It slumbered, perhaps, but even so, it breathed with mysterious vibrations that hummed beneath the soles of her feet as they circled the base of the hill. The tor was alive.

"These stones don't belong in this spot," Murdoch concluded, examining what might have been a fallen dolmen similar to those of the island's temple. "Someone has deliberately carried them here."

The lane they were wandering down was shaded and overgrown with shrubs and trees that Lissandra could not identify, but she knelt to examine a thriving bed of Saint-John's-wort. "We have these herbs on Aelynn. I have seen thyme and milkwort as well. Might the stones conceal a portal carved by our ancestors?"

"My thought exactly. Although there is nothing under this one. But perhaps we're close. Let me See."

She watched in awe and fascination as Murdoch stood so still that he seemed to take root, like the oak she knelt beneath. In his plain brown frock coat, doeskin breeches, and tall boots, his dark hair neatly queued at his nape, he appeared like any other man in this country, yet unnatural energy poured from him, sinking deep into the earth as surely as the roots of the oak.

Abruptly, he pulled from his trance to sit down on one of the stones and tug at the boots he'd borrowed from Ian's wardrobe. "They interfere," he said curtly at her questioning glance. "All this flummery keeps me from feeling the air and the earth as well as I should."

She understood. They were never so close to the earth as when undressed and in each other's arms. The hampering clothing prevented their connection to nature as much as it prevented them from feeling the caress of each other's hands. They needed the mist touching their skin and the soft soil rubbing their toes.

She helped him tug off the boots and stockings. She caressed the bottom of his feet, and he shivered, tensing with the bond between them. The air throbbed with expectation.

"Keep touching me," he muttered through clenched teeth, staring into the clouds. "I can feel more. I think I can feel the entire universe."

As they would if they shared the temple bed together.

Remaining seated, Murdoch planted his soles firmly on the soil, and she ran her fingers over his long, shapely feet, circled one strong ankle with both hands, rode her palm up his calf and shin. He shuddered along with the earth.

"Close, we're close," he whispered, his voice no more than the wind in the trees. "I feel water draining from the core, through the rock. The chalice is there, where the springs rise."

Spellbound, Lissandra listened and memorized his words as his spirit guide took him deeper into the bowels of the earth. She'd never seen Murdoch go into a trance. He looked more omniscient Oracle than human as his harsh features settled into serenity. The sun glowed from within and without. His eyes were shuttered by long lashes, and the breeze blew around his head, swirling his hair in loose tendrils.

Like a warrior of old, he should be naked to the sun. She clung to his bare leg, willing him to find the focus that so eluded him, praying her energy could somehow guide his.

"The chalice resists me," he said in sorrow, as if from a dream. "I am not strong enough for it. Danger! There is menace all around. No, I can't—"

He jerked abruptly back to the moment, rubbed the sweat from his brow, and stared blankly at the shaded grove.

Lissandra could sense his distance. She sat still, waiting, shivering with cold inside, though the day was mild. She knew it often took time to absorb everything Seen. Disturbing him now could cause him to lose valuable insights.

Finally, he rested his hand upon her head, and she felt safe to rise from her knees and sit beside him.

Murdoch wrapped her in his strong embrace and rested his chin on her hair. "You must go home now. Send Trystan here. Your life, and the one you carry, are too precious to risk."

"You don't intend to wait for Trystan, do you?" she replied. "You think it's too dangerous for either of us, and you intend to go alone. That is very noble of you, but you forget one thing." She leaned her head against his shoulder.

His eyes were dark with world-weariness when they looked down on her. "And what is that, my princess?" he asked in a voice tinged with irony.

"That we are joined as one. Even if we have not said the vows, I will feel your death as surely as my own. 'Whither thou goest, I will go,'" she quoted in the same sardonic tone. "For I refuse to suffer the torment of your absence for the rest of my life."

Her declaration knocked the cynical expression from Murdoch's face. He stared at her in stunned astonishment.

Lissandra meant what she'd said. What they had shared was so profound, so earthshaking, that she knew she would be as uprooted as the oak if she could not be with him.

# Twenty-seven

"Then take me back to Aelynn and let the Council stone me," Murdoch said, collapsing on the fallen dolmen and staring at the stockings in his hand as if he didn't know what to do with them. Lis had knocked all the stuffing from his head. *She wouldn't go home without him?* One of them had to be mad—she for claiming such a thing, or he for believing it. "At least you'll be safely home where our spirits can live on."

"Spirits live here. I can feel them."

Lis set her chin stubbornly, and Murdoch knew he was in trouble. The last time he'd seen her do that, she'd been twelve and he'd refused to let her follow him to the rock cliffs where he and Ian wished to practice diving into a waterspout. The next thing he knew, she was flying off the cliff on her own—not because she was trying to imitate them, but because she'd seen a patch of some valuable herb growing where she couldn't get at it otherwise.

She'd only broken her wrist that time. This time could be much worse. Once Lis decided that an action affected Aelynn, she was beyond reason—witness her search for his worthless carcass.

"I am not an Oracle," she told him, reading his mind clearly without actually Seeing into it. "I am of no great use to Aelynn. As much as it makes me weep to say it, the child I carry is not of Aelynn, and his destiny may not be there. I put my trust in the gods to protect him. But the gods have declared their intent for you, and it is my duty to guide you home. This much I know."

"Can you be that blasted certain of what your damnable gods want?" he demanded. "Do you have any idea of what we risk if we go inside that hill and I see you endangered?"

"You will lose control, make the earth quake, and bring the whole hill down on our heads," she retorted. "That threat wears old. We survived a sea battle without sinking. I'll take my chances."

He was an idiot for loving her false bravado. Where Lis was concerned, he'd always been an idiot.

Jerking on his boots, he scowled and tried not to remember the heated power of her hand on his foot. Lissandra coursed through his blood. Denying her was akin to denying himself. She was his moral compass. And she was telling him what he didn't want to hear.

"I don't want it to be this way," he said angrily. "It's much easier risking my neck than yours."

She kicked his boot with her soft shoe. "You're not listening again."

"Because I don't like what you're saying." Boots on, he rose to tower over her. "Why don't we send Trystan down the tunnel and see if it falls on his arrogant head?"

"You know where the tunnel is?" Her face lit with excitement instead of the dread he felt.

"The water has carved several tunnels from the limestone formation beneath here. The entrance closest to us has been widened by human hands. There are no supports. It is wet, dark, and deadly. We have no right to disturb the spirits inside."

"But you See the chalice there?"

Murdoch stared up at the magnificent bowl of the sky, the clouds scuttling across the surface, and knew he did not want to die now. He wanted to take Lissandra for his wife, have many rowdy children with her, and live life to its fullest.

For the first time in years, he felt a satisfying future within his grasp.

And his Sight said they might never come out of this hill. They could die for a damned chalice that he wasn't sure he completely believed in. For a country that had banished him.

For a woman he wanted more than life.

Selfishly, Murdoch dragged Lis into his embrace, crushed her against him, and took her mouth with all the force he possessed.

And she wrapped her arms around his neck and took everything he gave and returned it threefold. He wanted to weep at the beauty of her spirit.

They both jerked apart at the sound of boots tramping the hill toward them.

"Badeaux," Murdoch said, without looking up. Reluctantly, he released Lis.

A moment later the stocky miner trudged around a bend and into view. Huffing from exertion, he leaned his hands against the knees of his leather breeches while he caught his breath, then straightened. "Good, I found you before you did anything foolish."

Murdoch could feel Lis's questioning glance, but he had no answers. He'd sensed danger in his vision, but as usual, the danger could come in any form—human or otherwise. "I'm not much inclined to foolishness," he responded coldly.

"Ah, but the lady is," the old miner said, coming

abreast of them. "Women are like that. My wife wasn't one of us, and she tried to protect me from the committee that wanted my neck."

He stepped past them, into the nettles and briars, where he began scuffing his boots against the dirt and stone. "So even though she had her citizenship papers and swore oaths of loyalty and all that other humbuggery they place so much pride in, they killed her just the same."

"She died in prison protecting you?" Murdoch asked, testing the man's mental shield. As Lis had warned, it had corroded with time and grief, but it was still sound enough to shut Murdoch out.

"Aye. I could not go near her for fear of arrest, so I had friends bribe the guards in hopes of saving her. All for naught. They wanted me, and they would not let her go. In the end, it would not have mattered. She was frail and sickness killed her. By the time my friend reached them, the children were dead, too. Bastard peasants, may their revolutionary souls rot in hell." He casually rolled a large boulder to one side as if it were no more than a child's toy. "Here we are."

Lis squeezed Murdoch's hand, and he understood she warned him that the miner's mind was not stable. But Badeaux had just uncovered the opening Murdoch had sought through his vision, and he hadn't paused once with doubt.

"The tunnel is not safe," Murdoch warned, trying to think of some way of keeping the miner out. Or was Lis right, and the gods had sent Badeaux here for a purpose?

"That's why I'm here," Badeaux said smugly. "It's men like me who built these tunnels. I know the stone and the earth and how to hold them together. I sense no gold here, but if this is where you wish to go, then I can help."

Lis tugged Murdoch's arm, warning him again, but he had few options. Aelynn needed the sacred chalice. He didn't want to risk Lis or the child she carried, but his own gifts were more focused when connected with others, and a miner's energy should be an ideal protection against the tunnel's dangers.

Murdoch traced the aquiline bridge of Lis's nose with his fingertip and stared deep into her worried eyes, trying to reassure her. "This is best," he murmured. "You can rest here while we explore. Trust me."

"But the dream . . . ," she protested. "It showed both of us."

"Bring her along—it will be safe enough now that I'm here." Badeaux stepped back from the opening he'd uncovered beneath the boulder, gesturing for them to enter first.

Murdoch resisted. If the miner could roll the boulder that easily, he could just as easily entrap them by rolling it back. Murdoch might have the strength to move it, but he had an equal chance of causing destruction if his fury got the better of him.

"Between us, we can move mountains," Lis whispered. "Surely the gods would not lead us so far only to kill us. And if we must die, I'd rather we did so together."

"You are a morbid creature." He scowled down at her.

"'Whither thou goest . . . ,'" she repeated cheerfully. And without further warning than that, she stepped into the dank air spilling from the long-closed tunnel.

Cool air flowed around Lissandra as she took careful steps over the rocky ground. She could hear water trickling, but she could tell this part of the tunnel had been widened by tools and not water. Ancient torch marks darkened the ceiling only inches above her head.

Behind her, Murdoch wrapped his hand in her braid and tugged gently, with no intent to hurt. "You really mean to be the death of me, don't you?"

"I almost was, once," she whispered, letting her despair show. "Because of me, my mother nearly killed you. We've wasted too much time already. Don't make me lose more worrying over you."

"What I did, what your mother did, was not your fault," he said firmly. "If it is purity of heart the chalice requires before it will go home, then you are the one who possesses it, not me. Let us rescue a chalice."

She nearly stumbled beneath the weight of relief. "We are stronger as a pair."

"I'll not deny that," Murdoch agreed. "I just deny the need for both of us to die."

"That's fine, then," she said cheerfully, setting off down the tunnel in the glow of their flames. "Let's not die."

"No one's dying here," Badeaux agreed, following them in.

Lis sighed in relief when the miner did not roll the boulder back in place. She could still see the light at the end of the tunnel. His good humor after days of gloom, however, was odd. Perhaps he needed earth over his head to stabilize his disturbed thoughts.

"You do realize fearlessness is next to foolishness, don't you?" Murdoch grumbled, placing a hand at the small of her back to support her as they traversed the uneven path, Badeaux huffing and puffing behind them. The tunnel inclined uphill.

"Would you like my mother's lecture on fear being

wasted on our sort?" she asked, just to hear human sound rather than echoing blackness.

Having heard that lecture countless times, Murdoch switched his line of attack. "I don't suppose you See us walking out of here?"

"Have you ever received such a clear message?" she countered. "All I know is that I'm supposed to go with you. If we have lessons yet to learn before we can take the cup home, then let us learn them quickly." Eagerness and anxiety warred behind her brave words.

The tunnel narrowed. Water coated the rocks they touched. But the ground was more dirt than rock, hard-packed and rutted from human use. Lissandra felt the tor's power even stronger here, so strong that it distorted her perceptions. Murdoch appeared larger than life, like one of the ancients strolling through the real Olympus. His broad shoulders sheltered her. His formidable energy was a force field more durable than the one around Aelynn. Even ordinary clothes could not conceal his naked strength.

And the warrior was *hers*. The realization melted every remaining icicle that had once guarded her heart. "Can you sense the chalice yet? Or the altar?" she asked.

"Why would you seek such things when we have both on Aelynn?" the miner grumbled. "The pair of ye are as daft as the madmen who think they can overthrow an entire country."

Lissandra let the miner complain. She had little patience with someone who had not concerned himself with his homeland for so long that he did not know what was happening there.

Murdoch held her more closely as he let his senses roam through the narrow corridor. "The hill is not large. The chamber is close, but the footing may be treacherous."

Water dripped on her nose from the low roof. Murdoch had to stoop to walk beneath it. Cool air flowed around them, and she shivered. "If the Ancient Ones were tall, then they did not traverse this path."

"Like us, they would use what was available. It's not impassable. Can you feel the vibrations, hear the hum? The holy lines of energy our ancestors followed pass through here with such force that the potential for miracles or disaster is enormous. I think if we drew a straight line south, it would connect directly with Aelynn."

"Then it's almost like being home."

"Except we cannot walk through a volcano." Murdoch raised the light in his palm and eased more cautiously past a boulder carved in ancient runes.

The tunnel widened into a high, narrow chamber. The trickle of water rang more loudly. Lissandra glanced nervously at the arched limestone ceiling where a crack down the middle occasionally dripped. She didn't possess much earth energy, but even she knew limestone was fragile and splintered easily.

"Don't you worry," Badeaux said, apparently following the path of her gaze. "I can hold that ceiling in place just as I'm shielding you now. Not a rock will fall with me about."

Murdoch held up the flame in his hand to better illuminate the shadows at the back of the long chamber.

Directly beneath the peak of the tor was an altar very similar to the one on Aelynn.

Serenely waiting on the altar, surrounded by an incandescent glow of blue light, sat a glittering, jeweled chalice—the answer to all their prayers.

# Twenty-eight

Having the sacred Chalice of Plenty within his grasp was so overwhelming, so awe-inspiring, that Murdoch would have fallen to his knees had Lis not flung her arms around his neck and kissed him.

He hugged her tight and let anticipation run wild. All things were possible now. If Lissandra was right and the gods were truly with them . . .

He might have Lis to himself, might be able to return to Aelynn. He might even start believing her nonsense about the gods in his ring. *Might.* It was a powerful word.

If the gods would let him take the chalice home . . .

Badeaux whistled, breaking the spell of awe that had enraptured Murdoch and Lis.

"I certainly didn't sense that down here," the miner muttered. "How can that be?" he asked, more to himself than to anyone else.

"I fear it will disappear if I profane it with my touch," Murdoch murmured against Lis's hair, pressing a kiss to her brow to reassure himself that this moment was real. Her excitement fed his, and he was almost ready to dance her around the room.

"If our vision runs true, the chalice won't come with us if it isn't meant to," she warned, returning him to the practical. "If it is similar to the Arthurian tales, only the rightful king—the Oracle—will be able to hold on to it."

Turning in his arms, Lis leaned her head back against his shoulder, and together, they studied the gleaming silver object. The jewels on the cup's base glittered with reds and blues that would sparkle like fire in sunlight.

"The dream was more clear than most," he agreed, "but I assume we must test it. I, for one, will not willingly forgo the chance of a lifetime without at least trying."

Badeaux looked at them with suspicion. "You knew this thing was down here?"

"It's the reason we're here." Murdoch didn't think the old miner even recognized the Chalice of Plenty. It had seldom been removed from the Oracle's protection. If Badeaux had left the island as a young man, it was conceivable he'd never seen it. Murdoch saw no need to explain to the miner.

"The vision showed me trying first. Shall I?" Lis asked.

"You are far more pure of heart than I am." If anyone deserved to be Oracle, it was Lis. Swallowing his fear, clinging to hope, Murdoch dropped his arm from her waist but stayed at her side as she stepped up to the altar.

He held his breath while her long fingers stroked the stem lovingly—before curling around the silver and lifting. The cup resisted her pull, even when she used both hands.

Just like in their dream.

"The power here gives it strength." She rubbed the cup again, testing its tenacity. "Seeing it here like this, I can believe all the legends they tell of this place."

Murdoch resisted touching her while she continued

to test her will against the chalice. Despair etched his heart when the cup wouldn't move.

"Let me give it a rip," Badeaux exclaimed. He reached for the sacred chalice as if it were a mug of ale, again breaking their state of awe and reverence.

The miner grabbed the stem and tugged. At the profanity of his handling, the chalice illuminated the chamber with the power of a thousand candles, and flung Badeaux backward as if blown off his feet by explosives. He landed hard on the dirt floor.

With a cry of alarm, Lis dropped to her knees to check the old man's pulse and under his eyelids. "He's still alive!"

Murdoch refrained from expressing the sarcasm on the tip of his tongue. He had no great wish to be flattened by the gods for his irreverence, if that was what had just happened to the miner. The gods were obviously a feisty bunch. Testing the chamber with his earth sense, he decided the miner's energy shield wasn't needed in here, for the moment. "Let him sleep, then."

She hesitated, then nodded agreement.

There was no reason for the miner to see him fail. Murdoch had never felt so paralyzed as he did now, with so much riding on his next step.

Taking a deep breath, repeating the lessons Dylys had taught him, he cleansed his mind of all impure thought and reached for the sacred vessel that might free him from the prison in which he'd lived these last years.

Callused from a lifetime of swordplay, his broad hand covered the stem from bowl to base. He lifted. The chalice remained fixed to the altar.

Before he could let disappointment crush him, or think of another method of challenging the damned gods, the floor shook, and he whipped around to see the

Minutor struggling to his knees, holding the back of his head. "Stop that!" Murdoch commanded in irritation.

The old miner rubbed his furrowed brow, then shook his shaggy head as if to clear it, and stared at no visible personage. "Louise!" he said clearly.

Glancing at the cracked, unshielded ceiling, Murdoch placed himself between the dazed man and Lis. If the miner splintered the rocks in his stupor, Murdoch needed to intervene, except he hadn't tried to repair anything since childhood—for good reason. He couldn't maintain his focus long enough to pull together the broken parts and hold them in place to mend them.

Badeaux blinked and disregarded Murdoch's protective stance. Stumbling to his feet, he rubbed the bruise on the back of his head and viewed the chamber with an odd detachment. "The gods approve of my plan! I was right to follow you. Praise be to Aelynn and all that is holy."

His change in manner was so startling that Murdoch and Lis both froze in place.

Eyes glowing oddly, Badeaux removed two pistols from his capacious coat pockets. "Who better to halt a war than the high priestess of Aelynn?"

Clearly, the man's grief-stricken mind had cracked beneath too many strains.

Enraged at the miner's threat, Murdoch sought a menacing calm in hopes of finding a peaceful solution that wouldn't get them all killed. Hand on his sword hilt, he attempted to See past the miner's disintegrating mental barriers, but he could feel only his pain. If Lis could touch him, she might be able to Heal whatever had been jarred loose in the miner's head. He needed to disarm Badeaux first.

"We do not interfere in the Other World," he cautiously reminded the miner.

"I would think I'd have your support in this," Badeaux argued as if they discussed the price of grain. "The French rabble are killing all that is beautiful and prosperous in their country. Did you think your priest in the village was a man of God? He was just another thief with an arsenal to kill aristocrats and steal from the rich, just like the blackguards who stole my Louise."

"You led the committee to the priest!" Appalled, Lissandra stated what they had already surmised but had had no way of proving. "They almost killed that good man!"

She tried to step around Murdoch, but he pushed her back. Something in the old miner's head was out of alignment. Until the guns were out of Badeaux's hands, he wouldn't let Lis near him. Here was the danger he'd sensed—not a physical danger that he could battle with sword or lightning. He suppressed a shudder of dread. He didn't want to kill the demented old man. Spilling Aelynn blood would profane this holy chamber.

Badeaux shrugged. "I hoped the committee would lead me to the lady. I saw her in Pouchay and followed, but she hid too well."

"Why *me*?"

Murdoch winced at her astonishment. Lis had been sheltered in her mother's shadow for so long, she truly had no idea how valuable she was. In an effort to curb his temper, he clutched the hilt of his weapon and struggled to find some means of disarming the miner. Pistols inside a crumbling tunnel were as hazardous as his volatile earth powers.

"Isn't it obvious?" the Minutor retorted. "An Olympus can call on an army of skilled warriors. You can end the Revolution!"

"The lady is pledged to uphold the laws of Aelynn,"

Murdoch protested, still fighting his rage that any man, much less one of Aelynn, would threaten Lis. "You know she cannot do as you ask. The Other World must fight its own battles."

Lis pinched him, but Murdoch ignored her warning. She might be able to speak for herself far better than he could, but Badeaux had gone past reason.

The miner shrugged. "She can persuade the Council otherwise. I've seen her family do it, but if that is not her wish, there are other means. It looks to me as if you are her other half, a warrior who can fight on terms the Other World understands. Between us, we can force the Council to cooperate. Give me your support, and I'll hand the weapons to you."

"Of course we'll aid you," Lissandra said sweetly, before Murdoch could react.

Her innocent tone should have told anyone who knew her well that she was about to produce an ax and chop off a toe. Murdoch respected her abilities enough to suppress his anger and see what she intended.

"You miss your wife and children terribly, don't you?" she continued. "I cannot begin to imagine so great a loss."

The old miner actually wiped a tear with the back of his pistol-wielding hand. "I am nothing without them. All I've worked for, all I am, is gone, and I am left here, gutted and alone. Knowing I have the means to save others from this suffering gives me purpose."

She bled the man's heart with her Empathy.

This was not a formidable enemy to be struck down with lightning. Murdoch relaxed his tense stance and waited for the man to hand over his guns to Lis.

Contrarily, she stiffened behind him, and her words were less sweet in reply. "We will take you home with us, and you may present your case to the Council. They must know what is happening in this world."

What was she sensing that he could not? Murdoch asked himself. Wary, he watched for weaknesses.

"Your man here may talk to the Council," Badeaux acknowledged. "But I am a businessman who understands that I need collateral to obtain what I want. We'll wait here for his return. It should only take twenty-four hours or less to make the trip. We can give him a week to persuade the Council to reason."

As he grasped that the crazy old goat meant to hold Lis hostage to his demented scheme, Murdoch's rage shot from simmer to white-hot. He whipped out his swords faster than the human eye could see, and used them to hold the miner and his guns at bay. For Lis's safety, he forced his rage into his grip on the hilts, but he had no means of knowing how long he could restrain his wayward energy. "I go nowhere without Lissandra," he announced with the command of a general. "She has made you a reasonable offer. You do not need to continue holding weapons on us. Set the pistols down gently."

Murdoch could disarm the miner with his eyes closed, but the unstable pistols falling to the floor might discharge, or his own rage could cause the gunpowder to explode. He had to force the miner to set the weapons aside.

The vision of death he'd Seen darkened the corners of his mind. Just as he stood to gain everything he'd ever wanted—this demon had come to steal it from him. Murdoch wanted to roar at the injustice.

The Minutor snorted. "Don't think I didn't watch you using those blades on the giant last night. I don't trust you. That's why I carry these pistols. Go, talk to the Council. Leave us here. I understand these rocks far better than you ever will. There is more than one tunnel and more than one way in and out, so you cannot trap me. I am a gentleman and will see that no harm comes to your amacara."

Rage filled every pore of Murdoch's body and steamed out of his nostrils. Pebbles started to fall from the roof. Lissandra squeezed his shoulder to hold him steady. It would be far simpler to slice the bastard into ribbons, but he curbed his temper until the hard metal of his sword hilt cut into his palms.

If refraining from drawing blood was the price he had to pay to save Lissandra, he would pay it. He held his weapons and his temper, and, in this case, he submitted to her superiority in communication.

"Murdoch cannot go back without me," she chided. "If you had any contact with our home, you would know that. As an Olympus, I am the one with the powers of persuasion. You said so yourself. Let us all go together."

The miner's eye color shifted from the green glow of justice to the dark midnight of vengeance and obsession. Murdoch's gut churned as surely as his hand steadied on his sword hilts. In a ploy to placate, he lowered the blades to the ground and took a step closer, thus placing himself within reach of the miner's weapons.

"I go nowhere without Lissandra," he repeated. "If you can bring the cup back with you, the Council is certain to listen to reason. Why don't you trade your puny Other World weapons for one of far greater strength, the chalice?"

As expected, the Minutor again glanced greedily in the direction of the jewel-encrusted goblet.

With a speed that even a trained Aelynner would have had difficulty following, Murdoch grasped the miner's wrist and wrenched the firearm free from the old man's ineffectual grip. With his other hand, he pried at the smaller pistol, doing his best to point it away from Lis.

Cursing, the Minutor fought back with surprising strength. In an attempt to free himself, he accidentally joggled the trigger. The ball shot wildly, hitting the ceiling, and ricocheting off crumbling stone with hollow echoes. Lis cried out as the reverberations cracked the brittle limestone over their heads.

Reflexively, now holding both the miner's guns, Murdoch spun around and dropped to his knees to cover Lis as she sank to the floor.

With an explosive crack, the ceiling began to crumble and fall. Beneath the shelter of his body, Lissandra moaned. Setting the pistols aside, Murdoch caught her waist and pulled her closer, attempting to reassure her while he used his energy to divert the shower of stone from their heads. He could not divert all that fell, but he could protect the space they occupied.

A slab of rock crashed into splinters near the chamber's entrance. Murdoch winced and tried to make himself bigger, wider, anything to shield Lis. The avalanche of stone dislodged mud patches and loose rocks on its way down. Another shudder of vibrations and the remainder of the ceiling collapsed over the chamber entrance, leaving open only the space around the altar where they crouched.

With another moan, Lissandra fell limp in his arms. Heart in his throat, Murdoch held her tight while pebbles and dirt rained down on his back.

The Minutor shouted his fury, and another hail of pebbles and a slide of earth followed. The air filled with dust and dirt until each breath threatened to choke Murdoch's lungs.

As the cascade of rock slowed, Lis remained still and silent. He couldn't feel her essence as strongly as he should. Terrified he'd lost the most beautiful spirit on earth, not knowing how since he'd taken the brunt of the fall, he turned her over, supporting her waist and pillowing her head with his arm. His entire soul roiled in fury and anguish; he dared not let her inside the chaos of his mind until he knew what was wrong.

The hot, sticky flow of Lis's blood covered his hand.

His rage spiked, and the ground rumbled.

*Control*, she whispered inside his head, as if her spirit had settled there instead of where it belonged.

The air was so thick with dust, he could see almost nothing. Heart pounding as if it would depart his chest, Murdoch could barely find Lis's wound, much less Heal it. He could hear the Minutor coughing and scuffling, so the old man still lived. And Murdoch wanted to kill him, slowly and torturously. Which would require letting the miner live a while longer because Murdoch had better things to do—and he needed help doing them.

"Lis is hurt, you fool!" he shouted, stanching his anger for fear of shattering more rock. His head began to pound from his effort at restraint. "We need light and air. How great are your earth gifts?"

A faint glow suddenly illumined the rock faces of the chamber, revealing the disaster within. The entrance was completely blocked. Above them, the chamber's roof was now a sagging tangle of rock, earth, and old roots that could disintegrate with a sneeze.

"Your fault," Badeaux said. "We'll die in here."

Fear choking his throat more than dust, Murdoch ran his hand over Lis's beautiful hair, searching for the wound. He thought he'd protected her. How had he failed?

Dust turned her silver-gold strands to gray, but he saw no blood. Her face was pale, and she was so weak, her mind was open to him, open and blank. He entered softly, with soothing words, and located the pain piercing her spine where the ricocheting pistol ball must have entered.

His head nearly split open trying to conceal his horror and grief at the immense realization: she had stopped breathing and her body lay lifeless in his arms.

*A Minutor should have abilities to support the roof*, Lis's spirit murmured inside his head. *First things first.*

Had he been in his right mind, he might have laughed at the sensation of pure Lis whispering through his head. But his grief was inconsolable, and he was nearly as mad as the Minutor. Her body was *dead*. She inhabited his *mind*. May the gods help them.

"Shield the roof," he ordered aloud, "or I will see you die more unpleasantly than this."

The old man only whimpered and curled up inside himself. The earth roof strained from the weight of the tor above. Collapse and total destruction were imminent.

That he had not actually Seen death in his vision meant there was yet a glimmer of hope. Murdoch clung to that hope. If he could simply drill through the man's dementia to the knowledge inside his head ...

*Strength*, he prayed to the gods. *Aelynn give me strength.* And the patience not to strike out in fury. And the discipline to think everything through and carry it out in perfect order without destroying everyone in his anguish.

Sweat dripped in filthy rivulets from his brow at his effort to hold his energies and maddened grief inside. Still holding Lis's lifeless body, Murdoch honed his despair and anger into a razor-sharp focus to probe the miner's eroded shields—much as Dylys had done when she'd attempted to sever Murdoch from his powers.

To his amazement, as the pressure mounted inside his mind, he felt a Healing energy join with his, easing his pain and enhancing his power so that he could hold his focus steady.

The Healing energy wasn't Lis. He knew her spirit as well as his own, could feel her slipping away from him with every moment that he delayed. The soothing force bathed him in reassurance, aiding his concentration.

He had to mend the miner's mind first, help him shield the chalice and Lis, before he could surrender to the terror roiling inside him. Aiming the Healing energy as he would his rapier, Murdoch transferred it to the stricken miner.

The resulting connection to the other man's mind gave him some understanding of how Lis felt when she unmanned an attacker by grabbing his nose and softening his wits. Murdoch could feel and taste the shattered paths and anguish of the miner's memories.

Concentrating so hard he thought he'd topple, Murdoch traced the pathways, rebuilding what was broken, erasing what was irreparable—mending as he'd never done before.

He had no notion of how or why he knew to do what he did, but the action of submitting to a greater force than his own was all that kept Murdoch sane, giving his rage and grief a pure, shining focus. In a final burst of light, he removed the last obstacle that was preventing the miner's sanity, and released the good memories that had been blocked by the bad.

The Minutor howled in grief and agony.

In Murdoch's arms, Lis didn't respond to the cry,

which told him more than he wanted to know. Tears sliding down his weather-toughened cheeks, he prayed as he never had before. Could he Heal her? A spine wound was so serious. . . .

"Shield the roof, Guillaume!" Not knowing if his insane mental surgery had worked, Murdoch tried not to shout too loud. The mysterious outside energy had abated as quickly as it had come, leaving him to his own resources. It was a bad time to be convinced that he needed the minds of others—or the power of gods—to direct his energies.

Instead of retorting, the Minutor wept copiously, in great gulping sobs.

But Murdoch felt the miner's force field rising across the roof, and he quickly sent his own strength to join it. They were still imprisoned, but the showers of pebbles stopped. The Minutor's reason had returned enough for him to use his powers for self-protection.

"Aelynn be praised," Murdoch murmured in true gratitude, no longer doubting the gods, because there was no other rational reason for the miraculous feat he'd just accomplished.

With the pain between his ears easing, he turned his attention more fully to the woman in his arms. But when he tried to reach her thoughts, there was nothing in her head—or his. His grip tightened, but she didn't respond. Her breathing was undetectable. He couldn't find even a pulse.

*He had lost Lis!*

Despair and defeat flung him back to that grievous night of Luther's death, when he'd lost all. He'd collapsed in surrender then, putting his life in the Oracle's hands, begging to be put out of his misery, and she'd nearly destroyed him. As Lis's death and that of his child would destroy him now. If this was a test of his faith, he had failed. *Again.*

She deserved to live, to laugh in the green valleys of home, to have children who loved her. Let the gods take him, if only they'd let Lis live.

"Lissy," he called desperately inside her head, looking for lures to recall her spirit. "Lis, we can go home. We'll be there in a few short hours, if I have to blow the wind myself." He needed her to hope and cling to him—as the mysterious force had entered and aided him.

Murdoch let down his shields and poured his soul into her. He offered everything he'd held back all these years. He would trade all he possessed and more for a response. A man of few words, he abandoned his head and sought to speak from his core.

"Lis, you walked into my heart the first time you flung your childish arms around my legs and welcomed me to your home," he pleaded. "I adored you when you invited me to your favorite tree branch, even after you knocked me off because I was obnoxious.

"I admired your stubbornness even when you rightly rejected me. You have claimed me so thoroughly; you have been my heart and soul and conscience for longer than I can remember." Urgently, he sought words her spirit might hear and welcome. "I'm sorry I didn't listen to you, do what you taught me sooner. I'll be anything you want, do anything you say, if you'll just live. Please, Lis, come back!"

When he still received no response, Murdoch threw back his head and howled his silent appeals to the heavens, fully opening the heart he'd kept closed for so long. "Aelynn, I am yours to do with as you wish. I'll please all the gods in the firmament, but Lis is too precious for the world to lose. For Aelynn's sake, for the sake of all your people, please help me Heal her. You may strike me dead afterward if that's your desire, but please, let Lissandra live!" Tears streamed down his cheeks and onto her breast.

The blue glow in his ring abruptly coalesced and shot from the stone into a single beam of light, nearly startling him into falling backward. In moments, the dim womb of the chamber shimmered with cerulean brightness. The chalice gleamed and began vibrating so hard that it rattled on the altar slab. In awe, Murdoch felt energy plunge downward through the chalice and burst into the chamber, enveloping him with magnetism, pushing him into the light.

No longer fighting his fate if it meant keeping Lissandra, Murdoch surrendered his soul and prepared to slip down any path that welcomed him.

# Twenty-nine

Lissandra's spirit guide fluttered anxiously in the clouds, her face a stern mask of concern and impatience. The impatience was typical. The concern was not. As always when she sought guidance, Lissandra floated ethereally in the blue light of the heavens, waiting for direction.

At first, she saw nothing but the azure incandescence. The light was so peaceful that she wanted to linger and relax on its soothing waves. But some undefined insistence tugged at her more than her spirit guide's fretfulness.

Visions were so damned difficult to understand. She struggled to follow her spirit's pointing finger, but for some reason, her mind didn't move as smoothly as usual. Languishing in oblivion seemed easier.

A strange tranquility flowed over her, allowing her to release the heavy responsibilities she'd carried for a lifetime.

A blinding white light abruptly illuminated the sky, capturing her fascination. Even her spirit guide quit her anxious dance and waited in respectful regard. Lissandra followed her gaze, and her heart swelled with joy.

Her mother and father smiled on her with approval. She thought she might burst with an outpouring of tears, gratitude, and delight—until a strong tug of a more earthly sort caused her to gasp and almost slip back into herself. She resisted, needing to see her parents again.

Her mother's waist-length hair hung loose over her shoulders, and she looked years younger and happier. She raised a palm of benediction, then blew a kiss.

Dylys had never done such a thing in her lifetime. But the pure essence of her love was familiar, and Lissandra wrapped it like a protective cloak around her.

Her father was smiling, something he'd seldom done in her memory. His strength hugged her, as if in farewell. Tears spilled down her cheeks as she felt a ghostly kiss of approval upon her brow.

The earthly tug was more desperate now, fraught with grief and terror, pulsing with a love far stronger than the faint one fading into the light. The urgency was both strange and familiar, and she studied it with such curiosity that she didn't feel her parents' departure. She knew they were with her, in her heart, and she could call on them if she must.

With slow comprehension, she grasped that the soul bleeding with anguish elsewhere needed her more than her parents did. Someone required Healing. *As she did*, she realized with wonder. She hurt when he did, and vice versa. How extraordinary.

And necessary. Through unseen hands, a life force flowed into her body. Healing energy eased her paralysis and gave her strength. For a brief moment, she glanced longingly to the place where her parents had been. Her spirit guide tapped her toe.

A blast of pure heat wrenched her soul back into her body.

Spluttering, cursing her guide for being so hasty, Lissandra wrinkled her nose and tried to sit up—only to find herself wrapped thoroughly in Murdoch's body. . . .

*His* spirit was completely inside *her*, as if it was meant to be.

She laughed and embraced him with her mind, knocking him backward and driving the breath from his lungs. In a joy she could feel straight through her heart, he hugged her *inside and out*. What a miraculously strange—and comforting—feeling!

Relaxing as she had done in the clouds, she curled up against Murdoch's familiar broad shoulder and slept, knowing she was where she belonged.

In wonder, Murdoch ran his hand over Lis's slender back. The wound had disappeared as if it had never been. Beneath his hand, he'd felt the lead pulled out of her as iron to a magnet. If he looked, he might even find the slug on the floor.

Awe wrapped him in belief. *The gods had answered him!* Him, the unworthy warrior.

Lying on the cavern floor, beneath his blissfully sleeping amacara, Murdoch studied the cup shining on the altar—a creator of marvels, a chalice of plenty. Perhaps it was meant to stay here, in the world where it was needed most. Could Aelynn be saved without it?

Watching Lis breathe again, feeling the strong beat of her heart against his chest, experiencing the relief and joy of her running through his mind, Murdoch knew a gratitude so great that he swore he would do whatever the gods asked of him. Otherwise, he might never move again. It felt too right to hold her like this.

But, of course, it was all wrong, and he was being selfish once more.

*An Oracle directs his energy to others first.* He wasn't

certain whether that was Lis or her mother speaking to
him. He understood now that the universe contained
many spirits wiser than his, and he was empowered to
access their wisdom, if he would only listen with an open
heart and mind—and if he could refrain from blocking
them with infantile tantrums.

This new knowledge gave him the direction he
needed to drop down from his giddy, mindless joy to the
reality of their situation. "Badeaux, are you still alive?"
he called.

The whimpering had stopped, Murdoch realized, and
he listened anxiously, not just because he feared the ceiling would fall without the Minutor's aid, but because
he'd been inside the man's damaged mind and understood the tortured depth of the grief buried there.

"Don't know," the older man mumbled. "What
happened?"

If the miner was really lucky, he would have lost
his memory of all that had transpired. The grief would
Heal faster without the pain of recollection. "We were
touched by the gods."

"More like bludgeoned," came the grumbling reply.

Murdoch laughed. That had probably been the fault
of his inexperienced Healing, but no point in correcting
him. "You said there are more tunnels. Are any acces-
sible from this chamber? We seem to have destroyed the
one we entered."

He tried not to hope too hard as he carefully adjusted
Lissandra in his arms so he could sit up with her. She
stirred, and just that movement brought a foolish beam
of joy and relief. She was alive. And so was he. Anything
was possible as long as they both lived.

"There's a door behind the runes," Badeaux finally
said. "Other side of altar."

Taking a deep breath, Murdoch gradually eased from Lis's sleeping mind, praying this wasn't all a dream that would disappear upon waking. She snuggled her nose against his neck.

He used his earth sense to locate the hollow behind the altar. He could almost see the carving in the stone. The blinding light of the chalice and the blue light of the gods had evaporated, leaving only the dim illumination the miner provided. He would wonder the whys and wherefores another time, after he carried Lis to safety. "How does the wall move?"

Badeaux crawled through the rubble that separated them. Coated head to foot in dirt and dust, his eyes hollow, the Minutor gazed wearily at the wreckage he'd created, then down at Lissandra. "Is she dead?"

"No, she's Healing. But I suspect the air here isn't healthy for her." Murdoch watched cautiously, waiting for any further signs of the man's mad obsession. "Can you get us out?"

The old miner seemed more dazed than crazy. Furrowing his already wrinkled brow as if straining to recall his thoughts, Guillaume studied what appeared to be a solid rock wall.

Murdoch waited patiently for the miner to rediscover the power within him. Amazingly, he realized that no matter how much energy he'd expended to restore the Minutor's wits and bring Lis back to life, his head was completely clear of the pain of overexertion. Did this mean he now had the ability to control his energy all the time? Had he been Healed?

He would experiment later. Safety came first.

Ignoring the chalice on the altar, the old miner laid his hand against the stone and ran his fingers through the cracks and crevasses.

Energy began to build within the chamber once again.

Murdoch hurriedly laid Lissandra down and covered her completely with his body. If the ceiling caved in, she wouldn't feel it, at least. He pressed his hands over her head, hoping they would shield her.

She woke, of course. "Interesting position, but the bed is hard," she murmured sleepily. "I think I have a stone in my back."

"Hush; don't distract Guillaume." He pressed a kiss to her brow and prayed.

Years of cynicism had been stripped away in these past few minutes, leaving the raw, tender hope that Aelynn *really* watched over them. And that he owed the gods his life for saving Lissandra's.

Even more astonishingly, he could now distinguish among the different energies flowing through him: the thin, indestructible chord that was Lissandra; the tough, frayed rope that was Badeaux; the shining force of the chalice; and the deep, dark powers of the earth.

This must be what it felt like to be connected to others and not left adrift, alone. There was power here that he could feel and use. Power greater than his swords or lightning.

As the Minutor struggled to discover the secrets, Murdoch drew on the energy of the holy force lines and channeled them to the miner to enhance his more humble abilities.

An opening appeared where the miner had laid his hands. The ceiling didn't crash. The earth didn't tremble. Murdoch's head didn't hurt.

Lis stared up at him in amazement. "What did you just do?" she whispered. "I felt it, but I do not understand it."

Murdoch snorted and rolled off her. "Neither do I, and don't count on it lasting. The power in here is drawn from the earth's core and is so potent, it's a miracle the hill hasn't launched itself to the moon."

Refusing to feel awe or even relief until he had Lis safe, he stood and held out his hand to help her up.

She accepted his offer of aid without argument, dusting off her ragged tunic as she did so. He cherished the fit of her slender hand between his fingers. Better yet, he loved that she trusted him so thoroughly that she no longer needed to argue over his need to take care of her.

She sent him a wry glance that said she felt this new unity, too.

Through the open door, a blast of cold, damp air swept the dust from their noses.

"The chalice?" Lissandra waited for his decision.

"I still have a very different opinion of Aelynn's role in the world," Murdoch warned, "but if the Council will allow me to go home, I want to raise our children there."

Her smile of joy and acceptance was a balm to his troubled soul.

Understanding better now that Lis was his connection to humanity, he wrapped one arm around her. With his other hand, he grasped the Chalice of Plenty's jeweled stem, and tugged with all his strength.

He staggered backward, unprepared when the weight abruptly lifted from the altar.

Lissandra's laughter chased away the dust motes.

They emerged into sunlight on the far side of the tor to be greeted by the grim faces of Mariel and Trystan. Astonishment replaced the couple's fear when they recognized the chalice in Murdoch's hand. Amelie stood with them, and she gave a cry of joy as she jerked free of Mariel's hold to wrap her arms around Murdoch's trousered leg.

His dark hair streaked with gray dust, his cheek bleeding, his coat torn into a disreputable rag, Murdoch looked the part of ruthless scoundrel or worse. But he held the gleaming chalice with the same loving care with which he would carry a child. Lissandra linked her hand around his elbow and let her joy speak for her.

He had saved her life at great peril to his own. Any doubts she may have harbored in the dark crannies of her soul had been swept clean in a brilliant burst of blue flame.

Murdoch gently laid the chalice in Lissandra's hands, and knelt to gather Amelie into his arms. She chirped and petted him, pelting his cut cheek with kisses.

Lissandra gulped back unexpected tears at seeing the grim soldier brush away a child's frightened tears. She rocked the chalice as if it were her own babe. Murdoch had saved them all.

"How did you know where to find us?" Guillaume asked, limping out after them, looking much the worse for wear. His pistols had been buried in the stone, and he did not appear to remember them.

"After that quake, even the fish in the sea knew where you were," Mariel replied drily.

She was as pale as any ghost, and Trystan did not seem much better. The pair had been terrified, and perhaps frustrated with helplessness, not knowing what was happening.

Lissandra touched their hands in gratitude and sent them Healing strength. "I am sorry we frightened you."

Looking a little steadier, Mariel leaned against her

husband and covered her swollen belly with her hand. "I swear, the sun went dark, the earth trembled, and even the children wouldn't stay in the nursery until I promised to come see what it was all about."

Trystan examined Murdoch with curiosity. "You look different."

Lissandra had already seen the peace in Murdoch's eyes. With Amelie in his arms, he stood straight and tall, without the nausea and weakness that had followed his earlier use of his gifts. That his rage had not shattered the tor from within said it all.

The chalice—or the gods—had restored his ability to focus inward without pain.

Murdoch merely nodded at Trystan's observation, and carrying Amelie like a shepherd would his lamb, he set off down the path toward town. Looking at the world as if it were new again, Badeaux obediently followed.

"The gods have anointed Murdoch," Lissandra explained. She didn't think he fully understood or accepted that yet, but the blue of his ring now glowed in his eyes. "He passed the chalice's test and has been ordained our new Oracle."

The astounded reaction of their small audience of friends was sufficient to suggest the outrage that would inundate them when she made the same announcement to the Council that had once banished him.

# Thirty

Lissandra had insisted that they needed new garments for their arrival on Aelynn, and Murdoch had foolishly allowed her to choose the fabric and do the sewing. In the future, he would know better than to give her imagination free rein. He felt conspicuous in his elegance.

She'd chosen a finely woven navy blue cotton for him. The color was a shade brighter than his old uniform, and she'd adorned it with gold trim along the hem and V-neck. Thankfully, she'd left the matching trousers plain, although instead of drawstrings, she'd wickedly added a placket and garish gold buttons. But the Other World design was covered by the thigh-length top and belted with his scabbard.

For herself, she'd chosen vibrant red. Murdoch cast a sidelong glance at her as the ship docked, and they waited for the plank to be lowered. Except for the ugly gowns she'd appropriated in France, she'd always been her mother's shadow in shades of white and gray. He was certain she intended to make some statement with her bold choice of color, but a female's idea of sartorial elegance was a puzzle he would leave to the gods.

He simply appreciated the way the ridiculously fragile silk draped and clung across her breasts and over her hips. She'd fashioned a wide belt of gold braid. Even without the bone corset, her breasts were high and firm and her cleavage visible. He would be like a rutting stag until he had the garment off her.

Perhaps that was her intent—to distract him from the grim elders who were stalking through the jungle and lining up on the shore to meet them. Ian had learned enough of Mariel's ability to speak with dolphins for meager messages to be sent back and forth between England and Aelynn. The Council had been forewarned of their arrival.

Murdoch glanced over at Badeaux to see how the miner fared after the long hours at sea. He seemed rested and eager to return to his rightful home, where with luck his emotional wounds would someday Heal. He seemed to have little memory of events at the tor, and he now spoke of his lost family with love. The vengeful hatred that had driven him appeared to have dissipated.

They'd left the shoemaker and Amelie in Glastonbury, happily designing boots for Ian's stableboys. They'd already made friends and would fare well in time. If only Murdoch could See as much for himself.

Returning his attention to his homecoming reception, Murdoch located Ian and Chantal waiting on the beach, waving with genuine pleasure. At their feet, their young son dug in the black sand. A sturdy, dark-haired fellow, he'd exhibited no evidence of either his father's or his mother's gifts, or so Lis had told him. He'd missed a great deal during his absence.

Briefly, resentment flared and the longing for acceptance by his countrymen pierced Murdoch's soul. But he'd learned the hard way that life was too short to hold grudges. He would do what he must to remain a part of Lis's life—even if that meant enduring the interrogations of the Council.

Filling his lungs with the sea air of Aelynn for the first time in four years, Murdoch embraced the moment of homecoming. One of the disadvantages of Seeing the future was that he'd never learned to enjoy the moment or take pleasure in memories. He would no longer be so careless. Right here and now, he had his heart's desire at his side, the chalice in his arms, the approval of the gods, and friends to welcome him. He wanted to fall to his knees and weep in thanksgiving for these gifts. He hugged Lis and fought back tears instead.

Feeling fully at home inside himself, at last, Murdoch grasped Lis's elbow and led her down the plank to the dock. The earth didn't tremble and the sea didn't rise in rejection.

He was wary at recognizing the light of awe and grati- tude in the eyes of several of the Council members as they regarded the chalice in his arms. The chalice was holy. He wasn't. He didn't want their adoration, just their cooperation.

Perceptive as ever, Ian had already studied them, no doubt gauged their actions, their appearances, their tem- pers, and come to a correct conclusion. When Murdoch attempted to hand him the chalice, Ian lifted his son in one arm, and placed the other around his wife, making it clear that he would not accept the holy relic.

"Murdoch LeDroit, you have the gratitude of every- one on the island for returning the Chalice of Plenty," Ian said. "Welcome home."

Retaining the chalice, Murdoch responded promptly, "While I have your gratitude, I will ask for your blessing and permission to take Lissandra for my wife."

The last time he'd asked that, the day had ended in thunder and lightning and death.

Around them, the gathering Council members fell ominously silent.

Lissandra tilted her head and waited politely for her brother's reply. Murdoch was confident she would do as she liked in any case, but she would pretend to listen for permission for the sake of tradition.

"We have formalities that must be met before a marriage can take place," Ian said carefully. "You have my permission to begin the proceedings."

With deliberate mischief, Lis set the cat among the pigeons. "As you can see by the chalice, the gods have made their choice, and I choose to have our new Oracle anoint me for the altar."

Gasps of shock traveled so swiftly, Murdoch was certain even those living on the other side of the volcano heard them. To announce him as Oracle in the same sentence as their marriage ought to blow the volcano sky-high. Sardonically, he eyed the peak for hot coals spewing in protest, but Aelynn remained cloaked in a smoky gloom that chilled the brisk breeze.

"I'll have you appointed High Priestess of Drama," he murmured threateningly into his intended's shell-like ear, while maintaining his tranquil expression.

"If I must spend the rest of my life here," she said lightly, smiling at the varied expressions of shock around them, "let me have my fun, please."

Chantal whistled a merry tune and rolled her eyes to the heavens, perhaps in anticipation of fireworks or lightning.

Untangling his son's grip on his hair, Ian looked on them with wariness and appreciation, and addressed his sister with a touch of sarcasm. "Perhaps we should declare a week of celebration and festivities so the alleged

Oracle's intended won't become bored and ask him to shatter the temple and build a new one."

"That's my prerogative," Murdoch declared, deciding the public display they'd created was sufficient homecoming. "See what happens if my claim is denied."

Having used up all his restraint, he shifted the chalice to his shoulder and caught Lis's elbow to drag her down the path to . . . *where*? He had no home any longer.

Lis took care of that dilemma, striding deliberately toward the path leading to the temple and the cave where the chalice belonged.

The one the Oracles called their own.

Lissandra had known that establishing Murdoch as Oracle wouldn't be an easy matter of declaring it aloud and installing him in the cave with Aelynn's treasures. To her, the discussion of who was Oracle seemed a minor hurdle compared with the desperate need to solve the ills afflicting the island, but her brother's concern about her welfare deserved an audience.

Leaving their son with a nursemaid, Ian and Chantal hurried in Murdoch's footsteps, obviously intending to continue the discussion in private—and taking precautions in case their chat turned explosive.

Trystan the Guardian and Kiernan the Finder followed behind Ian, probably to act as guards. Lis prayed they also came as Murdoch's friends.

Behind them on the beach, Chantal's father wielded his oratorical skills to persuade the elders to let Ian deal with her shocking declaration about Murdoch as Oracle. Really, all the Council had to do was look at Murdoch and see the truth in the blue spirit light of his eyes, but people saw what they wanted to see. And in Murdoch's fine-honed edges, they saw something dark, dangerous, and deadly. For good reason, Lis had to admit. Not everyone would appreciate his decisiveness, and he wouldn't have patience with those who disagreed with him. He was not Dylys, and compromise would never come naturally to him. But he had the strength of the gods that they needed.

"They're right, you know," Murdoch murmured as he strode beside her. "I am a warrior, not a man of peace."

"As is every man on this island," she replied without doubt, delighted that he followed her thoughts. "And probably most of the women if their loved ones are threatened. Who better than a warrior, who knows the horror of war, to guide a nation to peace?"

"May I humbly suggest a warrior who tempers his hunger to fight with the wisdom of knowing when to hold his fire?" Ian asked from behind them.

"That is what gods are for," Lissandra retorted. "And Councils. Collective wisdom is necessary to shape our path. Why don't you take your brilliant insights to the Council and show them the light?"

"Because I know what each will say, and I'm not interested in hearing it again. Your story is far more intriguing," Ian declared. "Do you really expect Murdoch to be content anointing bridegrooms, influencing the Council, and delivering edicts?"

He'd listed some of the administrative tasks of an Oracle that even Ian had no interest in performing.

They had arrived at the foot of the volcano, on a high cliff overlooking the sea not far from the sacred temple, where the private abode of the Oracle was located.

Lissandra waited for Murdoch to speak his thoughts, but he only smiled grimly and raised his eyebrows, waiting for her to open the door blocking the entrance to the cave. The magic seal securing the door required knowledge he didn't yet possess.

"You could break it open if you wanted," she said crossly, not entirely understanding why she was irritated. "You don't have to pretend you're here at my request or Ian's."

In the blue tunic she'd made to match his eyes, with his hair tightly bound and slicked back from his face, Murdoch looked as regal as any king. He needed only a thin gold crown upon his head for any who looked upon him to kneel before his power.

And he waited for her to open the confounded door—as if she were his subject.

Ian watched them with amusement. "Still uncertain about who rules whom?" he asked drily.

"No," they both replied as Lissandra broke the seal and Murdoch opened the door.

"They're newlyweds," Chantal said. "We had a few issues of our own when we started out."

"A few?" This time it was Lissandra's turn to raise her eyebrows. "You nearly caused the Council to rise up in arms against your marriage, and the two of you had to live off the island until recently. I'm surprised no one has stoned you in these past weeks."

As they entered the high-ceilinged front room of the Oracle's hideaway, Chantal's laugh filled the airy cave with warmth even before Murdoch lit the logs in the fireplace. "Ian keeps the Council busy by setting them to look for outdated laws he can throw out." Chantal checked the larder and brought out cheese and dried grapes.

"And Chantal has been searching the island for music prodigies to add to her chorus. Watching Council members condescend to sing next to hearth witches has been entertaining." Ian leaned against the doorway and watched the domestic scene with an affectionate gaze.

Trystan and Kiernan entered warily, crossing their arms and leaning on either side of the doorway. Murdoch scowled, the chalice still held in his embrace. When no one objected, he set the holy cup on the humble trestle table, then took up a stance next to Lissandra, fists at his waist and legs spread apart.

She knew his blue eyes gleamed brightly in the dim interior, and she watched as first Ian, then Chantal acknowledged that the darkness had left him. Over these past days, Trystan had already accepted the change.

"Murdoch hasn't made the earth quake or mountains topple since we found the chalice," Lissandra said when no one spoke. "But I make no promises if you deny us what we want."

"I would hear the words from LeDroit," Ian said gravely, watching his old friend.

Lissandra had never done anything so undignified as to stick her tongue out at her older brother, but he tempted her greatly.

"There is nothing to be said," Murdoch growled. "I am what I am. You can accept it or not. But you have no choice in what Lis and I decide between us."

"She is my sister. I know her heart as well as my own. Unlike Mariel and Chantal, Lissandra belongs on Aelynn. If you say vows with her, then leave, she will waste away. I cannot let that happen."

Lissandra gripped her hands. Leave it to Ian to reach the crux of the matter immediately.

She turned to watch the bronzed flesh over Murdoch's cheekbones pull taut and waited for a flare of anger that did not come. He no longer trampled lives to

achieve his selfish goals, but he certainly didn't qualify
for sainthood either.

She completely trusted the man Murdoch had become. She opened the peculiar channel between their
minds so he could feel her faith, and some of the tension
left his posture.

"I want what is best for Lis," he acknowledged. "If
the gods have chosen us as amacaras, then I must trust
in their decision. If I am to accept that I am their chosen Oracle, then my place is on Aelynn. The Council can
choose to banish me, but in the absence of your mother,
I doubt there is anyone here, other than you, capable of
physically forcing me to leave."

Both Trystan and Kiernan stiffened, their hands falling to the hilts of their swords. Any battle between Ian
and Murdoch would be bloody. Lissandra didn't want to
know which side their friends would fall on. She waited
for her brother to accept what was so obvious to her.

Ian gestured for his friends to relax. "The Council
has good reason to fear you, LeDroit. Of all of us, only
you have the power to destroy this island with a careless rage. Even the fact that you were the only one of us
capable of wrestling the chalice home will cause trepidation. They will not accept Lissandra's word that you
have changed."

Murdoch nodded curtly in acceptance of that argument.
"Normally, I would take that as a challenge to battle. I can
prove that I am mightier than any man on Aelynn, and I
believe I can do it without bringing down lightning."

Ian waited.

Murdoch glanced at Lissandra. "I can see that the
volcano darkens our skies. You've said it rumbles, that
the weather has become erratic, the crops are failing,
and even Waylan the Weathermaker has been unable

to bring a balanced amount of sun and rain. And these problems are the basis of grave discontent."

Lissandra's heart beat faster, and nodding, she regarded him with wonder.

At her approval, he turned his attention back to Ian. "I have seen for myself what happens when one class of people holds all the wealth and power to the detriment of others. It is happening here, the same as in France. My mother scraped by as a hearth witch when I was a child. Even though I bought her a plot of land before I was banished, the Council will not acknowledge her voice. Nor does it acknowledge the voices of all the other landless people who clean your houses and till your fields. The weather is not the only basis for discontent."

"One of the many reasons I have the Council scouring our laws for outdated ones," Ian agreed without resentment. "It's best to start small and open the floor for discussion. Your mother is doing as well as can be expected, from all reports. She won't speak to me."

Murdoch snorted. "She probably won't speak to me either. I came by my temper honestly. What *will* meet her approval is not me proving my ability to beat you to a pulp, but me proving my ability to be productive."

Even Lissandra fell silent at that declaration. He was completely, totally correct. A mighty battle of weapons would only raise alarm and uncertainty. Returning health to the land or stability to the weather would sufficiently relieve the Council's apprehension.

"You have a suggestion?" Ian asked warily.

The wicked tilt of Murdoch's lips warned of the direction of his thoughts, and Lissandra pressed a hand to her belly in a protective gesture. "Planting your potent seed off the island, without the temple, does not count," she warned before he could say it aloud.

"I am mightily proud of my accomplishment, just the same," he replied with a grin, to the music of their audience's gasps.

Satisfied with the lovely blush on his intended's cheeks, Murdoch returned his attention to the only man with the power to destroy him. For Lis's sake, he could never harm Ian. Besides, he respected the man and considered him a friend. He wanted Ian's approval. He had known he could not walk into Lis's arms unchallenged. He could only pray the gods stayed with him through the ordeal ahead.

Ian turned to his sister with concern engraved upon his brow. "You carry a gifted child not of Aelynn?"

"The spirits of our forefathers are spread wide and far," she acknowledged. "You chose to live near them when you chose your Other World home."

Ian and Chantal exchanged glances. Chantal had been barren in her marriage before she'd wedded Ian and had borne only a son conceived at the temple since then.

Murdoch smirked in understanding. "It is almost time for you to consider conceiving another. Wouldn't you like to be able to return home and hope to achieve what we have done?"

"We are all testing the limits of our powers," Ian replied. "Tell us how you will prove your productivity— aside from the ability to produce Aelynn children without Aelynn."

Murdoch quit smirking and his look encompassed the men he'd once called friends, as well as the people he would call family, should he be so blessed. "I need to test the volcano."

"That way lies madness," Trystan said bluntly into the stunned silence. "Even if the gods do not kill you for your temerity, the volcano's sides are frail and given to collapsing."

Murdoch waited. If he had learned nothing else from Lis's company, it was to listen to others with patience, even though he knew he was right. He kept his smile to himself, but Lis's frown in his direction said she'd felt it.

"How will you test a volcano?" Kiernan asked.

As always, the vision he'd Seen was murky, but he knew he needed to gather strength from as many sources as were available. His experience in the tor had finally taught him humility—he knew he needed help, and he couldn't always count on divine intervention. "I cannot say until I get there," he replied. "But for whatever reason, the volcano is broken."

He heard the women gasp, but he kept his gaze intent on Ian.

"You have Seen this?" Ian asked. At Murdoch's nod, he turned to Lissandra with concern. "He walks into hell. What will happen to you and the child if he does not come back?"

Murdoch tucked his hands under his armpits and forced himself not to explode with the need to justify his actions. He wanted Lis to believe in him. He wanted her to stand beside him, even if she thought him crazed.

"I don't think any of you understands what Murdoch can do," she said quietly. "He has already channeled the power of the chalice and saved my life and that of our child. He has healed a madman—talk to the Minutor who returned with us if you do not believe me. Murdoch has worked miracles that we have never dreamed of because he's willing to fight for what he wants and has the imagination to See the whole of what he does." She sent him a look of love and laughter. "His downfall is that he lacks the humility to see the necessity in communicating what he knows."

As much as he longed to kiss her, Murdoch clenched his fingers into fists, hiding the tension they revealed beneath his arms while he waited as the others laughed at Lis's final remark. They still looked at him warily, unwilling to take the word of his mate—even when his mate was Lissandra, the Queen of Sensible.

"If he saved your life, it is no doubt because he endangered it in the first place," Kiernan objected.

Murdoch refused to defend himself. They had to accept him as he was—a man without words who could prove himself only through action. He'd spilled his guts for Lis and the gods. He had no desire to repeat the performance for disbelievers.

"You look through eyes clouded by affection. You do not see my sister as she really is," Ian admonished Kiernan. "Consider that Lissandra has done what the rest of us could not—returned with both Murdoch and the chalice. That he managed to deliver her safely despite her willfulness speaks well of his ability to deal with her as no other can. My concern lies in the chance of losing the one man who's capable of controlling her."

Murdoch allowed himself a laugh at Ian's perspective. It felt good to have at least one man who understood him—and Lis. "To risk Lissandra is to risk my soul," he admitted. "But as she has made clear, she is my equal and my match. You must give her the same freedom to do as she wishes as I have."

Lissy tugged one of his fists free from where he'd hidden it, and wrapped her slender palm around his fingers. He watched proudly as she glared at the room bursting at the seams with muscled men. "I have no idea what Murdoch intends," she said, "but I have seen what he is capable of, and I will do whatever he asks if it means re-storing Aelynn to normal. The gods are truly with him."

He lifted his eyebrow and looked down at her. "And if I tell you that you must stay here, where it is safe?"

"I will follow anyway," she said sweetly.

That succeeded in raising an uproar of discussion that carried well into the evening hours.

# Thirty-one

Letting his spirit roam, Murdoch studied the stunted growth of what should have been his mother's lush field of wheat. He'd sought her out as soon as he was able, but she wasn't home. And apparently she refused to return home until he left. Which he wouldn't do until he'd earned the right to the Oracle's residence. He came by his stubbornness fairly.

His brash statement to Ian about the broken volcano had been based on his visions, but he needed to plant his feet in the soil and feel Aelynn in his veins before he could even grasp the scope of the problem here.

The volcano hadn't quaked since their arrival two days ago, but he didn't remember the smoke being as thick and constant in his youth as it was now. The ashes raining down on the land reminded him of the poor Breton village after he'd nearly destroyed it with the unintended fire.

So far, his mother's people and the landless rebels who defied the Council had left him alone out here. They were waiting and watching to see what he would do. Word had spread quickly of his claim to the title of Oracle. As ever, he was caught between the worlds of his amacara's powerful family and the voiceless one of his parents. He didn't know how to bridge the gap between the two classes any more than he knew how to heal the dying land.

From his spirit's lofty perch on a celestial plane, he studied the distant elevation. Until these last few years, the volcano had been quiet. It had not unleashed its fiery power since the times of the Ancient Ones. The blackened lava had eroded in the winds and rain of the centuries, revealing the skeleton of earth and stone beneath the molten ash. Jungles grew up the mountainside now. Coffee and cinnamon trees flourished on the lower foothills, but higher up, the soil was too thin for farming, and fiery fissures had opened.

With his feet rooted firmly on the earth and his spirit free to roam, Murdoch's conviction grew that the gods had merely tested his obedience with the tor. Now they would test his strength and wisdom—and his confidence in himself. He was inexorably drawn to explore Aelynn's uppermost reaches.

Not only his fate but the fate of Aelynn rested on his shoulders. Until now, he'd thought an Oracle simply another pampered leader who told people what to do. He hadn't realized that in actuality, an Oracle stood between life and death—just as a warrior must do.

Persuaded that he'd learned all he could and that only one solution was possible, Murdoch emerged from his trance, uprooted his feet from the wheat field, and replaced his hoe in the shed where he'd found it.

He returned to the Oracle's cave, which Ian had politely left for his use. The Council was having tantrums over Murdoch's access to the sacred residence, but even they had to agree that since he'd returned the chalice to the island, he wasn't likely to sell it to the highest bidder, so the island's treasures were presumably safe with him.

They might think differently if they could see him now.

After wrapping the sacred object in old velvet, he tucked it into a canvas satchel. He prayed that he understood its purpose.

He added foodstuffs from the larder to the satchel, along with herbs and unguents. Dylys had taught him well, and he knew her cabinet inside and out. She hadn't taught him all that Ian and Lissandra—as potential Oracles—had needed to know, but he'd listened and learned just the same. He prayed fervently that he understood the gods' intent, and that he could carry out his task without mishap.

With care, he wrapped his swords in cloth and canvas that would shield them from tarnish and deposited them in the hidden chamber behind the cave's inner room. He verified that the Sword of Justice, the island's other treasure, was still safe in its hiding place, then laid his weapons alongside it. If he understood the gods, he would no longer have need of such blades.

He was at peace with the idea. A warrior had to be strong, and he'd proved the strength of his sword arm. By using physical prowess to accomplish what he believed, he had almost sold his soul. Now he had to prove the strength of his convictions by other means.

Night had fallen by the time his preparations were complete. His step was light and quick as he took the path through the temple grove and up the mountainside, the same path he'd traversed as a child, when the island was his entire world.

If he was wrong, this might be his last exploration.

Lissandra bent over the young Diviner and her newborn daughter and tucked them in while the proud papa looked on. "She is so beautiful. You are very fortunate."

The mother beamed despite her exhaustion. "She is fortunate that Aelynn sent you home in time to assist in my labor."

"I should never have waited to take my wife into town. I knew the nearest Healer was too old to climb these hills. It's all my fault," the father said gruffly.

Lissandra smiled and touched his burly arm. "You tended your crops as you must if you wish to feed your family. There is no shame in that. Perhaps Aelynn saw that I was home and sent the child early so your wife might be up and well in time for the harvest."

Tears sprang to the young man's eyes, and he hastily hid them by rubbing as if he had a lash in one. "Aelynn be praised," he muttered.

His wife had fallen sound asleep and could not repeat the prayer.

"Return Aelynn's gift by helping others when you can," Lissandra said. Swaddling the newborn to give it security and warmth, she left her in her loving father's arms.

The young family had a long night ahead, one she would normally have shared so the parents could learn about their new bundle of joy from experienced hands.

But she had sensed Murdoch climbing the mountain and could not linger. Even though they had not said the vows, the bonds of amacara held them, and she felt the direction of his pull. She'd sensed him even when she'd been engrossed in the child's delivery. The inner connection that had opened between them in Glastonbury was disconcerting at times.

Murdoch's excitement told her he'd found a solution, and she wanted to be there to watch—should he survive the ordeal. The cliff was impossibly high, the path much too tortuous. He could crash into the sea before she reached him.

Heart thudding, she stopped in the village to tell the local Healer of the birth so she could send someone to help the new parents.

What should she do now? She was unaccustomed to making her own choices.

The path down to her home would take hours. She was exhausted and drained by the daylong process of bringing a child into the world. She needed rest. But she wouldn't get any while the man she wanted more than life itself pretended he was a mountain goat and climbed to Aelynn's peak on a dangerous journey.

That Murdoch had left her the choice of whether to follow him invigorated her more than sleep. She could dutifully tend to her people as her mother had taught, or she could risk following Murdoch on another heart-stopping adventure with the potential for either disaster or blinding success.

She chose Murdoch. Whatever happened, she wanted to be at his side, to see the world through his eyes so she could open her mind to new ideas that her previous isolation prevented.

Requesting food and drink of the Healer, Lissandra partook of some and added the rest to her sack of herbs. She rubbed her feet briskly with a refreshing unguent, let the Healer massage her shoulders to relax the muscles, then set out into the night as if it were dawn.

Murdoch was risking his life for Aelynn. She just didn't understand how or why. Her Finding skill seemed connected more to Murdoch than to the object in his knapsack, but once she took the dusty lane out of the village, she identified the chalice he carried.

Dawn had thrown out its first orange glow before she felt him stop to rest. Weary in every bone of her body, she'd like to do the same, but not until she'd caught up with him. His desire poured through her like the flow of hot lava.

Once they said the vows of amacara, she would never be able to resist his call again. She no longer feared taking that step. When done freely—by choice—it was not bondage, but a covenant. It seemed as natural now as it had seemed unnatural before.

She arrived as the dawn hit the mountainside, illuminating the lightning-sculpted boulder below her. The sun's light disappeared as she slipped into a canyon between walls of ancient lava near the peak.

He'd timed his trip well. No one would have noticed their progress between jungle and canyon at night. And now that it was day, no one could see her behind the wall. If they were missed, they could be Found, but who would miss them? It wasn't as if either of them stayed in one place for long. It was rather exciting knowing they could escape from the demands of an entire population and find privacy up here.

Stripped to the waist, Murdoch was waiting for her when she arrived. As always, his bare torso loomed large, even against a mountain backdrop, but it was the peace in his eyes that took her breath away.

Taking her heavy satchel and setting it aside, he wordlessly wrapped her in his embrace and poured his Healing energy into her aching bones. She all but melted into the familiar hard planes of his chest and shoulders.

"You are a woman above all others, and I adore you with all my heart and soul," he murmured, stroking her back.

"If you brought me here because you could not restrain your lust a moment longer, I will push you off this mountain," she warned, although she didn't mean a word of it. To be in his arms was a pleasure she could never have too much of.

He laughed gently into her hair, then, with his finger, lifted her chin so he could kiss her. Desire flowed through her lips and tongue and downward, feeding the air she breathed and the blood warming her womb.

"Too soon, you will not be able to climb this hill," he murmured, stroking her belly. "I had to do it now. I cannot wait while the Council debates our future. The island's balance must be restored immediately."

She studied him with interest. He looked peaceful, accepting, not worried or anxious. Weariness crinkled the skin about his eyes, but their color was still the bright blue his ring had once been, startling against the dark hue of his face. She stroked his stubbled jaw, and he smiled in the manner that made her bones melt all over again. "In what way is the island out of balance?" she asked.

With a bleak look, he gestured at the peak. "The volcano is awakening."

Alarm was her first reaction. The smoke did seem to be thicker, blacker, but then, she'd seen it at her mother's funeral and accepted it as an omen from the gods. "I don't understand."

"Feel the heat rising through your sandals." He waited for her to test the soil.

She frowned. "Perhaps the earth's crust is just thinner in this place."

He shook his head. "I felt it down below, too. The effect has apparently been gradual. You haven't noticed the severity because you haven't been away as I have. Besides, I feel the earth's energy more than you do. The heat is roasting the soil, killing the crops from below, and the ash and smoke are keeping out the sun's warmth, changing our weather."

"We've known there was danger, of course," she said slowly, feeling her way around his explanation. "But one can't put a lid on a volcano. If it is really awake, must we flee?"

He hugged her tighter and pointed at the ground. "I draw my strength from Aelynn and the volcano's power. Your mother didn't destroy me so much as separation from my home did."

Lissandra pondered the mystery until his perception seeped into hers, and she stared at him in wonder. "While you were here, you drained the heat and fire and kept the volcano in balance. Once you left, the energy had nowhere else to go!" Which confirmed that her mother had been terribly wrong to banish him. She hugged her elbows to contain her sorrow at the years they'd lost.

He nodded. "While I was gone, the pressure built."

"And how will you release it?" she asked, images of steam and fire filling her head. "Throw a tantrum and blast the stars?" Perhaps her mother hadn't been wrong. Perhaps Murdoch had needed those years away to understand how fragile their world was.

"I could do it that way." For a moment, mirth erased the solemnity of Murdoch's gaze. "But there are more pleasant alternatives. How do you think I unleash my fire when I do not let my rage explode?"

Lissandra blushed clear from her hair roots to her toenails. "Our lovemaking releases Aelynn's fire?"

"That's one theory. Ian and the Council will not approve. What do you say?"

"I say we test your theory."

If possible, Murdoch's eyes glowed an even brighter

blue as he gathered her in his arms and swept her from her feet. "I have the traditional herbs and unguents with me. There is a small grotto with heated water waiting inside." His mockery fled, and his expression grew more serious than she had ever seen it as he asked the words she had thought never to hear: "Will you marry me?"

# Thirty-two

"Marry? Here? Not in the temple?"

Murdoch chuckled as he lowered Lis to a bed he'd made of his sack and the heavy blanket he'd brought for this purpose. He heard no displeasure in Lis's voice, only perplexity, and his relief knew no bounds. She wasn't concerned about marrying a muddled man from a farmer's home so much as the proper conduct of the ceremony.

She believed in him more than he believed in himself—or in this new self, leastways. "We can marry again in the temple, if you wish, but we've already created a non-Aelynn child. We don't need the spirits of our elders from the altar. Or Ian's permission. If I am the chosen one, then I must lead as I see fit."

She accepted that with a nod and curled against his shoulder when he lay down beside her. Long ago, this land had been under water. Even now, soft sand filled its hidden caverns. The blanket gave as comfortably as any mattress.

"And will you tell me why we must say our vows here, above the world, in such an unorthodox manner?" she asked.

"It won't be entirely unorthodox. We have a grotto and incense and the traditional herbs and wine. The only

thing different is the location. If I am to draw off the volcano's heat, I would rather expend the flames high above
habitation, where I can cause no harm. I've learned not
to explode fireworks around other people," he said with
sadness, squeezing her waist.

"How did you become so wise?" she murmured
sleepily. Her long lashes swept her cheeks as she closed
her eyes.

"From you." He kissed her lids. "From the chalice.
From spending hours with no thoughts but Aelynn's.
We'll rest now. The moon is full tonight. It will be an
auspicious start for our future."

"Have I told you how much I missed you these last
days?" She settled in more comfortably against him.

"Have I told you how much I love you?" he returned,
but she was already asleep and didn't hear his heart-
spoken declaration.

He didn't know if a man as cynical and battle scarred
as he was deserved the love of a woman as understanding as Lis, but he knew a rare and precious gift when he
was given one. If the gods allowed him to claim her tonight, he could do no less than return the gift by saving
the island—or die trying.

"Ohhhh, this feels so nice. It's a good thing we slept
first, or I'd fall asleep and drown." Lissandra leaned
back in the sandy volcano-heated pool inside the cave.
Steaming water lapped at her breasts and soothed muscles aching from the climb. Her legs floated effortlessly,
brushing Murdoch's.

The desire between them seemed capable of turning
the pool water to steam.

To keep the pressure building inside her to a mini-
mum, she tried not to look at him too often. After they'd

woken from their nap, they'd dined on cheese, dried fruits, and toasted bread, not exactly a wedding feast, but she tasted nothing while enrapt in fascination with Murdoch. His dark hair brushed his powerful shoulders, and his beard-blackened jaw emphasized the luminous quality of his blue gaze. She didn't think she could get enough of staring into the brilliant blaze of his eyes. His mobile lips quirked every time he caught her staring at them, as if he recognized the absurdity of this mark from the gods on a man once destined for black deeds.

Sitting beside him where she couldn't gawk so easily, she was enthralled by the muscular power of the arm dwarfing her shoulders, the iron-thewed thigh pressed against her soft one, and the proud jut of his masculinity just below the water's surface. Heat obviously did not wilt Murdoch's ardor. She understood now how fire fed his energy.

"You are certain you desire our bonding?" he asked, proving his thoughts didn't match his body's needs. "There is still every possibility that I will fail and have to leave Aelynn."

"That you have to ask sorrows me," she murmured in despair. "That we belong together is the only thing in this world of which I'm certain."

His relief produced a gust of warm air through the chamber. "The vows are permanent and eternal. I had to be sure. *You* must be sure." He drew her so close she almost went up in flames right then.

"Couldn't we change some of the ritual now that you are Oracle?" she asked, wishing she could lower herself onto his lap and have done with this delay. "I am as cleansed and purified as I'll ever be, and I'm tired of waiting."

He chuckled and leaned over to kiss her lips. "As purified as any newlywed would be while contemplating a wedding night."

She sank into his kiss with bliss, wrapping her arms around his strong neck, mingling her breath with his. One short move ...

He set her back to his side again. "I don't know how much of the ritual is important for us, but I don't think we should risk straying too far from your mother's lessons. Some tradition has a purpose. Ian believes the dried mushrooms aid the vision of conception, and the other herbs reduce the dangers created when our gifts merge. Since you've already conceived and have many of my abilities, I don't know if this is entirely necessary, but I'd rather take no risks."

"We only have one wedding night," she agreed. "Shall I anoint you first?"

"I think we'd better do it together," he said wryly. "I would not wish one of us to take advantage of the other before we're fully prepared."

She laughed. The oils and unguents were as highly erotic as the aphrodisiac elixir consumed directly before the ceremony. Normally, the Oracle and his or her priest or priestess would apply them, but normally, one of the newlyweds wasn't the Oracle.

Standing ankle deep in the shallow edge of the pool, they held the pots of ointment Murdoch had prepared. The scent of sandalwood and eucalyptus swirled around them as they began massaging the musky balm into each other's shoulders.

With their backs done, they turned to face each other and start on the front. Murdoch's powerful biceps took twice as long to cover as hers. Lissandra struggled bravely to concentrate on the marriage prayers she recited aloud as she rubbed in the ointment, but her entire body quivered with each stroke. His muscles tensed when she rubbed them, and if she dared look down . . .

Murdoch began to massage her breasts, and her knees came undone. She grabbed his arms to steady herself.

"I take thee, Lissandra, as wife, keeper of my soul," he murmured, covering her breasts with his hands, warming the balm until it tingled her skin and stirred her womb.

Murdoch's pledge seemed to sink into her with the oil, to become a part of her that she could never deny. "By Aelynn's will, I take thee for husband, keeper of my body and soul," she repeated as naturally as the desire rising through her.

Lissandra spread the balm across Murdoch's broad chest, absorbing his heartbeat beneath her hand. He was a god among men. She might be the only woman in the world who saw the vulnerable man beneath the strength. "I take thee as amacara, father of my children, from now until the gods decree."

His body strained to join with hers, but by sheer determination, he held her at arm's length. "By Aelynn's might, I will not take another. You are my amacara, keeper of my children. Free me, Aelynn, for I am yours to do with as you will."

At this final vow, an explosion of white-hot radiance illuminated the cave, and a rush of scorching wind nearly bowled them over.

Lissandra gasped and clung to Murdoch. Head tilted to the heavens, eyes closed in prayer, he gripped her waist, and the wind died to a warm breeze. The blast of fiery light diffused into the misty silver of a full moon outside the cave. The binding had been done.

Unafraid, she continued the ceremony as she had been taught. Kneeling, she began to rub the balm into thighs the thickness of tree trunks. Normally, without the aphrodisiac, the recipient would not be already aroused. Normally, of course, it wouldn't be the bride anointing the groom.

As she massaged his abdomen and lower, the moon's silver light glowed brighter, until she felt it on her skin, and her woman's place swelled and ached with need. But she resisted the temptation. For now.

When she reached his feet, Murdoch lifted her and performed the same service for her, smearing the cream into her thighs and calves and even her toes with unbearable tenderness. She was no more than molten jelly by the time he finished.

Standing to his full height, he reached for the wedding potion on a rock ledge above her head.

The chalice! He was using the Chalice of Plenty for their ceremony. She nearly laughed aloud at Murdoch's audacity. He would not be a fainthearted Oracle.

"By Aelynn's will, I give thee my love, my honor, and my respect for always, into eternity," he said solemnly, lifting the sacred vessel to her lips.

Lissandra stared into his eyes and saw the heavens reflected there. *Love.* Murdoch had said he *loved* her. Her man of few words seldom expressed his feelings. That he proclaimed them now on this solemn occasion when it was not required brought tears to her eyes.

Accepting his offer as the sacred promise of commitment he meant it to be, she sipped the heady mixture until her wits spun. Then she took the chalice from him and repeated this new vow with the strength he had invested in her. "By Aelynn's will, I give thee my love, my honor, and my respect for always, into eternity."

Murdoch shivered and closed his eyes as if to let her pledge sink in and mend his wounded heart and soul, before he lifted the chalice and drained the honeyed elixir dry.

A steady breeze rustled chimes around the island. The silver moonlight pulsed with a magic of its own. While the heated water clouded the air with foggy tendrils of steam, Murdoch set aside the cup and reached for her with the force of the gods gleaming in his eyes.

Wrapping her arms around his neck, with the volcano's heat enveloping them, Lissandra experienced the first thread of fear at his dangerous experiment. Would he cast out the volcano's fire through her? Would he split the heavens asunder?

But her head wasn't steady, and her desire was too strong to worry about earthly matters. Trusting in him, she floated off the ground in Murdoch's arms, her hair trailing into the water as he carried her out of the pool, into the bed of moonlight.

"Take my fire," he murmured, laying her down on the velvet cloth in which he'd carried the chalice earlier. "Take it and dispel it into the heavens, back to the stars where it belongs."

His voice vibrated through her as he knelt between her legs and she opened wide to accept him. When he leaned over to place his tongue there, Lissandra cried out her rapture. Flames licked her skin, exploded along her nerves, poured through her blood. She shook and quaked uncontrollably like the earth, reaching for the one steady rock within her grasp, Murdoch's arms.

With an athlete's grace, Murdoch moved over her, the dark strands of his hair mixing with her pale tresses. She clutched his biceps while the mountain trembled. He applied his heat to her nipples, and desire built again, rushing like wildfire to her womb until she arched and thrust her hips and urged him on.

He pressed his lips to hers, sent the fire rushing down her tongue. Her tears of joy dried into paths of salt from the raging inferno that would fuse them into one. She dug her fingers into bulging muscle and fiercely pushed her hips upward into his straining sex.

He spread her knees wider and drove into her.

Murdoch didn't waste energy howling his ecstasy at having finally reached the enveloping core that was his wife, his amacara, his Lis. The blending of their bodies and souls and minds was too intense, too shattering for him to do more than silently absorb the thrill.

The essence of her flowed through his veins, feeding his flames without scorching, expelling his heat into the atmosphere. While his sex thrust and claimed hers, his hands instinctively angled her hips. The contractions of her muscles aroused and coaxed, and his mind sought the spiritual mending of becoming one with the Healer who made him whole.

He didn't want release if it meant leaving the haven Lis offered. Angers, frustrations, and tensions he'd hauled around with him forever now mysteriously evaporated, leaving him buoyant with joy and pleasure, truly free for the first time in his life.

Lis's healing hands stroked his tough skin. She sank her fingers knowingly into his buttocks to adjust his rhythm to a more erotic one. Murdoch nearly lost his restraint completely when she massaged deeper.

He opened his eyes and stared down into her entranced expression. The cave was ablaze, but not from moonlight. Awareness wrapped around them even as his body pounded harder, more frantically.

At the final climactic moment, when he buried his sex deep inside her and his seed shot from his loins, his shuddering release sent his spirit soaring. In triumph, her spirit joined with his, and while fire and flame spewed into the night sky from the volcano's peak, they slipped from their replete bodies to meet in the clouds.

"You think of yourself as a giddy butterfly?" Murdoch asked in amusement, watching the play of light on Lissandra's translucent spirit wings.

"I should have known you would prefer to be a naked gladiator." She perched on his broad chest.

They had no bodies, no real form, and no sensations up here, but the pleasure of their minds couldn't be contained as their bodies below slipped into the languor of satiation. Murdoch luxuriated in the unplanned moment. "I've always thought it best to face the world prepared," he admitted.

"Naked isn't prepared. It proclaims your virtue and fearlessness." She hesitated. "I can see and hear through you as I never have before. It is as if you've opened my eyes to a larger world and my ears to the voices of many."

"Touching minds is a curse and a blessing." He lifted his hand so her spirit form could alight on it. "It made me wild until I learned to close people out, but now I See that I must learn to concentrate by connecting with other minds as I once used my sword to direct my power."

At this admission that he still needed aid to focus, she glanced worriedly below. "Can you tell if we have succeeded in dispelling the mountain's heat?"

He glanced down from the clouds. The night sky blazed a fiery red and orange. Aelynn's peak glowed with burning embers and billows of steam. "Either that or we blew up the island."

Her butterfly image moved threateningly to his nose. Their words and actions were mere thoughts, but he understood her warning and mentally grinned. "If you want any more of what we just did, I don't think you'll unman me."

"If we've blown up the island, there won't be any more of what we just did."

He turned serious, Seeing as much through Lis's mind and eyes as his own. "Between the two of us, we've let off a little of the pressure, but not enough."

Losing her laughter, Lis zapped back to her body, dragging Murdoch down with her. They faced each other on the blanket, the night sky outside the cave glowing in reds and oranges.

"What now?" she asked. "Years more of intemperate weather?"

Murdoch took a deep breath and exposed his worst fear. "I think we need *everyone's* help."

"Everyone? How?" Lis asked in dismay.

He closed his eyes and pondered impossibilities. Could he believe the gods trusted him enough to do this? If they hadn't killed him yet . . . "I think I can touch all their minds from here, if they would open their shields to me."

"We need the aid of the masses, the hearth witches and hedge wizards," she said with understanding. "The Council might be more powerful, but most won't willingly let you in. You need to reach the lesser enabled, the ones who do not guard themselves so heavily."

He opened his eyes and stared into hers. "The landless are the ones I'm most connected to," he said softly. "Between us . . . with both of our connections . . ."

To his relief, she didn't hesitate. "We are all one people. We are all Aelynners. The time for division is over."

He still watched her with concern. "You understand I've never connected with anyone but you and Ian. I have no idea what will happen."

She shrugged. "We will save the island or die trying. Let us blow your fire into the heavens. Use me—use all of us—as you must."

She understood his fears and matched his courage. Together, they could do anything.

Murdoch covered her with his body, propping his weight off her with his forearms. "We will join with just our minds this time. I'd rather not let the entire island see or hear our private moments."

She laughed. "And what do you think they thought when they saw our fireworks?"

"That I didn't kill anyone. Yet." He rested his brow against hers. "Open your mind to me, *mi ama*. I need your help."

"We all need each other," she murmured in return, doing as he requested. "Let's start with Ian. Once he understands, he can help with the others."

As expected, Ian was awake and watching the volcano's fiery explosion with trepidation, as was more than half the island. When Murdoch touched his mind, Ian responded in relief and curiosity. They'd never had this power before unless they were close enough for their weapons to touch. Lis was the missing piece Murdoch had needed all these years, the conduit between him and others, the channel of communication he'd never known.

She suggested visiting Chantal next. Ian reached out to Trystan and Kiernan. As each of them opened his or her mind, they expanded to a whole new network of friends, family, and acquaintances, spanning the entire island from all sides of the volcano, all ages, genders, and classes—until they had the awareness of almost the entire population, except those of narrow and closed mind.

Humbled by the enormity of the trust and power they placed in his hands, Murdoch spread their energy over the volcano, let the fire flow through him and into the universe.

The night sky glowed as if the sun had come to earth.

# *Thirty-three*

W hen they came down from the mountain three
days later, the sky shimmered with brilliant blue,
raindrops glistened on tree leaves, and the air was clear
enough to breathe again.

The Council waited grimly for them in the meeting-
house.

Murdoch squeezed Lis's hand. In his mind, she appeared more queenly than all the royalty of Europe.
She wore her silver-gold tresses loose and flowing down
her supple back, crowned only with a circle of jasmine.
They'd bathed and dressed themselves in the rich garments she'd created for their earlier homecoming. The
only difference now was that she wore a pendant bearing the onyx and black pearl he'd chosen for his family
stone, and he wore an armband of the white pearl and
ruby of her family.

Standing tall and stern, Ian blocked their path where
the jungle's edge met the village clearing. His gaze took
in the symbols of their joining, but his comments reflected his more worldly concerns. "The last nights have
been inspiring," he said drily. "The entire island steams,
in more ways than one. I believe the midwives will be
very busy nine months from now."

"Too bad we missed the spectacle," Lis said with an

airy wave. "I'm sure the night sky illumined with fire must have been a miracle to behold."

"Had you not given us warning, Waylan and Trystan would have loaded their ships and sailed us away, thinking the volcano was about to erupt."

In his earlier days, Murdoch would have taken offense at Ian's tone, but now he could see through Lis's heart and understood the awe and respect in her brother's irony. "You will note that we carefully avoided scorching populated areas," he said in the same cool manner as Ian, although knowing he had finally earned Ian's respect warmed him clear to the marrow.

"May I extend our gratitude for your thoughtfulness?" The sarcasm was automatic, covering Ian's examination of them for signs of damage, internal or external. "The wells are gushing water. The wheat in the field must have grown a foot these last few days. The Council may argue for the sake of arguing, but after you miraculously rebalanced Aelynn by drawing on our mutual energies, you can demand anything you want. Have you chosen your course?"

Politics and war had not been on his mind in the days he'd had Lissandra to himself, but Murdoch nodded. "If you approve of our marriage, I will tell them the course I See."

Lis hesitated, looking questioningly from one to the other. "I know it is tradition for the spouse of the Oracle to become Council Leader, but I hope you do not See me in that role."

Murdoch lifted her hand to his lips and pressed a kiss there. "You are the other half of me, the wise half, the priestess who speaks my thoughts more clearly than I. You are my channel to understanding others. I can't work without you, but I recognize that you are a Healer and a student of science by nature. This Oracle prefers that we each do what we are best at. Aelynn needs people like you to study who and what we are and what we can become. Your heart isn't in Council leadership."

She beamed in delight at his understanding—and at the freedom he offered. "In other words, I'd bore them to death before I'd persuade them to my reasoning," she teased.

Murdoch smiled. "I think the time has come to choose our leaders for better reasons than marriage or wealth."

Ian laughed, and the cool gloom with which he'd greeted them dissipated. "That argument could engage the Council into eternity, leaving you free to do whatever you will from henceforth."

"I did not say I wouldn't aid the decision." Murdoch tucked his wife's hand into the crook of his elbow and led the way down the hill toward the Council that had never accepted him. With all doubt dispelled, he looked forward to a battle of wills.

To his amazement, he discovered he was more comfortable in his island home than anywhere he'd roamed. He'd had to leave to understand that he belonged in this place.

Waiting at the side of the road, an aging Agrarian carrying a basket of plump purple grapes studied them through narrowed eyes, watching to see how he would be greeted.

Having just used the minds of these people without warning, Murdoch was surprised by the man's offering. He'd never coveted the gifts people gave to an Oracle, and he'd been humiliated when the Breton villagers had thanked him with their food. But through Lis's eyes, he understood that the farmer offered the fruit of his trade in exchange for the benevolence of the gods—through Murdoch.

As Oracle, he was a vessel of the gods, as he'd forcefully demonstrated these past few nights. He still found the title almost laughable, but Lis squeezed his arm, and he had to accept that he had been granted great favors, and it just might be in his power to pass them on.

He nodded acceptance of the gift, and the farmer fell boldly into step beside Ian. Murdoch snickered at the sight of a mighty Olympus walking with a farmer—that would never have happened when he'd been here last. Perhaps he actually could make a difference.

Hesitantly, as if uncertain of her reception, a young hearth witch bearing the rowan broom of her trade waited beside the path. This time, both Lis and Murdoch smiled and nodded at her. Solemnly, she stepped up to join the Agrarian.

Murdoch almost laughed aloud at his wife's smug expression. She couldn't have said "I told you so" any louder if she spoke. Engulfed by her warm acceptance, Murdoch relaxed and marched onward toward the Council House.

Waiting beside her cottage, an Herbalist nodded her approval of his entourage and handed Lissandra a bouquet of thyme, rosemary, and basil still glistening with the morning dew. Encouraged by the others following them, she joined the parade.

Murdoch felt Lissandra's tears of happiness as surely as if they were his own. *He was no longer alone.* His previously withered heart expanded to encompass the entire island, from the newest innocent babe to the grumpiest, corrupt old man.

By the time they reached the Council door, he was smiling so broadly it was a wonder he didn't crack his face. Behind him walked a procession of the most menial laborers, the weakest invalids, and the most common artisans. Even untrained adolescents stepped proudly with their elders, their faces scrubbed and their eyes gleaming. No king could have a more royal reception.

Trystan and his warrior-trained friends waited at the door of the Council House, wearing their ceremonial finery minus their swords, Murdoch noted with relief.

"Lord Vulcan," Trystan greeted him with laughter in his eyes. "You have provided spectacular entertainment these last nights."

"That's what fire gods are for," Murdoch replied with a shrug, although he felt the acceptance of his old friends with keen gratitude.

"We can declare an annual Day of Pyrotechnics should we survive these next hours," Ian said drily, before throwing open the double doors of the Council chamber. He stood aside to let Murdoch and Lissandra enter first.

When it became apparent that Murdoch didn't intend to stop his humble followers from entering, Trystan held open one door while Ian held the other. Their strapping comrades lined up along the aisle to allow the ragtag procession to stream through the crowd. A few of the younger bachelors even bowed their heads in respect as Murdoch and Lissandra passed by. Once, they had been Murdoch's friends. He hoped this meant they would be again.

At a signal from Ian's wife, a flood of harmonious voices lifted in song, politely drowning out the Council's gasps of outrage at the unruly procession entering their hallowed ranks. The gasps turned to murmurs of bewilderment as the parade of laborers sought places among the seats of the nobles. The boom of drums, large and small, erupted to accompany the chorus, and the joyous noise drowned out any vocal objection.

Beside Murdoch, Lis stifled a giggle. They dared not open their minds to each other for fear others sensitive to thoughts might pick up on their exchange, but he didn't need to hear what she was thinking. He needed only to know that she was enjoying the spectacle—and that she felt confident enough not to hide her soft heart behind haughty dignity any longer.

The last of their humble supporters fanned out among the landless bachelors in the rear of the room. Auburn hair gleaming, handsome Nevan the Navigator looked startled to be standing beside a young maiden with flowers in her hair. Dark, intense Kiernan the Finder surrendered space for a hunched old woman and the young boy who served as her crutch. Appearing his usual surly self, the fierce and scarred Waylan the Weathermaker gave up his bench for a gnarled fisherman and his winsome daughter.

As Murdoch assisted Lissandra to the dais, he sensed that some of their parade had not taken seats but had boldly followed them to the front where the influential and wealthy squirmed and looked over their shoulders and whispered angrily among themselves.

Ian, as elder representative of the most powerful house on the island, waited until the last moment to join them on the dais. Now, as Murdoch stood beside Lis and faced the crowd, he almost choked in shock to see his mother taking a seat newly vacated by Alain Orateur, Ian's father-in-law.

Marina LeDroit was not a tall woman, but she held herself with the same regal authority as Lis. Murdoch understood why his mother had given him up to Dylys for teaching, but in doing so, she had expected great things of him. And—until now—he had failed her.

As he'd hoped, she had waited to see if he proved himself.

From beneath her braided crown of silvered hair, she glared at him as sternly as he remembered. Only this time, with Lis squeezing his arm, he could see the love and approval in the curve of his mother's lips. A flood of emotion swept over him in a tidal wave. He clamped his hands on Lis's shoulders to steady himself.

Ian stepped up to the podium. The drums and choir ended their song. Out of respect for the Olympus name, most of the audience quieted. Murdoch assumed Ian mentally nudged the recalcitrant into silence. He hoped if Ian returned to England, he wouldn't have to practice that subtle trick, or his warrior's strength might slap a few souls senseless.

"I am here to announce the marriage of my sister, Lissandra, to our new Oracle, Murdoch LeDroit."

The words were no sooner out of Ian's mouth than the room once again erupted in an uproar of cheers and shouts and bellows of fury.

Murdoch adored the way Lissandra turned and slanted her eyes to look at him expectantly, with just the tiniest gleam of mischief despite her serious expression. She was anticipating his next move. If the unruly crowd would not respect this solemn moment, he would have to provide a fitting show for his wife's entertainment.

An Oracle's place was to envision the future and guide the Council Leader wisely. Since they were currently without a chosen leader, it was up to Murdoch to call the meeting to order. Remembering Lis's earlier cynical comments about raising the roof to demand respect, he couldn't resist this opportunity for showing off his new techniques for managing his anger.

With his hands on Lis's shoulders, Murdoch channeled his contentment through her narrow focus and, with the strength of their joined minds, amused himself by raising the thatched roof from the rafters. A flurry and squawk of doves and swallows flapped in startlement, darted over the audience, and flew out windows and doors as well as the gap between thatch and timbers. He hid his grin. He still had the ability to enjoy tweaking arrogant noses.

The crowd fell silent in shock and stared upward, waiting to see if the roof would fly away or fall on their heads and wipe out the population.

"Peace!" Murdoch thundered, and gently lowered the roof now that he had their full attention. "If I can be welcomed home by the noble family I have most harmed," he bellowed at his obdurate audience, "then I believe you owe them enough regard for their centuries of leadership to listen to what they have to say."

Several of the wiser heads nodded agreement, and the audience grudgingly remained silent. Not all of them had joined their energies over these past nights. He still had to reach the rebels.

Murdoch released Lissandra so she might step forward. He knew she didn't like oratory, but she was an Olympus, and had learned what was expected of her.

"All of you saw the spirits of the gods leave the island upon my mother's death." She paused to let them recall the moment of awe and horror. "I followed them to France, where they led me to the man my parents raised as their own. To this man. To Murdoch LeDroit."

Lissandra turned her gaze to Murdoch's mother. Ian stepped down to offer Marina LeDroit his arm and lead her up to the platform.

"I do not question the decisions of the gods," Lissandra continued. "They led me to Murdoch LeDroit, and they led Murdoch to retrieve the Chalice of Plenty. They have chosen him as my amacara and my husband. They have selected him as Oracle as surely as they have chosen him to discharge the dangerous volatility of the volcano—with your help. You may prefer to reject the decision of the gods, but the Olympus family will not banish Murdoch again. He is here to stay. And while I am speaking, I would like to apologize for our appalling neglect of the woman who brought our Oracle into the world, Marina LeDroit. I hope you will be hearing more of her in the future."

She turned to give Murdoch's mother a chance to speak. But the older woman with tears in her eyes merely shook her head, hugged her tall son, kissed Lissandra's cheek, and stepped aside. A housemaid all her life, she had no experience in public speaking.

In the back of the room, a few of the common folk began to applaud. More followed. Trystan and his worldly friends stomped and whistled their approval. Before Lissandra knew what was happening, thunderous applause, hoots, and shouts rattled the rafters.

The more noble, landed families did not follow suit, but even among their stern faces, she noted a smile or two of approval and a few nods of reluctant respect. She could ask no more. She stepped back to let Murdoch take his place.

"If you're an Oracle," challenged one angry nobleman, "then tell us what you did to make the crops grow so we do not repeat the suffering of these past years!"

"Don't banish your hotheaded youth would be my recommendation," Murdoch replied drily. "Our volcano is a fragile resource, one we must learn to use wisely.

When Luther Olympus and I regulated Aelynn's fire, all was well. With both of us gone, balance was lost. The excess heat dried up your wells, and the vapors created clouds that chilled the island, resulting in more demand for heat, which reinforced the unbalanced cycle."

The hedge wizard who had first joined the procession stood up. "You used *all* of us equally to restore balance these past nights. Tell us what that means."

Murdoch nodded. "I needed *all* our people to vent four years' worth of pent-up energy. Every person on this island is a valuable resource. If we continue working together toward one goal, instead of individually and at odds, the weather will return to normal. I am beyond grateful to all of you who joined together to make this happen."

An excited murmur rippled across the audience, followed by whispered doubts. One and all, they knew the volcano wasn't the only problem they faced. .

"Will you lead us into war?" a loud voice shouted from one of the first rows.

"I will not lead you anywhere," Murdoch replied quietly. "I am not here as a warrior, but as teacher and student, as an Oracle should be."

Lissandra admired the luminous gleam of her husband's eyes and the stalwart straightness of his spine as he faced an audience who had once condemned him and were still wary of him.

"I have tested my endurance and skill in the Outside World," he continued. "I no longer need to play the games of boys and challenge others to prove my superiority. My father was an Agrarian. My mother sets houses in order. I am a caretaker by birth and a warrior by training. The gods have blessed me with abilities beyond those common ones, and it has come time to study and practice them. In order to do so, I ask your forgiveness for the sins and wildness of my youth and your acceptance and guidance in the future that knocks even now at our door."

Only a man of great character could humble himself to ask for the forgiveness and acceptance of his enemies. Had Lissandra any doubts at all, they would have been banished at this moment. With his words, he freed them all to find their own strengths. Tears of joy slid down her cheeks as she tugged Murdoch's arm so that he would lean down for her kiss.

"I love you," she murmured, not caring who heard.

"Which Olympus will be Council Leader?" Alain Orateur called, crossing his arms over his chest and waiting for the answer looming large in all their minds. Alain had led the Council these past two years in the absence of any traditional leader.

Chuckling, Lissandra stepped behind Murdoch, and Ian joined her, along with Murdoch's mother. They flanked him, letting him take the brunt of the brawl to come.

Murdoch didn't protest their departure. Nor did he seem to notice it. His broad shoulders blocked her view of the crowd, straight and stiff and . . . vacant. She knew if she looked into his eyes right now, they would be glazed and empty, as hers were when her spirit fled her body.

A second later, he jolted back to the moment as if he'd never left.

"An Orateur can talk an audience into believing the moon is blue," he said, "but that does not mean believing in blue moons is a wise choice. I speak not only for the gods but for all the people on this island"—he nodded at the men and women who had followed him in—"when I say that we need a leader who is strong enough to defend what is ours and to provide justice for those who are too weak to defend themselves."

Rustles and murmurs of anticipation filled the chamber in the silence as he paused to give them time to absorb what he was saying.

A blue light tinted the sun from the windows, casting an odd glow over the chamber, one that Lissandra recognized well. In awe, she listened as the gods spoke through Murdoch—as she'd never heard them speak through her mother.

She took the hands of the two people beside her as Murdoch announced, "It is not my place to choose the Council Leader. Over these next years, let the Sword of Justice and the gods choose who leads us—all of us"— his gesture swept the room—"into the next century."

Astonished silence was followed by roars of agreement that raised the roof without need of Murdoch's aid. He was opening the door of opportunity to every man and woman on the island to earn a place as head of the Council.

The choir broke into a triumphant melody accompanied by excited drumbeats and a clear crystal flute that could come only from Chantal. In the rear of the usually staid and solemn chamber, a farmer swung a maid in a dance of joy. Liking the idea a little too well, some of the bachelors turned to the other young women and an impromptu reel spilled across the room and out the door.

The drums beat faster and the choir shifted to a dancing rhythm.

Eyes laughing, Murdoch turned and swept Lissandra from her feet. Before she could even think to protest, he was dancing her across the dais in dizzying circles that felt *right*.

She flung her arms around her husband's neck and

threw her head back to let her happiness flow free as she swirled weightlessly in his strong arms—dancing, at last.

"I want laughter and music to greet all celebratory occasions," he murmured against her ear. "And I want every day to be a celebration for you."

Leaning back so she could admire her husband's expression of relief and hope, Lissandra smiled. "Let us have music *and* dancing. I think I like this form of entertainment."

He laughed and swirled her around again.

Wind chimes all over the island tinkled as the earth moved to the rhythm of their feet.

# Epilogue

Lissandra hugged Chantal and Ian and then Trystan and Kiernan while the ship preparing to sail for England bobbed in the harbor. "Please, you are not so far—you must return as often as you can," she told them all. "I want to see the babies, and we must find some way of schooling them here as well as there. They must know their heritage."

Smiling almost benevolently, Murdoch hugged her waist. "We will start a boarding school for all the hellions who disrupt the Outside World. Perhaps we should send Kiernan hunting for Crossbreed Teachers."

"Our home in England is yours," Chantal said softly. "You must visit there as often as we do here."

Even as he spoke with Trystan and lifted Ian's son to his shoulder, Murdoch tugged Lissandra against him and gave her his strength to reply.

She shook her head at Chantal's invitation. "I go nowhere without Murdoch, and as Oracle, he can never again leave Aelynn. Our traveling days are done. We leave that to you and Ian and all those who wish to follow you. All our worlds are changing."

"For the better," Murdoch reassured them. "The more knowledge we accumulate, the more effectively we can teach our children to face changes in the future.

Then, it might be safe for Aelynn to rejoin the rest of the world."

With tears in her eyes, Lissandra watched her family and friends board the ship that would take them out of her reach. Until Murdoch had taught her it was healing to release the emotion inside her, she'd been unable to weep her farewells. She had no such trouble any longer. She waved until the ship sailed through the invisible barrier and disappeared from sight.

And then she buried her tears in Murdoch's broad shoulder and let him wrap her in his love and ease her anguish.

"I will melt if you cry any more," he said gruffly, swinging her into his arms. "Must I make you angry so we can return to normal?"

She laughed into his shirt. "Will you make it thunder if we fight?"

"I will not," he said, carrying her along the path that led to the privacy of the Oracle's cave. "I am a peaceful man these days."

She made a face and nibbled on his ear. "And what did the peaceful man decide we should do about adding a nursery? Will you build it yourself or ask the gods to do it for you?"

"I think we'll wait to see if the child is a monster as great as me or a rational human unlike either of us before I decide whether or not to raise him in a cave," he grumbled, although his tone reflected pleasure more than irascibility.

Lissandra laughed aloud, replacing the sorrow of parting with dreams of their future, as her all-knowing husband knew any new mother would do. "Oh, I have Seen our *daughter*. She is a red-haired witch. The two of you ought to get along splendidly."

Murdoch spun her in circles with glee. Lissandra shrieked, but he threw her over his shoulder to carry her the rest of the way up the hill.

"A redhead! We haven't had a true redhead on the island since . . ."

"My mother," she reminded him drily from her upside-down position. "Just because her hair turned gray early does not mean she was always gray."

She kicked his thigh and wiggled until he set her in front of him. He bunched his fists at his waist and grinned down at her, his eyes blazing with blue light, his dark hair falling over his shoulders.

"We will call her Marina," he commanded.

"We will call her Dylys!" She knew this game well. She wrinkled her nose, tagged his shoulder, and raced for the safety of the cave.

"Over my dead body," he roared, racing after her.

"That can be arranged, my love!"

Laughing, Lissandra fled to the Oracle's bedchamber and let her gown fall to the floor before Murdoch burst through the doorway.

He ran after her and stopped short to stare at her hungrily as candles flamed to life around the room.

"As long as we are overthrowing traditions, it is only fair that we profane the sacred chamber of the Oracle with physical pleasures," she taunted.

"I'll build a bigger bed." With that, he tumbled her to the narrow cot and plied his kisses against her throat until she screamed with laughter and purred with pleasure.

The fire of Aelynn burned steadily.

Read on for an excerpt from
Patricia Rice's next book, the first in
her exciting new historical romance series,

## AN HONEST SCOUNDREL

### A YOUNGER SONS NOVEL

### Coming in July 2010

*The daughter of middle-class gentry, her parents recently
deceased, Abigail Merriweather gave up her fiancé to
take charge of her four young half siblings, only to have
the executor of her father's will relieve her of parental
duties because she's female. Assuming no man in his
right mind would want to marry a spinster with only
a farm for dowry, much less take on a ready-made
family, she has applied to her father's distant relation, a
marquess, for aid in having the children returned to her.*

"I need a man," Abigail declared, so decisively that a squirrel leapt from the fence and hid under the hedge. "I need to marry a rich solicitor," she amended, applying her hoe to the rhubarb bed. "A responsible gentleman who loves children and would take my case to the highest courts. An upright, respectable man with enough wealth not to worry about the expense!"

Rather than cry more useless tears, Abigail was stubbornly contemplating solicitors and selling her pony cart for fare to London when the mail coach rattled to a halt on the tree-lined road. The mail wasn't delivered personally to Abbey Lane, but she couldn't prevent her heartbeat from skipping with hope. Perhaps a letter of response from a marquess required hand delivery. She wouldn't know. She'd never received one.

Please, let him say he would help her fetch the children back. If she couldn't find a rich solicitor to marry, she needed a wealthy London gentleman like her father's distant titled cousin, who might be willing to fight for her cause.

The coach lingered, and she hurried toward the gate, hoe still in hand. Perhaps their guardian had relented and sent the children home for a visit. The coach might stop out here for young children—

"Keep the demon hellion off my coach until you've tamed or caged her!" a cranky male shouted.

"I hate you, you bloody damned cawker!" a child screamed.

Despite the appalling curse, Abigail hurried faster. She did not recognize the voice, but she recognized hopeless desperation on the verge of tears. She would not let harm come to any child under her notice.

"Your generosity will not be forgotten," a wry, plummy baritone called over the thump of baggage hitting the ground.

Abigail almost halted. Sophisticated aristocrats with rounded vowels and haughty accents were not a common commodity in these rural environs. She wasn't young or foolish enough to believe the heavens had thrown a wealthy noble onto her front lawn in answer to her plea.

Her innate social insecurity kicked in, and she froze until a small figure darted through the hedgerow, dragging a ragged doll and shouting, "Beetle-brained catchfarts can't catch me!"

"Penelope!" the gentleman shouted. "Penelope, come back here this instant."

Oh, that would turn the imp right around. With a sniff of disdain at such parental incompetence, Abigail intercepted the foulmouthed termagant's path, crouching down to the child's level and murmuring, "If you run around behind the house, he won't find you, and Cook will give you shortbread."

Tearstained cheeks belied the fury in huge, long-lashed green eyes as the child gazed warily upon her. With her heart-shaped face framed by golden brown hair that was caught loosely in a long braid, she could have been a miniature princess, were it not for her threadbare and too-short gown. And the outrageous expletives that had just polluted her rosy lips.

"Hurry along now. I will talk to the rather perturbed gentleman opening the gate."

The child glanced toward the gate and, setting her jaw in mulish determination, raced across the lawn to the three-story brick cottage Abigail called home.

"Penelope!" A fashionably garbed Corinthian caught sight of the child and gave chase.

Abigail almost gaped at the intruder's manly physique, accentuated by an impeccably tailored, long-tailed frock coat, knitted pantaloons, and Hessians polished to a fare-thee-well. She thought her heart actually stumbled in awe—until alarm startled her mind into ticking again.

She might be inclined to be generous and reserve judgment of a man who had made a child cry. But the gentleman's expensive coat and boots in the face of the child's pitiful attire raised distressing questions.

She was even less inclined to be reasonable when he seemed prepared to run right past her as if she did not exist. She was painfully aware that she was small and unprepossessing. And she supposed her gardening bonnet and hoe added to her invisibility in the eyes of an arrogant aristocrat, but she wasn't of a mind to be treated like a garden gnome.

She stepped into the drive and held the hoe so it would trip the elegant stranger if he didn't pay attention. He might be large and fearsome, but no man would intimidate her into abandoning a hurt child. He halted in startlement at her action.

She scarcely had time to admire his disheveled whiskey-colored hair and impressive square chin before he ripped the hoe handle from her grip and flung it into the boxwoods. He was formidably male from his whiskered jaw to his muscled calves and smelled so deliciously of rich male musk that she trembled at the audacity of her impulse.

"The little heathen first, introductions later." He broke into a ground-eating gallop that would have done a Thoroughbred proud.

Discarding her disquiet, she hastened up the drive in the intruder's wake. Dignity and her corset prevented galloping. And her short legs did as well.

She arrived at the kitchen door to a scene of chaos.

Plump and perplexed, Cook stood with a tray of shortbread in her hand while the threadbare princess darted under the ancient trestle table, apparently shoving the sweet in her mouth while dodging chairs and the gentleman.

Miss Kitty yowled and leapt from her napping place on the sill, knocking over a geranium.

And the gentleman—

Abigail thought her eyes might be bulging as she regarded the captivating view of a gentleman's posterior upended under her kitchen table. She had never particularly noticed that part of a man's anatomy, but garbed in knitted pantaloons, his was extraordinarily . . . muscled. And neither her insight nor his action was pertinent.

She sighed in exasperation and daringly yanked a green coattail as the gentleman tried to squeeze his broad shoulders between the workbench and the table in an attempt to reach the child. "Honestly, one would think you'd never seen a child have a tantrum before. Leave her be. She won't die of temper."

Caught off guard by a rear attack, the intruder stumbled sideways, caught Cook's chair to steady himself, and knocked over a steaming teapot. He gracefully managed to catch the pottery before it crashed to the brick floor, but not before scalding his hand with its contents.

Abigail winced and waited for the flow of colorful, inappropriate invectives that the child had to have learned somewhere.

The gentleman's throttled silence was more evocative. Dragon green eyes glaring, he carefully returned the pot to the table, clenched his burned wrist and ruined shirt cuff and, ignoring Abigail's admonitions, again crouched down to check on the runaway.

If she had not already noted the family resemblance of matching cowlicks that tumbled hair in their faces, Abigail would have known the two strangers were related by the identical mulish set of their mouths.

Bumping his head against a kitchen table while holding his scalded wrist, Fitz tried to recall why he'd thought learning to be an earl required turning over a new leaf. The moldy, crumbing old foliage he'd lived under all his life had been perfectly adequate for the lowly insect he was, although he must admit, his impulsive actions in the past might occasionally give the flighty appearance of a butterfly.

He snorted. In the past? If kidnapping his own daughter wasn't flighty, it was the most ill-conceived, absurd, and possibly the stupidest thing he'd ever done, as even the child recognized.

"I want my mommy." Beneath the table, Penelope stuck out her mutinous lower lip.

He peered in exasperation at the whining, scrawny six-year-old bit of fluff he'd accidentally begot in his brainless years, when he'd thought women would save his wicked soul.

The child had his thick brown hair and green eyes, so

he knew she was his. The petulant lip and constant demands obviously belonged to her actress mother—may
the woman be damned to perdition.

And yet, he was stupidly drawn to the imp of Satan
who so resembled his neglected childhood self. He suffered an uncomfortable understanding of her rebellious-
ness. After all, she'd been ignored for years by a mother
who had run off to marry a rich German, and a father
who thought good parenting required only servants. Fitz
still preferred servants, but he obviously needed to find
more competent ones.

"I will find you a better mother," he recklessly promised, if only to persuade the child to emerge from beneath the table so he didn't appear any more beef-witted
than he already did.

"I want *my* mommy!" Big round eyes glared daggers
at him.

"You have a daddy now. That ought to be enough
until we have time to look around and pick a pretty new
mommy for you." What in hell did she expect him to
say? That her mother didn't want her? There was one
truth that wouldn't pass his tongue.

"Mommy says you're a worthless toad sucker. I don't
want you for a daddy," she declared.

Her real mother would never have lowered herself to
such a common expression. Understanding dawned. "If
you mean Mrs. Jones, she is a slack-brained lickspittle,"
he countered, "and she is *not* your mother. Do you think
I'd pick dragon dung like that for your mother?"

He ignored the choking laughter—and outrage—of
his audience in his effort to solve one problem at a time.
The child's mother had chosen the nanny. At the time,
Mrs. Jones had seemed affable and maternal and all

those things he imagined a good mother ought to be. Not that he had any experience with mothers or children.

He couldn't even remember *being* a child. An undisciplined hellion maybe, but never an innocent. What the devil had he been thinking? That he wouldn't repeat the mistakes of his father? And his grandfather? They hadn't been called Wicked Wyckerlys for naught.

Still, he tried another tactic, plying the silver tongue for which he was known. "But I need a daughter very much, Penelope, and I would like you to live with me now."

No, he wouldn't, actually. He'd always assumed the child would be better off almost anywhere except with him. Therein lay the rub. There was nowhere else for her to go. Perhaps shock at inheriting a bankrupt earldom had scrambled his wits.

He feared the banty hen breathing down his neck was prepared to dump the entire pot of steaming tea on him. If he'd learned nothing else in his life, he'd learned to beware vindictive women, which seemed to include all pinched, spinsterish females with time on their hands.

"If you will remove yourself from my table—" Right on schedule, the hen attacked, kicking at his boots in a futile attempt to dislodge him.

"I want my mommy," the child wailed in a higher pitch, rubbing her eyes with small, balled-up fists. "You *hate* me!"

"Of course I don't hate you," Fitz said, too appalled to pay attention to the hen. "Who told you that I hate you? You're all the family I have. I can't *hate* you."

Sensing she'd shocked a genuine reaction from him, Penelope wailed louder. "You hate me! You hate me! I hate you! I hate y—"

"If you will give her time to calm down . . . ," the increasingly impatient voice intruded.

He didn't listen to the rest of her admonition. "Do the theatrics usually work with Mrs. Jones?" he asked, deciding on a nonchalant approach that generally shocked furious women into momentary silence.

At his unruffled reception of her tantrum, Penelope stared, taken aback. Fitz crooked an eyebrow at her. At last, a little control over his battered life.

"While this is all very entertaining," the little hen behind him clucked, "it will not get dinner cooked."

He winced at the reminder of the utter cake he was making of himself. So much for impressing the household with his usual currency of sophistication and charm.

The hen ducked down until Fitz was suddenly blinking into delectable, blueberry eyes rimmed with lush ginger lashes. A halo of strawberry curls framed dainty peaches-and-cream cheeks. Whoa, was that lusciousness what she'd been hiding beneath her ghastly hat? His gaze dropped to her ripe, rosy lips, and he nearly salivated as he inhaled the intoxicating scent of cinnamon and apples. He must be hungrier than he'd thought.

Ignoring him, she looked pointedly at Penelope and barked like a field sergeant instead of in the syrupy voice he'd anticipated. "Young lady, if you will refrain from caterwauling like an undisciplined hound, you may wash your hands and take a seat at the table."

Apparently expecting to be obeyed, the pint-sized Venus stood up, and her unfashionable but sensible ankle boots stalked away from the table. Fitz stared back at his daughter. Over their heads, he could hear the exquisite little lady commanding her troops.

"Cook, I believe we will need your burn salve. And sir"—she kicked his boot heel just in case he didn't realize he wasn't the only man in the room—"if you will step outside a moment, we will have a little talk while the salve is prepared."

"Just keep remembering she eats sweets, not people," he whispered to Penelope before backing out to face his punishment.